CITY OF MASKS

CITY *of* MASKS

A CREE BLACK THRILLER

DANIEL HECHT

BLOOMSBURY

For information address Bloomsbury,
175 Fifth Avenue, New York, N.Y. 10010

Published by Bloomsbury, New York and London
Distributed to the trade by Holtzbrinck Publishers

Cataloging-in-Publication Data is available
from the Library of Congress

ISBN 1-58234-341-1

First U.S. Edition 2003

10 9 8 7 6 5 4 3 2 1

Typeset by Hewer Text Limited, Edinburgh
Printed in the United States of America by
RR Donnelley & Sons, Crawfordsville

This book is dedicated to Christine Klaine,
neighbor, friend, and collaborator, who came to me
with a terrific idea for a series of novels about this most
unusual lady ghost buster . . .

1

C REE – AN UNUSUAL NAME. An Indian tribe, isn't it – up in
Manitoba or someplace? Your parents named you after them?"

"No. A nickname. Short for Lucretia, which by the time I was five
years old struck me as too old-fashioned to live with. You're welcome to
call me Ms. Black, Mr. Beauforte." Cree smiled but put enough of a
point on the comment to suggest that more personal inquiries were
unwelcome. So far, Mr. Beauforte's smug and insinuating manner had
not exactly endeared him, or commended the Beaufortes as prospective
clients, whatever Edgar said about cash flow.

"No, 'Cree' – I like it. Very charming. Unusual." Ronald Beauforte
nodded with satisfaction, as if pleased to find something to irritate her
with. He was a handsome man with a brush of gray at his temples, dressed
in a well-tailored charcoal business suit, top two shirt buttons undone, no
tie. Now he sat back in his chair, legs crossed, pants cuffs tugged to reveal
just so much of his argyles and no more, the steeple of his tanned fingers
making a fine display of several fat gold rings. The Louisiana accent was
not so deep: Clearly, he'd spent a good amount of time outside his home
state, Cree decided, maybe an Ivy League education. When he'd first
come in, Cree had noticed the appraising flick of his eyes over her body,
the glimmer of appreciation. She was willing to give that the benefit of
the doubt, but already the excess of relaxed confidence had begun to
bother her.

"Now, Cree, please explain just what it is you do. I confess I have
never before had dealings with a . . . what would you call yourself? A
ghost buster?"

"I suppose that's one way of putting it — "

"So, what, you're going to come to Beauforte House with those, what do they call it, ectoplasm tanks on your back, the space suits and what all? Like the movie?" He smiled a skeptical crescent of white with glints of gold at the back.

Cree paused, trying to think of a way to take control of this conversation with any grace. And failing. Finally, she opted for the candid approach: "Listen, Mr. Beauforte, you're skeptical. You've made it clear that you've come to me only to honor your sister's request and that you consider her concerns foolish. That's fine, and, truly, I can understand why. But this *is* what I do for a living, you have my references and therefore know I am well regarded in my field. And you *are* here. So if you'd like to proceed, we'll need to discuss this on a serious and professional level. Do you think we can back up and try to get off to a better start?"

It was a risky approach to an arrogant bastard. Edgar would be stinking furious if Beauforte stomped out of here. As he'd reminded her before he left: "Yes, Cree, our priority is research, but we are *trying* to fund our work through client fees, and right now we could use some revenue!"

And, yes, the Beauforte family did look like a good candidate for the role of cash cow.

But what the hell, Cree decided, you can't let people push you around. She took a breath and let her tone stiffen: "We can begin with your calling me Ms. Black."

Beauforte's face twitched through an instant of indignation, but in the end the gambit seemed to work. One of the benefits of studying psychology: You could apply it to the living as well as the dead. Ronald Beauforte was, after all, the son of a powerful Southern matriarch, on some level still reflexively obedient to female authority and heir to some residual Southern custom of gallantry in dealing with the gentler sex. He straightened in his chair, dipped his gaze briefly, and nodded his acquiescence.

"Ms. Black, my apologies. I have been told that I speak con-descendingly at times, especially when I'm feeling a tad out of my depth. Thank you for reminding me of this failing, and do forgive me. Please proceed."

A trace of the supercilious smile remained, Cree saw, showing he was humoring her – *Ah do so like a little gal with spunk.* But she nodded. It would have to do.

"Thank you. As I told Lila, it's not an easy process to describe. Part of the problem is all the traditional folklore about ghosts, haunted houses, the 'undead,' and so on, which gets in the way because it colors people's perceptions of what they experience. My colleagues and I take a more systematic and scientific approach. We don't claim an objective under-standing of human consciousness, or . . . the spirit, or life after death. But we do apply in-depth historical research, psychological analysis, empathic techniques, and, whenever possible, technological means to verify and identify what most people call 'ghosts.' Our goal is paranormal research, but we usually have access to the . . . the object of our interest . . . only when someone calls us in to get rid of it, so – "

"Something of an irony in that, isn't there?"

Cree liked him a little better for having noticed. "Definitely. The majority of our clients are people like your sister – troubled by inexplicable and frightening presences and wanting to be shut of them. So, yes, on one level, I suppose we are 'ghost busters.' We prefer to think we *alleviate* hauntings. Hopefully for the benefit of the haunting entity as well as the living."

"And 'we' are – ?"

"Myself and two associates. You met Joyce Wu, my assistant, in the outer office. My partner, Edgar Mayfield, is in Massachusetts conducting a preliminary review of a case. Sometimes we bring in consultants or network with various research institutes. But we're a small firm."

"'Partner' as in business partner only or – "

"That's correct."

"Mm." Beauforte sorted that away. "And just what are 'empathic techniques'?"

Except for the near foray into Cree's marital status, these were all reasonable questions for a prospective client to ask, and Beauforte's inquiring about the empathic issue spoke well of his intelligence. But his tone irritated Cree. Every word seemed honed to show her he felt above all this, was going through it for form's sake only.

"Again, it's difficult to explain. One thing we've learned is that hauntings are not experienced by everyone – there needs to be some particular psychological vulnerability, sometimes a special connection to the situation, on the part of the person experiencing the haunting. That's why one person can experience something and another person, in the same room, experience nothing. It's very, very subjective, a matter of each individual's psychological and neurological states. So one of our goals is to share our clients' emotional state, which increases the like- lihood we'll experience what they do and allows us to learn more about the nature of the haunting. We want to know what that special link or vulnerability is and why it's troubling. And if there *is* another entity involved, we try to share *its* experience, too – to learn what happened to that person, why his or her revenant is compelled to do what it does. We try to learn what it wants."

" 'Revenant'?"

"Just another word for 'ghost.' Someone lingering in some form after death."

It was all getting to be a bit much for Beauforte, and he shook his head, openly incredulous. "So you are, in effect, what . . . something of a *psychotherapist* for ghosts?"

Cree just gave him a bright smile. "Yes. That's a fine way to think of it, yes."

"I had heard, of course, about this New Age thing in Seattle, but – "

"I'm originally from back east."

Beauforte seemed to need a moment to digest what he'd heard. Tapping his fingers together, he looked around the office, then gazed through the windows that took up most of the southwest wall.

Cree gave him time, tried to see things through his eyes. Outside, the rooftops of Seattle sloped away to a terrific view of water and mountains. Elliott Bay and the Sound were a somber deep blue today, and beyond them the Olympic range was majestic and aloof, but the sky was an exuberant, playful blue scattered with clouds that seemed sculpted with sheer whimsy.

Beauforte was frowning slightly, as if engaged in some internal calculus that gave him difficulty, but perhaps he wasn't really such a smug bastard. His skepticism was understandable; likewise his unfamiliarity with Psi Research Associates' methods. He had every right to vet what he considered a wacky Seattle outfit before handing over money – there were plenty of idiots and con artists in the field. And however dubious, he *was* going through with it, honoring the request of his sister Lila, who had called Cree last week, sounding very distraught and desperate. Clearly there was more to him than the persona he apparently felt he had to project.

Cree hoped their offices made an appropriate impression on a potential cash client. They'd had the walls resurfaced and painted last week, which gave the place a crisper look, more professional and credible. When all was said and done, she thought the third-floor, three-room suite represented PRA well: the reception room and front office, Ed's big lab-cum-tech warehouse at the back of the building, and this, Cree's office, a gracious, high-ceilinged corner room with hard-wood floors and mahogany wainscoting. And of course the priceless windows. Sandwiched between First Avenue and Post Alley, the old brick building was not in terrific repair, but it had come through the recent earthquake with little more than cracks in the plaster. The other occupants were low-key – a law office and an architectural firm – and Cree felt it was an appropriately professional, discreet headquarters for a firm like PRA. Even with the rent reduction given by the landlord, Ed's rich uncle, they were paying more than they would for comparable facilities elsewhere: The view was expensive. But for Cree the good light, the big sweep of land and sea, were necessary antidotes to the other side of the profession.

Whatever he'd been thinking about, Beauforte seemed to have come to some decision. "So how's it work?" he asked. "You just come on down there, take a look, do some kind of . . . exorcism . . . or what?"

"Well, we start with just what we're doing, an initial conversation. If you or your sister think you'd like to proceed to a preliminary review, you pay us a retainer, and then we go to the location. We tour the site, conduct interviews with witnesses, and do some historical research. Once we have an idea what we're dealing with, we design a strategy tailored to your specific situation. This can range from us doing nothing – if, for example, we discover that all you've got is squirrels in your attic – to an intensive process that can take many weeks. For that, we have a standard contract that clearly defines our fees. Really, it's not so different from contracting with, say, an interior decorator."

This was putting as mundane a face on it as she could manage in good conscience, verging on an outright lie. In fact, an in-depth investigation and remediation often turned into a wrenching experience for both client and researcher.

Beauforte chuckled sourly. "It's not squirrels in *my* attic, thank you. It's my sister who's got the squirrels." He tapped the side of his head with one finger. "No disrespect intended, Ms. Black, but as I've made clear, I do not believe in any of this business. Hell, if you live in New Orleans, you know every damn house is 'haunted' – at least according to the tourist brochures. It's a whole local industry. And as far as that murder, there isn't a house in that town hasn't seen something sensational over the last couple hundred years." He looked down at his hands, frowned at some imperfection and picked at it. "I don't mean to sound flippant. Fact is, we – my mother and myself and Jack, that's Lila's husband – we're worried about Lila. She's been very upset since her . . . episode. Unstable. We persuaded her to see a psychiatrist, but it isn't helping." For the first time since he'd been here, Beauforte sounded as though he might be sincerely concerned.

"Why don't you tell me more about the situation? Lila was reluctant to go into any detail over the phone. You mentioned a murder – what's that about?"

Beauforte took a deep breath and recovered from his lapse into candor and compassion. He checked his watch, gave his head a toss that suggested both impatience and resignation. "Our family home was the, ah, site of a rather famous murder. I'm surprised Lila didn't mention it when she spoke with you." He snorted, then went on with histrionic sarcasm: "And I suppose it's the tormented spirit of the victim that roams those dark halls – "

"Mr. Beauforte."

One eyebrow came up. "Sorry. But be forewarned, that's probably just about what Lila's gonna tell you."

"And I'll look forward to hearing her point of view when I interview her. Maybe we ought to just start with the basic information. The house – I gather it's been in your family for a long time – ?" Cree readied a legal pad and poised a pen over it.

Once he got going, Ronald Beauforte managed to tell her a great deal. The house had been built in 1851 in New Orleans's Garden District by Jean Claire Armand Beauforte, a wealthy sugar producer and military officer who later distinguished himself as a general for the Confederacy. During the Civil War, the house was seized by Union troops under the terms of a law that permitted the Army to occupy absent slave-owners' property. When hostilities ceased, it was restored to General Beauforte's family for another generation, but they sold the house in 1897, after which it was owned by a succession of progressively poorer families. Like most historic buildings in New Orleans, its condition mirrored the economic hardships of the region, the long swoon from Reconstruction right on into the Great Depression. So the house endured many years of improper maintenance and neglect and then stood abandoned for another decade until 1948, when it was repurchased by Ronald Beauforte's father, great-grandson of the famous general. By that time the roofs were practically falling in, the plaster raining from the walls, the sills gone to wet rot; a big live oak had come down in a hurricane and damaged one wing. Beauforte's father spent a small fortune restoring and modernizing the house, slave quarters, and carriage house. According to Ronald, many historic houses in New Orleans shared a similar arc of interrupted ownership, decline, and restoration.

Ronald and his sister Lila were both born into the big house and lived there until they left for boarding school and college and began their own lives. Their father died in 1972, but their mother stayed on there until her

7

stroke in 1991. The house was empty for about a year, as Charmian Beauforte went through rehabilitation and tried to determine whether she could live in it again; finally, deciding she needed closer medical supervision and more modern conveniences, she opted to move to a retirement complex. They rented out the house for seven years, until the tenants encountered their "unfortunate circumstances." For eighteen months afterward, it had stood empty again until Lila Beauforte Warren, Ronald's sister, decided she wanted to move back in, reestablish the Beauforte name and bloodline on the historic premises.

Cree jotted notes as Beauforte expounded, impressed by his knowledge of the house and its long history. She realized how little she knew of the places she'd lived — the apartments in Philadelphia, the suburban ranch houses, the student dives, the old farmhouse near Concord where she'd spent those happy years with Mike, even the little house she lived in now. Next to nothing. She wondered with some envy how it would feel to trace your roots so clearly to a one locale, a single proud structure. To have your world pivot on such a durable axle. *Depends on what kind of place it is*, she decided.

" 'Course," Beauforte finished, "Lila's plan has one little fly in the ointment — her damn ghost. She doesn't want to move in again if she has to cohabit with tormented spirits and the rest of it." Before Cree could formulate a question, Beauforte raised his hand. "And *don't* ask me about *that*. *She* swears it's haunted, she wants somebody to unhaunt the place. She found out about you guys on the Internet or someplace, and I was coming to Seattle on business and therefore got delegated to check you out. You want the fine print on the supernatural end of it, you're going to have to talk to her. She won't reveal the details, and anyway I'd refuse to dignify her claims by repeating them."

"But you were going to tell me about the 'unfortunate circumstances' of your tenants."

Beauforte checked his watch again and looked out the window as if to verify the time by the slant of light across the rooftops. "You no doubt heard about it in the news, even up here. The Templeton Chase murder?"

"That does ring a bell, but – "

"Well, we'd rented the house to this fella Templeton Chase – Temp – popular news anchorman on a big New Orleans TV station. Pretty wife, well-off, seemed like a good tenant after Momma moved out to Lakeside Manor. So one fine day after they've been there seven years, Mrs. Chase comes home to find Temp in the kitchen shot in the head. Caused a big stir."

"Right, I vaguely remember. So how'd it turn out?"

"Well, later on, some dirt came out about Temp having some under-the-table connections with big crime elements, I can't remember all the details. So some people said maybe it was a whack job." Beauforte's face darkened and became more guarded. "I don't know how the police are doing now, but for us, surprise, surprise – kill somebody in a house, high-profile grisly murder, your rental value really takes a dive. End result is, Beauforte House is sitting empty again, almost two years now. We cleaned it up good and did some remodeling, but after a year of advertising and no takers, we took it off the market. Can't say as I blame anybody."

"I thought you didn't believe in ghosts."

Beauforte cleared his throat. "Has nothing to do with ghosts. You want to sit your kids down to breakfast in that kitchen nook where somebody got his head blown off? Where they had to scrape Temp's brains off the wall?" His expectant look suggested that he'd deliberately tried to upset her with the gory details.

Cree nodded. For a moment, inside, she felt the familiar empathic dip and swoop toward the chaos and darkness, the tortured psychic space that would surround the murder. She pulled out of the dive, looked quickly to the sunlit landscape to anchor herself. She wondered if Beauforte had seen her mood change.

When she'd steadied, she decided to return the provocation. "Why not? Haul the corpse away, clean up the gore, even give the walls new coat of paint. Then eat your breakfast. Why not?"

"The idea just does something to the, ah, ambience, wouldn't you say?"

Cree shrugged. "What's the matter with the ambience? What could possibly remain to discomfort a person?"

He opened his mouth to respond, then shut it again. Finally he grinned sourly and said, "Touché." Then the smile faded and he looked at her appraisingly. "So, Ms. Black. Would it be safe to say the 'empathic techniques' you referred to earlier are your, uh, personal area of expertise? Your primary responsibility in your firm?"

"You're very observant." Yes, he'd caught her sudden slide and recovery.

"Which brings up the question, why would an attractive, intelligent woman like you *want*, actively *seek out*, involvement with places and situations like that? How the hell'd you ever get into this line of work?"

Cree felt herself stiffen but managed to shrug with an attempt at nonchalance. This was a place she didn't go with clients. "A longtime interest, that's all."

Beauforte's eyes showed he'd caught the dodge. But he nodded, accepting it, then checked his watch again and stood up. "Well, this has been one of the strangest conversations I have ever had, but I can't say it hasn't been educational. In any case, I have a meeting to get to. Ms. Black, we'll go as far as to pay for one of your preliminary reviews. Hell, maybe if we can convince my sister we've done something, that'll fix her head. Chalk it up to the placebo effect." He paused, opened his lapel to take out a checkbook and a fat Mont Blanc fountain pen, then flipped open a pair of half-lens glasses. "That is, provided it's something you can do soon. We, uh, feel it's become a matter of some urgency – given my sister's state of mind, you understand." He put on the glasses but peered over the top of them with a blue gaze calculated to drive home the point: His sister was not coping with whatever had happened to her.

Cree tapped on her keyboard to bring up her calendar. "There are a few things I need to take care of, and as I said, my partner's in Massachussetts, so he's not available . . . It's short notice, but I think I can juggle things to get down there by the end of the week. Is that soon enough?"

"Sooner the better. Your retainer for this 'preliminary review,' how much would that be?"

"Five thousand dollars, plus expenses – airfare, hotels, and so on."

Beauforte began to write out the check.

"Mr. Beauforte, there is one other thing you and your family should be aware of." The obligatory caveat. It was in the contract, too, just so clients couldn't say you hadn't warned them.

"Oh? And what's that?" Bent over her desk, he paused, eyes alert.

"Part of our process is to do extensive investigation into the personal and family histories of our clients. It will be especially important in this case, since the house has been in the family for several generations. Should we take on this case, we will need to have candid, in-depth discussion with you and your sister, your mother, and any others who have known you, your father, or your grandparents."

"Isn't it Temp Chase's family you want to talk to? Isn't he the supposed ghost?"

"We don't know that yet. One of the problems facing a serious researcher is that the history of a place is very much . . . *layered*. We'll need to be like archaeologists, delving down through those layers of time. If there is a haunting entity, it could be the residuum of a homeless person who died there while the house was empty back in the forties. Or the wife of General Beauforte, say, or one of those Union soldiers who occupied it. Or someone from any time in between. And sometimes it can be . . . older still."

Beauforte nodded equivocally. "Okay, I get the idea."

"Your family's history is particularly important for two reasons. One is simply that they've been the house's primary occupants. The other is the issue of the link – why it is your sister who has had these experiences, why she's particularly vulnerable or sensitive. We'll need access to family archives, photo albums, and genealogies . . . My point is, this can become very personal, and some clients find the process intrusive. And sometimes . . . unpleasant details emerge. But let me stress that this *is* an essential component of our work. And our contract includes strict confidentiality clauses that – "

"Ms. Black." Beauforte took off his glasses, squared his wide shoulders, and drilled his eyes into hers. "You have never been to New Orleans, have you?"

"No."

"When you do come, you will discover that we Beaufortes are held in *highest* esteem by our community. For the simple reason that there is nothing less than honorable in our history. Nothing in the slightest unsavory." He finished writing the check, ripped it free, and flipped it onto Cree's desk. "Your warning is unnecessary and verges on being offensive. The Beaufortes have nothing to hide."

"Of course not, Mr. Beauforte." The smile she gave him was meant to be reassuring and businesslike, but it felt wan and wry on her face, the best she could manage. She felt a rush of sympathy for him: He was either a man who knew very little about the human condition, or a man who worked very hard in what would always be a futile effort to stay above it. "No insult was intended," she said, wanting suddenly to console him. "Of course not."

2

AFTER HE LEFT, CREE jotted a few more notes, started a file on the case, and brought the retainer check out to Joyce. The outer office was smaller but had enough room for a row of file cabinets, a big bookcase, Joyce's desk, and a couch and coffee table. A small counter held cups, napkins, and a coffee brewer that filled the suite with a tempting smell.

Joyce looked up. "Good-lookin' guy, huh? Clark Gable with a little more meat on his bones."

"If you like the type." Cree handed her the check.

"Which I take it you don't?" Joyce looked at the check and whistled. "Hallelujah. We'll get paid for at least another couple of weeks."

"He wants us to provide the placebo effect," Cree said dryly. "For his sister."

"A skeptic, huh?"

"Also a model of probity and integrity, from a family without a smudge upon its name. But the site is historic, and the case has other interesting features. It might be a productive one for us to investigate. I was thinking I might try to get down there for a preliminary before – "

"Cree." Joyce's face showed concern, and she reached out to take Cree's hand. "You're speaking with a Southern accent."

"Shit."

Cree shut her eyes and let Joyce rub her hand, feeling the stabilizing effect of physical human contact. Thank God for Joyce, who took seriously the job of keeping Cree anchored in herself, in her own body and identity, in the here and now.

It was so easy to drift. Before she knew it, she was resonating with another person, the way an old piano will sing ghost notes from the vibration of your footsteps as you walk by. The tendency even had physical manifestations: She often took on clients' limps and gestures, felt their aches and itches. When her sister had delivered the twins, Cree had been doubled up with sympathetic labor pains.

You had to keep the empathic connection manageable, or you'd lose yourself. In their work, it was a useful talent that allowed her to perceive things beyond the ordinarily inviolate walls of individual identity. But in daily life, it was more like a disability, some exotic disease. It required constant vigilance. If you weren't careful, the sheer mass of human presence in the world could crash over you, a tidal wave of emotion that would drown you in the hungers and hopes and fears that were all around, everywhere, always. Or, as had just started to happen, it could subtly, stealthily erode you. Without her even noticing it, her borders had blurred and she'd absorbed some of Ronald Beauforte, *becoming* him to a tiny degree, picking up his accent and who knew what else. And she didn't even like the guy!

Cree hated imposing her penchant on her friends and colleagues. It made her feel fragile, dependent – a sickly child. And yet it was essential to their work.

"Sorry. Thanks." Cree took a deep breath and blew herself a Bronx cheer, retrieved her hand, and briskly slapped her own cheeks as if putting on aftershave. One of Pop's gestures, she remembered. " 'The rain in Spain falls mainly in the plain.' Better?"

"Much." Joyce's almond eyes checked her face critically and then looked back to her desk, apparently reassured. "Listen, Ed called while Clark Gable was here, I figured you didn't want to be disturbed. But he'd like you to call him back ASAP. Also your sister called, wants a return buzz." Joyce handed her the phone slips. "But don't forget there's Mrs. Wilson coming in ten minutes."

Right. Cree had forgotten Mrs. Wilson. Ronald Beauforte's visit had put her off balance, and anyway it was seldom that two clients came to the office on the same day. She took the slips, gave Joyce a kiss of gratitude, headed back to the office.

Joyce didn't get involved with the supernatural end of the work, but she kept Cree and Edgar on track, managed the business end of things, archived their files, and did the lion's share of historical and forensic detective work. Like Cree, she was an East Coast transplant to Seattle. Her accent gave away that she'd grown up on Long Island – talking to her on the phone, people assumed she was a New Yorker, probably Jewish, and, given her deep contralto, probably large. They were always surprised to come to the office to hear the same voice coming from the small, delicate Chinese woman behind the desk. But Joyce Wu was a person of contradictions, and her appearance was misleading, too. She looked to be in her early thirties but was in fact forty-two, four years older than Cree, possessing some enviable longevity gene that kept her skin smooth and hair glossy. And though she was small and slim, she was as strong as any man Cree knew, something of a fitness freak. The first time they'd gone jogging together, Cree had done four miles with her, working hard to keep up with Joyce's lithe stride, before letting her go on for another three.

Mrs. Wilson. Right. The woman who had called for an appointment last week and who had refused to reveal any aspect of her situation, about which she seemed very uncomfortable.

When she came in, she looked very much as Cree had imagined her: an elderly woman, portly, expensively dressed, and nervous. She had a large, lugubrious, kind face beneath a well-coiffed cloud of gray hair, and an endearing humility. Cree invited her to sit and offered her some coffee, which she declined.

Mrs. Wilson's spotted hands fidgeted with the strap of her purse. "I do hope you can help me," she said.

"I will certainly do my best. Please tell me how."

"It's a little . . . awkward."

"I understand. Many of our clients feel the same way at first – your situation may not be as unusual or awkward as you think."

"Our discussion is confidential?"

"Absolutely."

Mrs. Wilson's watery hazel eyes caught Cree's and retreated. Another quick glance and retreat. "Not so long ago, I lost someone dear to me. Very dear." Pause.

"I'm so sorry – "

"I don't know anything about the 'afterlife.' I'm not religious, never have been."

Cree nodded.

"And I'm seventy-three years old!" Mrs. Wilson looked at Cree searchingly, the glistening eyes finding the courage to linger this time, as if trying to convey what her words did not.

Cree put it together: *My loved one has died and left an emptiness that hurts and frightens me. I am old and don't know what I believe. I am old and thinking about my own ending, facing big questions.*

Cree waited. But so did Mrs. Wilson, who apparently expected Cree to take the lead. After another moment, Cree came around the desk and took the chair next to her. Mrs. Wilson was now clenching her purse hard against her buxom front, and Cree put a hand on one tense forearm. "Why don't you tell me about the person you lost."

"My splendid prince. He died two weeks ago." Mrs. Wilson faltered, and the big face crumpled. Cree's heart went out to her: "splendid prince." Such a romantic term coming from this powder-smelling, proper-looking, fireplug-shaped old woman. She fumbled in her purse, took out a laminated color photo, and gave it to Cree with a trembling hand. "My companion for eighteen years. My splendid prince."

It was a dog.

Cree was no expert in dog breeds, but the scruffy little brown dog in the photo looked anything but splendid or princely.

"You're surprised, I can see you are. Yes, he's just a mutt. I first called him Splendid Prince to be funny, to tease him. As if he were some noble pedigree, you see. But that is exactly what he became to me."

Cree was speechless. This was very touching. Absolutely no words came for a full five heartbeats. Finally she managed, "It must be a terrible loss. I'm very sorry."

"That's why I hoped that you might be able to . . . put me in touch with him, wherever he is?"

Oh my, Cree thought.

It took another half hour to soothe Mrs. Wilson and convince her that she and Ed weren't mediums, they couldn't go looking for the souls of the departed. She left the dog issue out of it, just stressed that PRA got involved only when there was reliable evidence the departed had already chosen to return. No, sorry, Cree couldn't refer her to someone else. She urged her to be cautious if she continued her quest, wary of unscrupulous people who might take advantage of her grief and desperation.

As she was leaving, Cree felt a sweet-sad chord in her chest and spontaneously bent to give her a hug and a kiss on one doughy cheek. Mrs. Wilson looked grateful for the contact.

Cree forestalled Joyce's questioning look with a raised finger and went to call Edgar. It was only four o'clock, but it would be seven back east, and she wanted to catch him before he went to do any night fieldwork. She went to his room so she could use the videophone and get a look at his face, which she missed whenever they worked independently.

Edgar's room was three times the size of Cree's, with naked brick walls and a pair of tall windows facing the building across the alley. His desk and file cabinets occupied only one corner of the room; the middle was taken up by the counters, computers, and rack-mounted electronics of the lab he used for processing physical evidence gathered at field sites. The remainder of the room served as storage for the equipment Edgar used for his end of their work. He had taken the minimal kit needed for a preliminary review to the Massachusetts job, leaving the bulky stuff behind, a mix of off-the-shelf, high-end high-tech and Edgar's own adaptations of various technologies: infrared cameras, radar motion detectors, ambient-light night-vision photographic equipment, sound recorders, visible-light video and film cameras, air-pressure- and temperature-monitoring equipment, seismic vibration sensors, ion counters, electromagnetic-field-measuring devices, a forensic gas chromatograph, microscopes, skin galvanometers, voice-stress analyzers, the

17

electroencephalographs, tripods, toolboxes, and bulky aluminum travel cases.

Edgar's playground. More than three hundred thousand dollars' worth of equipment. They'd gotten some of it used from various donors, received some grants from the Society for Psychical Research and the odd eccentric millionaire, including Ed's uncle, but the outlay had left them with some hefty debts. One big reason for Ed's concern for revenue.

And so far, it had produced very little in the way of empirical evidence.

But you had to try. Credibility ultimately rested on scientific evidence, some hard physical proof. Something that all of Cree's emphatic talents couldn't provide.

Cree sat at Edgar's desk and used his videophone to dial the number Joyce had given her. Within seconds, the screen bleeped and there was Ed's familiar face. Cree looked into the little ball-shaped camera on top of the monitor and waved.

"I thought it might be you," he said. "Hey – you look different. You got your hair cut."

"Just a trim. I'm surprised you noticed."

"Are you kidding? It looks terrific." Edgar smiled, a grin that crept up the right side of his face. Cree had always liked that smile, the touch of irony in it.

Ed was into technology, but he was not at all the proverbial nerd. He was too handsome, in a long-faced way, and his intelligence was by no means confined to machines. The tilt of his smile gave it away: the streak of sadness or resignation that came with knowing the human condition only too well. His lanky body, long face, and sandy hair gave him the look of a minor member of the British royal family, which he exploited to do an outrageous impersonation of Prince Charles.

"How did the meeting with Beauforte go?"

"He's sort of a smug son of a bitch. But I think there might be something for us there. I agreed to do a preliminary, got a retainer check. Full fee, you'll be happy to hear."

"Great! Well, I should be done here in a week. I can go down there if you'd like, or we could both go – "

"I thought maybe I'd get down there later this week," Cree said. "Maybe before you return. I can clear the time." Edgar looked disappointed, so she explained: "He says his sister – she's the main witness – is very disturbed. I got the sense the family's only coming to us because they'll do anything to calm her down, she's really going pieces. Plus, I was thinking, here's the paying customer you said we needed, so it would be good to follow up right away . . ."

Edgar nodded, unconvinced.

"Okay," Cree admitted, "I got a feeling that we should move on this. A buzz. I don't know why." Still Ed said nothing, but a little ripple of concern passed over his forehead, and Cree decided to change the subject. "How about your end? What're you getting?"

His face brightened, sheer enthusiasm for the hunt replacing his doubtfulness. "Multiple occurrences, multiple witnesses with excellent credibility. The entity appears to be a perseverating fragmentary, displaying both visual and auditory. A couple of reports of tactile, but those're from my least reliable witnesses."

Cree nodded, and Edgar went on, using a shorthand vocabulary that in all the world only Cree would understand. A perseverating fragmentary was an entity with a limited repertoire of activities, an apparition appearing in the same place and doing the same motions again and again. They called it fragmentary because the entity was not a complete human personality, but a lingering, very limited mental construct. Such a manifestation was almost more the experience itself than a being – a disconnected mental and emotional matrix that somehow repetitively played out independently of a corporeal body or much of a self-aware consciousness. What people referred to as "ghosts" could range from merest shards, no more than a roaming impulse or hunger, to virtually complete personalities.

That Ed's entity had been seen, heard, and maybe felt on several occasions by more than one person did suggest it would be a promising study. If it were perceivable by several senses, and was robust enough to be witnessed by several people, it would give Cree more to work with and possibly allow Edgar's equipment to register verifiable physical phenomena.

"So what's on for tonight?" Cree asked.

"Well, I'm going back to the site. I'll do some infrared and visible-light work. One of the witnesses has agreed to come with me and wear the polygraph setup, too."

"She good-looking?"

Edgar rolled his eyes, and the grin appeared. "She is, very definitely. But she's also thirty years older than me and happily married." Then his smile evaporated. "Actually, I'm not looking forward to it. The place bugs me. Creeps me out."

"Any reason in particular?"

Edgar's eyes moved to one side. "Just the feeling of the house. I'm not in your league, Cree, but I do have a couple of functional nerve endings."

"I've noticed. I rely on it daily, Ed. Tell me about the feeling."

A kink of trouble had formed between his eyebrows, and Edgar rubbed at it with both big hands as he tried to put words to the feeling. "This . . . loneliness, I guess. Something very . . . stark there."

Oh, yes, Cree thought. *That.*

When she'd first started spending time in haunted places, she'd been as frightened as anyone else by the fear of scary things, the dark, the unknown – grisly deaths, nightmarish visions, awful secrets, moving shadows. That unrelenting sense of imminent danger. But you got a grip on that after a while. What you didn't get used to was the existential stuff: The scary things might spring out and hurt you or make you crazy, but the maw of loneliness Ed spoke of, that abyss of emptiness, could swallow your soul.

They both came back from that. They talked some more about the Massachusetts entity and then about the equipment she'd need to take with her to New Orleans. Cree got on the radiophone and Ed walked her back into the storage area, showing her where to find everything. But he seemed increasingly reluctant, and at last she pointed it out to him.

"You're not too happy with me going down there on my own, are you?"

"I'm just thinking . . . why don't you come out here first? Help me finish this preliminary. I could use your insight. Maybe we could take an extra day to see the sights of Boston, then both go to New Orleans – "

"I don't think the client can wait. Anyway, we'll have plenty of time to work on these together if we end up taking either case."

She didn't mean it to, but that sounded cold, and Ed didn't answer right away. She was glad they weren't on the videophone now and couldn't see each other's faces. Edgar's desire for her company was sweet but poignant and difficult. Though he never imposed his feelings on her, he didn't try to hide them, either. He was a terrific person, and she gave him most of the credit for their ability to navigate daily through the complex of emotions, working as friends and business partners despite what amounted to a very unequal relationship.

"I'm also a little worried about New Orleans," he admitted hesitantly. "*You* in New Orleans."

"Why's that?" Knowing why. She got defensive and angry when this stuff got stirred up.

"I've been there. Great town – 'The Big Easy.' Fun party town. Rich and colorful history, a great mix of cultural traditions. But it's got some places you should probably avoid. More than most cities, Cree."

He wasn't talking about bad neighborhoods. New Orleans was well known among legitimate parapsychologists and sensationalist amateurs alike as a place where some particularly grisly things had taken place. The horror of LaLaurie House, where Madame LaLaurie tortured and butchered dozens of her slaves in an attic room, was only one of many examples.

"I'm fine. I'm strong now, Ed," Cree said. Then it caught up with her and she bristled at his concern. "I think I can probably handle it."

Now he coughed, cleared his throat, feeling awkward. "Of course! It's just – you've been a little, you know, *susceptible* recently, more than usual . . . Shit, Cree, I can't always figure out how I'm supposed to – "

"Yeah."

She said it gruffly, and they both fell silent. On one level, she was doing great. But, yes, she had been more "susceptible" recently. Why? Maybe something to do with Mike, this time of year, she wasn't sure.

And yes, she could imagine that it would be tough for Ed, tiptoeing around her vulnerability, trying to protect her without treating her like an invalid. Still, it pissed her off. Not at Ed, he was doing his best. At herself. At the complexities of life. At the reminder that she was fragile, thirty-eight and single, a perpetual widow with a lot of unresolved crap. Why did she get so tough on Ed when he brought it up? Maybe because neither he nor Joyce fully understood that, yes, she had to be careful, but she also had to *resist*, had to fight back. You had to push the boundaries and hope you got tougher as time went on.

"Where'd you go, Cree?"

"I'm here."

Which was so obviously not true that he had no choice but to roll with it. "Right," he said, with more resignation than sarcasm.

Cree had drifted back toward his office, and though she was out of range of the videophone camera she could see his earnest face in the monitor. He looked downcast and worried. He clicked a ballpoint pen in and out, inspecting the tip, then looked hopefully up at his own monitor. Still not seeing Cree, he looked away and rubbed his forehead again.

"You take care of yourself, though, okay?" Edgar had pivoted his chair, and there was something touching about seeing him in profile. Like watching him talking to himself. "You'll keep in close touch with Joyce and me, right? Call in the cavalry if you need us?"

"Yeah," Cree said again.

And then she hurried over to the videophone, wanting to make things better between them, but by the time she got there he'd hung up, and now it was her turn to look at the bland gray-blue of an empty screen.

3

DEIRDRE DIDN'T ANSWER WHEN Cree tried to return her call, so after leaving a message she decided to stop over there on her way home. A dose of normalcy seemed in order, and anyway she was feeling something like a nutritional deficit after going four days without seeing the twins.

Her sister had married a carpenter who when he wasn't renovating other people's homes had gradually restored their own, a fine Craftsman-style house in the heart of the Queen Anne district. Between Don's carpentering and Deirdre's teaching, they did well, and their place was something of a testament to building on what you've got, sticking with it, in both marriage and domicile. The house was pleasingly proportioned, with ivory clap-boards and goldenrod trim, fronted by a small yard exploding with rhododendrons and California lilacs: a place loved and loved in.

Cree went up the walk between mounds of blossoms to the front porch. No one answered when she rang the bell, but she could hear muffled music through the door. She banged on the glass for a while and was glad to see feet and then legs and then all of Zoe skipping down the stairs, a slender girl with chin-length yellow hair that clashed with her Sonics jersey.

"Hi, Aunt Cree."

"Hi, Niece Zoe."

Following Zoe into the living room, she wondered how those straight hips managed to hold up low-riding bell bottoms at all. She tossed her purse onto the couch and then threw herself after it, immediately feeling better.

"Come here," Cree said. "Gimme some girl bones, kid." She made a grab and managed to snag Zoe, who didn't resist much as Cree pulled her onto her lap and hugged her. Both girls had started to shoot up and were skinny as witches' brooms, all angles and ticklish skin. Now Zoe's butt bones dug painfully into Cree's thigh, sharp as two elbows. Cree inhaled the sweet smell of her as she rocked her back and forth.

"So where's your mom?"

"She went to Larry's Market to get some fish and stuff. We're being responsible."

They probably were, Cree agreed. Ten years old, it was at least a possibility. "And where's your sister?"

"HYACINTH!" Zoe exploded like a trench mortar. "She's upstairs. HY!" Zoe leaned away so she could finger one of Cree's earrings, inspecting it with a critical expression. "She's got her music on. HYA-*CINTH!* YOUR *AUNT* HAS COME TO *SEE* YOU!"

Cree's ears rang. "You know, I never really noticed it before, but you got quite the voice on you," she said. "Especially from this close."

"I get plenty of practice, believe me." Zoe tossed her head contemptuously toward the stairs. An indictment of her sister.

They were supposedly identical twins, and were both blonde, skinny, moon-faced, verbal, and vivid. But they were not at all alike. Hyacinth seemed to Cree like a cheerful garden of pansies, cosmos, and marigolds on a breezy day, her moods varying but only the way the flowers sometimes toss their heads in the wind and sometimes go still, come vibrantly alight in the sun and then dim as clouds passed over. Zoe was more like fireworks, intense and intermittent, searing colors bursting aloft, etching the sky with brilliant trails and flashes and as quickly fading into utter darkness.

Hyacinth came into the living room, barefooted and wearing a yellow dress. She frowned at Zoe. "I'm not deaf," she said primly. "I just wanted to hear the end of that song. Hi, Aunt Cree."

"She actually *likes* Britney Spears," Zoe said, appalled.

"I do not! Just that one song."

Cree gathered Hyacinth onto her lap, holding the two of them like a big, loose armful of reeds and twigs, awkward and pokey. Too big to fit, now. For a moment they jostled and squirmed, and then Zoe broke loose and went to sit on a chair nearby.

"So, have you been finding any ghosts recently?" Zoe asked.

Cree thought for a moment. She had never tried to conceal what she did from the twins, but she made it a policy not to get too deep with them. You could gloss over it somewhat, but in the end you were dealing with death, and what happened after death, and the often sad and scary compulsions and fixations that lived on, and living people's fear. The girls didn't need all that.

"Well, actually, I wanted to ask you two for some advice. On one of my cases." Cree decided that if she didn't mention names, telling them wouldn't really constitute a breach of confidentiality. "A very nice old woman came into my office today with a most unusual request."

That got their interest: They both loved a challenge, a problem to solve. Hyacinth slid off Cree's lap and sat sideways on the couch so she could see Cree better. She bent her long stems under her and tugged her skirt hem over her knees. "What was it?" she asked.

"She wanted me to make contact with a loved one who had died? And before I could tell her what we really do, she showed me his picture. And it was a *dog*."

Different responses: Zoe rolled her eyes, Hyacinth made an expression of sympathy.

"Do dogs . . . *can* there be ghosts of dogs?" Hyacinth asked.

Cree shrugged. "I've never encountered one. But I don't see why not."

"So what are you going to do?"

"That's what I wanted to ask you guys. She was such a nice person. I wanted to help her, but I couldn't think of how."

"I know how," Zoe said. "You could do this, like, séance, and pretend you'd made contact with the dog. You could tell her the dog's ghost was happy and still loved her and would stay with her always."

"Hmm. Yeah. But I don't like to lie to people. And then if she believed me, she'd want me to do it again, and pretty soon – "

Zoe scowled. "You could just tell her to get a new dog. I mean, that's what she needs!"

"No," Hyacinth said immediately. "That would be disloyal! And Aunt Cree couldn't suggest it without offending her, like her precious dog could be so . . . replaceable. She doesn't want just any dog, she misses *that* one."

"That's what I thought, too," Cree agreed. "You can see it's a quandary."

The girls put their chins in their hands and thought about it, taking it on face value, in their different ways allying themselves instantly with solving the problem. Cree looked at them and loved them fiercely. There had been times when she'd envied Deirdre her marriage, her living husband, her relatively normal life, and most of all these two. In tougher moments her longing hurt and knotted up dark inside, but more often it was like this: acute gratitude that these two girls were in her life. The best imaginable nieces.

They spent a few minutes coming up with suggestions of increasing complexity and unlikeliness, and then the phone rang. Hyacinth bounced off the couch to go to the kitchen to answer it.

Zoe watched her leave the room, then turned to Cree. "That's her boyfriend. You can tell by how fast she jumped up."

"Boyfriend! Really? At ten years old?" Cree could just see down the hall to the kitchen, where Hyacinth leaned in the doorway. She had cradled the phone between ear and shoulder and was speaking quietly into the receiver, very involved, swinging the coiled cord like a jump rope.

Zoe nodded. "At least I *think* it's a boy. But he looks like some kind of, like, *rodent*. The sad part is, I think she's in love with him *because* that's what he's like. She's so softhearted. 'Mommy, look, he followed me home, can we keep him?' " An acid caricature of a cutesy kid. "Pathetic."

Cree pretended to peer at her doubtfully. "Twins, huh. Which one were you, again?"

"Very funny," Zoe said acidly.

"You really are a *menace*, you know that?"

Zoe just nodded again in sober agreement. " 'Me-nace 2 So-cie-ty,' " she intoned. Then she sniffed indignantly, and her eyes widened in accusation. "*You* should talk!"

"Really like a rodent?

"I can hear you guys perfectly, by the way," Hyacinth called down the hall.

When Deirdre came in, banging through the door with a double armload of groceries, purse, key ring, newspaper, Cree and the girls took the bags and they all went to the kitchen to put things away. The two cats came to get underfoot as they opened and slammed cupboards and drawers and refrigerator.

"Leave the fish out," Deirdre ordered. "That's dinner. And one of those lemons, Hy."

"The girls were very responsible," Cree told her. "I can personally attest."

"This old lady wants Aunt Cree to hunt for the ghost of a dog," Zoe said.

Another minute of chaos and Deirdre paused to look her daughters up and down. "You know, girls, it's awfully crowded in here. I think Cree and I have this under control. Why don't you go get started on your homework and let us catch up. I'll call you when it's time to set the table." She turned back to the cupboard to stack cans of cat food.

The twins left, carrying the cats. Cree folded the shopping bags as Deirdre put on an apron and began washing vegetables. The music began again upstairs, this time the insistent, battering beat of Zoe's rap. Cree leaned against the counter, watching her sister's face in the mirror over the sink as they conversed. Deirdre was thirty-six, two years younger and, even in the thick-soled jogging shoes she always put on after work, three inches shorter than Cree. Now she was dressed in her teaching clothes, a white blouse and a practical floral skirt with a faint handprint of chalk dust on one thigh, a silk scarf at her throat, looking very much the middle school teacher at the end of a long day. Cree knew from experience that people seeing them side by side would recognize them as sisters but wouldn't be able to say which was older. Deirdre had prettier, more delicate features, made dramatic by darker hair and brows, but her face showed deeper lines of both worry and laughter, the paradoxical marks of teaching and motherhood. When they'd been in their teens, Cree had often felt largish and plain by comparison. Later, she'd discovered that men could fall just as hard for a fuller-bodied woman, and that had evened things out.

"Monday, huh," Cree inquired.

"It certainly is that." Deirdre put the greens in the salad spinner, set it aside, and began scrubbing some carrots. "What's this about a dog?"

"It's complex. I was just asking the girls for advice. Joyce said you called – anything urgent? I left a message."

Deirdre glanced at the blinking red light on the answering machine she hadn't had time to check. "Not urgent. Just that Mom called this morning. She likes to call up for heart-to-heart chats when I'm running around trying to get ready for school."

"Uh-oh. What was on her mind?" When their mother called Deirdre, it often had to do with Cree, and vice versa.

"She told me the doctor said she has congested coronary arteries."

"Well, we suspected as much."

"Yeah. So she's supposed to go in for an angioplasty – where they blow up this little balloon in your artery? She says her friend Marie Haskell had one last year, and it was no big thing."

"But you're worried?"

Deirdre turned her back to the sink, leaning against it with her arms crossed. "Well, yeah. You know."

"Was she?"

"She plays it down. But I'd say, yes. Can't blame her." Deirdre frowned, then brightened. "And then she talked about you."

"I figured."

"She told me her new heart doctor is a total dreamboat and is your age and recently divorced." A tight grin. She turned back to the sink but kept her eyes on Cree's in the mirror. "She thought maybe next time she went to see him, you could come with her – ostensibly to help her, you know, decide on treatment or whatever, did I think that was a good idea? I figured you deserved fair warning."

Cree laughed and gripped her head in exasperation. "So what was your verdict? Good idea?"

"Uh-uh. No comment. I'm staying completely out of it." Deirdre applied herself to the carrots.

It was all lighthearted, supposedly. Mother's concern for her widowed daughter's singleness, childlessness, strange profession, and bouts of existential anguish. Mike had died nine years ago, and Cree still wore her wedding ring. No, she hadn't gotten over it, didn't have a clue how to let go of the sweetness they'd had, and given what had happened when he'd died there was no way to explain to Mom the confusions that came with meeting other men. She was married forever to a dead man and devoted to a metaphysical quest, like some kind of nun in a strange religion with herself as its only adherent. You could laugh all you wanted at people's concern and matchmaking reflexes and the rest, but you still couldn't deny the pang of truth that came with it.

Deirdre had been watching Cree in the mirror again and must have seen her expression change. "Sorry," she began, "I didn't mean to – "

"No, it's all right. I'll call her. Thanks for the heads up."

They let it settle for a moment. Deirdre finished the carrots and set Cree up to slice them as she went to work on the fish. The girls were laughing together upstairs.

"Stay for dinner?" Deirdre's light tone sounded a little forced. "Don will be home soon – "

"I don't know . . ."

"Cree – "

"Really, Dee, it only hurts when I laugh. Just a little stitch, right here." Cree grimaced and put her hand on her heart. Pushing it all one level deeper in an effort to let Deirdre off the hook. "Okay?"

29

"Okay," Deirdre said, smiling again. "But it would still be nice if you stayed for dinner."

When the salad was washed, the rice on to boil, and the fish ready for the oven, Deirdre poured them each a glass of chardonnay. They sat on the tall kitchen stools, relaxing. Deirdre looked as though she deserved a moment to let her shoulders down.

"So when's Mom supposed to go in for the angioplasty?" Cree asked.

"Three weeks."

"Good – I'll be back by then." At Deirdre's questioning look, Cree explained. "I'm going to New Orleans, flying out later this week. Just got a fat retainer for a preliminary investigation, probably only take four or five days. I'm looking forward to it – I've always wanted to go there."

"You know Don and I went once," Deirdre said. "Back before the girls were born. Our wild youth – we thought it would be fun to go for Mardi Gras."

"Right, I remember. How was it?"

"Hmm. Strange, actually." Deirdre's pretty forehead drew into a small frown.

"How so?"

"It was really . . . well, *wild*. We went down there to party, but this was more than we'd bargained for. It's like the whole city goes crazy. Everybody's in costume. Everybody's wearing a mask. It's got a lot of morbid overtones, and it's very . . . pagan. And it's amazingly uninhibited – I mean, literally, people screwing in the streets and on the balconies. Seriously, in full view!"

"That's the whole point of masks – license. If your identity's hidden, nobody can hold you accountable for your behavior – you can act the way you'd really like to." Cree swigged her wine and chuckled. "I didn't know you had such a prudish streak, Dee!"

"No, really, Cree. We found it a little, I don't know . . . sinister. The city has this *doubleness*. Don started calling it 'the city of masks.' I don't mean just the parades. The whole town puts on a show, a welcoming facade, but it has another face: poverty, resentment, crime, corruption.

Race issues. Nothing is quite what it seems. Even the woman who ran our b-and-b – charming, matronly Southern hostess, we got to know her pretty well, even went out for drinks with her? We were there for three days before I came into the bathroom and saw her with her wig off, shaving her chest. She was a man!"

"So?"

Dee snorted. "So nothing. Except that he took the opportunity to make a pass at me! And I'm standing there, still trying to put it together, and I just blurt the first thing that comes to my mind? I tell him, 'No, thanks so much, but I'm not a lesbian!' "

They both laughed, and then the phone rang.

Deirdre answered it, listened. "Sure, just a moment." She went to the hallway and called, "Hy – telephone!" She covered the mouthpiece with one hand and whispered to Cree, "Boyfriend!" She listened until Hyacinth picked up. Sober again, she told Cree, "I don't mean to rain on your parade. It's a fascinating place. You just have to, you know . . . watch yourself, that's all."

4

TUESDAY WAS A SCATTERSHOT day. Cree felt like a dragonfly, darting and flitting as she prepared for the trip: getting airline tickets and hotel and rental car reservations, checking wardrobe, juggling appointments, and making phone calls to carve out the time away.

Aside from the routine travel preparations, there were those specific to her trade. She reviewed the psi literature to learn more about past cases in New Orleans. She asked Joyce to buy a few books on Louisiana history and culture. She selected some equipment from the metal shelves of Edgar's room, checked it, and packed it carefully in a big foam-padded aluminum case.

Even that was fairly routine.

Another dimension of preparation underlay all the bustle. For the empath there was always a quiet taking stock, a taking of one's own measure and readiness, and a grappling with the resulting ambiguities. Then there were the contacts made with loved ones and colleagues, all freighted with an unspoken burden – hellos with contingent good-byes hidden in them because the person who leaves for a ghost hunting expedition, the way Cree did it, might well not return. Not as the same person, anyway.

It was almost eight o'clock before she had time to stop in and see her mother. She was still undecided whether to bring up the handsome cardiologist thing, but it would be good to see Mom, especially at work. She drove to the little civic rec center Janet Black managed, parked, went up the broad steps and into the invigorating stink of sweat and floor varnish, the rubbery smell of basketballs and athletic shoes.

The racket in the entry hall told her that she'd guessed right: One of the teen league games was in full swing. The building echoed with the drub of balls, the squeak of shoes, the whistles of referees, the cheers of a small crowd. A girls' game, she saw as she paused at the gym door. The players milled for a moment and took positions for a foul shot, arms out, legs braced, eyes wildly alert. The shot hit the rim and bounced away, and then everyone was moving again, blue shirts and red shirts skirmishing, refs sidling and jogging. The numerals of the scoreboard clock counted down.

Mom sat at the scoring table. She looked joyful and suitably officious, very much in her element here: a woman in her early sixties, wearing the tan uniform shirt and slacks of the rec department, gray-shot hair tied back and out of the way. She lifted her reading glasses to make a notation, then let them fall against her chest on their red sports band. Her eyes went back to the game for a moment before she spotted Cree at the door. They exchanged smiles.

Cree made her way around the wall of the gym and slid into a folding chair next to her mother. This was Janet's preferred view of her domain: dead center in the big room with its high, trussed ceiling and glistening yellow floor. Fold-out bleachers lined one side, half full with the small but enthusiastic crowd; the teams hunched on low benches along the sidelines.

"Good game?"

Janet nodded. The crowd cheered for a scoring attempt, and she had to lean close to Cree's ear to be heard. "For sheer drama, nothing beats a middle school girls' basketball game. Not the NBA, not the WBA, nothing. This is something of a grudge match. The reds lost last time, and they've been building this up – the big rematch, right? But then their star player got hurt a couple of days ago. Fell off the stage during a play rehearsal at school and broke her foot. That's her over there."

At the red team bench, a tall girl slumped miserably, her foot in a cast, crutches against her shoulders.

"So now the poor reds are out there trying to 'win it for Jen,' Lord help us. And they're getting pounded."

The clock showed two minutes to play, and the reds were getting desperate and frustrated, hustling too hard. Several looked as if they were biting back tears. They were behind 42 to 30.

The battle veered close to the scoring table. The ball bounded over the line but was swatted back by a lunging red, and the crowd screamed. The reds recovered, charged the basket, shot, missed. A blue grabbed the rebound. Cree could feel the collective burning of flushed cheeks, the swelling of knots in throats.

Blue scored twice in a row, red managed to pick up a basket, and then a foul stalled the inevitable. Janet had to attend to her record keeping. When the buzzer sounded, the careening players went slack suddenly like marionettes whose strings had been cut. The blues hugged each other in the middle of the court as the reds slumped toward their bench. The bleachers began to empty as people stood, stretched, massaged sore buttocks; mothers hustled younger sibs to the bathroom. Smokers hurried for the front steps.

Janet discussed something with one of the coaches, then fielded a question from a ref. When they left, several parents approached the table and needed to talk to Mom.

Cree leaned back and tried to let her shoulders down. The blue team went to the locker room. The reds had found the far corner, where they sat on the boards, consoling each other and drinking from plastic squeeze bottles as their coach gave them spiritual guidance – about coping in the face of great loss, presumably. Scattered around the edges of the gym, pairs and trios of high school kids flirted, girls flouncing their hair, boys posturing and punching each other in the arms. Toddlers ran aimlessly in the broad expanse of yellow floor, exhilarated by the space and noise. Slowly, the building began to empty.

Janet had done an exemplary job of "getting on with her life" after Pop died. She had mourned hard and then called an end to it. Now she carried her lingering grief gracefully, honoring his memory but never permitting her daughters to pity her. It was no accident that she had chosen to work in a rec center, where the river of life ran quick and bright every day, cleansing the psychic space of shadows. To Cree, the building felt full of sparks: the residual hot, clear feelings of kids at play and the tempestuous but transient emotions of competition – the reds' defeat made a dull ache in her chest, but already it was ebbing. Mom was queen here, managing the program calendar, score-keeping when she could afford the time, refereeing whenever she had a chance, at least before her arteries clogged enough to make the exertion dangerous. She liked the epicenter of activity, here under the bright lights.

At last the big room began to quiet down. The teams left, Janet's assistant rounded up balls.

"God, I am beat," Janet said. "The excitement is too much for me. Oh Lordy." She palmed her eyes for a moment, then turned to give Cree a kiss. "Hello, Cree."

"Can you leave soon?"

"Yeah. The cleaning crew will be in tomorrow morning. Let's give it another five minutes and I'll close up."

Cree dug in her bag and pulled out a wax-paper-wrapped parcel. "I brought you some salmon. From that fish guy you like."

"God, I'm hungry enough to eat it raw!" Janet hefted the package appreciatively before leaning to put it into her own bag. "I'm glad to see you. What prompts this unexpected visit?"

Nothing, she could say, *just wanted to see you.* Or *I'm leaving town for a few days, just wanted to touch base.* "Dee says you're going to have an angioplasty."

Mom's eyes changed just a little – guarded to hide concern over the procedure, Cree wondered, or the plot with the cardiologist? "Well. All my friends are having them. I figured I had to keep up appearances."

Cree smiled. "But how do you feel?"

"Me? I feel great." She paused and gave it a little disclaimer. "Just get out of breath, and these little pinches in my chest. Same old stuff."

"I'm flying out to New Orleans on Thursday. I'll be back before you have to go in."

"What's doing in New Orleans?"

"A job. I'm not sure of the details, but it looks promising."

Janet nodded. "Well, I'm jealous. Your father went once and had a blast. He and I were always going to go back, but we never quite managed it."

"What was Pop doing in New Orleans?" Cree asked.

"Oh, his ship docked there when he was in the Navy. He never admitted it in so many words, but I believe he drank his way up one side of Bourbon Street and whored his way down the other. He was twenty. That was 1950, it's no doubt very different now." Janet shrugged. "C'mon. Help me close this barn down."

They gathered their things. Cree tagged along as her mother returned the score sheets and clock controls to her office, then checked the bathrooms, the locker rooms, the basement. They turned off lights as they went.

"Oh, I meant to ask you. I was hoping you could come with me to the cardiologist. Talk through the procedure with my doctor and me, the recovery and so on. Help me get the medications straight – you know how I am, I – "

"I'll go with you if you want me to. But I can't make promises about the cardiologist. Even if he is good-looking."

Janet smiled as they came back into the gym, dazzlingly bright after the back hall. "Damn Dee anyway."

"You want to go out for something to eat? Or we could go to your house and I'll fix that salmon – "

"You know I just want you to . . ." Janet petered out. At a loss, she gestured at the big bright space, the purity and simplicity of it, all the good ghosts. *Embrace life*, she probably wanted to say. *Find something like this.* But she just came up with, ". . . be happy."

"I know."

They got to the front hall. Janet unlocked the switch cover and cut the gym lights and then the hall lights. The building was dark now and somehow much bigger. They went out onto the front steps, where Janet shoved the doors shut and checked them with a hard yank.

The sky was deep purple velvet, the street a harder dark pierced with blue streetlights and the metallic reflections of parked cars. Halfway down the block an SUV with a dead black windshield crouched, motor idling, just its parking lights on. The city made an encompassing whisper, a vast vacuum of white noise.

"Mom," Cree began.

"Mm-hm?"

"I love it in the gym. With all the people there. All the noise and distraction."

"It's not 'distraction,' Cree – "

"But let me ask you something. Can I?"

"Cree, it's not 'distraction.' It's called 'life'. If I push at you sometimes, it's because I want you to *enjoy* it. I'm sorry if – "

"Mom, how do you feel right now? With the lights off, the gym all dark. If I wasn't here right now, and you were going to go out into the dark and go home alone as you usually do. As strong?"

"Well, this is not the safest neighborhood in Seattle . . . an older woman, alone, naturally I – "

"Not that part."

They were still standing in the pool of light at the top of the stairs. Janet looked up at Cree. "You mean, am I like the older waiter in that Hemingway story? '*Nada y nada y pues nada*'? A little, probably. Sure. So what? 'It is only insomnia, many must have it.' Or however it goes." She snorted.

"I'm just saying, see, this is what *I* need to look at, this side. This set of feelings, you know? That's what I need to figure out. I don't want to fear it. I don't want to ignore it, or pretend it's less important than . . . back in there. That's all." Hearing herself, Cree realized she was too serious, too urgent. She'd turned this visit into one of those cloaked good-byes.

Janet didn't answer for a moment, just stood looking up at her, concerned. After a while, she grinned a tight, small grin, to show she accepted the point, she got it. Mom always got it. She sighed. "What I don't understand is why you come to me as some kind of . . . *oracle* if you're not going to listen to what I tell you. And I'm no good at being a damned oracle anyway."

"I don't come to you as my oracle, Mom."

"What then?"

"Hmm. More of a good luck charm. My lucky talisman. Gotta rub up against you once in a while." Cree took her arm and hugged it against her side.

That seemed to please her. She shook her head, confounded. "What *is* it with mothers and daughters?"

Cree shrugged. "Beats me."

Janet tugged her toward the steps. "Okay. So I'm full of shit for the cardiologist caper. So take me home and let's eat something. If you promise to be a good girl, I'll tell you some other scandalous tales about your father. Deal?"

Cree wondered what it cost her to treat of him so easily, so cheerfully. Maybe not much – everyone was constituted differently in those matters.

She promised to be good.

5

L ILA WARREN'S EYES WIDENED. "Oh, I don't think so. I can't go back. No, I really don't think I can go into that house again."

"Even in the middle of the day? Even if I'm with you?"

"You have to understand, I'm . . . it has upset me badly. Very badly. It's been over three months now, I thought maybe I'd be getting over it, but I'm not. It's only getting . . . worse." Lila's speech carried only a moderate accent of the Deep South, the stretched and rounded vowels

They were talking across a low table and a pot of tea in the second-floor sitting room of Lila Beauforte Warren's house, on the northern end of New Orleans. From the windows, Cree could see over the grassy slope of the levee to the scattered trees of a shoreline park, and then to the vast flat blue of Lake Ponchartrain. The border between water and sky was straight as a ruled line and completely empty.

Lila's house was not one of the lavishly ostentatious piles Cree had passed as she drove here in her rental car, but rather a contemporary, somewhat smaller copy of a Greek-revival plantation house. And that described Lila herself, Cree thought: a contemporary, miniaturized version of a Southern businessman's wife. The sense was reinforced by the minute watercolors hung here and there, neatly framed, that Lila admitted were her own. The hand-sized floral still lifes were tiny and unobtrusive, yet their rich hues and slightly ominous darker tints suggested that a great deal of feeling had been compressed to fit within those little frames.

Perhaps Lila's diminution came from her current uneasiness. She was clearly struggling to cope with some recent, troubling experience. But there was also something habitual there, more deeply rooted. She had obviously lived with some kind of uncertainty and diminished sense of herself for a long time. Cree could see it in the rounded hunch of her plump shoulders, her small, uncertain hands, the tentative way she set the tray on the table and then rearranged the teapot and cups as if unsure she had put them in just the right places. Her eyebrows were uneven: One of them tilted up slightly at the center, enough to suggest a hint of alarm or doubtfulness.

And yet she was still rather pretty, Cree thought. She had shoulder-length, graying-blond hair that seemed to rebel against the controlled hairdo she'd chosen, a face with full lips and a generous but nicely upturned nose. Her knee-length blue knit dress, her makeup, the simple pearl necklace and earrings – all were good matches for her natural coloring. From the photos on the mantel, Cree could see that though she'd always tended toward the plump, she was one of those women who carry their weight mainly in bust and hips, retaining an enviably narrow waist.

The tea had had time to steep, and now Lila Warren poured a wavering stream into two fine china cups.

"Mrs. Warren – "

"Please call me Lila. I hate formalities. If we're going to get to know each other as well as you say we'll have to, we might as well start with that. Lemon? Sugar? I can get some milk if you'd prefer – how thoughtless of me not to have – "

"Lemon is fine, thank you. Lila, this is a lovely house. If your experience has been so upsetting, why do you still want to move back into Beauforte House?"

Lila sat with her cup hovering, saucer held beneath it. "That's a very good question. And it's one my brother has asked. He would be quite happy to sell the house. Before this all happened, I just thought it would be good to keep it as the family center, our historic home. My children all have the Beauforte middle name, there's a lot of family pride there. My youngest son just went off to college last fall, my last baby out of the nest, and I began to *think*, you know? About what a family is. About what it means to have a place where you all know it's home? Where everyone comes back to? I would very much like to provide my children and grandchildren with . . . that. It's not easy to explain if you don't share the sentiment."

"Makes perfect sense even to me, and I'm a gypsy, myself – we'd lived in five or six different places by the time I got out of high school. What does your husband think about going to live in the house?"

"Oh, Jackie. Well, he would like nothing more. Different reasons, I'm sorry to say. Jack is in real estate himself, you know, and he's very . . . how shall I say this? He's status conscious. Jack comes from an upriver suburb, and though he's done very well for himself, even married a Beauforte, I don't think he's ever felt he's really *arrived* in New Orleans. Living in one of the finest, most historic houses in the Garden District would do wonders for his . . . position." The uneven brows dipped disapprovingly: Lila clearly found this motivation rather crass.

Cree nodded, sipped her tea. "Still, this seems to have upset you a great deal – "

"So why fight it, is that what you're saying?" Lila's hands shook so her cup and saucer chattered, and she put them down. But she straightened in her chair and drew her shoulders up. "Because you can't just *take* things! You can't just . . . run away with your tail between your legs! I think I've done enough of that already in my life. Sometimes you have to just tough it out. I guess I got my back up." It all came out in a rush, and afterward Lila looked rather surprised at herself.

Cree admired the blaze in her eyes. It was good there was this much fight left in the outwardly docile, fragile Mrs. Warren: She'd need every bit of it if there was an entity at Beauforte House.

"So in that spirit – no pun intended – " Cree prompted. The moment was probably as good as it was going to get for what came next. She turned on her cassette recorder and placed it on the table between them. "Just hang on to that feeling, okay? And tell me what happened."

Lila began haltingly at first, finding her way into it with difficulty.

She had avoided the house after the murder, letting Ron take charge of cleaning up and remodeling the kitchen where the shooting had occurred. She couldn't bear to think about it. She had gone along with the idea of renting the house out again, but when that didn't work it became clear they had to do something with the place – as Jack pointed out, an empty house goes to ruin.

In September, she and Jack drove over to take a look, feel it out. A beautiful day, the house cool inside despite the hot weather, so spacious and fine. The kitchen – well, yes, that was difficult. Just thinking about what had happened. But they were churchgoers, didn't believe in ghosts. And Ron had done a good job with the remodeling, making the kitchen extra bright and cheerful.

They began the move in November and were settled in time for Thanksgiving. All three kids came home, Momma was there, some friends of the family, Ron and his girlfriend du jour. A wonderful homecoming to Beauforte House, a renewed sense of family.

"And I didn't even last a month!" Lila said. "I was uneasy from the start, and it just got worse and worse, and then there was that, that last episode. After which I couldn't set foot in the house again. Didn't even make it to Christmas. Fortunately, we hadn't sold this house yet, so we could move back in here."

"But the effects of the experience are still with you."

Lila's small, plump hands were clasped close against her stomach, fingers massaging the opposite wrists as if they ached. "I've – did Ron tell you? – I've been seeing a psychiatrist."

Cree nodded. "Has it helped?"

"He tells me I should have a CT scan, look for something wrong with my brain! He says we have to start with me accepting that what I experienced was some kind of hallucination or delusion or whatever. And I can't do that, because *I know what I saw!*" The anger gave way to doubt again. "But damnation, between him and Jack and Ron – I mean, I'm not sure, maybe I *am* having a nervous breakdown! Maybe I *am* going crazy!"

"Have you ever had a breakdown before? Any history of mental illness in your family?"

"Nothing in the family. I had a little tough spot when I first went off

42

to boarding school, but that was thirty years ago! I may be unassertive or whatever you want to call it, but I have enough damned *spine* to not break down. I come from a proud family. I raised three children. But I've never had . . . anything like this." Lila winced back tears of frustration.

Again, Cree was touched by her. A woman oscillating between the poles of fear and dismay on one hand, and that fierce resistance on the other — not unlike Cree herself, it occurred to her, bouncing between her almost overwhelming "susceptibility" and the need to confront it, master it. No, you couldn't run away with your tail between your legs.

Cree poured herself a second cup of tea. "You've had a very unusual experience, and it isn't easy to communicate those feelings. And I know that while seeing a ghost is frightening, what's more upsetting and confusing is the way it challenges your view of the world. Changes how you think of life, death, your place in the scheme of things. That in itself can be devastating."

Lila looked grateful that someone understood. "We always went to church! The ghost stuff, that was for voodoo people, or for the tourists — I always felt superior to it. And now look at me!" Starting to falter again.

"Just remember that feeling you talked about earlier. Get your back up. Please, tell me about it. Just tell it as you experienced it. Help me understand."

Lila rallied and began again.

She was uneasy the first day they spent there. It was one thing when the movers and painters and cleaners were coming in and out, but once everybody left it felt different. It was a bigger house than two people needed, twenty rooms plus the former slave quarters and carriage house, so she and Jack had really set up to live in about half the house, leaving the rest unused but mostly still furnished with the period furniture her father had installed. How Momma had lived there all those years with just a housekeeper, she didn't know.

The sense of unease grew until by the time she woke up in the middle of that first night and had to go to the bathroom, she couldn't bear to get out of bed. They had left the lights on in the hall, turned down on the dimmer switch, but it didn't help. There was this feeling of *expectation*, the sense that something was just about to happen. And it didn't help to have the murder to think about. But after a while she had to get up, leaving Jack asleep in the bed – always a deep sleeper, Jackie. She went out of the bedroom, and just as she turned into the hall she saw something move, slightly, right where the hall opened into the big room at the top of the front stairs. Something small, down near the floor. Beyond it, the darkness of the big central room loomed, the doorways of the front rooms just visible as rectangles of shadow on the far wall. She froze, choked with fear, and squinted at the thing from twenty feet away, trying to make out what it was in the dim light. She could see only a couple inches of it, flat on the floor and just emerging around the corner – brown, rounded, smooth, a little shiny. Oddly familiar, but incomprehensible.

Then it shifted again, tucking itself a little farther back out of view, and suddenly she made sense of what she was seeing. The toe of a shoe! Someone was standing just back of the corner, in the darkness of the big room. Waiting.

Telling it to Cree, her eyes got wide, a twitch tugged at her right cheek, her uneven brows danced out of control. Her chest was pumping in shallow, uneven breaths.

It was the most terrifying thing she had ever seen. She felt like she was going to be sick. Afraid to make a sound, unable to take her eyes off the shoe, she backed up. She made it to the bedroom doorway and went quickly to rouse Jack. He seemed to take forever to make sense of what she was whispering, Lila glancing over her shoulder and expecting to see whoever it was coming into the bedroom. But at last Jack got up, put on his robe, got his shotgun out of the armoire.

When they got out to the hall, the shoe wasn't there any more. Jack called out; no one answered. He noisily jacked a shell into the chamber and warned whoever that he was coming after him with a gun. Still no answer, no sound. And when they went around the corner, no one was there. No shoe, either. Jack gave her skeptical scowl but dutifully went through the whole house with her.

They found nothing. All the doors and windows were locked. The security system was armed and in order. Everything was just as they'd left it when they'd gone to bed.

"Jack thought I'd imagined it. But, honestly — a shoe!" Lila's lips worked in frustration. "Who would imagine they saw the toe of a *shoe?*"

Cree just nodded. "What sort of shoe was it?"

Lila looked brought up short by the question, but she thought about it for a moment. "Well. A man's shoe. Brown leather, a dressy sort of shoe, I think. But I could only see the toe."

"A modern shoe? As opposed to, say, a shoe from the nineteenth century?"

"I really couldn't say. I . . . just don't know."

She made it through that night, persuaded she had imagined the shoe. But the next day Jack went to his office, leaving her alone at the house. There was still moving-in work to be done, putting things away, hanging a few paintings. A couple of friends called, she had nice chats with them. She turned on the kitchen TV, just for some noise. But the sense of unease grew again. There was a sense of something fluttering, some movement somewhere, but every time she darted her eyes to a doorway, window, or mirror, she saw nothing. It *ate* at her, nibbled at her calm, very nerve-wracking. Still, she managed to get the kitchen squared away, then went to the library to finish putting books onto the shelves. She also wanted to wax Daddy's old square grand piano, make the rosewood shine the way she remembered it.

She was working in the library when she heard a curious creaking sound. Not like wood, not like a floorboard, more like something under great pressure. A grating screech. It seemed a familiar sort of sound, but it wasn't until she'd listened to it come and go for a half an hour that she realized what it reminded her of. When her daughter Janine had been a teenager, she'd had a tooth-grinding problem, had to be fitted with a guard — some hormonal or peer-stress thing, the dentist said. Lila would hear it at night, a horrible sound, the sense of enormous pressure brought to bear in that poor girl's mouth. *Skreeeeeeeak.* That's what this sound was like: two hard surfaces grating together with tremendous force.

45

It seemed to be coming from the other end of the library, where two leather reading chairs bracketed her father's fine claw-foot table. She went over there to hear it better, worried that maybe it had to do with some structural problem in the old house, subsiding or something. Or termites – did termites make noise in the wood? When she got closer, she could tell it seemed to be coming from near the floor, but it stopped as soon as she bent to listen.

She waited, but it didn't start again until she resumed working. She made a mental note to talk to Ron about it and tried to put it out of her mind. It seemed to intensify, nagging like the fluttering motion, eating at her.

Jack came home, she cooked some dinner. Jack was in good spirits; he took a satisfied turn through the house to survey his new domain. Afterward they went to watch TV in the former music room, at the end of the east wing, which they'd set up as a den.

Sitting now in the bright, lake-facing sitting room, Lila was getting shakier, to the point where Cree almost interrupted her. Her empty teacup still hovered in front of her, wavering wildly. But obviously she was getting to something crucial, best to let her continue. Cree's empathic radar was going crazy, too, as some big terror moved into Lila like a gathering storm.

Much later, Jack asleep in front of the TV, Lila got up to go to the kitchen. When she passed the library, she heard the creak, louder now, and went to investigate. Down there near the claw-foot table. She bent down, hearing it so clearly she expected to see the damned termite, or whatever, right there. And then she saw what was making the noise.

The claws! Four carved legs of the table ending in eagle talons, each gripping a solid glass globe a little smaller than a tennis ball. The claws were *alive*. Lila saw the horny wooden fingers move, working their grip, clenching the glass with tremendous pressure, releasing, clenching. All four feet. The sound like teeth grinding. The table crouched like a horrible living animal suddenly transported into her house.

A sharp *clack!* made Cree jump. Lila's teacup fell to her lap, the slender porcelain handle still ringing her index finger. The tension in Lila's hands, just trying to tell this, had broken the little ear off the cup.

"Oh, God!" Lila whispered. She hastily retrieved the cup, set it clattering back on the tray. There was a spot of blood on her finger, and she dabbed distractedly at it with her napkin.

This was too much. Cree knelt beside her, took her shoulders, kneaded them, rocked her gently. "You okay? Let's back away from it now. Maybe we can try again tomorrow, or whenever you're up for it. We don't have to do this now."

But Lila was still in that moment, staring sightlessly across the sitting room. She whispered, "So of course I ran to get Jack. And I made it all the way to the TV room door before I realized *I couldn't tell him*. Because what I'd seen *was* crazy. That's what he'd say. That's what *anyone* would say — I couldn't tell anyone! And that was the moment I realized I was *alone* with this. This whole . . . problem."

This close to her, Cree was feeling it all herself. Lila Warren's experience played in her chest, painfully poignant and terrifying. She could feel the curve of Lila's hopeless shoulders in her own spine, feel the woman's tremors twitch her own cheeks and brow.

One thing she knew for certain: This woman was as fragile as the teacup and starting to go pieces.

Lila took Cree's hands in her two trembling hands. She looked desperately into her eyes and whispered, "What do *you* think? Do you think I'm crazy?"

And to Cree's great relief at that moment there came a thump and clatter from below, and a man's voice calling upstairs: "Peaches? Lila, darlin', I'm home. That ghost buster gal show up yet?"

So instead of having to answer, Cree settled for a look of sympathy and complicity.

"We're upstairs, Jackie," Lila called shakily.

Still kneeling at her side, Cree quickly smoothed Lila's hair, then took a napkin and patted the tears from her cheeks, wiped away a smear of lipstick from the corner of her mouth. Got her in order as Jack's feet thumped up the stairs. And by the time he came in, a business-suited, ruddy-faced, chunky man just under middle height, they were standing on opposite sides of the coffee table and Lila was mustering a housewifely smile that almost worked.

"Hello, Mr. Warren, I'm Cree Black," Cree said, offering her hand. "I'm very pleased to meet you. But I'm embarrassed to admit that I've been kind of a bull in a china shop here – I've broken one of your teacups!" And she showed him the little porcelain ring.

6

THAT NIGHT, BACK AT HER hotel, Cree opened her laptop and took notes on the interview. She'd booked a week at the Clarion, on Canal Street, the backbone avenue of New Orleans and a good central location from which to conduct research. She had chosen it sight unseen from Seattle for its reasonable rate and had been pleasantly surprised to find the building clean and well appointed, her room big and agreeably modern. It had watercolors of French Quarter scenes on the walls, a queen-sized bed with a reasonably firm mattress, a well-stocked minibar, and cable Internet hookup. Best of all was the absence of too much psychic ambience, meaning it would serve as a place of respite from the rigors of her job. From her seventh-floor window, she had a good view of the traffic on Canal: six o'clock and though it was well past Mardi Gras, flocks of tourists were drifting toward the river and the French Quarter, wide-eyed couples holding hands and looking around with a mix of excitement and uncertainty. Cree had every intention of joining them once she'd gotten her notes done.

Do you think I'm crazy? The word *crazy* didn't quite mean anything to Cree. The world could be chaotic and so could minds. You could be absolutely rational in one part of your mind and utterly nutso in another, and the universal coexistence of the two was what made the human race so marvelously interesting – and so dangerous.

But the phenomena Lila reported didn't fit with any of Cree's expectations or experience. Lila's psychiatrist was absolutely right to insist on brain scans and blood work – a tumor or an unnoticed stroke could induce hallucinations not unlike schizophrenia and would need

49

immediate treatment. The scariest part was that Lila had barely started to recount her ordeal. If what Cree had heard was just the tale of Lila's first forty-eight hours at Beauforte House, she shuddered to think what the rest of the month had been like.

Jack had been cordial, full of a Realtor's bogus bonhomie, but he'd also been assessing Cree with a critical eye. When she'd left, he'd made a point of coming out to the driveway with her.

"Uh, Ms. Black, I don't know just how to say this," he'd told her. "But as you can see, my wife is not in the best condition at this time. We are all very concerned."

"Understandably."

"Now, she's seeing a highly regarded headshrinker, and it's important to us that she follow through with her therapy. This ghost business – it's all just a bit much for me. I don't mind telling you I'm skeptical. Of people coming back from the dead and all that. And therefore, I'm skeptical of someone like yourself who claims to get rid of them. I don't believe any of it." His accent was much stronger than Lila's: *Ayund theahfoah, Ah'm skeptical* . . .

Cree paused at the door of her car and thought about that. A breeze bustled in off the lake, balmy and soothing, tossing the live oaks and the towering date palm in the Warrens' yard.

"What *do* you believe, if I may ask?"

An indignant expression froze Jack Warren's habitually jovial face. "Why, I was raised to believe in our Lord Jesus Christ!"

"Me too." Cree nodded. "I especially take strength and solace in his return from death, don't you? His resurrection and everlasting life?" She gave him a steady, sincere smile, and in the end he had no choice but to swallow his protests and nod in agreement.

"Point is," he went on, "we can't have anything getting in the way of my wife's recovery. That's my only concern. Me and the kids, we want our Lila back. You're here because we're willing to do anything, even call in a witch doctor if we have to. Anything to set her mind at ease. But –"

"You're worried that by taking her claims seriously, I'm jeopardizing her other treatment. Which depends on her accepting her experiences as delusional."

"The thought occurred to me."

"I couldn't agree with you more. I'll certainly encourage her to continue with her therapist." Cree opened her car door, tossed her purse onto the passenger seat, but didn't get in. "I hear your concern. You want your wife to be happy and stable. You're worried that my dredging up her experience again, acting like I believe her, will make her worse. And you're warning me that if you see that happening, I'm out of here. Is that a fair summary of what you're trying to say?"

Jack tucked his chin. "It's not my habit to be so, uh, blunt, but yes. That about says it."

Cree got in and shut the door. "I have absolutely no desire to encourage any self-destructive or delusive behavior. We're on the same side here, Mr. Warren."

Cree had driven away trying to sort through the several levels of that short conversation. Jack Warren wasn't as sophisticated or cosmopolitan or assured as Ron, or even, despite her disarray, Lila. His accent was deeper, his suit didn't fit as well, he was clearly trying harder – as Lila said, a man feeling perpetually on the outside of New Orleans's wealthier society, looking in. His concerns for his wife's well-being were no doubt sincere, but they were complicated by his desire to live at Beauforte House. And though he certainly wanted his wife "back," she suspected he wanted her returned to him in the form he was used to: timid, compliant, self-effacing, supportive. Which Cree could not promise. Lila would come through this a stronger person, or not at all.

Wanting to make a credible first impression, Cree had dressed in a businesslike outfit of skirt, white blouse, silk jacket, nylons, and moderate heels, but after fifteen minutes at her computer she suddenly realized that if she didn't get out of them she'd go crazy herself, run screaming down the hotel halls, flinging clothing left and right. She stood up and peeled off the layers, then took a quick shower. Still naked, she went to the minibar, found a Heineken, opened it, drew a satisfying swallow, and stood for a moment in the middle of the room, rolling the tension out of her shoulders. Through the gauze curtains, the busy street seemed very alluring. New Orleans!

Jeans and a T-shirt, she decided at last, *walking shoes.* Feeling much better, she dressed and carried the beer back to the laptop.

Lila's experiences, from what Cree had heard so far, were anomalous, particularly the table's claw feet clenching their globes. The shoes were possibly a spectral manifestation and the most scary kind, too – the furtive and secretive kind, the kind with some weird *agenda.* Just the thought made Cree shiver. But that type was very rare; put it together with the table coming alive, and you had to consider other alternatives.

One was that Lila Warren *did* have a brain disorder, or *was* facing some normal-world psychological crisis. She was certainly a woman arriving at certain physical and situational passages: last kid just off to college, the empty-nest syndrome. Maybe the beginnings of menopause? Moving to a too-big, too-empty house, redolent with memories of her distant childhood. The clash of past, present, and that long, looming future as Jack Warren's little wife. The strong possibility of a medical dimension here upped the stakes and greatly increased the level of Cree's responsibility: Her actions now would have direct bearing on the mental health, the survival, of another person.

Another possibility was that the experiences were epiphenomenal: that is, Lila's perceptions *were* psychological in origin, not delusory per se but rather "side effects" of being in the proximity of a real extracorporeal presence. Cree's sometime mentor, Mason Ambrose, had lectured her from time to time on the diversity of epiphenomenal effects. They could include anything, as the witness's hyperstimulated mind, triggered by subconscious perceptions of inexplicable phenomena, churned out images, sounds, feelings, sensations. Dr. Ambrose's several papers on epiphenomenal manifestations stressed that though the perceived images were not "real," as symbol-rich products of the witness's subconscious they could be very helpful in determining the nature of the actual haunting entity and the witness's link to it.

There were other possibilities, progressively less likely. One was that the things Lila experienced were indeed the manifestations of some awful revenant, part of a once-human being locked into its own scary imaginings. In effect, the ghost of a crazy person. That would be a hard one – hard to study, hard to communicate with, hard to shake out of Lila. And very dangerous for the empath who tried to make contact. Madness could be contagious.

And – something no parapsychologist should ever forget – there was always the chance that there was some truth to all the tales of powerful malevolent beings, shape changers capable of, say, masquerading as tables. True, for all the terrors she'd witnessed, Cree had never experienced anything of the sort, and she was intellectually, emotionally, and philosophically resistant to the idea. But though she and Ed tried hard to be systematic, to map the invisible world and to establish a taxonomy for the range of entities and occurrences, to match experience with accepted scientific theory, it was an uphill struggle. If she'd learned anything from the last nine years, it was that paranormal events were enormously diverse. And given that devils and goblins and nightmare spirits and unnamed creatures of the dark had inhabited every culture's legends and folktales throughout history –

Okay, Cree told herself pointedly, *enough of* that, *thank you*. She slapped her computer shut and stood up quickly. A little shaky, but that was just low blood sugar – time to look for something to eat. Further speculation would have to wait until after her next interview with Lila.

Now it was time to hit the streets of New Orleans, see what all the fuss was about.

A breeze played in Canal Street, flipping Cree's hair around with gusts that were one moment balmy and the next chilly and river scented. She was tired, but it felt good to be on her feet, in casual clothes, off-duty, with an unfamiliar city to explore. Starting with a restaurant, her stomach insisted. She surrendered to the street, to the flow of people moving toward their Friday night meals, entertainments, adventures.

From studying maps during the flight, Cree had a rough idea of the layout of New Orleans. It was nicknamed "the Crescent City" because the original French colony had built outward in an arc around the sharp northern bulge in the Mississippi River. Now the city occupied all the land between the river and the southern belly of Lake Ponchartrain. At its center was Canal Street, a broad boulevard with a wide median up the center, running straight to the river and dividing the historic French Quarter from the Downtown district. Down the streets to Cree's left, the buildings were mostly three stories tall, fronted with the Quarter's famous ironwork balconies, while to her right loomed the glassy modern facades of skyscrapers, skyline cut crisp against the lingering sunset. Somewhere beyond downtown was the Garden District, newer by a hundred years than the French Quarter but still old enough to be the site of many of New Orleans's finest historic buildings, including Beauforte House.

Tomorrow, Cree reminded herself.

She looked covertly at the street map she'd folded into her purse. No question, she didn't want to get anywhere near the infamous LaLaurie House. Fortunately, she found, it was on the eastern end of Royal Street, which would allow her to enjoy most of Bourbon Street without getting too close.

Bourbon Street: Crowds of pedestrians filling streets and sidewalks. Bright lights, the pulsing beat of music. The buildings on either side had a pleasantly dilapidated look to them, their flaking, flat facades coming right down to the narrow sidewalk with no intervening lawn at all. On the upper stories, balconies were hung with ferns and bougainvillea, and many of the second- and third-floor windows were warm with light, revealing high ceilings and moving figures. Strings of colorful beads were caught on railings, gutters, streetlights, no doubt flung by Mardi Gras revelers. At street level, the wide-open doors and windows of restaurants gave glimpses of tables stretching away into dim interiors echoing with the gabble of conversation. Bars, trinket shops, strip joints. Cajun food, seafood, Creole food, Italian food, po'boys. The smell of meat broiling, piss, beer, garbage. The sharp, sweet scent of fruity mixed drinks and stale cigarette smoke rolling out of doorways on air-conditioned gusts.

Jazz, crawfish, and booze, Cree thought, *the themes of Bourbon Street.*

And sex, she added. Another block farther up and every other doorway advertised sex shows – topless, bottomless, men, women, old-fashioned burlesque, female impersonators: *You Have to See It to Believe It! Live Love Acts*. Randy music from curtained doorways guarded by handsome barkers in top hats and tails. Windows full of photos of lush-bodied nudes. Sex toy and video and leather shops. Every ten steps, another pounding bass rhythm made war with the last: music for the bump and grind, Zydeco, hard rock, Dixieland jazz, rhythm and blues, Top 40, Zydeco again.

Flux, Cree thought. So many experiences crammed into the same psychic locale. The flux was nice, a buzzing place where it seemed she could find balance. This was one of the things Mom found at the gym. Tugged in every direction, she could stay steady where she was. Yes, she could still hear the whisper of endlessly layered history here, the quiet stories breathed by dark attic windows and deep courtyards, telling of the thousand thousand lives passed and deaths met in these rooms for two hundred and fifty years. But it was drowned out by the tumultuous noise and chaos of the street, the air of libidinous license, the endless rushing waterfall of immediate emotions and experiences. Sex, food, drink, music, money, dancing, talk. All the hungers.

Three-for-ones! signs advertised. *Hurricanes! Drinks to Go! No Cover!*

Everything Live! one sex emporium sign bragged, and Cree smiled and thought, *Well, hey, that's some relief. Considering the alternative.*

When she couldn't ignore her stomach any longer, she picked a restaurant at random. She was led upstairs to an outside balcony, where from her table she had a terrific view down Bourbon Street, a corridor of sagging balconies and thronged pavement, alive with activity and light, that stretched as far as she could see. She ordered a beer and a mixed seafood plate, and watched the trade coming and going at the female impersonator club across the way.

About half the people passing – the more uptight tourists, especially families with kids – tended to walk in the middle of the street, clumped close together with eyes fixed on the pavement, uncomfortable, embarrassed, disapproving. But the other half seemed to catch the sexualized charge of the place. Young teenage girls thrust out their chests and found excuses for lots of movement, as if announcing to their scrawny boyfriends or gawking brothers, *I've got those, too, you know!* Middle-aged pairs, to-go drinks in hand, paused for deep kisses and daringly intimate caresses. It wasn't Mardi Gras by any means, but she got some idea of the licentious mood Deirdre had mentioned. Even old couples sashayed to the music and bumped hips flirtatiously as they walked.

Cree decided that maybe human beings were okay after all.

She drank beer out of a plastic cup, ate deep-fried oysters and shrimp, a slice of blackened fish, and a cup of jambalaya. Finishing up with another beer, she felt fatigue come-on as the night air picked up a chill. Still the street grew more crowded, the music louder, the barkers more aggressive.

Cree watched a woman her age beckon to her man as if she wanted to say something over the din of the crowd, and when he bent to hear her Cree clearly saw her tongue slip into his ear. The man leaned into the sensation for a few seconds before they pulled apart, laughing. He swatted her rear, and they continued up the street, hip to hip, arms firm around each other's waists, with obvious plans for later. Walking right next to them, an alarmed-looking husband and wife shepherded their two children quickly along, holding the kids' blond heads against their sides with eyes mostly covered.

Which kind is Cree Black? she wondered. At first, a little of the reserved type, she decided, defenses up; but after not too long, definitely more of the other. Not that she had anyone to share that mood with.

And with that thought she suddenly found herself sliding. Cree Black was sitting up on a balcony, alone, watching the passing parade from above. No plans for later but that solitary hotel bed, probably drifting off to sleep doing some reading on the habits of the dead.

Nine years. And counting. When was she going to get around to turning her full attention to the living? Mom was right. Everybody was right.

It had all turned around on her, the gaiety gone sour. Bourbon Street now struck her as frantic, squalid, false. A city of masks, as Don had said.

Desperation masquerading as pleasure. She quickly pushed back her chair and stood up, wanting nothing more than to get the hell out of there. She left a tip, went to the register to pay. The cashier was a handsome guy in his early thirties, dark hair and brown eyes, earring in one ear, T-shirt showing good biceps. He smiled at her and seemed to take his time making change. "Here on business?" he inquired mildly. "Or just for pleasure? Seeing the sights?" An easy glance at Cree's face to let her know he was fishing, in a low-key way.

"Business," Cree told him curtly. "A business trip."

7

THE BUSINESS WAS EITHER something scary happening in some-one's head or something scary happening in an old house in the Garden District. Before going to her appointment with Lila Warren the next morning, just to get an idea of what she was up against, Cree drove over to take her first look at Beauforte House.

Following her city map, she headed out Magazine Street, through downtown and then through a wilderness of highway overpasses and interchanges. That gave way to a dilapidated but charming older district, and then as she continued west the style and feel of the neighborhoods began to change dramatically. The buildings grew in size and improved in appearance; greenery intruded and diversified. By the time she crossed Jackson, the houses had become huge and much more like Cree's image of classic Deep South architecture.

From her reading, Cree knew that the Garden District grew from an invasion of Americans who began moving to the city after the United States purchased the Louisiana Territory in 1803. Before the railroad era, the Mississippi was the artery of trade and transport, New Orleans the center of economic activity, for the whole middle of the continent. The river and lush agricultural lands had been good to the original French and Spanish settlers, allowing them to convert a swampy backwater into a thriving financial and cultural center ruled by a wealthy, cosmopolitan Creole aristocracy. In the decades following the purchase, upriver sugar and cotton and timber growers and American shippers, merchants, and entrepreneurs arrived in increasing numbers to get a piece of the action.

But finding little space or welcome in the Creole-dominated Vieux

Carré, they settled mainly in their own town to the west. Coming from a different culture and determined to let the natives know it, they built lavish houses that turned the traditional local architecture inside out. Where the typical mansion in the old town was deep and narrow, presenting a flat facade to the street but wrapping around a gardenlike interior courtyard, the new houses were centered in lush lawns and gardens, spreading into their lots with wings and galleries. Many were built in variations of the Greek Revival style, with thick white columns in front, or, later, the Italian-influenced style with slender pillars, more elaborate decoration, and rounded window tops.

Some were the size of small mountains, Cree realized as she cruised Second Street. Matching the houses, massive live oaks spread their branches in gnarled aerial tangles. Date palms rose tall above, and flowering trees and shrubs lined the fences that bounded each lot. Most of the houses were splendidly restored and maintained, and the cars on the streets and in the driveways were Porsches and Mercedeses: The Beaufortes weren't the only people with money around here. So this was what Jack Warren aspired to.

Beauforte House was one of the big ones. Cree approached it with a tingle of anxiety, but in fact it was a pleasant-looking place, yellow with white trim, graciously proportioned, a modified plantation-style house with a central block and asymmetrical wings on either side at the rear. Its lot was bigger than most of the neighboring yards, more overgrown with green, surrounded by a head-high wrought-iron fence. Next to the front gate, a darkened bronze plaque labeled the property a national historic site. When Cree rolled down her window to look it over, she was met with a gush of humid, blossom-smelling air. Nine-thirty A.M., and it was already getting hot.

Yes, a nice-looking place. True, looks could be deceiving, but it was easy to understand why Lila still wanted to live there, despite what she'd experienced. The house had . . . what? *Texture*, Cree decided. Presence, weight, depth. It looked securely anchored in its place, belonging like an old tree or something geological. It was *real* – unlike the plasticized, minor-league opulence of the house that Lila and Jack now called home.

It all tied in with Lila's tiny, self-diminishing watercolors and the compressed yearning for *more*, for an outward-blooming life, that Cree felt in her. Whatever else Lila was coping with, part of her spirit was straining against the containment imposed by her Tupperware-tight world.

Cree left the Garden District and drove to the Warrens' house, where she was surprised and disappointed to find Jack's cream-colored Mercedes in the driveway. She had hoped to get to the tough stuff with Lila today, which was likely to take a lot of coaxing, encouragement, and refocusing. Jack's being there could distract Lila, or, worse, functionally censor her.

She got another surprise when she rang the bell and Jack ushered her into the foyer. Lila was there, holding her purse, dressed as if ready to go out.

"I want to go to the house," Lila said. "This morning. Right now before I chicken out again."

Cree just tipped her head inquiringly.

"We had a big fight last night after you left," Lila explained.

Jack began, "Honey, do we have to – "

"A knock-down, drag-out humdinger," Lila continued. She had the red, puffy eyes of someone who had been crying, but she also had a look of angry determination, as if she'd hit bottom but had found some gritty resolve down there to sustain her.

If Jack had been keeping any cool at all, he lost it now. He was taking huffing breaths as he stood looking at Cree with his elbows out and fists dug in at his waist.

"As long as we're determined to air our dirty laundry with an audience present," he said, "I told my wife I didn't think it was wise to continue with this . . . this *charade*. She was a damn shambles after you left, but she still wasn't goin' to tell me just what it's all about, what the *hell* she is so afraid of over there. I told her this thing is ruinin' our marriage, and I also told her I want Ms. Cree Black to butt her ass on out of our family life!"

"Jackie!"

"I mean, encouraging her, this thing of – "

"And I told Jackie he was right," Lila interrupted. "He's entitled to know, I owe him that. But I can't go over it and *over* it with every last person, it's . . . it's too much. So we *agreed*, Jackie, that today we'd go to the house and I'd tell you both, I'd show you. Get it done with. And that after we've heard Cree's opinion, *I* will decide what to do for my own peace of mind!"

Jack spun away, frustrated. Lila just looked beseechingly at Cree with those haunted eyes.

Cree scrambled to adapt. Obviously, she'd landed smack in the middle of a marital crossfire as well as a metaphysical and psychological crisis. She'd really have preferred to hear it from Lila without Jack there, but that option had obviously been negotiated out of the picture. Best to roll with it, make it work to everybody's advantage. If these were the terms for getting Lila to Beauforte House, she'd take them. Anyway, there might be therapeutic value in Lila's telling her husband the whole story.

"Mr. Warren?"

Standing with his back to her, arms crossed, he took a moment to answer. "Yeah."

"Does that sound like a plan you can live with?"

"Yeah." Grudgingly.

Lila looked both relieved and terrified.

Cree told them she needed a moment to explain her process and introduce them to some of the technology before they drove over. She went out to the car, popped the trunk, and got out the big, aluminum-clad equipment case. When she came back, they all sat in the living room as Cree talked it through.

She explained that she wanted to hear everything Lila could tell about her experiences, with as much detail as she could recall. She also wanted to see the house, particularly the rooms where Lila had witnessed anything. She'd be glad to hear any history of the house that Lila thought relevant, but her main focus would be Lila's perceptual, mental, and emotional experience.

"Lila, Jack, I know you're both religious people, and I know the idea of there being . . . unknown entities . . . touches on belief and faith and can sometimes seem at odds with religious tradition. I'd be happy to go into the metaphysics of this with you later, but today let me just give you a basic idea of the science I'm going to be starting with."

She waited for nods from both of them.

"One of the consistencies we've encountered in our research is that paranormal or 'supernatural' occurrences seem to require a particular state of mind, or sensitivity, on the part of the person perceiving them. This doesn't mean the person is going crazy. Think of, oh, the radio telescopes we use to look at distant galaxies. They are instruments designed to pick up very subtle, but real, electromagnetic activity. Or the instruments we use to detect solar activity like gamma rays or X rays – we can't perceive these things with our senses, but the right instruments can. You following me so far?"

A less-than-heartfelt nod from Jack: *If you say so.*

"Today we're going to focus on your mental and physical state, Lila, because so far you're the 'instrument' that's perceiving these subtle phenomena. You're the one 'tuned' to the right frequency. Many ghosts are not readily perceivable by more than a single witness, so if I'm going to see this one and interact with it, I need to come to know you pretty well. In fact – this may sound strange – you may even find me talking or moving a little like you. It's all part of my effort *think* like you, to take on your mental and emotional state as a way of 'calibrating' my own perceptions, sensory and otherwise. Does that make sense?"

A halfhearted nod from Jack, some quickening interest from Lila.

"And beyond what you can consciously recall, it's likely that your body and your unconscious mind remember many things. So, Lila, if you agree, I'd like to fit you out with a kit that'll give me readings on your vital signs. I'll explain it now, but once you're rigged I want you to try to forget about it. Just focus on remembering your experience."

Cree lifted the case to the coffee table and opened it to reveal the foam-encased devices Edgar had so painstakingly adapted for the peculiar needs of ghost hunting. She hesitated over the voice-stress analyzer but decided that under the circumstances it wouldn't reveal anything she didn't know. Instead, she pulled out a fat, flesh-tone plastic finger clip that dangled an electronic plug.

"This is just like the clips you get when you go to the hospital. We'll put one on your forefinger, and it'll continuously take your pulse rate and blood pressure. The information will be fed to this" – Cree held up a strap of nylon webbing attached to a small black box not much bigger than a wristwatch – "which you'll wear like a bracelet. The box is a little radio-sending device that'll relay the data." She handed them to Lila, who turned them over in her hands uneasily.

"Relay it to where?" Jack asked.

Cree handed him a bigger, titanium-cased box with a number of output plug receptacles and a series of knobs for adjusting sensitivity levels.

"This is a receiving and recording device – I'll be carrying it in a fanny pack so you don't have to be too burdened, Lila. It'll digitally record the readings from your monitors. Later, we'll print the readings out on a roll of graph paper, just like an EKG, so we can review and precisely measure your responses."

Jack passed the recorder to Lila, who gave it only a distracted glance and set it back on the table.

"We also like to use some other medical monitoring technologies, and my partner uses a wide array of sensing devices that measure and record environmental phenomena. But that'll come later. At this stage, the most complicated gear we'll use is this." Cree took out a harness of elastic fabric and wires. "This coiled wire goes around your chest, and this band around your waist against your skin. The first one will tell us your breathing rate and depth. The other – you see the little metal buttons? Those are electrical contacts that'll tell us about your skin conductivity levels."

"That's a, what do they call it . . . a galvanometer?" Jack said.

"Basically, yes – "

"Like on a lie detector?"

That froze Lila up, Cree saw. Wide eyes showed she took it as a betrayal by the one person who claimed to believe her.

63

Cree got to work on damage control: "Yes, it's adapted from polygraph technology. But 'lie detection' is a myth – there's no such thing. All any of it does is measure degrees of metabolic arousal, caused by unconscious agitation – telling lies is only one of many psychological reactions that can cause it. And that's *not* what we're after here, Lila. As we walk through the house, and you tell me things, this'll let us know what frightens or upsets you. What triggers intense unconscious mental activity. Lila, remember, you're our instrument here, right? This is just a way for us to better understand what the instrument is telling us."

She hoped that sounded reassuring, but Lila didn't look any happier.

They drove down in two cars, Cree alone in her rented Taurus and the Warrens together in the Mercedes. Following them, Cree could see Jack's head bobbing and swiveling as his right hand gestured vehemently. Obviously, the argument wasn't finished yet. But by the time they got to Beauforte House, it had apparently settled into the comparative calm of emotional exhaustion. The Warrens met Cree at the iron gate wearing chastened expressions.

They went up the broad stairs and between tree-thick pillars onto the front porch, which Jack explained was called a "gallery" in New Orleans. The day had turned quite hot, but when Jack opened the front door a wave of cool, stale-smelling air poured from the interior. And suddenly the deep, shadowed porches and dense vegetation made sense to Cree: Down here, shade was all that kept houses from turning into ovens.

They went into a large entry hallway, where Jack took a moment to disarm a blinking security panel. A proud staircase rose along the left wall; double doors opened to rooms on either side. As Cree's eyes adjusted to the poor light, she could see more of the interior: fourteen-foot ceilings, tall windows covered by full-length drapes, antique furniture, darker doorways at the rear.

Open the curtains, let in some light, it would probably be a pleasant place, Cree thought. But the whispers were growing, like a chorus singing in the far, far distance. Very faintly, she felt the subliminal jitter, the sense of some activity just out of view or hearing. The vague, irrational sense that something was about to happen.

Yes, there was something here.

That recognition came with a thin blade of fear but also a tingle of excitement, the thrill of the hunt that she and Edgar shared. Cree's right hand found the controls on the fanny pack, turning on simultaneously the receiver-recorder and a voice-activated audio recorder. While one recorded changes in Lila's vital signs, the other would record anything said in the coming interview. Both were equipped with a chronometric tagging system so that the polygraph readings and voice track could be precisely synchronized, second by second, later.

Jack led them into the right side room. He flipped a switch to turn on a little galaxy of lights in a chandelier hung from the center of the ceiling.

"We keep the drapes closed 'cause with no one here we want to keep pryin' eyes off all these antiques," he explained. "Anyway, too much light'll degrade the old fabrics and finishes."

The electric lights allowed Cree a better sense of the space, but they gave the interior a depressing, underlit, yellow cast. The slotted daylight around the curtain edges was bright, almost harsh, by comparison.

"I'm . . . not sure where to start," Lila said in a tiny voice. Her earlier grit was gone, and now she looked around like a pursued creature trying to decide which way to run.

"Whatever is easiest," Cree said. "Why don't you just walk me through the house? We can focus on specific areas later. You just tell me whatever comes to mind, I'll take a few notes as we go, and if I have questions I'll ask them. Does that sound okay?"

Lila nodded.

The room they were in was the size of Cree's whole apartment, perhaps thirty by thirty, and was joined at the back by a wide, arched doorway to a second room the same size. Windows lined the outside walls, defined by the daylight that sneaked around the drapes. A massive marble fireplace coping and mantel framed a small, black coal-burning grate, and fine cornice moldings detailed the juncture of walls and ceiling.

Jack gave a running commentary: "Originally, this front room would've been the guest parlor. Usually, it'd be closed by these sliding doors so's to be kept clean for social occasions, with the rear room serving as your main family living room. 'Course, for major social events the doors'd be slid open like they are now, making it one long room big enough for musical recitals, dances, and whatnot. These chandeliers are Baccarat crystal – they used to be set up for burnin' oil, then got converted to gas, and then finally to electricity. Those portraits, that one's Lila's daddy, there's Momma, there's her uncle Brad . . . these others are ol' General Beauforte, his wife and daughters, various relatives – Lila or Ron can tell you more than I can on that score. The carpets and furnishings are authentic period items collected at great expense by Lila's daddy. Ol' Temp Chase, he had a more contemporary style, so a lot of 'em we just locked in the storage room in the back after Momma moved out. There's central air and heating now, and wiring of course, but mostly this looks look just as it did back in 1851."

Shit, Cree was thinking. *Bring a Realtor along when you tour a house, you'll get a Realtor's spiel.* How to shut Jack up long enough to allow Lila to think?

Still, Lila managed to chip in, "We used to keep it open – Daddy liked a big room. And he and Momma entertained so often anyway . . . Naturally, with all these antiques, we kids weren't allowed to run crazy in here, but one time Daddy let Ron set up his model train tracks all through both rooms." She was still speaking in a small, shaky voice, but as Cree had hoped, being back here had triggered a mood of recollection.

They headed into the rear parlor, identical to the first, with four windows, coal stove and mantel, chandelier, all period furniture. Also a splendid, ten-foot-tall gilt-framed mirror with an unfortunate crack marring its heavy silvered glass. Jack talked briefly about the antique Turkish Ushak carpet and Chippendale tables, then led them into the hallway that continued from the foyer through the center of the house. The relatively dark hall had several doorways opening to rooms on the other side, and to a brighter room at the back – the kitchen, Cree saw. Through the open doors Cree saw a smaller room that was set up as a formal dining room, and a sitting room with very little furniture in it.

They paused in the hall while Jack flipped on more lights and told Cree that the moldings and fluted pilasters – flat Grecian pillars on either side of the main doorway to the rear of the house – were not really marble but wood painstakingly painted to resemble it. "And the doors themselves, they're all Southern cypress, hand painted to look like white oak. Faux finishin' was quite a popular art, back then – "

"Jackie." Lila's quavering voice interrupted him.

Jack pulled up short. "What, darlin'?"

"Jackie, I want you to stay with me."

He took a step closer to her. "Well, of course, honey, we'll just – "

"No – I mean after what I have to tell you. After you *know*. No matter what you think about it. Even if it's the craziest thing you ever heard."

Now Jack seemed to remember what they were here for. And gazing at the diminished, shaking creature that was his wife, he began to look a little frightened himself. Cree was rocked by a wave of sympathy for them both: two plump, staid-looking little people standing on the trembling verge of chaos.

" 'Course," Jack mumbled.

"Promise me you won't tell Momma? You won't tell Ron? No matter what? Both of you! I can't live with what they'd say, I already know what they think of me. You have to promise."

Cree promised. Jack nodded and moved as if to put his arm around her, but then, confused, seemed to think better of it.

Once she'd gotten their assurances, Lila seemed determined to plunge on, straight into it. She turned and stumped ahead of them down the remainder of the hall, a woman running on utter desperation and not much else.

The hall ended in a large kitchen that had obviously been remodeled not long ago, with white-marble counters, cheerful yellow walls, tile floors, and brushed chrome appliances. The pleasant breakfast nook was surrounded on three sides by windows framed by bright, flowery curtains. Where Temp Chase had blown his brains out. Yes, Ron had gone to considerable lengths to get rid of that unmarketable "ambience." Cree could feel it, just barely – the dark paroxysm, the convulsive pain and confusion that had been lived here. But she pushed it away, held it down: *Not yet.*

"This is the kitchen," Lila said. "Isn't it the prettiest kitchen you ever saw."

On her pad, Cree made a note of Lila's flattened affect. The recording unit in her fanny pack vibrated faintly, reminding her that the scroll would tell it definitively later. But watching Lila now she knew what it would probably show: ragged, generally rising indicators on all of Lila's signs since they'd come into the house, but not the telltale spikes and deep valleys that revealed a remembered or unconscious crisis. Not yet.

"Wasn't the original kitchen," Jack said. "Old days, they always kept the kitchen pretty separate – wood-fired stoves, too hot, and there was always the fire risk, so – "

Cree gave Jack a look and tossed her gaze to Lila. To his credit, he got the message.

"Down here is the library," Lila said. "Jack, remember I told you about that noise, I thought it might be termites . . ."

"You said you never heard it again. I sure never heard it."

"I did hear it. I heard it every day." Walking quickly, Lila led them down a side hall from the kitchen, into one of the wings. They passed a modern bathroom and a couple of closed doors Cree assumed to be storage rooms or closets, and then came to a large, dark room lined with bookshelves.

In the gloom, Cree could make out the glisten of dark, oiled furniture and the straight white teeth of a piano keyboard. She picked up a faint sense of presence here, but not the sense of nightmare Lila apparently felt. This felt keening . . . a piercing sweetness. Whatever it was, it was subtle, impossible to probe with the distractions of Jack and Lila present.

"Let's get some damn lights on in here," Jack said. He fumbled for the switch and bulbs came on in a smaller version of the chandeliers in the front rooms.

"Jackie, that table . . . that table was making the noise." Lila was unwilling to go farther than the doorway.

"What the hell — ?"

"It . . . it came alive. The claws."

Jack looked as if someone had hit him in the gut. He looked quickly to Cree, something like panic in his eyes. For a long moment, he didn't have a reply. Then he crossed the room to the table and bent to look at the wooden talons. The dark mahogany legs, Cree could see, were elaborately carved with scales or feathers, each one ending up in a gryphon's head just below the top.

Jack shoved at the table and turned back to his wife. "We'll get rid of the thing. We'll sell it. Hell, we'll toss it out on the trash today!"

Lila just shook her head. She was biting her lips, fighting to stay functional. "I can't. That was one of Daddy's favorites, Momma would never forgive me. Anyway, it wouldn't help. That . . . isn't all. There's more. A whole lot more."

8

LATER, CREE WOULD REMEMBER Lila's quavering narrative as one of the most remarkable and terrifying tales she'd ever heard. This was true partly because of what she said, but mostly the way she said it: that tortured mix of self-doubt and utter conviction. And all told against the backdrop of the old house, the dim rooms full of unrelenting whispers. Maybe most poignant of all was the emotion between man and wife, the ebb and flow of terror, concern, distrust, love, doubt, resolve, desolation, loyalty, guilt. Cree did her best to disappear, speaking only to murmur something sympathetic when Lila seemed about to fall apart.

They continued to walk slowly through the house. Lila took small, broken steps, as if she were a woman thirty years older, or as if she'd injured herself. Indecisively, Jack did his best to help her. Sometimes she stood for long moments staring into some extraspatial distance as she struggled to put words to what she had seen.

The day after the first incident of the claw feet was one of the most horrible she could remember. She was afraid to tell anyone what had happened, because she knew what they'd think. So what she did instead was dream up excuses to be away from the house. When Jack left to go to his office the next morning, she left, too, taking the other car to go shopping for a couple of lamps she'd decided they needed. She called some friends and tried to get lunch dates, but no one could make it on such short notice. She ate lunch at a restaurant and drove around town, even swung by the empty lakeshore house as if seeing its familiar, safe facade could offer some comfort.

What was going on? she asked herself. She'd lived at Beauforte House for the first fifteen years of her life and couldn't recall feeling this way. Sure, a few childhood scares — bad dreams, Daddy or Uncle Brad or the nanny telling a scary story that kept her awake for a while, that kind of thing. And yes, she could remember the family talking about there being ghosts at the place, but everyone who lived in an old house, which was most of her friends, did; it was casual and taken for granted you were mostly kidding. Everybody had a housemaid or cook or gardener who supposedly practiced voodoo, too, and nobody took that seriously except as a potential personnel problem.

And then Momma had lived there for all those years, hadn't she? Lila had visited regularly over the course of two decades and had never felt any greater stress than missing Daddy, or being ticked off at Momma for one thing or another, or the general nostalgia for childhood. And Momma had never acted as if there was anything terrible there. Momma had a few secrets, maybe, but it couldn't have been anything too troubling or she wouldn't have stuck it out. Not if it felt like this.

Which, it seemed to Lila, suggested two possibilities. One, this was about something that had happened after Momma had moved out — Temp Chase's murder. Or, two, maybe she was just going plain crazy.

She couldn't decide which was scarier.

But eventually there was nothing left to do but go home. She felt a little better — walking around downtown had refreshed her. She convinced herself that she'd just been feeling uncomfortable, knowing about the Chase murder, and it was making her edgy. Anyone would feel the same. With time, it would no doubt pass.

Back at the house, that idea lasted about one second. The flutter, the jitter, was there as soon as she walked inside. From the kitchen, she could hear the table claws clenching.

She unpacked the things she'd bought, determined to ignore it. Then she went to do something in the upstairs bedroom. She turned into the big room at the top of the stairs, and when she glanced down the hallway she saw something at the edge of one of the doorways, maybe thirty feet away. The shoe tip! And something else, too, along the edge of the door

71

at chest height. She stopped, feeling nauseous, and made herself look at it. Fabric – some kind of coarse brown weave, sort of raggedy. And it was moving, a slight, regular rise and fall. Breathing! She realized she was staring at part of the lapel and shoulder of a jacket. Worn by someone standing in one of the doorways. Someone who thought he was out of view.

It took a moment to shake off the shock. She wanted to run and call the police but was afraid to turn away from the intruder. Instead, she shouted out, "I see you! I see you there! You come out of there right now!"

Whoever it was didn't move. Just continued to hold there, breathing.

"I have a gun!" she lied. "You come out or I'll shoot you, so help me God!"

Standing in the big room at the top of the stairs now, Lila pulled out of the narrative to look wide-eyed from Cree's face to Jack's and back. "And I *would* have!"

"Why didn't you? Couldn't you have gotten Jack's shotgun?" Cree asked. She sighted down the hallway, lined by many doorways.

Lila shook her head. "Oh, I did. But not at that point. It's so hard to explain what goes through your head at a time like that! See, I . . . I *saw* somebody standing there. But then part of me was looking for a, I don't know, a *normal* explanation? I'm sorry, Jackie, for a minute I thought maybe it was *you*, home early and pulling some stupid prank. Or Ron. Or somebody else who maybe had some reason for being there, I don't know, a, a handyman Jack had asked to come in. Or then I thought, *No, Lila, it's your nerves again, just like the first time.* The security system was working when I came home – how could anyone have gotten in? I just didn't want to do anything stupid! I didn't want to call *attention.* You see?"

So she began to walk toward the doorway. When she was fifteen feet away, the lapel disappeared, slipping backward into the room. What she thought she was going to do, where she got the courage, Lila didn't know, but she kept on going until she stood in that doorway and looked inside. It was the room that had been her bedroom when she was a child, now set up as a guest bedroom.

There was nobody in there. The windows were closed and locked, and there was no other way out. She could see the empty floor under the bed. The only place someone could hide was the huge armoire that served as the room's closet. The doors were shut, but there was a key in the lock and she quickly turned it and yanked it out. Good, solid, old-time craftsmanship, heavy doors with strong lock and hinges. If someone was in there, he was stuck now.

She debated calling the police but then got afraid of making a fuss, of what people would think if they came with flashing lights and sirens and found nothing. Jackie would for sure hear about it, he'd tell Ron and Momma. So instead she went quickly across the hall, got the shotgun, and came back.

Jack had taught her how to load it, she'd even shot clay pigeons with him once in a while, she knew how to operate the gun. She jacked a shell into the chamber. Holding the stock tucked tight under her right arm, barrel straight ahead, finger on the trigger, she used her left hand to turn the key. She yanked open the doors and jumped back.

No one was there.

She felt only the briefest sense of relief. The absence of an intruder left vastly more frightening possibilities.

Lila made it through that day and the next. She heard the table clenching. She saw the shoe and the jacket again, a little more showing each time, but when she'd go to investigate, it would disappear. And now she'd begun to hear things – movement in the other room, the scrape of a chair, the brush of cloth. Sometimes she thought she heard a pattering, like a four-legged thing running, the clack of claws on the floorboards. It never happened when Jack was in a room with her, only when he was at work or in another part of the house. She began making it through her days and nights hour by hour. Any distraction helped; it was a relief when the new cleaning woman started coming twice a week, because for the first couple of times Lila had to show her around – that killed off part of a day.

Thanksgiving came, and Janine and David, the two youngest Warren kids, returned home for the holiday; Ron and his girlfriend and Momma

73

and Jack's parents all came over for the feast. Everyone commented on Lila's condition – "Oh, honey, you've lost some weight! You takin' proper care of yourself?" "Mom, you haven't been sick, have you?" – but having people in the house seemed to banish much of the tension.

Once the holiday ended, things got rapidly worse. Lila saw her watcher several times – the shoe tips and the lapel of the jacket. She began to sense flutterings at the corner of her eye all the time. She heard the relentless screech of the table's claws, and a couple of times she saw other things quickly resume their former shapes as if trying to conceal dire transformations from her: the faces in the family portraits leaving a faint afterimage of snarling, ogling monstrosities, a throw rug that had been a gnarled, warted, lizardlike thing. She became afraid to leave the TV on because the sound might camouflage the subtle noise of something sneaking up on her. Mirrors became particularly intolerable, because whenever she saw herself in them she always got the sense that another image, something terrifying, had just vacated the glass. And then there was her own face.

When she asked Jack how he liked the place – was he comfortable here – he said a guy could sure get used to it. People came up to him at the office and complimented him on his new digs, he told her cheerfully. That was pretty fine.

So far, Lila told herself, nothing she'd experienced was all *that* bad, she was a Beauforte, she should show a little *spine*. But it was wearing on her – the constant tension, the sleepless nights. Plus she was living a double life, trying to lie to Jack and Ron and Momma and everybody about how great she was doing and all the while being gnawed hollow on the inside.

They decided to hold a big Christmas party, with all the kids, some of Jack's family, some friends. Seemed like a good idea: She'd keep busy with planning, sending invitations, making calls for catering and decorations, and so on. But it didn't help. By the first week of December she didn't think she could survive until Christmas, let alone be able to play hostess. Things came to a head the second week of December.

Middle of the night. Jack asleep in bed. Propped up on the pillows next to him, unable to find sleep, Lila had been reading until her eyes burned. Just after she turned out the light, she heard a brushing or slithering sound. She lifted her head to stare at the fireplace, its little black coal grate just a square of shadow in the semidark. As had become their habit, they'd left the lights on in the hall, so there was enough light to see what was happening.

A shadow began oozing out of the stove – many slender tendrils of shadow, actually, worming out through the holes in the grate, groping in the air and then braiding together into a thick snake of darkness. It came out like smoke but seemed to collect weight, growing as a long tube of shadow along the floor, writhing, arching, swelling thicker until it was as big around as a horse's belly. It looked like a water moccasin. Lila could *hear* the friction of its body on the floor, the rasp of scales. She couldn't breathe, couldn't even scream until its knotting coils had filled half the room.

Jack woke up groggy, groping for the bedside light. "Lila? Peaches? What's goin' on?" he mumbled. Lila managed to find her lamp and snapped it on. When light filled the room, the snake didn't disappear instantly but rather took a second or two to fray into separate tentacles and suck back into the stove.

Lila was pointing at the fireplace, but there was nothing for Jack to see. Shaking with her own pulse, she could only tell him it was a bad dream. She'd had a bad dream. She was sorry she'd wakened him. Bad dream.

She had always hated snakes. The visitation had given her a shock, and the next day she felt sick, almost too weak to get out of bed. The housekeeper came for half the day, so that one wasn't so bad. But the next day Jack had to leave on a business trip, a realty seminar put on by the national affiliate company in Dallas. Jack couldn't skip it – he was supposed to make a presentation.

Lila was left alone at the house for two days and nights.

"Do I really have to do this?" Lila moaned.

"Only if you want to," Cree said. "It will certainly help me, and I think it would help you, too. But it's up to you. Always."

They had come to the bedroom she and Jack shared, a big room that was now about half furnished. A huge antique canopy bed dominated the wall opposite the fireplace, and two large mirrored armoires stood against the other walls. A pair of French doors opened onto a small balcony that hung among the branches of a magnolia tree. Through the dark green, waxy foliage, Cree could make out the backyard, bounded on the far side by a hedgelike thicket, the iron fence, and then the wall of the next house. Cree noticed that the mirrors on both armoires' doors were broken, big spiderweb cracks from some heavy impact, and in combination with the broken mirror downstairs it struck her as a significant detail. But it wasn't the right moment to ask Lila about it.

Lila was shivering. She reached shakily for one bedpost and sat down on the edge of the mattress.

Jack moved to her side, looking chastened. "I didn't know," he mumbled miserably. "I didn't really . . . get it. How bad it was. Or I wouldn't have gone."

Lila stared at the coal stove as if she could still see the shadow snake emerging. The separate muscles of her face ticced, one above her eyebrow, another that tugged the corner of her lip.

"I don't have what it takes for the blow-by-blow. I can't give you all the buildup. I can't tell every detail. I can't." Looking up at Jack, Lila took his hand and massaged it lovingly as if, Cree was surprised to see, she were suddenly worried about *him*. But when she went on, it was in that flat, almost mechanical voice, reciting it to get it over with: "That night I saw a wolf in the house. A black wolf. Yellow-green eyes. He just rounded the corner at a run and came bounding down the hallway. I barely had time to jump back in here and slam the door. I could hear him snuffling all along the crack and at the keyhole. I could see the shadows of his paws and muzzle under the door. And then I could hear him saying my *name*, this raspy, whispery voice, God help me I could hear the sound of those . . . long wolf lips kind of fluttering as he called my *name* over and over, and I thought, *Oh, God, just let me be dead! Don't make me listen to this!*" Lila's desperation had crescendoed again, and she struggled to find the impassivity that would let her go on. "And of course I knew there aren't wolves in New Orleans, and wolves can't *talk.* Which meant I was crazy. So I stood in here for a long time. After a while I didn't hear him. So when I got my courage up, I went out again. I was going to leave the house, go sleep at a hotel. But down at the corner, where I'd seen the shoe, there was the edge of someone's clothes again! That awful raggedy jacket. I'd been seeing a little more of him each time, and this time I could see part of his face above the clothes, the side of his cheek, with hair, a beard or something. And I was going to come back in here and get the gun and shoot him, I didn't care if it was a hallucination or whatever, I didn't care if I was going to wreck up the house. But then the face turned, and I realized that what I could see wasn't right, it was sort of . . . square, shiny but hairy. Not human. More like a bristly snout. And that's what it was. He stepped out, and he had a pig's head. It was a boar-headed man. I peed myself. He had a wet snout and bristles going down into his shirt and these little tiny bright eyes. And he came straight for me. And I ran down the hall, I was going to go for the back stairs. But he came after me so fast, I knew he was going to catch me. So I turned into my old bedroom. I tried to shut the door on him, but he pushed it aside so hard it knocked me down. And – "

Lila stopped, panting shallowly. She sat curled slightly forward, hands tight over her stomach, knees pushed together hard. A defensive posture held so hard the whole bed vibrated with her tension.

The sudden silence startled Cree. Jack's face had flushed red and his eyes bulged as if there was a huge pressure inside him.

Cree gave it a full minute, but Lila didn't move. "And – ?" Cree prompted gently.

"And that is all I am up for today," Lila said flatly. She wasn't speaking to either Cree or Jack, just telling it to the world at large: *Enough.* Still she held herself rigid. *The way a hunted rabbit freezes,* Cree thought, *hoping it will disappear into the background.*

And then Lila exploded: "Isn't that *enough?* I mean, doesn't that give you the general idea? You want more? What is the point?" And she broke suddenly, a tree going over in a gale. She folded over her knees, crying wrenchingly.

Agonized for her, Cree almost went to her side. But some instinct told her to wait. And after a moment Jack took the initiative.

He bent and held her shoulders and rocked her tenderly. "Come on now. Let's get out of here. Let's go home. Come on, darlin'."

For a long time Lila stayed bent double as if her back had cracked under the strain. And then she unfolded without a word and numbly let him lead her out of the house.

9

CREE GOT BACK TO HER hotel room feeling sticky and nauseous. Lila's wrenching tale had shaken her. The tension was contagious, and when they'd emerged from Beauforte House into the baking heat of daylight, Cree realized that she'd been sweating heavily the whole time.

Throughout Lila's narrative, Cree had picked up her feelings, resonated with them to an unprecedented degree. And Lila's experiences were fantastic. They didn't jibe with anything Cree had encountered in her own work or with accounts from any other legitimate researchers of parapsychology.

If Edgar were here, he'd ask her to put words to the feeling – both a good friend's curiosity about her special talents and a scientist's recommendation to try to articulate even the most subjective experience.

The only thing she could compare it to was the one time she'd seen a tornado. She and Mike had been driving to visit his parents in Southern Illinois and had heard the warning on the car radio, telling them that funnel clouds had been sighted nearby. Cree thought it would be fun to witness one of nature's most powerful phenomena. So despite Mike's misgivings, they pulled over and got out to sit on the hood of the car, where they had a good view of seemingly endless wheat fields beneath a troubled sky. First the light turned a sick yellow as the clouds clotted at the horizon, fraught with occluded lightning. Around the car, sudden turbulences followed pockets of calm so still they felt airless. The scattered trees along the road alternately shivered and then sagged submissively, and the grain fields dimpled and cratered and went still again as if some gigantic, invisible creature had landed and rolled and bounded up again. Then an obscene nipple formed in the overcast and suddenly a snake of cloud was there, groping toward the earth a couple of miles away. And as the funnel vortex solidified and began to rove, Cree had recognized her own arrogance: That mindless hunger and power wasn't fun or interesting or anything but terrifying, and there was nothing in her thoughts but a prayer the rooting snout wouldn't turn her way.

That's how Lila's psychic "weather" felt.

And the scariest part was that she knew Lila had quit before recounting the really bad stuff. Lila had a lot more to tell.

The three of them had driven back to the Warrens' lakeside house, where Cree recovered the polygraph harness and other gear. Lila clearly needed to rest, so they didn't discuss anything, but Cree made an appointment to meet them at their residence again later in the afternoon. On the way back to the hotel, she had stopped at a restaurant and stared at the lunch menu for ten minutes before realizing she couldn't eat anything.

Now it was just one o'clock and she felt used up, shaky, sick.

She was about to take a shower, try to scrub away the feeling, when the phone rang.

"I'm just checking in to see how our cash cow is doing." Joyce's pragmatic-sounding New York voice, so good to hear. "Do you think there's something there for us?"

It took a moment for Cree to decide what to say. "I'm not sure. We've got a really traumatized witness. So far, I'm thinking this is probably psychological. But we were just at the house, and I did, you know . . . pick up that . . . there might be something . . ."

"You're sounding very faint, Cree. I can hardly hear you."

Cree made an effort to speak into the receiver: "I think this might be a case where the witness has other issues, maybe even a brain disorder. We were just at the house . . . I haven't looked at her tapes yet."

"You don't sound too good. You taking care of yourself?"

"I'm okay."

Joyce made a skeptical sound. "So is New Orleans as terrific as they say? Hint, hint – don't you need me to come help with research?"

"Not yet. We'll see, maybe I'll have a better handle on this by tomorrow."

"All right. In the meantime, I've got that list of research resources you asked me to compile. New Orleans is *very* into its history and architecture, so there's quite a bit – historical societies up the proverbial ying-yang, universities, museums – "

"Great. Well, e-mail it to me. Also, Joyce, there's a murder case I'd like to know more about. Took place two years ago – a New Orleans TV news anchor, Templeton Chase. Can you do a search on that and prepare me a brief?"

"Love to," Joyce said. And she meant it: Joyce loved the forensic dimensions of their cases and was very expert at digging. Cree didn't look forward to Joyce's reaction when she found out the murder was unsolved but figured her love of investigation would bring her around in the end.

"Look for something in your mail tonight," Joyce said. "Let's see . . . in other news, Ed called, he's excited about the situation there. I gave him your hotel number, so you'll probably hear from him. Your sister called, ditto. Oh, yes, and that Mrs. Wilson left a message while I was away from the desk. What're we going to do about that, Cree? I mean, I know this is a weird field anyway, but – a *dog?*" She signed off with a wet-sounding kiss.

There was a lot to do before meeting Lila and Jack at four. Cree made a mental list. Several times since touring the house with Lila, Cree had caught herself gripping her own wrists and anxiously kneading them, a gesture of Lila's she'd unconsciously appropriated. Yeah, you needed to identify with the client, but you couldn't do any good for a person who was going to pieces if you went to pieces along with her. So, first on the list, very definitely: Get shit together.

That meant taking a shower and spending half an hour naked on a towel on the floor. Deirdre was the one who had suggested she try yoga as a countermeasure for the dangerous confusions of her work, and it had proved a real help. Cree's routine began with *pranayama*, breathing exercises that focused her mind on the simple act of drawing air deep into her body and exhaling completely. Now she was able to shed some of the whirlwind thoughts and emotions, and after a few minutes a glow of energy began to burn in her stomach, just below her belly button. Once the breathing rhythm and the tummy-*chakra* glow were well established, she segued into neck rolls and other basic stretches, and then moved through a series of *asanas*, holding each position until the warmth spread up into her chest, her neck and scalp, out her limbs and into every muscle and nerve. She finished by sitting in lotus position, hands held on her lap in the *dhyana mudra*, mind just hovering. *A vast silk banner rippling gently in boundless space, buoyed in the subtlest uprising breeze*, she thought. Then she let go of that, too. Found a timeless time of no words, no images at all.

And after a while she was back. By the time she unhooked her ankles from her thighs, her skin had goosebumped from the hotel room air-conditioning, and she felt pretty sure she could handle the rest of the day. She got up and put on some comfortable clothes.

She cleared the desk of tourist literature to make room for the polygraph register and tape recorder. Then she turned on her laptop and plugged in the portable roll-paper fax machine Edgar had adapted. When the computer had booted up, she opened a program that imported data from the register's tape and exported it as digital data the fax printer would convert to graphic images. The little machine began its stuttering mumble and started spooling out paper. A quick glance at the first foot or so told Cree that everything was working as it should: five jagged lines superimposed on an index grid measuring intensity levels against the passage of time.

They'd been in the house for just over half an hour, so it would be a long scroll; Cree figured it would require about fifteen minutes to print. As the paper folded loosely back and forth on the floor, Cree rewound the audiotape and reviewed the notes on her pad. She drew an approximate floor plan of the whole building from memory, then traced the route the three of them had taken through the rooms, blocking out the places where Lila had seen the shoes, the smoke snake, the wolf, the pig-headed man. It was a good enough schematic to make some sense out of Lila's data, but as soon as possible it would be essential to locate accurate architectural plans for the house.

When the scroll finished printing, Cree ripped the paper free, creased the rounded bends, and set the haphazard zigzag stack on the right side of the desk. She unfolded the first three feet. Along the bottom of the paper, the time was printed out in five-second intervals, showing that she had pushed the start button at 11:04:32.

At first the scroll seemed to verify Cree's earlier expectations of general, increasing agitation across all indicators, with the lines breaking into earthquakelike jagged spikes when Lila told of the really harrowing stuff, or when they'd entered the rooms where she'd had those experiences. But she quickly got a surprise: Lila had experienced some kind of crisis of subconscious unease barely three minutes into their tour of the house.

11:07:20. Cree turned on the audio recorder and listened to the first few minutes, matching the recorder's digital clock readout with the times on the polygraph scroll. From the speaker came the rustli of Cree's clothes as she adjusted the fanny pack, the echoey sound of the footsteps in the front hall. Lila: "I'm not sure where to start." Cree reas ring her. More noise of movements. Then Jack's voice, explaining out the chandeliers.

Lila's first period of acute agitation occurred as they stood in t front parlor. The episode lasted only a couple of seconds, and then Lila igns had stabilized again as she reminisced about her childhood.

What had caused it? Cree puzzled over it briefly, then listened to at section of the tape again. No great inspiration came to her, but still felt a growing buzz of excitement: These anomalous readings were ofte the most revealing. The problem was to figure out what caused them Sometimes, yes, the witness's signs responded to what someone was saying, but the stimulus could as easily be the part of the house they were in, or something in the room that their eyes happened to fall upon. Or even the subliminal perception of some other presence.

Cree jotted a note on the scroll, underlining the moment for future reference, and then jumped as the phone rang. She paused the audio playback and answered.

"This is Cree."

"Ms. Black," a man's voice began, "I'm Paul Fitzpatrick, the psychiatrist who's working with Lila Warren – perhaps she mentioned me? Do you have a moment?"

"Of course." Somehow, Cree wasn't at all surprised. She knew what was coming.

"I'll get right to the point. Jack Warren just called me, very upset. He tells me you are some kind of spiritualist or medium who – "

"No. I'm a psychologist who does parapsychological research."

"Fine. In any case, he says that Lila is having a crisis and that you're going to meet with them later today?"

"That's correct."

"The Warrens requested that I be there. Frankly, Jack thinks your involvement is damaging to Lila. And I'm inclined to agree with him." Despite the potentially hostile content of what he was saying, Dr. Fitzpatrick kept an even, moderate, professional tone. He had a nice voice, Cree decided, warmed with only a hint of a Southern accent.

"And what does Lila think?"

A pause. "That's a fair question," Fitzpatrick admitted. "At this point, I'm not sure. But I intend to help her sort it out. I wanted to talk to you now to enlist your cooperation, as, I hope, a person of conscience. To assure that there is not any kind of an upsetting . . . scene . . . if we decide – "

"If *who* decides to get rid of me?"

Another pause. "You've made your point, Ms. Black – "

"Excellent," Cree said. "Then I'll see you at four. I look forward to meeting you. And thank you for calling." She hung up.

Maybe it was some lingering high from the yoga session, but Cree didn't feel particularly pissed off at Jack or Dr. Fitzpatrick. You couldn't blame people for being dubious; Cree herself had been a lifelong skeptic until that day with Mike nine years ago. And when the change had come it was a painful, wrenching epiphany, neither expected nor welcome, that she wouldn't wish on anybody. Fitzpatrick was simply doing his job: Lila's problems could very well be purely psychological, and the intrusion of a supernatural theory could derail a therapeutic process big time. And Fitzpatrick really hadn't come across as too much of an asshole.

In any case, Cree reminded herself, you had to develop a thick skin for skepticism, or parapsychology wasn't the field for you.

She put it out of her mind and focused on Lila's tapes, unfolding sections of scroll and listening to the audio, sometimes rewinding and listening again, jotting notes as they occurred to her. It took over an hour, but when she was done she felt she'd identified several features worthy of further attention.

The first was the high level of agitation in the front parlor, when Lila had outwardly seemed relatively calm. The kitchen itself stood out because neither Lila's verbal narrative nor vitals showed any particular escalation of tension – the readings suggested that whatever Lila subconsciously knew or felt or perceived, it wasn't obviously connected with the Chase tragedy. Of course, conclusions were premature at this point.

Cree picked up another anomalous peak that had come when they were in the former slave quarters, though Lila had not recounted anything important there. Why would Lila react to this space – what did she remember or sense about it? Or were her signs unconnected to the place and simply responses to something she was thinking about?

In the hallways and rooms where she claimed to have seen things, Lila's readings showed classic features of fear, anxiety, panic, confusion. By the time they'd gotten to the master bedroom and she was telling about the pig-headed man and the awful changelings, her signs had become chaotic, wild and ragged to a degree that would frighten a cardiologist, let alone a psychologist – extreme but appropriate responses to remembered trauma.

Given what this data was telling her, Lila had shown amazing determination and strength to do as well as she had. The woman did indeed have a core of great resilience and self-control. How to get her to trust it, take assurance from it?

Cree checked her watch and realized it was time to head over to the Warrens'. She refolded the scroll and put her notes away for further review. One thing she knew for certain, though: Whatever else the scroll might reveal, it had already proved that Lila Beauforte Warren really had experienced something deeply, profoundly disturbing. Now it was up to Cree to determine just what that was.

10

CREE ARRIVED AT THE HOUSE a few minutes before four to find a black Jaguar parked carelessly and nearly blocking the end of the Warrens' driveway. She was just parking on the street when another car approached and also paused in front of the house, an older BMW with a vanity plate that read *SHRINK*. It didn't take much to deduce that the driver was Dr. Fitzpatrick. They both parked, got out, and approached each other warily.

Fitzpatrick was a long-limbed man around Cree's age, with thick brown hair and a congenial face that reminded her faintly of Alan Alda. He wore white linen pants, a white shirt with its sleeves turned back on his forearms, and an unruly blue tie.

They met at the end of the driveway and stopped to look each other over.

"Dr. Fitzpatrick, I presume," Cree said.

"Hello, Doctor Black." He smiled at her surprise and explained "After we talked on the phone, I took the liberty of doing a bit of on-line detective work on you. I'm very impressed with your credentials. And relieved."

He extended a hand, and Cree shook it, thinking that his doing research in advance was better than their getting inside, going territorial, and having to lay out their résumés side by side to see who had the longer list of honors and degrees.

"Relieved?"

"Yes. That you have sufficient background to understand why multiple approaches – conflicting approaches – to therapy can be injurious to the patient."

The unspoken conclusion being, *and will therefore back out of this without an embarrassing tussle.* Still, Fitzpatrick's tone was amiable and respectful. It was hard to take much offense.

They started walking up the drive. "How much has Lila told you about what happened to her at Beauforte House?" Cree asked.

"Not much. We've only just begun, really. And she's a . . . a reluctant patient."

"I brought a cassette of what she told me when we were over there this morning. If she's willing, I'll lend it to you."

Fitzpatrick bobbed his head unenthusiastically. As they skirted the black Jaguar, he rapped the sleek hood with his knuckles. "This is Ro-Ro's car: Looks like Jack has decided to gang up on you, Dr. Black. Got the whole posse here."

" 'Ro-Ro'?"

Fitzpatrick laughed at himself. "Ronald Beauforte. The nicknames are something of a convention in certain socioeconomic circles hereabouts. I'd guess his being here means Jack has enlisted him to help chase you off, too."

Cree was just thinking that the impending session was looking less and less like the one she'd intended for this afternoon. And then the door opened and Ro-Ro stood there with his supercilious good looks, beckoning them inside.

"I'm flattered that you think I deserve such a big production," Cree told them. They were in the living room, Cree seated on the couch with Jack and Dr. Fitzpatrick ranged on a pair of facing chairs, Ronald standing at his ease to one side of the room. Cree had been a little disconcerted to hear Ronald greet Dr. Fitzpatrick as "Fitz," as if they were good buddies. "But isn't there someone missing?"

"We thought it might be better if we talked without Lila here," Jack said. "You saw what she was like. She can't take any more of this ghost business. We were wrong to bring you here."

"Your wife is stronger than you think, Jack," Cree told him. "She's going to surprise you."

"You can keep the retainer," Ronald put in, "if that's what – "

"She's never been all that strong," Jack said. "She's always been easily upset."

"I can vouch for that," Ron agreed. "There's some history here." He turned to the credenza behind him and began fixing himself a drink from one of a number of liquor bottles on a tray there.

Cree watched him, thinking, *Ro-Ro*. Once you'd heard the nickname, it was hard not to think of him that way: an aging Southern bon vivant clinging to upper-class frat-boy mannerisms.

"I have no problem with returning the retainer or discontinuing my research," Cree said, "provided I hear from Lila that that's what *she* wants."

Jack and Ronald turned to look at Fitzpatrick, as if that was his cue to respond. But before he could, Lila appeared in the doorway. She was still wearing the same gray skirt and white blouse, rumpled now as if she'd been sleeping in them. She did look like hell, Cree saw, haggard and red-eyed, a wisp of hair hanging down over one eye and giving her a demented look. And yet the back that had looked so broken at Beauforte House was ramrod straight again.

Jack stood up, instantly solicitous. "Darlin' – "

"Sit *down*, Jackie." Lila glanced over at Ronald, who was looking on with a sardonic grin and swirling whiskey around his glass. "Ro-Ro. Of course you're here. Do make yourself at home, won't you? Care for a drink?"

"Maybe I will, thanks." Ronald blinked languidly and took a sip.

"I am not a cripple," Lila said. "I won't be discussed in my absence by some . . . cabal, however well meaning. *I* am the one who will decide what I need to do for my own mental health."

Jack and Ronald frowned briefly, different kinds of frowns, but Fitzpatrick's expression was one of both interest and, what – pleasure, maybe, at Lila's assertiveness.

"And what *do* you think, Lila?" he asked mildly. "You've had a harrowing experience today. What's the best way to get you to feel better?"

"I want to figure out what the hell these ghosts are. And why they're bothering me. And how to get rid of them for good."

Jack shook his head. "Lila . . . Peaches, the things you told us today, those can't be *real*. They may be scary as hell but they aren't *real*, they ain't even regular ghosts. They're – "

"They're all in my head, right? Hallucinations, because I'm going crazy. That's what I've been thinking, too. But after we got home today I remembered something. Jackie, I want you to think back to that night I woke you up, back in December. When I was so upset and said I had a bad dream? I told you and Cree about it today?"

"Yeah, the snake."

"Yes. Now Jackie, can you remember what happened? Can you *admit* what happened?"

Jack looked puzzled, glancing quickly from Ronald to Dr. Fitzpatrick as if seeking support. "What happened? I heard you scream, I woke up. I didn't know what the hell was going on, you snapped on the light and said you'd – "

And then Jack stopped abruptly. His eyes went thoughtful and then a little alarmed.

"No," Lila insisted. "*You* said – ?"

Jack looked at her with dismay. Lila waited him out, and at last he dropped his eyes. "I said . . . I asked somethin' like, 'Is that smoke?' "

Lila stared at him, then Cree, a look of desperate triumph or vindication: She had described her giant water moccasin as oozing like smoke.

"I – I was still practically asleep, the light blinded me! Doesn't mean – "

"You *saw* the snake! Just for a second. *You* saw it, too. If there'd really been smoke, we would have smelled it! It would have lingered in the room. There's no reason there'd be smoke, that old coal heater hasn't been used in fifty years. You saw it, Jackie!"

Cree felt a pang in her chest. Lila's plea for verification was a cry for someone to share her experience, for proof she was not really as alone as she felt.

Jack couldn't look at her, but he couldn't back down, either. "Baby, if there'd really been a big damn snake, wouldn't *it* have still been in the room?"

"Can I ask a question?" Cree interrupted. "Lila, have you seen or felt any of those things here, at this house?"

"Never." She gave Cree a grateful look.

"Jack, has Lila acted . . . that way . . . here at this house or anywhere else? At any time?"

Jack thought about it, pouted. "Can't say she has," he admitted. "I mean, she's been *upset* since we moved back in, after that business over there, but . . . no."

"Why would that be, do you suppose? Why would she encounter her hallucinations only in Beauforte House?"

Ron sipped his whiskey, thoughtful now. Jack threw out his hands, palms up, at a loss, then looked to Fitzpatrick. "Help me out here, Fitz."

Fitzpatrick shrugged. "I think these are issues we can iron out later. The real point is, Lila, if I'm hearing you right, you still think your best course is to explore the supernatural, um, possibility? Even though there's a good chance you have a brain disorder, and even though the process upsets you, you feel that it would be a beneficial therapeutic approach?"

Lila nodded.

"And you'd like to continue working with Dr. Black?"

"Now hold on a minute here," Ronald said. He frowned as he set his glass down and stepped closer to the circle of chairs. "Not half an hour ago, we all agreed – "

"Ronald," Lila said, "*you* agreed, not me. I'll tell you what I agree to. I want to get to the bottom of this. I want to do whatever I have to with Cree. And if you want cooperation from me about the house or *anything* else, you'll damn well cooperate with me and with Cree's research on this! Jackie, same goes for you. If you want me to continue with Dr. Fitzpatrick, it's conditional on me working with Cree until such time as *I* say it's not the right thing." Lila's decisiveness was clearly a major effort that was fatiguing for her. But she rallied one more time to glare at her brother and her husband. "Am I making myself clear?"

Ronald shook his head, disgusted, and shot an accusatory glance at Cree as he went to pour himself another drink. Jack just sat for a moment, hands on knees, puffing out his cheeks as he blew air through pursed lips. And then he meekly got up and went over to the credenza himself, muttering, "I think maybe I'll join you, there, Ro-Ro."

Lila hovered, still defiant but looking suddenly uncertain again, her power ebbing.

There was a long moment of strained silence, and then Fitzpatrick loudly smacked his hands on his thighs and stood up. "Well. That settles that, then, doesn't it?" And he grinned widely to no one in particular.

Cree and Dr. Fitzpatrick left the house fifteen minutes later. Outside, the lowering sun had stretched the shadows of houses and trees into long diagonals, and the air had cooled nicely. They paused at the end of the driveway, and Cree was about to shake Fitzpatrick's hand when he unexpectedly tipped his head toward the green slope of the levee and asked, "Ever been up there?"

"No. This is my first visit to New Orleans."

"You want to take a walk? I was just thinking, you and I have a few things to talk about. No time like the present. Good weather, grab it while you've got it."

Cree looked up at the sunlight on the grass, the blue sky, the tops of trees just visible on the other side. Lila had ended her bravura perfor-mance by asking Cree to begin a full investigation and handing her a retainer check for another five grand — a convincing statement to Ron and Jack about who was in charge. She had also given Cree and Fitzpatrick permission to discuss her case with each other.

Cree was tired, but the lakeshore did look inviting, and the sooner she began a dialogue with Fitzpatrick the better. "Just let me get my other shoes from the car," she said.

She changed into her walking shoes and met him at the end of the street, and they climbed up the steep embankment. At the top, she was rewarded with a vast view of water, bordered by a wide strip of green parkland that stretched out of view to the left and right. The flat top of the levee was almost level with the second-floor windows of the houses in the neighborhoods behind it. Here and there along its zigzagging length, people came and went, suggesting that beyond keeping flood-water out of the city it doubled as a walking and bicycling path. On the lakeside, the lawns were thronged with people picnicking, playing catch, lounging, wrestling with dogs, flying kites. The breeze that bustled off the lake carried the scent of smoke from portable grills as it tugged at Cree's skirt and hair.

"This is nice," she admitted. It was a relief to be surrounded by lots of space, free of close interiors so congested with emotions and history. To let the wind and sun sweep it all away for a moment.

Fitzpatrick stood with his hands deep in his trouser pockets, eyes shut, face turned to the sun. Yes, a little like Alan Alda, Cree decided, but more edgy. More dash or darkness – an attractive combination. The wind made his hair crazy and pulled his tie fluttering over his shoulder.

"I come running here a couple of times a week," he told her. He still hadn't opened his eyes. "When it gets hot, which is basically from here on in, this is the coolest place in town. The wind helps. You jog?"

"Pretty regularly."

"Thought so," Fitzpatrick said.

Cree heard the oblique flattery in his comment. He was low-key and unselfconscious about it, and left it alone afterward. To her surprise, she liked the way it made her feel. They began to walk along the levee into the lowering sun.

"I expected you'd be part of the lynch mob, Dr. Fitzpatrick. Why weren't you?"

"Might as well call me Fitz. Everybody else does."

"I noticed. I take it you have social contact with the Beaufortes?"

"Some. I'm not real close – friend of the family, I guess you could say. My father was a lifelong friend of Richard, that's Lila's father, and Charmian. But we're all in the same krewe, travel in some of the same circles – old families, you know. When this all blew up and they were looking for some . . . advice . . . on Lila, they came to me. She was amenable."

" 'The same crew'?"

"Krewe, spelled with a *k* and an extra *e* at the end. It's a club, or maybe you could call it a fraternal organization. All we really do is plan our Mardi Gras parade and festivities. Probably sounds silly to an out of towner, but around here it's a pretty big thing." He grinned as he looked at her to gauge her reaction, but after they'd walked on a few more steps, he sobered. "I didn't join the mob because it became obvious to me that you have Lila's best interests at heart, and because she seems to trust you. She has a hard time talking to me – there's a lot of denial there, and a lot of shame. She's a damned Beauforte, and Beaufortes don't *have* weaknesses or breakdowns. But I could see you two had established good rapport. And she needs an ally now, very badly."

Cree nodded. *Rapport* was hardly a sufficient term, though; rather, an inexplicably deep sympathetic resonance. At its core was the feeling that they had something crucial in common. Both were deeply shaken by an unexpected, undesired, undecipherable revelation that necessitated re-interpreting the laws of nature and reassessing the meaning of person-hood. Caught between an absolutely convincing experience that was utterly at odds with normal life and the beliefs of a skeptical world. Prone to shattering vulnerability, yet determined to find the strength to confront it and master it.

They passed a couple of kids playing on the lake side of the levee, two boys about the same age as Zoe and Hyacinth, the low sun burnishing their black skin with gold highlights. Wide grins and lots of fidget and goofus, a dog barking at them from below. They each had a square of cardboard ripped from some box, and were sliding on it down the grass of the embankment – sledding, Cree realized, in a land that had never known snow. It took a lot of paddling and kicking get to the bottom. Their cheerful abandon felt sparkling to Cree, effervescent.

"I was also too curious to lynch you outright," Fitzpatrick went on. "I looked you up in the American Psychological Association roster. Ph.D. from Duke, master's from Harvard, won the prestigious Haverford

Fellowship. Which, I have to tell you, turned me green – I applied for that bastard but was deemed unworthy. Fact is, I'm dying to know how you got into parapsychology. From your résumé, I wouldn't think you were the type."

"I don't think there is a 'type.' I had a paranormal experience nine years ago that changed my outlook dramatically. My life has been something of a . . . an ongoing field study to understand it ever since." Cree stopped, surprised at herself. Ordinarily, she didn't go anywhere near her own upheaval. Fitzpatrick must be a great psychoanalyst, she decided, his sincerity and unjudgmental interest easily drawing out his patients.

"You going to tell me what it was?"

"It's complex," Cree said lightly. "Maybe some other time."

Fitzpatrick nodded, the good shrink knowing when not to push further.

They had come to a street that cut through the levee. The grassy mound was capped by a cement wall of the same height, mounted with two massive steel doors that were open now but could obviously be slid shut on their steel tracks. Fitzpatrick led her down the slope to the flat lawn, then along the street to a road that ran close to the shore. A steady stream of cars and pickups rolled by, people driving with windows open, music racketing.

"Saturday evening, good weather," Fitzpatrick told her, "this is the place to see and be seen. Cruise along here, go back around Robert E. Lee Boulevard, and do it again."

They turned left to continue along the shore road and soon came to a bridge over a little river. All along the bridge, people of all ages and colors stood trailing strings into the water, lounging against the railing, laughing and chatting, listening to music from boom boxes.

Fitzpatrick saw her curious look. "Mudbug season," he explained. "Crawfish. Regional delicacy. Just tie a turkey neck to a piece of string. Crawfish latches on, you just pull him up and toss him in your bucket. Or you can put down a little wire cage. After a couple of hours, you've got enough of 'em to go over there and steam up a pile and eat 'em fresh."

He gestured to the wide sward of grass ahead, where several families sat around grills mounted with big pots. Cree caught a whiff of swampy smell in the charcoal scent.

Once they had crossed the bridge, Fitzpatrick led her right to the water's edge, where a seemingly endless concrete breakwater went down in steps to the waves six feet below. Scattered along it, people sat with their lines in the water. Down close to the waves and mostly out of view of the general melee, lovers cuddled discreetly in the slanted sunlight.

Fitzpatrick had dug his hands deep into his pockets again. "So you want to tell me about Lila's experience?"

Cree told him the story, starting with the shoe tip and ending with the attack by the boar-headed man. She didn't interject any of her own opinions.

"Holy shit." Fitzpatrick looked shaken. "Damn! That poor woman."

"That wasn't all of it. Lila ended her narrative very abruptly. She's still keeping something to herself."

"Do you have any idea what?"

Cree did – Lila's body language and her sudden compassion for Jack suggested what came next. But she'd wait until she heard it from Lila before jumping to conclusions or sharing assumptions. Cree just shook her head. Instead, she told him about the polygraph scroll and how it corroborated Lila's trauma.

Fitzpatrick was staring at the lake's western horizon, his forehead troubled, his hands still in his pockets. "Got to get those brain scans," he said. "Soon." He shot a sideways glance at Cree. "So – don't take this the wrong way – how do you explain ghosts that are seen by just one person and no one else? Without explaining it as a psychopathology?"

"Most ghosts *are* seen by just one person. It's just a matter of variations in sensitivity. Not so different from other senses – any audiologist will tell you that some people hear higher sound frequencies than others. Wine tasters have verifiably more acute senses of taste and smell."

"But, I mean . . . a boar-headed man, a talking *wolf*? Are those typical denizens of the otherworld?"

"There's only one world – this one. It's just bigger and stranger than we know."

Fitzpatrick nodded, accepting the point.

"And the answer to your question is, I've never encountered creatures like Lila's. I'm not sure what to think. Except that, as I'm sure you know, reality and psychology mix and recombine in an endless number of ways." Cree went on to explain the idea of epiphenomenal manifestations.

Again Fitzpatrick nodded, but his brows knit in doubt or puzzlement. "I don't have any background in your field. Zero. I've never had a paranormal experience. I haven't any idea what your diagnostic methodology is, or what your models of psychology are. I'm coming at this from a strictly psychiatric paradigm, and from here the whole thing of ghosts doesn't make sense."

"What exactly doesn't make sense?"

Fitzpatrick took his hands out of his pockets long enough to grapple the air as if trying to wring the right words from it. "Any of it! I mean, what *is* a ghost?"

"It's a loose and imprecise term for a set of phenomena we don't understand well. There are many forms of ghost, and they probably manifest through many different mechanisms. But most are not so much beings as they are experiences. Essentially, you might say, most ghosts are mental constructs."

"Mental constructs! So, really, you're saying that ghosts are psychological in origin." Fitzpatrick sounded relieved at being back on more familiar turf. "Meaning you're basically a . . . a practicing psychiatrist who specializes in patients who think they're seeing ghosts!"

"Not at all! Ghosts are completely and objectively real. I mean that in the sense that life and self and the world are also mental constructs. There's a hidden link between material reality and consciousness, a link between mind and world. And that's what I'm most motivated to explore."

He looked at her with keen appreciation. " 'A hidden link between material reality and consciousness' – God, I love it!" Then sobered and turned thoughtful. "That's really the . . . crux, isn't it? The place where philosophy, psychology, medicine, and religion converge. Even physics, nowadays . . ."

Cree nodded. Fitzpatrick caught on fast.

"Okay," Fitzpatrick went on, "so ghosts *do* have an independent existence outside the minds of those who perceive them – "

"Yes and no." Cree smiled at his confounded expression. "Most ghosts appear to be residual, fragmentary elements of human consciousness – intense memories, traumas, feelings, or just drives – that continue to manifest independently of a living body. They may require a living human consciousness to manifest themselves."

"But not all ghosts?"

"Some are more fully integrated personalities, more complete beings. And I suspect there are other entities as well, I'm not sure what to call them. There's a possibility that some ghosts are rare forms of geomagnetic phenomena. Some might be manifestations of nonhuman entities – most cultures have at one time or another believed there were spirits of the earth, or of animals, or local gods of one kind or another. But I don't know."

"But you've . . . experienced . . . ghosts. The more human variety – you've *met* them?"

"Often."

"Oh, man." Fitzpatrick shook his head, frustrated but grinning. "So what's it like?"

"Different every time. It takes a while for me to get there. Usually, it starts with moods or vague feelings. I'm highly synesthetic, so the . . . impressions or sensations come across to me as sounds of a particular color, or tactile feelings of a specific odor, or, I don't know, maybe vertigo that's like citrus mixed with sadness – not easy to translate. Further along, I experience their specific thoughts, sensations, and emotions. In some cases, it can be just like a conversation."

That was it for Fitzpatrick. Abruptly he turned aside and threw himself down on a bench that faced the rippling expanse of water. At a picnic table forty feet behind him, a family was busy with a big pile of steamed orange crawfish, breaking the little lobsters apart and bickering noisily. Sprawling at one end of the bench, Fitzpatrick gestured for Cree to sit also, and then laughed at himself. "Okay. I'm out of my depth. I've run out of academic terminology. I have to go back to when I was a kid. Question: If ghosts are just these . . . pieces of a personality, sort of floating loose, how come they wear clothes? How come they even look like human beings?"

Cree chuckled with him. A childish question, and a good one. "They don't always. But if they do, it goes back to their being mental constructs. And for better or worse, our sense of ourselves is that we have human forms and wear clothes. How do you picture your mother – the way she looked when you were a kid?"

Fitzpatrick thought about it. "Yeah. I sure don't picture her without clothes."

"Now take it a step further picture yourself back then "

"Yup. I'm a little freckly guy wearing blue corduroy overalls. Damn!" Fitzpatrick thought for a moment. "Okay, another question. How come they hang out in particular places? Why do they haunt particular houses? Why don't they just, I don't know . . . drift off into space?"

Again Cree laughed. Fitzpatrick had set this up nicely – being honest about his skepticism but truly trying to understand, easing it with good-natured self-deprecation. He'd set this up as a game of twenty questions, not an interrogation.

"Well, maybe a lot of them do just dissipate. But most ghosts are highly localized, haunting a specific place such as a house, or even just a specific *room* of a house, and nowhere else. My colleague Edgar Mayfield has a theory that localized haunts happen because the ghost came into existence in a particular geomagnetic field, a particular locale. He thinks an intense human experience can make an electromagnetic imprint on a local field, like a recording that can be played back only in that environment."

"You sound a little dubious about such a mechanistic explanation."

He *was* perceptive. "Yeah. I tend to think of it in existential terms. As a mental construct, especially one reenacting a specific experience, a ghost thinks of itself not only in terms of a body image – male or female, with a specific face and wearing specific clothes, for example – but also in terms of a particular physical environment. Usually it's the perimortem environment – the place the person was in at the moment of death, which is a very poignant moment. But often crucial memories replay at that moment, too, so it can be confusing for me. If you had died suddenly back at the Warrens' house, and your consciousness perseverated in some way, you would most likely manifest elements of their living room along with your own body image. A ghost is just an echo of a whole being's experience at a crucial moment, complete with an environment, smells, sounds, objects, thoughts, feelings. I experience the ghost's *world* as much as the ghost itself. That's because 'world' is in fact equally an artifact of consciousness."

Fitzpatrick was nodding thoughtfully, and Cree got the sense he had not only followed the line of reasoning but also appreciated its ramifications. "So this is really a very . . . metaphysical field. And that's the part that attracts you, isn't it? You're after the big truths."

Cree smiled, pleased to be understood.

"And you tune in, um, you sort of *commune* with the ghost. You share its experience?"

"The ghost and the people who perceive it. They reveal a lot about each other. It's not so different from standard psychoanalysis. People who come to you for treatment have unresolved issues that trouble them, right? As a psychiatrist, you're a detective of the subconscious – you go and try to figure out what's unresolved or dissonant between their emotional world and their situational world, what's missing, what's longed for and refused, and so on. And when you identify that issue, you help patients resolve it in a way that lets them get on with their lives."

He chewed on that for a moment. "If you're that sensitive, don't you also pick up on the experiences of living people? Doesn't a living person generate a powerful field?"

"Oh, yeah." Ruefully.

That troubled him. "So . . . what's the difference between a ghost and a living person?"

Cree felt suddenly jarred. She glanced up to see that the landscape had dimmed around them, the sun now partly eclipsed by distant buildings and trees, the light beginning to drain out of the sky. She looked at her hands and found them knotted on her lap.

"I'm still working on that one," she said.

"Seems like a kind of lonesome perspective," he said quietly. Very serious now, he watched her closely. "And all this connects back to your own, personal paranormal experience, doesn't it?"

Cree bit her lips and nodded.

"I read in one of your bios on the Internet that your husband died some years ago . . . Did that influence your – "

"It's not something I'd like to discuss right now." Strangely, though the pain was there, she didn't recoil that hard from his probing.

He nodded, aware that he'd pushed it too far. But he didn't labor through apologies, just let it go easily, gracefully. And Cree had to admit he must be a damned good shrink. Maybe even a decent human being. Throughout their conversation, his presence had seemed to her as open and clear as the breezy day. Now, appropriately, it became somber, the same hue as the band of blue-black deepening at the horizon.

They sat for a while longer, watching darkness infiltrate water and sky. Cree felt her melancholy grow, but it was a serene moment, and she let it take her. She thought it spoke well of Fitzpatrick that he could sit and share silence with a virtual stranger, as if they'd both found the same state of mind. The sense was reaffirmed when, without either saying anything, they got up simultaneously and started back the way they'd come. The park was quieter now, the crawfishers mostly gone from the bridge.

"You've given me an enormous amount to think about," Fitzpatrick said. "But there's a lot we haven't discussed, and we should meet again to compare notes on Lila. And to figure out where this goes from here. For my part, I'd like to hear your tape of her narrative, and then tomorrow I've got to see if I can move up the schedule for her cranial diagnostics. How about you – what's your next step?"

"I'm going to spend some time at the house. Probably go over there at around ten tonight."

"Huh," he grunted. "Want company?"

That surprised her, and it took her a moment to sort through it. "Dr. Fitzpatrick, I can't rationally defend everything I do or think or experience. My job requires just as much method, *and* just as much empathy, intuition, and guesswork as yours does. What I'm saying is, I don't mind company, but I have no need of distracting or dogmatically skeptical company."

He mulled that over as they climbed the levee again and headed back along its top toward the Warrens' house. The breeze was chilly now, and lights had come on in most of the houses. Cree wondered what Lila was doing. Talking to Jack? Cooking dinner for the two of them? Washing the dishes? How would she be girding herself to face another night in a world turned so deceptive and uncertain?

They shuffled down the landward slope onto the street, where Fitzpatrick stopped to find his key ring and beep his car doors open. Cree went to her car, found the audiotape of Lila's narrative, and came back to where he stood flipping his keys into the air and catching them.

"How about relatively open-minded, very curious company?" he asked.

Cree looked at him as he waited for her reply. In the mixed streetlight and sunset glow, he looked amiable, gently irrepressible, and, yes, relatively open-minded. Face it, a cute guy.

But she shook her head. "Some other time, I think. Tonight, I'd better go alone." She tossed the tape to him and he caught it easily. She started to walk away and then found herself turning back toward him. "Hey," she called, "thanks for showing me the lake and the levee. It really is lovely."

He nodded, waved, and dipped into his car. When he drove past her, he gave her a little good-bye beep on his horn.

11

By the time Cree Black and Paul Fitzpatrick left the house, Lila was too furious with Ro-Ro and Jack to stay in the same room with them, and too uncertain she could keep up the facade of defiance. So she went into the kitchen and made up a marinade, then boned and skinned the dinner chicken and put the meat in to soak. Something useful to do with her hands, that always helped. The men sat together drinking whiskey in the living room, leaving her some time to be alone, to try to think.

Her thoughts scurried like panicked mice trying to find shelter. Wherever they went, it was scary and troubling. The only place of some reassurance was Cree Black.

The ghost hunter was not at all what Lila had anticipated. Somehow, she'd expected a smaller woman who'd exude the self-dramatizing, snake-oil-scented aura of mystery Lila had seen all her life in the palm readers, Cajun fortune-tellers, and self-proclaimed voodoo queens at the street stalls around Jackson Square. Instead, Cree Black was disconcertingly straightforward. She was tallish, with brown hair worn in a simple, loose ponytail, and a face that would probably be very pretty if she accented her features with some makeup. She had green-hazel eyes and a level, direct gaze that was sympathetic without condescension, appraising without judgment. Her clothes were comfortable looking, tasteful but not flashy. She had a steady, quiet voice, and though there was definitely something vulnerable about her, she also came across as unflappable.

More than anything else, it was clear she *believed*.

Lila hadn't felt that supported or affirmed since . . . forever, practically. Not since Josephine. She had been unflappable, too. Where had Josephine gotten her strength? "Our Lord Jesus Christ," she would say. She had always been so devoted, so active in her church. Her long, serious face, the color of dark, aged mahogany, was full of piety and moral resolve and that fierce unswerving loyalty and love for Lila. So much more certain than Momma's love, so unqualified. She'd know how to fix this. She had always known.

Lila hadn't seen Josephine Dupree for almost thirty years, and yet she could remember her face well enough to realize that the old nanny and Cree Black had something in common. You could see it in their eyes: They had both stared hard into the unfathomable. The infinite.

It was Cree's belief that had given Lila the strength to be so assertive when Ro-Ro and Jack and Paul had called their little powwow. It also helped that there was something of a science or a vocabulary for this kind of thing, that there was known precedent and maybe a method for dealing with it. It wasn't just herself alone in an uncharted wilderness.

Her thoughts were interrupted by a knock at the kitchen door frame, and there was Ro-Ro, who must have had his fill of whiskey.

"Hey, little sister," he said, trying to look nonchalant.

"Go home, Ronald. I'm busy, you're just about potted, and I don't need whatever it is you're selling."

He grinned appreciatively. "My God, you *do* sound just like Momma when you talk like that!"

Lila just reached up to the array of copper-bottomed cookware that hung above the island, selected one of the three-quart pots, and measured in water for rice.

He watched her, frowning at being ignored. "Except I don't believe Momma's hands ever shook like that in her whole life."

"I guess that makes two of us missed out on the good genes. Because you don't exactly measure up to Daddy, either."

Ron twitched his head as if dodging something she'd thrown. He came into the room to stand beside her at the counter. "Listen, Lila, can't we just make some kind of a deal here?" His voice was quieter and though she could smell the whiskey he'd drunk, up close his eyes didn't look like a drunken man's eyes at all. "This thing of living at the old house – look what it's doing to you. Right? If I said, 'Hey, okay, let's sell the place and I'll take less than my half,' would that help? If you and Jack took sixty to my forty? Momma'd go for that, I'd bet."

"I've got to get dinner up. You're in my way." She opened a cupboard door so that it swung into his face, and he had to step away to keep looking at her. Her hands clattered among the spice jars, not certain what they were looking for.

"You trying to go back to the good ol' days? Is that it? Think you can re-create your youth?"

She was bringing out jars without even knowing what they were, setting them on the counter. "Yes, I'm sure that's it. Something *you* wouldn't understand, Ro-Ro, given your arrested development. Having never relinquished your adolescence in the first place."

He grabbed her hands and pulled them down to the counter, stilling the frantic reaching and sorting. "I was *at home* while you went off to school! Remember? I had to do a lot of growing up and coming to grips, real fast. Maybe I have the misfortune of remembering some things you don't."

His pain was real, too, she saw, and suddenly she felt terrible about provoking him, wounding him. She'd rather see him smug and insulated than laid so bare and vulnerable. Her heart panged with sympathy so powerful it was as if she'd been stabbed. In the intent look he was giving her, she could vaguely see her remembered big brother, once her best friend, protector, ally. She turned her hands in his and held on desperately, all her defiance going out of her.

"I'm sorry!" she blurted. "I'm just all shook up today. I don't know what you're trying to say to me!"

"You don't remember a goddamned thing, do you?" He was whispering, and though his words were harsh, his eyes were only intently curious and his hands held hers softly. "You really don't?

105

I'm always trying to figure how much. How much you might be pretending."

"Pretending? I'm not pretending anything!"

Clearly, she'd misinterpreted him. He flicked his eyes at the ceiling, a token look to God Almighty for the strength to forbear, then looked around the room as if trying to find the words that would allow him to say what he meant.

At last, his face very close to hers, he said, "Lila, put the shoe on the other foot. What if . . . let's say you knew there was something that happened – something I did, something that put me in danger. How would you handle that? What would you do?"

"Well, I don't know . . . it depends, I – "

"If you knew I could barely live with having done it," he whispered, "if you knew it was something I could never ever do again. Wouldn't you try to protect me? Wouldn't you try to keep it from catching up to me? Wouldn't you look out for your family? Even though you think I'm the lowest scum lowlife in the world, isn't blood finally thicker than water?"

"Well, yes, of course, Ronald! Is that what this is about? You did something that – "

He shook his head, frustrated. "I just want you to think about that. What I just said. What you just answered."

Jack stumped past the kitchen doorway and went into the bathroom in the hall. In a moment they heard the clank of the toilet seat and the sound of his urinating. It sounded as if he'd left the door open, and Lila wondered if he was drunk or just didn't know company was still present.

"Does it have to do with the house?" she whispered. "Is that it? Is that why you – ?"

"You're just not getting this, are you? Just think about what I said, goddamn it!" Ronald took his hands away from hers. He glanced over at the doorway as Jack flushed and ran the tap, and when he looked back at her he was angry again. He shook his head in disgust, made a flinging-away gesture in her direction, and strode away.

Lila heard Jack's voice in the hall as Ronald headed toward the front of the house: "Hey, Ro-Ro. Done with your sibling heart-to-heart? Sure you don't want to stay on for supper, now?"

Ron's answer was to slam the front door.

Lila squeezed a glob of cerulean blue into the dimple in the little plastic palette. This was probably hopeless. In the past, she'd found some comfort in painting, but that, like everything else, seemed to have been taken from her. She wished her hands would stop shaking.

The sun was setting, sending long shafts of peach-colored light through the west-facing window of her second-floor studio. The room had been a walk-in closet before she'd set it up to get her painting stuff out of the rest of the house, and it was cramped, too small for the worktable, drafting stool, easel, bureau, and shelves she'd put in. The table held several jars of brushes, a cubbyhole for her paint tubes, and the easel she almost always used, a little table-mounted tripod just the right size for smaller canvases.

Just outside the door, she heard a floorboard creak and knew it was Jackie, finding excuses to walk by, wanting to talk to her but not mustering the resolve to intrude into her sanctum. She'd fled to her closet as much to get away from his well-meaning, ineffectual concern as to paint. Especially after the drinks he'd downed with Ro-Ro, he'd be too maudlin and suffocating to bear. Though his compassion for her was genuine, it was so infused with male condescension for the weaker sex and so diluted by his own insecurity as to be worthless. It meant his solicitousness was really something of a shoehorn by which he hoped he could ease her back into her prior state of mind, her prior role, their prior life. And she didn't fit any more.

She worked her way through the blues and into the greens, a circle of rainbow on the white palette, then began with the earth tones.

As she'd feared, returning to the house and telling about the horrors had awakened it all again. The frightful images, the awful memories kept springing suddenly up into her thoughts. The world had become a frightening place, as pliant as a dream, where nothing held certain, where things twisted and distorted and became other things – bad things. But unlike a nightmare, you couldn't wake up from it.

And though she'd clutched some slight reassurance from her meetings with Cree Black, it had all been swept away by her talk with Ron, which seemed to promise another horrible secret, another awful transformation. He'd been trying to say something and couldn't find the words, or she couldn't hear them right, and he'd given up on her. It sounded as if he'd been pleading with her, asking her to understand that he could be in danger. "Something I did . . ." The only thing she could think of was Temp Chase, the horrible murder. Was he suggesting that *he* killed Temp? That somehow her moving back to the house could expose him? How could it possibly?

She wrestled with it for a time: If she knew that Ron had killed someone, would she protect him from the consequences of his crime? No. Yes. Maybe. Depends.

It didn't quite make sense. Even if Ron *had* done something like that, he'd never let anyone hear a hint of it, he'd never show his hand even if he was falling-down drunk. No, that wasn't quite it, that wasn't exactly what he was trying to say.

Of course, maybe that whole talk in the kitchen was just Ron being Ron, being manipulative and greedy and trying to prevail upon her sympathy and family loyalty to get what he wanted. Exploiting her confusion and distress right now. That she could easily see. Except he'd seemed too sincere, too vulnerable. But what, then?

She realized she had a tube of paint in her hands and didn't know what color it was or whether she'd put any on the palette yet. She read the label, alizarin crimson, and squeezed some out. Yes, it was time for the reds now. One after the other, they came out like half-congealed blood. The pigment got on her trembling fingers when she tried to replace the caps, and the idea of so much red on her hands, flowing from her, struck her as appealing.

There was always that, wasn't there. There would be respite in that, surely.

Behind all the specific images, the snake and the table and the wolf and even the boar-headed man, loomed a dark, impenetrable storm cloud, turbulent and cruel. And perhaps the scariest thing was the knowledge that though she saw or felt that cloud only now, after the events at the house, it was a familiar menace. It had been there before the ghost. It had always been there. She had lived her whole life in its shadow. And she didn't know what it was.

She completed laying out the paint, set the palette aside, and wiped her hands clean on a towel. From the shelf she selected a canvas board the size of a hardcover book and propped it in the table easel. She stared at it, trying to imagine what she would paint on it. It seemed at once too small and too vast an expanse to deal with.

The floorboards creaked in the hall, Jackie just happening to pass by. She felt a twinge of compassion for him: The poor thing was beside himself.

She'd better get control of herself, she decided, stop all this hysterical, self-indulgent, overblown dramatizing. She was only making things worse for everyone. *Show some spine! Manage your house, manage your family, manage your mind. Don't call attention. Look at the state Jackie is in. Think of the kids! Consider the others. Consider the Beauforte name. Consider your own self-respect! If you can't change it, and can't master your feelings, then ignore it. What choice do you have? You just do what you have to do. Get on with it. You have to take hold of your problems and fears and willy-nilly emotions and hysteria and confusion and stuff them back inside where they belong. Where they don't show.*

After another moment of staring at the blank canvas, hating herself for her weakness, she put it away and took a smaller one from the shelf. This was scarcely larger than her hand, one of the boards she'd had the frame shop make up specially. "I paint miniatures," she'd explained to the man. "Oh, yes, I know just what you want," he'd told her. "Many of our housewife artists want the same."

She stared at the little rectangle of white and then decided that it was too big, that what she really needed was a matchbook-sized one. No, a postage-stamp-sized one.

No, a dot. A nothing.

12

IN THE DARKNESS, THE HOUSE seemed bigger, more formidable and somehow more distant, tucked back into the foliage. All the nearby houses had warm lights in their windows, and many had gas lamps flickering on their porches, but Beauforte House struck Cree as hollow and forlorn, lost in the leafy shadows thrown by streetlights. She wondered if it had been wise to turn down the cheerful, if distracting, companionship of Paul Fitzpatrick.

She shivered involuntarily as she opened the iron gate and shut it behind her. It wasn't just the darkness and the empty windows; reading Joyce's materials on the Chase murder had filled her mind with bad images that were hard to dispel.

Joyce had e-mailed a note chastising Cree for not telling her earlier that this case might involve an unsolved murder, which they'd all agreed added unacceptable dimensions of risk and complication to a case. But as Cree had hoped, she'd done the work anyway and had attached a good collection of news stories about the incident: a cluster of articles from two years ago and then increasingly sporadic items from the following months.

The basic facts were simple. After his eleven o'clock show one night, Temp Chase had come home, sat down for a snack, and been shot dead by somebody who came into the house. His wife had been gone, visiting her parents just north of New Orleans, and had returned to find the body. Later articles revealed that Temp Chase's outwardly perfect life had some serious flaws. He had a drinking problem; he had recently lost money in bad investments. Even his prestigious job at WNOW, New

Orleans's largest TV station, was in jeopardy; he'd been news anchor there for twelve years, but station management had been talking about replacing him with someone younger. There were rumors he'd been consorting with organized crime elements in New Orleans and Baton Rouge.

People died by all kinds of means, but murder victims made for bad ghosts. Not in the same league as suicides, but they were the psychic residuals of people torn suddenly from life, unwilling to let go, dying in an explosion of pain and fear and agonized clinging. Hard for an empath to endure.

So why come here at ten o'clock at night, alone, vulnerable? Cree asked herself. She almost chuckled when she realized the mental voice she'd used was Fitzpatrick's continuing his game of twenty questions. She answered in her own voice: *Because while it scares the crap out of me, and my partner thinks it'll kill me one day, I love this. Being at the edge of the ultimate mystery.*

Of course, she knew it wasn't that simple. Edgar knew, too, Deirdre and Mom knew. There was a lot more, the Mike stuff, probably a death wish thing, too, but that was all too sad and complex and this wasn't the time to get mired in it.

She turned on her little flashlight, casting a tight spot of light on the door handle, then used the key Lila had given her to unlock it. She pushed it open. The house exhaled its stale breath. She stepped inside, shut the door behind her, and disarmed the security system as Jack had instructed her. She turned off the flashlight.

Darkness.

It would be easy enough to turn on the lights, but she left it as it was. She took a few steps into the hall, the dark absolute and cottony quiet.

Fitzpatrick would not understand what had to come next. It was not rationally explicable or defensible. It was unpredictable and took many forms. Cree could imagine him asking more of his "childish" and completely reasonable questions: *Why do people almost always see ghosts at night? Aren't they wandering around all the time?*

Because, Cree answered, *in the dark our other senses come more alive.*

Because at night our neurochemistry changes. Because the competing sounds and sights of human activities quiet down, and we can see and hear subtler things. Because the bright mental beacons of the living are quenched in sleep all around, and we can sense fainter, more fitful glimmers. Because in the disorientation of dark we become aware of our own unconscious activity. Because we let go of the ordinary and are no longer bound or protected by it.

Serious ghost hunters did their work in the dark.

Her eyes adapting, she began to make out slivers of mercury vapor light around the curtains in the big room to the right, and she walked toward the silvery outlines. It was at the far end of this room that Lila's signs had shown that first anomalous reading. Cree walked slowly back there and stopped.

The dim faces of Beauforte relatives and ancestors stared back at her, and she felt the flutter, a dark moth beating softly, relentlessly, at an invisible window. But that was all. Something staying just beyond reach, nameless.

After a time, she moved on into the rear parlor, where her vague reflection in the broken mirror startled her, and then felt her way into the hallway and the kitchen. It was a little brighter there, with its light yellow walls and windows that opened to the yard. At the far end a black rectangle loomed, the door to the hallway that led into the north wing.

She turned to the right, toward the breakfast nook where Temp Chase's head had exploded.

All around her, the old house seemed to inhale and hold its breath. Then she felt a wave rock her, a pressure front of compressed images and feelings, striking and passing too quickly to understand.

"That you, Temp?" she whispered.

There was no answer, just a fading aftertaste of fear, confusion, and surprise. She gave it several minutes, but nothing else happened and the feeling waned. After a time her heartbeat stopped shaking her, and she realized she felt oddly impatient, preoccupied, wanting to move on. As if some other part of the house were calling her.

She let it guide her. Through the back hall to the library. She walked silently with the flashlight in her pocket, her hands out to either side, palms forward, the still air moving through her outspread fingers, cool.

The library was pitch black. She found her way inside, located the piano bench with her thigh, and sat. From experience, she knew if anything came to her it would begin with the mood, the psychic weather, of the other presence. Vague at first, then defining itself as she probed its elements, it could happen fast or take weeks. If she were lucky and didn't recoil in panic and didn't get distracted, she could begin to see or hear it, tuning in to its experience of itself. If it preserved any interactivity at all, she could insinuate herself into its experience. Commune and, if possible, converse. Find its core impulse, its psychological engine. Free it from the bondage of its obsession. Break its tape loop.

A psychotherapist for ghosts?

Yes and no. A psychotherapist had to preserve objectivity, but the empathic ghost hunter had to abandon it to a large degree. To experience the ghost, she had to do more than identify with Lila, take on her attributes, feel what she felt – in a way, she had to virtually *become* her. And the same was true of the ghost: Before she could alleviate the haunting, she had to share the ghost's experience and learn what moved it, what obsessed it, why it lingered.

The crucial thing in either case was to preserve a strong sense of your own identity and local reality. In the case of the ghost, especially, you could resonate so completely you became absorbed into it and came undone. That was the danger: that the ghost would break apart *your* obsession, your own illusion of life and self, and free you from your corporeal bondage. Everyone who had ever witnessed a ghost instinctively knew that, feared it. It was the fear that underlay all fears of the unknown, and it was a very real danger – especially for a synesthesic empath who as often as not didn't mind the idea of dying, of being subsumed and obliterated.

What sort of ghost takes the form of a talking wolf, a man with a boar's head?

Cree sat, trying to still her conscious thoughts. Outside, a car passed on the street, the bass of its stereo system audible even here, deep in the big house.

Cree felt her mood drift toward a sense of melancholy, a vague impression of psychic motion. She let herself slip into it. Inside it were other emotions: a hard anger or wrath with overtones of righteousness, volatile, full of wild surges. But within that, she found something else, that keening again, a heart's call of sympathy or loyalty or protectiveness maybe, strong and clean and not at all bad. Regret, too. And confusion. It waxed gently and then waned, pale as a faint aurora borealis. Then it was gone.

For a moment she wondered if what she sensed was just Cree Black, alone in a strange house in a strange city, sifting through her own crap. But no, she decided, it had a foreign flavor. Something or someone was there, just very faint. Could be from yesterday or a hundred years ago, could have nothing to do with Lila's experience, or everything.

She waited but couldn't get a better sense of it. At last she decided she could do no more here. She left the library and walked silently back to the kitchen and to the front hall. At the bottom of the stairs, she felt a prickle along her back and neck, a tingle inside her elbows.

Something upstairs.

She went up the stairs with hands outstretched in the receiving pose. With the curtains open, there was more light here, the blue-silver of streetlights and the very faint, diffuse yellow of neighbors' windows. Light bleeding through the several doorways gave even the big, windowless central room enough illumination to navigate by. She turned left at the top of the stairs, toward the hallway that led to the master bedroom. The hallway of Lila's bounding wolf and pig-headed man.

She lingered at the end of the hall, standing just where the shoe tips had appeared that first time. She stared down the dark corridor and tried to conjure in herself the resonance she'd felt with Lila. But beyond the vague, pregnant sense that something was there, nothing much came. After ten minutes her feet hurt from standing, and she moved on down the hall into the big bedroom.

With the foliage over the windows, it was darker in here. She sat on the bed and stared at the fireplace, where the little coal stove was just a

114

square of blackness in the bigger mass of coping. The broken mirrors of the armoires reflected only black.

Time passed. The faint mottle of yellow on the ceiling vanished as the neighbors' lights were turned off. The darkness had a secret turbulence in it but nothing more defined.

She gave it another half hour but then realized that her leg had gone to sleep and her head was bobbing. She had started to drowse. She stood, breathed deeply, flexed the pins and needles out of her foot. When she pressed the button on her watch, the blue-lit dial told her that it was after midnight.

Obviously, despite her unusual projective identification with Lila, she wasn't ready yet. So far she'd found nothing of use. Really, not even a sure indication that Lila had experienced anything other than the symptoms of a psychosis or a neurological disorder.

She went into the hallway and headed toward the front of the house. For a moment she felt the fatigue of the whole busy week descend on her and debated calling it quits. But as she came back into the central room at the top of the stairs, she felt an intuitive pull. The left front bedroom. She crossed over to it, determined to give this one more chance.

Four steps through the doorway, she felt herself suddenly tugged − a feeling of vertigo as if she were swung or suspended on an elastic cord strung between two points. Immediately she saw where the sensation came from: the big mirror on the door of one of the armoires that served as closets in all the rooms. The mirror was seven feet tall and four wide and like the downstairs mirror was split with a single, long fissure. Now it looked like a window into some huge space − a dim, tapering corridor that stretched far beyond the walls of the house. Dim rooms and doorways and the silver-lit face and shadowy body of a woman.

It took her a moment to recognize what she was seeing: By some accident, the mirror on this armoire was aligned with a similar mirror on the armoire on the other side of the room. A mirror tunnel. Cree lifted her hand, a gently curving file of half-silver-bright, half-shadowed women lifted their hands. A chorus line of streetlight-gilded Crees hung in tapering space, diminishing with distance and darkness.

She realized that the door to the armoire was slightly ajar, just enough to align with the other mirror twenty feet away. Shut it and you'd see only the reflection of the bedroom wall. Cree stood at the center of the mirror tunnel, swaying. With the room too dimly lit to anchor her sense of balance, she felt almost dizzy, and without a contrast between solid walls the Dopplering tunnel looked very real. It was a disorienting effect, and it drew Cree into it.

Was this what Lila had seen, one of those nights? For a woman already on edge, the unexpected sight could easily cause shock and disorientation. Was that why so many mirrors in the house were broken – had Lila attacked them? She made a mental note to ask her next time they met.

As a psychologist, Cree knew that mirrors could be symbolically significant, patients' attitudes toward them revealing a great deal about their attitudes toward themselves. As a ghost hunter, she also knew that mirrors often figured in hauntings: Scary things were seen in them, scary things came out of them. Sometimes people fell through them into scary places.

Then, too, mirrors could help induce a hypnagogic state that brought on other states of perception. Cree had used them in several cases and found them very helpful. Thinking clinically, she'd decided that mirrors worked because they squirreled the visual sense and the centers of the brain that determined your body's location and orientation in space. And when they lost control, other perceptual and cognitive abilities could come to the fore. The disordering of ordinary perceptions had been known throughout human history to induce extraordinary mental states. The shaman's fasting, ritual dancing, and deliberately induced exhaustion; the prophet's self-imposed privations and solitude; the fakir's bed of nails; psychotropic drugs; meditation; clinical hypnosis – all were ways to blitz the senses and the reasoning mind. All were ways people sought truth.

Cree hovered in the mirror tunnel, staring into its depths. She became very aware of the big house all around her, hollow and dark and somehow *waiting*.

A long time later, half drowsing, she noticed vaguely that the woman in the mirror was gripping her own wrists and kneading them uneasily. The silver-blue face seemed to waver above hunched, defeated shoulders.

With the realization, she felt a sensation as abrupt and distinct as if someone had thwacked her in the temple with a finger. It brought her instantly wide awake, alert. Something was moving in the house. One side of the dim mirror corridor reflected part of the door into the central room and the faint outline of the door on the other side. A shape had flitted quickly across the far doorway. She held her breath, trying not to look at it directly. And soon there it was again. Maybe a man-shape.

Its stealthiness was frightening: something wanting to stay hidden.

She tried to calm her heart and struggled to keep staring fixedly into the tunnel, using only her peripheral vision to monitor the doorway. There was no movement there for a long time, but when it came again it seemed closer. Maybe in the central room now.

Part of her was screaming, telling her to run. The silver face of her reflection looked like a theatrical mask of alarm. The thing coming shook the psychic space like a storm front advancing fast. As the feeling swelled, Cree could distinguish some of its separate elements. Overwhelmingly, it was a sadistic, predatory excitement – wild, careless, charged with violent lust. Within that, anger and envy. But more than anything else, that exuberant, savage, *animal* lust.

She could hardly hold herself still. In the reflected doorway, the shape hunched and darted again, and Cree realized that the slightly musty smell of the room had thickened and soured into the rank scent of sweat, skin musk.

Her fear spiked intolerably, and before she was aware of doing it she had leapt forward and slammed the armoire's mirror door shut. Her flashlight had appeared in her hand and its beam flashed blindingly past her own eyes.

The tunnel vanished. All that remained in the mirror was a fractured Cree Black, chest heaving as she stood alone in a big, dim room. High ceilings, walls cut with streetlight glow and tree shadows, crazy angles of reflected flashlight beams. She spun around and held the light on the doorway.

Nothing.

It took her a moment to catch her breath. She berated herself for her cowardice, for closing the aperture between herself and whatever it was that moved in these rooms. But the *feeling* of the thing! That ugly sexuality. That desperation. That hungry carnality, swollen, tumescent.

She kept the flashlight on as she stepped shakily into the central room, scanning, probing doorways and shadows. A volatile darkness. She went quickly down the stairs, suddenly hating the house and wanting nothing more than to be out of it. At the bottom of the stairway, she leapt toward the entrance as if the animal thing were pursuing her. She opened the door, slammed it behind her, and didn't stop until she was out on the front walk among the gentle lights and noises of the Garden District. She turned to look back at the house, which seemed to hunker down in its shadows, baleful and loathsome.

No wonder the woman's a wreck, she thought. And again the other side of that hit her: Lila had to have enormous, hidden strength to have done as well as she had in the face of that. Whatever *that* was.

Cree slipped through the iron gate and shut it behind her, hoping she herself could find comparable strength.

13

Mmmph. Cree. Hi. What's, uh, what's going on?" Edgar's voice was deep and sleep muffled. It would be three A.M. in Massachusetts; even ghost hunters had to sleep sometime. Cree pictured him sitting up in some rumpled hotel bed just like the one she was sitting in, his long face bleary and stubbled as he squinted at the digits of some clock radio just like the one she was squinting at. The image made her feel better.

"I had a real good one. I mean a bad one."

"One of those, huh." He sounded muzzy but very much there. It wasn't the first time he'd gotten this kind of call.

"Yeah. Hey, I didn't mean to wake you up – "

"No – no, 's fine. Just a little out of it. You know." She heard him work his lips, trying to get them functioning. "You want to talk about it?"

Cree had thought she did, but now realized she didn't. "No. What I really want is for you to . . . tell me about something."

"Like, uh – "

"Something regular that happened. Something, you know . . . normal. Nice."

"Nice. Nice. Um." Ed took a moment to rally to the challenge. "Well, today I went into Boston. Never really been to Beantown, thought I'd check things out? Took the T to get around. So I'm there on the platform, waiting for my train, and I look up and there's a sign that says, 'Take the Blue Line to Wonderland.'" He chuckled. "It sounds so . . . psychedelic, or something. Shades of Alice, I don't know."

119

Cree chuckled with him. It was very *Ed* to find amusement in that.

"What the hell *is* Wonderland?" he asked.

"Dog-racing track. Up in Revere."

"Oh, and then there was this guitarist, playing on the street with his guitar case open, people throwing money in? Mother and her two kids stop to listen, right, and the kids are eating ice-cream cones? And one of the kids drops his cone into the case, *blop*, right on its head! The mother is mortified. So when she picks it up, it's got coins stuck in the ice cream, I mean it's *covered*, like those, you know, what do you call them – "

"Jimmies."

"Yeah, jimmies. What a mess. I mean, what could anybody do? Pick out quarters and dimes one by one, get your hands all sticky? Throw it away? The guy was trying to be nice about it. Fortunately the mother left him a fiver, so maybe it wasn't such a bad deal after all. Funny." He was silent for a moment. "Sorry, Cree. Guess I'm kind of sleepy. Can't think of anything really great."

"No, that's good," Cree assured him. "Thanks."

They were both quiet for a long time. She realized she'd been childish, expecting Edgar to solve her late-night insecurities by long distance.

"Maybe you ought to just tell me about it," he suggested. He sounded more like his regular self.

"The witness is really on the edge. She's been seeing animals and half-animal, half-human figures. Highly interactive. They chase her and call her name – "

"Oh, man. So you're thinking it's psychological?"

"Well, I was. But I went to the house tonight. I got a really light touch in the library, but then I went upstairs and something came at me, scared the living bejeezus out of me. I'm having a hard time getting rid of it. I didn't really get a good visual, but I got enough to know she's not just hallucinating. I suspect the animals are by-products of the stress of being around the real entity. Whatever it is."

"But it's a bad one."

"A nasty one," Cree confirmed. "And I've got this unusual degree of identification, I mean, I'm picking up her gestures, I'm – "

"You don't have to do it, Cree. There are lots of screwed up things in the world, it's not your job to take them all on. If this one really gets to you, you should just – "

"No. I can't just leave this woman high and dry. She needs some support on this. She's a person at a critical passage." Cree sensed dubiousness on the other end of the line. "Plus, this is totally selfish, but she and I have a lot in common, and I keep thinking if I help her, maybe it's an opportunity to . . . sort through some of my own stuff."

Edgar sighed. Cree knew what he was thinking: *Cree's losing her borders, the empath doing her job too well.* And he was right.

"And there are some unusual elements here, I want to find out what we're dealing with. And I don't like feeling afraid – that what's out there is so awful we can't even look at it." She knew Edgar agreed with that, philosophically anyway, but he still didn't say anything. So she switched gears, tried to put on a chipper tone. "Anyway. So how're things at your end?"

"Today's . . . Sunday? I could be in New Orleans by Tuesday."

"No. I mean, no hurry. I'm okay, Ed, really. There's a lot more I should do here before we bring in all the artillery. I was just checking in. I shouldn't have called so late."

"Uh-huh." Skeptical.

"I feel much better, now. Thanks, Ed. You're the greatest." She was dodging again, they both knew it, but every word was true. Who else could she call with the heebie-jeebies at three A.M.? "I'm sorry I woke you up. You always make me feel better. I don't know what I'd do without you."

"You'd do fine, Cree. The real question is, what're you going to do *with* me." Just a little sad, a little miffed, mostly resigned.

And there was no answer to that. Cree thanked him again and told him good night, hoping he'd heard her, hoping it was enough.

Lakeside Manor, where Charmian Beauforte lived, wasn't actually on the lake but several blocks below it, not that far from the Warrens' house and just east of the huge park that stretched down from Ponchartrain toward the center of New Orleans. It was a gated retirement community of splendidly maintained lawns, gardens, and waterways centered around a cluster of private residences and larger common buildings. Cree stopped her car at the gatehouse, waited as the guard verified her appointment, then drove through when he raised the barrier.

Charmian Beauforte's house was one of a dozen similar houses built along a short cul-de-sac. All were one-story modern structures of brick with white trim in what Cree now knew enough to think of as a neo-Creole cottage style. She checked her tape recorder and suppressed a twinge of trepidation: Over the telephone, Mrs. Beauforte came across as an aristocratic old bird, rather formidable. Whatever her stroke had done to her ten years ago, it hadn't subdued her pride or dulled her razor tongue.

It was almost eleven o'clock. Cree had awakened at eight to the muffled sound of jackhammers from a road repair crew starting up outside. She'd lurched out of bed and made coffee from the hotel brewing setup, sipping it as she looked down on Canal Street, seven floors below. A pair of cops did white-gloved mime to direct traffic around the road work, but the boulevard was choked with cars and pedestrians. Delivery trucks pulled onto the curb to disgorge supplies for the restaurants.

Daylight and the workaday bustle below brought with it a welcome relief from the troubling images of the night before. She still felt the murky hangover of nightmare, but she also felt oddly refreshed, confident. And it wasn't just the caffeine. Part of it was talking to Edgar: He really did give her strength and reassurance, more than he knew – his steadiness, the reliability of his concern and affection. And some of it was the residual high that close encounters brought, even bad ones: Mystery and danger had energizing powers, and she was a little addicted to them.

Whatever, she felt okay, and there was a lot to be done. After stoking down a diner breakfast of eggs and grits with a side of biscuits and gravy, she'd returned to the hotel and made phone calls. She'd scheduled the impending meeting with Mrs. Beauforte, then made appointments for later in the day with Dr. Fitzpatrick and with Detective Bobby Guidry, the lead investigator for the Temp Chase shooting. She'd tried to reach Lila Warren, too, but no one had picked up and she'd had to leave a message. That made her a little nervous, and she resolved to try again from Charmian's house.

A housemaid let her in and wordlessly led her to the kitchen at the back of the house. Cree found Mrs. Beauforte standing at the central island, arranging flowers in a crystal vase. Next to her on the counter was a bundle of untrimmed blooms, mostly roses. The kitchen was bright and immaculate, with a wall of windows opening to a backyard garden that was the obvious source of the flowers.

"Miz Black to see you, ma'am," the maid announced. She disappeared into another room.

"Ms. Black. How nice to meet you," Mrs. Beauforte said. She barely glanced at Cree before she selected a large rose, inspected it critically, and began trimming bits from it. "My son tells me you're already stirring up trouble." Each syllable was stretched and softened, the accent of South-ern aristocracy, and spoken in a cool, dry voice; either her sense of humor was equally cool and dry, or she wasn't trying to be amusing.

"Doing my best to, anyway," Cree said. "That's a lovely rose!"

"You aren't what I expected. I had the impression you'd be pale and delicate – one of those ethereal wisps with the devastated eyes, that otherworldly yearning. I can see why Ro-Ro's attracted to you."

The old woman liked to keep people off balance, Cree decided, throwing two or three provocations at you at once. "Actually, I do have the otherworldly yearning pretty well covered. But I got my father's big bones, and you're right, they disguise it pretty well."

"Mmm." Mrs. Beauforte pruned the rose stem at a sharp angle and inserted it quickly among the others in the vase. She picked up another and began inspecting it closely. Her apparent disinterest in her guest was deliberate, Cree decided, intended to show this out-of-town charlatan ghost buster her place in the order of things: a mere hireling, a member of the laboring classes. She felt a flash of pity for the housemaid.

Mrs. Beauforte's straight back and square shoulders gave the impres-sion of a bigger woman, but she was actually almost a head shorter than

Cree. Lila had gotten her mother's nose and chin, no mistake, but while Lila had plumped and softened with age, Charmian had gone dry and sinewy. With her crisp white blouse and pants covered by a spotless raw linen apron, her yellow Smith & Hawken gardening clogs, her helmet of sculpted gray hair, the acute focus she gave to her flowers, she projected competence and vitality. Again Cree wondered just how the stroke had impaired her.

"As I explained over the phone," Cree began, "part of my process is to interview anyone close to a witness or who has spent time at the site of the haunting? You're both, so you were first on my list?" She caught the questioning tone of her statements and berated herself for feeling so intimidated. "I've got a lot of questions for you about your family, particularly Lila, and about Beauforte House – "

"Have you been to Decatur Street or Bourbon Street yet?"

"I spent some time in the Quarter my first night here. It's fascinating."

"Then you know that ghosts and hauntings are a New Orleans tradition. Did you see the cemetery tours they advertise? The voodoo tours? For ten dollars, you can ride in a van with a bunch of other tourists to five haunted houses and listen to the driver recite terrible tales. You can visit Marie Laveau's tomb at midnight. You can even pay to witness a voodoo ceremony complete with snakes and chickens and half-naked trance dancers."

"Yes, I saw a couple of ads – "

"I could go to any of a dozen voodoo queens or Cajun witches and hire supernatural services. To cure or kill someone, cast a love charm, find lost objects, read the future." For the first time, Mrs. Beauforte lifted her eyes to Cree's, a shrewd gaze. "Or banish ghosts. For, oh, about fifty dollars."

Cree wasn't sure where this was leading. Yet another declaration of skepticism from a Beauforte? Or another routine to make sure Cree knew her place?

"Great," Cree said. "And I can go visit old people's homes and retirement villages in Seattle, keep them company for a few hours, entirely on a voluntary basis. Some are kind of cranky, but if you just humor them they usually come around."

Mrs. Beauforte's right cheek tightened, but otherwise her face remained inscrutable. "Is this how you endear yourself to your clients?"

"Not usually. But I bet this is how you've tyrannized your kids all their lives."

The seamed cheek tugged again as Mrs. Beauforte put down her clipper and began pulling off her gloves. The twitch grew and Cree realized it was the beginning of a sardonic grin. Mrs. Beauforte took off her apron and brushed unnecessarily at the front of her blouse.

"I think you'll do, Ms. Black," she said, drily appreciative. "You may call me Charmian. Would you care for some tea?"

When Charmian moved away from the kitchen counter, carrying the vase of flowers, Cree immediately noticed her limp. Her left leg seemed reluctant, the toe slightly outturned, a well-concealed clumsiness at odds with her otherwise impeccable appearance and movements. So she had lost something from that stroke after all. She limped ahead of Cree through a large living room furnished in a tasteful mix of contemporary pieces and expensive replicas of antiques. There were a few photos on the mantel, showing Ron and Lila and some children Cree assumed to be Lila's, but otherwise the room struck her as somewhat impersonal, with few telling curios or mementos.

Charmian led her to a sunroom in which a silver tea service had already been laid out, a wisp of steam escaping the teapot's spout, as if the resolution of their first clash had been anticipated. Charmian set the vase on a white wrought-iron table, primped the blooms, sat, and beckoned Cree to the chair opposite her.

The housemaid remained invisible. They let the tea steep for a few minutes as Cree presented an overview of her theory of ghosts and her investigative methods. She concluded by explaining why it was crucial for her to understand Lila's state of mind.

Cree's return to the subject of Lila seemed to give Charmian an opening she'd wanted. "Do you have children, Ms. Black?"

Charmian's non sequiturs were calculated, Cree decided. They surprised and seemed to deflect you, but ultimately wove back in somehow, and it was best just to roll with them. "No. I often wish I did, but – "

"Then it may be hard for you to understand what I'm about to say." With a steady, blue-veined hand, Charmian began pouring tea into two cups. "Whether they admit it or not, all parents harbor a secret hope that their children will be exceptional, will embody all their lineages' virtues and none of their failings. Now, of course I love my children. But I would be lying if I didn't admit they've disappointed me in many ways. Lila has always been prone to emotional frailty. She never had the . . . starch . . . I'd hoped to see in a child of mine. I've always believed you need a stiff upper lip and a firm chin to get by in this world, but she gives up too easily. She doesn't *demand* and therefore doesn't *command* respect. Her marriage to Jack Warren was just another example of her failure to respect herself or her family name. No doubt you're right, I tyrannized my children, I pushed them. But it was an attempt to get them to do their best. The world does not forgive those who squander what they've been given."

Cree thought of Deirdre's twins and how secure in themselves the girls were, and had to stifle the urge to argue parenting philosophy with Charmian Beauforte. Instead, she accepted the cup of tea Charmian handed her and took a sip of the richly aromatic brew.

"Why do you think that is? You're a powerful presence, there's a proud family history on both sides, Lila and Ronald were raised with every advantage. Why should Lila have been so . . . timid?"

"Perhaps it's those very advantages." Charmian's gray-blue eyes stayed on Cree's, conveying no emotion whatsoever. "Perhaps it's generational."

"How so?"

"Richard and I were born in 1929, right into the Great Depression. It took a terrible toll in New Orleans. The fortunes and holdings of both of our families were mostly lost. Under such circumstances, if pride is your only possession of value, you protect it fiercely. You learn to hold your chin up no matter what. My children were born in a time of plenty. Perhaps they never found their own strength because they never really had to."

Cree nodded. She could see it clearly in the wrinkles that creased Charmian's forehead and rayed from her shrewd eyes, the determined fold on each side of her mouth. And she could feel it in her – that iron resolve. It was impenetrable, inarguable, a solid, hard thing at the woman's very core. She wondered if Charmian had ever witnessed her daughter's hidden strength.

"How do you feel about Lila's wanting to move back into the house?"

"Naturally, I'd be very glad to see her living there."

"But it sounds as if Ronald is not equally keen on keeping it in the family – "

"Ronald has his own brand of weaknesses."

"Such as?"

The raying wrinkles at Charmian's eyes tightened. "Are such concerns really germane to the task at hand?"

"I don't know. But, generally, the more context the better."

Charmian thought about that for a moment. "His weaknesses are the same as those of many men of his class and age: bad investments and young women of unreliable character. He is unlikely to have children with his young flings, and posterity therefore doesn't loom large in his thinking. And he 'took a hit,' as he puts it, on Wall Street when the dot-com balloon popped. I don't know the details. But I suspect he sees the house as an asset that would do him more good liquidated, not as one that would serve a larger vision of himself and our family."

"So who actually owns the house?"

"I do. If we were to sell it, I would divide the money between Ronald and Lila." Charmian set down her cup and frowned. "This is not the sort of interview I expected to have with a ghost hunter."

"I'm mainly trying to draw a bead on Lila's state of mind," Cree reassured her. "What stresses might trigger her vulnerability to the ghost. If there's tension between her and her brother, for example – "

"So you believe there is a ghost at the house."

"What do you think? You lived there for, what, forty years. Did you ever encounter a ghost?"

Again Charmian's eyes held steady on Cree's. "What is a ghost, Ms. Black? A memory of times past that suddenly awakens with unbearable poignancy? Images of a loved one who's gone? The buried longings or regrets that one inevitably acquires with age and that sometimes spring unexpectedly to life? Those I lived with constantly, as I do here. But if you mean the species of ghost you specialize in, no, I didn't. Of course not." The old woman's gaze remained unrelenting, as if challenging Cree to refute what she was saying, or as if she had spotted Cree's inadvertent response.

"May I ask why you left? I know you had a stroke, but you seem very healthy . . ."

Charmian sighed. "What you see today is the result of years of deliberate effort. For the first few years, I had very little use of my left arm or leg. The doctors were concerned that I was prone to another stroke. Here at Lakeside, I have every imaginable convenience and none of those wretched stairs. I pursue the best physical therapy available in the facility's clinic. There are medical staff in residence twenty-four hours a day if I need them."

"But do you believe in ghosts?"

"What on earth does it matter what I believe?"

"I'm just wondering why you're willing to grant me any credence at all, even to talk with me now. Ronald certainly doesn't."

"I'm talking with you because my daughter requested I do so." Charmian studied the vase of flowers critically and took a moment to adjust several of the roses. It was clear to Cree there was more there.

"And?"

"And at my age, I have learned not to discount the possibility that the world is stranger than people usually assume."

Cree nodded. "But when Lila tells you she's seen a ghost, what do you say? You either believe her or don't believe her. You either think she's nuts, or she's onto something. Which is it?"

"You're looking for yet another proof of my failure to support my daughter, aren't you. Another example of my supposed tyranny." Charmian's tone suggested anger, but Cree got the clear sense she enjoyed this kind of fencing. "Or are you really asking whether a ghost drove me out of Beauforte House?"

"Is that what happened?"

Charmian's poker face remained perfect, inscrutable. "Answering questions with questions – that's a technique used by both police interrogators and psychiatrists, isn't it? Do tell me, which role are you playing?" She held Cree's gaze for a moment, not really wanting an answer, then checked her wristwatch. "You know, I have a lunch date with some of the other residents at one o'clock. If you have any questions that are actually relevant to this . . . situation, we'd better get to them."

That was all right with Cree. Whatever else she had evaded, Charmian had clearly indicated that certain kinds of probing were not welcome. It was a point worth pondering, but for now it was obvious that further efforts would only antagonize her. So Cree poured herself another cup of tea and began asking the standard questions.

"One of my focal concerns will be the house itself," Cree told her. "I'd like to know more about its architectural history, especially any renovations. It's often hard to tell at first who a ghost is, or even what era it's from. But if I can put dates to when the floor plan might have been changed, I can compare the ghost's behavior to the layout of the house. A ghost walking through a wall, for example, suggests that it lived there when that wall wasn't there, or when there used to be a door at that place. We call it spatiotemporal divergence, and it's an important clue for the parapsychologist. Do you have any architectural schematics for the house?"

"My husband was very fortunate to find the original builder's drawings before we renovated in 1948. He made every effort to stay true to the historic plan of the house, so I think you'll find the layout has changed little, if at all."

"Do you still have those drawings?"

"We gave them to Tulane University, the School of Architecture archives. We felt that students and historians should have access to them."

"Excellent." Cree made a note. "And do you know anything about the people who lived in the house before you and Richard moved in? Family names, dates . . . ?"

Charmian shook her head. "It had stood empty for at least ten years. So many of the fine houses did then. Before that, I don't know. You'll no doubt find records of who owned it down at City Hall. But who actually lived there is another story."

"Do you remember hearing any anecdotes from before you and Richard moved in? Did you ever have conversations, with neighbors, say, about the prior occupants?"

"About murders, gruesome accidents, tragic illnesses?" Charmian's cheek twitched, a signal she was amused.

"Those, or whatever – marriages, babies born, illnesses, love affairs – ?"

"Or ghosts?"

"Sure." Cree just smiled at her.

Charmian shook her head. "We were newlyweds. If there was any gossip about unpleasantness at the house, I'm sure I did my best to ignore it. And if I ever did hear any, that was fifty years ago – I've long forgotten it."

"What about gossip from when the first Beaufortes lived there?"

That was a different matter. Charmian did remember some stories her husband had told her about when his great-great-grandfather, the general, lived there. Jean Claire Armand Beauforte had led Confederate troops in several important battles and returned a hero to his home city in 1865. The house had been empty for a time after its occupation by Union troops in 1862, but it was still in good condition. In the years that followed, New Orleans suffered under the exploitation of Yankee carpetbaggers, and the transition from a slave economy was difficult for both black and white. Still, the Beauforte name had prestige, and the general used it to his family's advantage. He sold off his upriver plantations and with the proceeds established a foundry that thrived throughout his lifetime. He died at the house in 1878, one of many victims of the yellow fever epidemic that swept the city that year.

His son, John Frederick, didn't do as well. The Reconstruction was hard on New Orleans, sending the city into a decline that it didn't recover from until the Louisiana oil boom and burgeoning war industries brought the economy back to life in the 1940s. Sugar and cotton prices fell. Trade on the river waned, and John Frederick was slow to modernize the Beaufortes' businesses. He kept the family going by selling off parcels of the land around the house, until by 1890 it stood on the urban lot it now occupied. When he died, his widow sold the property.

"I do recall a Beauforte legend from that period," Charmian said. "One that might interest you. John Frederick killed one of his servants."

"What!"

"John Frederick had been born in the era of slavery and never really adapted to the idea that his servants were now free people. It was not at all uncommon in those years. He believed in, shall we say, 'firm discipline.' Apparently there was a horseman, a big, strapping Negro, who gave him a great deal of trouble. One night they came to blows, and John Frederick beat him to death with the fireplace poker. Richard's father wasn't born until twenty years later, but he used to tell the tale with a . . . certain amount of pride."

Cree couldn't hide a shiver of revulsion. "Do you remember the servant's name? Or when this happened?"

"Lionel. Just the first name, Lionel. I believe this was in the 1880s."

"Was John Frederick charged for the murder?"

Charmian's mouth turned down as if the question were absurd. "A white man killing a truculent black servant? Not in that century! But I take it that's the sort of thing that arouses your morbid curiosity?"

It was the second time Charmian had made a point about the role of violence or trauma in hauntings, and Cree felt it deserved to be addressed. "There is often a morbid element to my job, it's true. But it has to do with how extracorporeal manifestations originate. My partner, Edgar Mayfield, has a theory that powerful emotions create electromagnetic 'broadcasts' that imprint naturally occurring geomagnetic fields. They're like tape recordings that replay under the right conditions. Not every emotion is intense enough to accomplish that imprinting. It makes sense that mortal moments are full of intense feelings, so often the ghost is a reenactment of the state of mind he or she had at death. But that varies greatly. People might feel shock and fear, or horror and anger. Or they might feel a surge of affection or concern for loved ones, or intense relief and ecstatic serenity. Quite often, they relive memories of important earlier experiences, recollections that may not seem directly connected with what happened at the moment of death. The range of perseverating experiences varies enormously."

"So conceivably, agreeable, or . . . happy emotions could also become ghosts."

"Absolutely. But usually perseverating emotions tend to be feelings that are *unresolved* – the frustrated need for closure or resolution seems to be a constant." Unexpectedly, the image of Mike's face, full of that yearning, came to Cree and her voice faltered. But she banished it and went on deliberately: "That's the one thing the folklore has right. Ghosts are most often created when the individual dies with something important pending, up in the air, unexpressed, and their dying emotions usually orbit around that yearning for closure. Positive emotions are not as often so unresolved. So my interest in deaths and so on really isn't my own morbid curiosity. It's just that I don't often get called to investigate a happy or benign ghost. I consider it one of the . . . downsides of my profession."

Charmian's gaze showed she caught the undercurrents in Cree's comments. She thought about it for another moment and then asked, "So the ghost that's ostensibly terrorizing my daughter, it's an unpleasant one? Of course it is – that's why it's so upsetting for her."

"I'm sorry, but Lila has asked me not to discuss the specifics with anyone." Cree almost gave her statement the inflection of a question, that irritating propensity for turning tentative around Charmian's forcefulness.

"Why on earth? I'm her mother!" Charmian tucked her chin indignantly.

"Because she's afraid you'll think she's crazy. That she's weak. She's very concerned with what you and Ronald and Jack think of her. She longs for your respect and doesn't want to lose what little she feels she has. I also think she wants to process this by herself, without anyone's interference, however well meaning. And I think that's a wise decision, because she needs to master this on her own terms."

Charmian raised one eyebrow. "I had no idea this was such a . . . nuanced process," she said drily.

Cree shrugged. "Can be."

The sweet scent of roses thickened as sun squares from the windows inched across the tiled floor. Cree steered Charmian back into more recent times, trying to assemble in her mind a list of the people who had inhabited the house. During Charmian's life there, it was a short list: Richard, Charmian, Ronald, Lila. Charmian's brother Bradford had stayed at the house for a time before he got his own place, and was a constant visitor. Houseguests stayed over now and then – friends and relatives. And of course there were the servants. Charmian remembered the names of many of them; she'd employed four different live-in housemaids and five or six groundskeepers from 1972 until her stroke in 1991. Before that, they'd had the same housemaid from the mid-1950s until Richard's death: Josephine, who'd been a mainstay of the household and nanny to both kids, raising them from birth until boarding school. Where any of them were now, God only knew. Only one person had died at the house during the forty-one years Charmian had lived there: Richard, who had died of a heart attack in 1972, leaving Charmian a widow.

Charmian's face became inscrutable again as she told about Richard's death. Then she paused and fixed her raptor's gaze on Cree. "You're a widow, too, aren't you," she stated.

Caught off balance, Cree just looked at her.

"It's not just that you call yourself *Ms.* Black but wear a wedding ring. Let's just say I recognize the . . . signs. When our conversation approaches certain topics. I know the symptoms. The style." Charmian raised her own gnarled hand to show Cree the gold band she also wore, and her unrelenting eyes took on a satisfied look. Pleased at her own insight, or at Cree's discomfort? Both, Cree thought. And maybe, just maybe, there was some genuine commiseration there, too, appreciation for this small measure of shared circumstances.

"I ordinarily answer yes," Cree confessed, suddenly tentative again. "But I've been wondering if there's a time limit for it. The way people who are recently divorced say, 'I'm divorced,' but at some point they say, 'I'm single'? Maybe I'm . . . single."

Charmian appeared not to have heard her. Instead, she moved her hand among her roses again. "You know, I only select the very best. A bloom past its peak will not have the scent, and it'll quickly shed its petals. So one gets an instinct for knowing when a rose is at its prime. For cutting it at just the right moment. And even then, perfection is a fleeting thing." She paused and then went on with certainty: "You are not past your peak, Ms. Black. You are in prime bloom, and you should not waste that bloom. At the same time, you are indeed a widow. Very much so. A most difficult dilemma, I'm sure. Oh, you conceal it well – the chipper smile, the quick recovery, the dogged persistence, the pretense that you haven't heard or been affected by insults. The blue-collar-with-a-Ph.D., wholesome, plain-Jane girl-Columbo act. But when all is said and done, they are all stopgap stratagems, aren't they. Because none can solve the fundamental problem – the best they do is postpone the reckoning. Yes, I *am* familiar with such."

Charmian leaned back to watch Cree's response closely. Her eyes took on that satisfied gleam as she saw she'd hit her mark, saw Cree's utter inability to think of a comeback. But there was the other glint there, too, the ancient, enduring thing that verged on commiseration. After a moment she stood up briskly, then quickly caught the edge of the table as her reluctant leg didn't quite get under her in time.

"And now I have to get ready for my luncheon with the ladies. Club sandwiches, bridge to follow. And then my physical therapy session. You can see I live a demanding life."

Cree had found her breath again. "Can we talk again soon?"

Straight-backed, regal, Charmian paused at the doorway to the sun-room. "Why, I look forward to it! I haven't enjoyed myself so much in years."

14

CREE CALLED AGAIN ON HER way out of Charmian's house, but there was still no answer at the Warrens'. The buzz of worry intensified. She checked her watch and decided there was time to drive over there before her appointment with Bobby Guidry of the New Orleans PD's Cold Crimes Unit. Torn between outrage at Charmian and concern for Lila, she drove west on Robert E. Lee Boulevard, then turned into the maze of residential streets just below the lake.

Damned old buzzard, Cree kept thinking.

There were no cars in the Warrens' driveway, and when she rang the bell, no one answered. She couldn't decide why it concerned her so much. Lila had a life; maybe she was, wisely, having lunch with friends, or doing something else that would get her mind off her troubles.

Guidry's office was at the police and courts complex on Broad at Tulane, which according to her street map meant she had to drive half the north-south length of the city once more. It left her with plenty of time to think about Charmian Beauforte. The dowager's parting remarks made it hard to focus on anything she'd learned that might be relevant to the haunting.

Roses, widows. Once pierced, she found it hard to ignore the wound.

Was it so obvious? Charmian's exposure of her would seem sadistic if it weren't so accurate: *Mustn't waste the bloom. A fleeting thing. Still very much a widow. Stopgap stratagems.* Suddenly Cree's eyes stung and she winced back tears, teetering on the brink of a self-pity she could neither abide nor afford.

Damned old vulture, she cursed inwardly.

She shook out her rumpled city map, checked it, and headed south onto St. Bernard. As it angled away from the park, the shaded boulevard passed through increasingly poor neighborhoods; Cree opened her window and drove slowly, looking out with desperate curiosity, inviting the buffeting breeze and the sights of the city to distract her.

Wholesome, plain-Jane girl-Columbo!

But there was some balm in watching the city flow by. Wherever you went in New Orleans, she decided, every area rich or poor, black or white, there was a consistent, distinctive texture. It was a look of dilapidation, decay, a kind of terminal funkiness she found irresistible: pale stucco crumbling off dusty red brick, sagging porch roofs held up by flaking pillars, trees grown close overhead and draping foliage onto roofs. Wooden walls painted in faded rainbow pastels, peeling to reveal generations of prior color schemes. Windows and doors gone to parallelograms, porch railings missing stiles, steps falling away with wet rot. Roofs shaggy with grass and even small bushes that sprouted from fallen leaves turned to loam. In some areas, formerly grand private houses had been converted into multi-unit apartments and now seemed to be settling into the soil like ornate steamboats abandoned and sinking in some lost bayou.

Behind every canted window, she could feel all the loving and warring that had ever taken place inside. The thousands of rooms, the millions upon millions of hours and days.

Somehow there was comfort there. *Take me in,* she called to it.

Spontaneously, she turned off St. Bernard onto a smaller street and then turned again, just to get deeper into it, to burrow in and nestle against its great, ragged bosom. Every building, every view, was jammed with color and detail, a visual density you seldom saw in Seattle or in New England, concocted from a mix of poverty, history, Delta humidity, and urban pollution. No wonder New Orleans was so aware of its past: It was always all around, reminding you – deep, richly textured.

Cree came to a section of particularly ravaged-looking one-story residences. From her reading, she knew they were called "shotgun" houses because they were so long and narrow, one small room wide and four or five deep: Walk in the front door, and you'd pass through every room to get to the rear of the house. Put two of them side by side with a common wall between, and you had a "double shotgun," each unit only a dozen feet wide, both front doors sharing the same rotting porch.

It was a Monday, so most kids were at school and adults at work, but still the streets were active. All the residents here were black. Cree was startled to see an impossibly tiny woman struggling to push a baby carriage along the uneven sidewalk. She wore medium-heeled pumps and a pink dress belted awkwardly at the waist, a battered hat with fake flowers on it, a gaudy, old-fashioned necklace, and bracelets too loose on her spindle arms. A midget? And then Cree realized what she was seeing: a little girl, dressed in her mother's or grandmother's clothes, playing mom. Cree missed the twins with a sudden pang and then she had sailed past. On the porch a few houses down, a couple of women chatted animatedly, slapping their thighs as they laughed and hooted at something scandalous. A middle-aged, hugely fat woman tottered laboriously along lugging heavy clusters of plastic grocery bags in both hands. Beyond her, three men wearing tool belts dug around the base of a falling-down porch propped up by two-by-fours; one of them turned and shielded his eyes against the sun to watch her.

Cree glided on, feeling like a voyeur, wishing she were invisible so that she could look and look and absorb and not be seen, not disturb or intrude. Here in the dense center of the neighborhood, she could feel its hum: a penetrating, warm, steady vibration like the muffled buzz of a honeybee hive deep inside the trunk of a hollow tree. The ghost of New Orleans. Of the living and the dead alike.

Yes, Charmian, she thought, *pleasant feelings have a life just as much as the awful, the unendurable ones.* Here it all mixed together, a patchwork quilt of rainbow colors as rich and dense as the decaying facades all around. Every dark and terrible thing was lived here: the frustration of poverty, numbing resignation, anger and resentment, cruelty and violence, jealousy and hatred, hopelessness and helplessness, madness. But also humor, joy, aspiration, love, tenderness, anticipation, glee, desire, celebration, strength – even here in the poorest corner of the decaying city, the light did not yield. It all poured together and did not cease.

Take me in, she called to it again. And it seemed to.

She pulled over to the curb and just stared up at a row of beat-up houses, feeling inundated and comforted. She couldn't recall a more seductive place, one that drew her into resonance so easily and thoroughly.

Of course, it occurred to her, maybe it wasn't so much New Orleans that had caught her in its web. Maybe it was just more of what Edgar had pointed out: her unaccountable susceptibility right now.

Her eye fell on the face of her watch and she got a sudden jolt. If she didn't hurry, she'd be late for her appointment with Investigator Bobby Guidry.

She had to mask her surprise when she met him. When she'd talked to him on the phone, his deep voice and strong accent had conjured the image of a tall, big-bellied bubba, with a gun on his hip and a wooden matchstick in his teeth. But Bobby Guidry was a tiny man who looked less like a classic Southern sheriff than a race-horse jockey at a wedding. He was dressed fastidiously in a dark charcoal gray suit with faint pinstripes, tie, and mirror-shined shoes, and though his black hair was probably natural, it was so thick and glossy it looked like a toupee. His small, blue-stubbled face wore what had to be a permanent frown of suspicion.

Guidry led her into the labyrinthine interior of the building and brought her to a metal desk in a big room with six identical desks in it, only two of them occupied. Windows lined one wall, and through them Cree could see one of the facility's parking lots, mostly full of white-and-blue police cruisers. Institutional beige walls, shiny linoleum floor, uniformed and plainclothes police coming and going: all in all, an atmosphere of industrious professionalism that was a good antidote for the stuff Charmian had stirred up.

Guidry gestured to a chair and asked Cree if she wanted some coffee. She looked at the half-full paper cup of curdled-looking mud on his desk and declined. Guidry remained standing, arms folded as he leaned back against his desk; even when she was sitting, Cree's face was nearly on a level with his.

"Well, you got exactly two minutes to explain why in hell I should tell you even one thing about the Chase murder." Guidry tapped the face of his watch as if marking the beginning of Cree's time. "You can start with who y'are, and why ya'll're down here all the way from See-attle."

Cree had anticipated this question. Telling Guidry she was a parapsychologist would be a good way to get the bum's rush out of here. Anyway, the Beaufortes had been very clear about their desire for confidentiality. So she opted for a small lie – a misleading truth, really.

"I'm a freelance writer, and I'm working on an article about the case. I've started my interviews with the Beaufortes because I needed their permission to get into the house. But everyone tells me you're the guy who can really help." Guidry looked doubtful, so she added quickly, "I don't think I need to know anything that will compromise your investigation."

"We'll have to see about that." Guidry's frown pinched his narrow forehead. "Hell, okay, shoot. But if I say no, you gotta take me at my word it's somethin' I can't tell you. Don't push on it."

Cree nodded gratefully and got out her pad and pen. "So I take it the case is still open."

"Oh, yeah, case's still open. But the name of my unit should tell you something – *cold*. I rode this damn thing up from the District Six office, and I can tell you it's basically been cold from day one."

"I read in some newspaper articles that you were looking into the possibility that Chase had organized crime connections. Have there been any developments in that area?"

"Wouldn't tell you if there had been." Guidry opened a drawer and found a stick of gum, which he peeled and folded into his mouth. "But to set the record straight, 'connections' may be the wrong term. You look at who Temp was talkin' to, who he knew, maybe he could be some of these guys' buddy. And maybe some favors got traded, highway contracts, with Temp's friends up in Baton Rouge – Southern Lou'siana

139

social networkin' has a tendency to get more'n a little inbred. But then you ask his people at the TV station, they say, yeah, ol' Temp, about twice a year he liked to pick out a choice item for some investigative reporting, and he'd been workin' up a piece on organized crime influence in the legislature. So maybe Temp was on the up an' up after all. But I can't tell you more'n that."

"Were there – are there – any other suspects?"

"No comment."

"What about the wife?"

"Looked at her, cleared her one hundred percent. Verifiably with her family that night, they had a baby shower for her sister, they all spent the night. Murder broke that gal up, too. Poor kid."

"Were any of the Beaufortes ever considered suspects?"

A clever look of dawning comprehension came over his face. "That what this's about? Ron Beauforte, or that ol' Charmain, they got you checkin' up on me?" He eyes narrowed as he chewed his gum animatedly.

Cree avoided staring at the neat little gnawing teeth. "No one's got me checking up on you! Absolutely not. Why would – ?"

" 'Cause we looked at the Beaufortes. Standard procedure – murder took place in their house. So we interviewed Ron and his sister and the old battle-ax. Especially Ron – everybody knew there were some sour feelin's between him and ol' Temp from back in '94."

"Can you tell me about that?"

"Oh, Ron got it into his head he'd give politics a try, maybe thought he could buy a good campaign for himself, ran in the Democratic House primary. Like I say, down here things get kind of looped around, family connections, money connections, hard to untangle. Ron and Temp kinda belonged to the same club, you know, but at some dinner party or other Temp let it be known that he preferred the other candidate. I never saw any harm in it, probably it was more Ron felt Temp had some kind of duty to support his landlord, maybe give his candidacy a boost. But Temp was a popular fella in this town, his word went a long way, the other guy got the nomination. Sure, we talked to Ron. But it sounded like they figured out how to get along afterward, Temp kept on rentin' his house. And anyway, Ron killin' a guy five years later, over somethin' like that – that's a bit of stretch."

Cree thought so, too. "How was he killed?"

"Bullet to the back of his head, close up."

"What kind of gun?"

"Some kind of forty-four. Can't tell just what 'cause we never found the gun, or any shell casings, either."

Cree was feeling that they'd drifted away from what she really wanted. She wasn't here to solve a murder but to get information that might help her identify a ghost. The more she learned about Temp Chase, the more she sensed he was irrelevant to the haunting that terrorized Lila.

But it was too soon to rule anything out. She plugged on.

What kind of person was Temp Chase? Guidry fished in a file cabinet and handed Cree photos of both Chases. Temp's was a studio shot of a man in his late forties: a hint of African ancestry in his café-au-lait skin and short black hair, a slight smile intruding charmingly on a look of journalistic sobriety. Jane Chase's photo was also a studio production, showing a much younger woman with pale skin airbrushed to perfection, full red lips, big raven-black hair. Both handsome, a perfect media couple. According to Guidry, "Whites liked Temp because he was pale enough to mostly pass," and his success spoke flatteringly about how progressive New Orleans had become; blacks liked him because he was "one of us" and a local boy made good. Guidry described him as gregarious, a climber, still popular but maybe not aging as gracefully as he might've, putting on a little weight. Born in New Orleans but studied broadcasting out east. His wife had been a model he met at a commercial shoot at the station early in his tenure there; she was eleven years younger. From Ohio, moved to New Orleans as a teenager when her engineer daddy took a job at the NASA assembly facility up in Michoud. Their marriage seemed okay, she never seemed to mind giving up her career to be housewife and manager of their busy social calendar. As for Temp's state of mind at the time of his death, Guidry thought he had to be going through some trouble. For one thing, the bosses down at

Channel 13 were considering replacing him with a younger anchor, or maybe the kind of male-female tag team you saw a lot of nowadays. When the organized crime thing had surfaced, Guidry had thought that with his career in broadcasting hitting a major bump, maybe Temp had gotten worried enough about his financial future to look for other opportunities, maybe with the wrong people. But whether that was how he'd managed to get himself killed or not, surely he'd known something was coming his way. Friends and relatives stated he'd seemed depressed and anxious in the weeks before his death.

A call must have gone out, because there was a flurry of activity in the parking lot as a couple of squad cars lit up and squealed away. Guidry watched disinterestedly until they were out of view, then looked back to Cree.

"What else you need?" he asked.

There was a lot more Cree would have liked to ask, but she sensed she was running out of time with the detective. "What happened when he was killed? I mean, the sequence of events that night?"

"Conjectural," Guidry said immediately. "Seems like the killer had the jump on Chase, he was shot close-range from behind, had a sandwich half eaten on the kitchen table. Pretty well taken by surprise, I'd say."

Surprise, Cree thought, a strong element in the gust that had blown past and through her in the kitchen. Of course, the experience of dying came as a surprise for almost everyone.

"I have just two more questions," Cree said. "When you interviewed Lila Warren, do you remember her state of mind? Was she very upset by the murder?"

Guidry had to think about that, chewing gum and staring into space. "Can't remember too well. Shocked, upset, not too happy to be involved, I guess, the way anybody would be. Cooperated fully but didn't have anythin' for me. She didn't know the Chases, didn't socialize with 'em. Nothin' any of the Beaufortes did or said rang my bells."

"If I wanted to get to know Temp better, how should I do it? I mean his personal style, the way he talked, dressed, that kind of thing?"

"The wife, of course, you could talk to her. But I wouldn't – I'd let her be. I wouldn't stir it up for that gal." Guidry's compassion seemed genuine. "Best bet'd be talk to Deelie Brown. She's the reporter did most of the stories in the *Times-Picayune*."

Cree made a note. "Any other advice for an out of towner wanting information on this?"

Guidry shoved himself away from the desk, indication it was time for Cree to leave. She stood and followed his thick, shiny hair toward the door.

"Sure, I got some more advice. Go ahead and write your article, but don't play amateur detective here. First of all, because you'll be wastin' your time – we been over this whole pile of bushwah with a fine-tooth comb every which way for two years, you won't find anything we didn't. Second, because if whoever did it notices you sniffin' around and thinks you *might* find somethin', then you've bought yourself a peck of trouble, haven't you? A word to the wise, is all."

Guidry looked up at her expressionlessly and extended a little, hard hand to shake. "And, hey – welcome to the City That Care Forgot," he said.

15

I N GLOUCESTER, EDGAR SPENT the morning at the site, setting up
equipment and thinking about Cree. The equipment part was easy.

The house was tall, weathered to gray, with a Wyethesque starkness
that was austerely beautiful. It had tall, narrow windows, elaborate
cornices in the Victorian tradition, and porches knotted with gnarled
wisteria vines that wound among the gingerbread. Generations of birds
had nested in its eaves and streaked its buckling clapboards with drop-
pings. Inside, the empty rooms smelled of dust, mouse piss, and old
wood, except when gusts of sea breeze rattled the windows and blew
drafts of clean, briny scent through.

Giving Edgar a little shot of adrenaline as the invisible cold moved in
the rooms. For all its charm, the place keyed him up. Put him on edge.

Part of the house's appeal derived from its proximity to the rugged
shore, Edgar decided, so different from the broad California beaches he'd
grown up with. From its windows and porches, or from the iron-railed
widow's walk, he could see up and down the coastline, irregular steep
headlands meandering to the north and south, interspersed with salt
marshes and sand beaches. New England seemed drenched in history.
With her synesthetic and empathic talents, Cree would love this place
and the seemingly endless layers you could sense here; but even a thick-
headed, cognitive-normal California engineer could appreciate it. Sometimes, staring across the ragged, winter-brown fields toward the water,
Edgar imagined he could sense prior presences: the early Native Americans, the probable Norse seafarers, the Pilgrims, the successive waves of
European immigrants who had lived and striven and died here. The vistas

brought back images garnered from grade school history classes: the
Salem witchcraft trials, the American Revolution, the whaling industry
with its far-flung wooden ships.

Whoever had lived here, from whatever era, their lives had revolved
around the sea – the cold, gray-green, salt-smelling North Atlantic that
surrounded the spit of land on which the house stood.

To the north, the fields sloped gently away toward the water, ending
abruptly in rocky cliffs. At low tide, the shore rocks humped out of the
water, shaggy with black seaweed and crusted barnacles; at high tide, they
lay like slumbering whales just under the surface, waves foaming over the
rugged tops. Straight east, the water tossed and rolled out to the horizon
line, where a lone freighter slouched slowly out to sea. To the south
stretched a vast, flat labyrinth of salt marsh, islands of grasses and reeds
interspersed with waterways that became stagnant pools and glistening
mud flats at low tide.

Lonesome, he'd told Cree. Especially without Cree here. Especially
today, when the gray-green sea was the exact hue of Cree's eyes.

He wished he'd done a better job of cheering her up when she'd
called. He wished he'd persuaded her to wait on the New Orleans
investigation, come out here first. Clearly, she'd felt some intuitive
attraction to the case, wanted to dive into it for reasons she couldn't
express.

The Wainwrights had offered to help him set up the equipment, but
he had turned down their well-meaning companionship, agreeing
instead to meet them for lunch. They were both avid talkers, eager
to tell every last scrap of information on the house, the history of the area,
the gossip in town, the ghosts they'd seen. Good company, but right now
he needed to concentrate, and he made a point of never letting a client
near the equipment.

With Cree's talents unavailable, he relied primarily on technology, and
even for a preliminary he traveled with enough gear to require he rent a
minivan to carry it. He began with the four tripods, and once they were
in position he began attaching the compact array of electronics that
would top each. The infrared sensors would reveal the presence of light

below the visible frequencies, and the multiple EMF meters would show electromagnetic activity in several spectral bands; the ion sensors would reveal electrostatic activity, plasma discharge, combustion, or radioactive decay. With sensors at all four corners, every cubic centimeter of the room would be covered; ghosts manifesting virtually any level of energy discharge or consumption would get caught in the act.

A gust of wind shook the house, and the sudden rattle of loose panes in the nearest window startled him. He shook his head at his own nervousness but had a sudden insight about why a haunted place put you so on edge. It had to do with the feeling of the *unseen* – that the world is so much bigger than most people cared to admit. Most human beings thought of physical spaces as delimited: a room, four walls, ceiling and floor, earth below, sky above. Simple. *But in reality we're walking around blind,* he thought. *We're groping our way in an infinite place full of unimaginable happenings. A ghost makes us uncomfortably aware of how tiny and how blind we are, how strange the universe is, how* right there *its unseen dimensions are.*

Cree would see that in more metaphysical terms. He wished he hadn't ended their conversation the way he had: *You'd do fine without me.* It sounded more like a goad or an accusation than he'd intended. He'd been tired, missing her, disappointed that she didn't seem to want him in New Orleans. And he was worried about her. Cree lived nearer the edge than anyone he'd ever met. And New Orleans, though he loved the place, had a sunny face and a shadowed one; bad surprises lurked in its darker corners.

Damn it, Cree.

It had been four years since he'd attended the American Psychic Research Society's Seattle conference. At the time, he'd claimed a defensibly limited belief in the possibility of extracorporeal manifestations, but he hadn't believed in love at first sight until the first presenter of the afternoon session came to the podium. She was a woman somewhat above middle height, not pretty so much as compelling: dark hair, mobile lips framed by a fine, strong jawline, eyes whose calm intensity registered even halfway back in the conference room. She'd been dressed in what he'd call casual chic – clogs, a tweed jacket over crisp blue jeans – but she'd spoken with such clarity, conviction, and compassion that her words carried great authority. Her lecture had concerned the importance of psychology in investigating paranormal phenomena, particularly the importance of the emotional and neurocognitive link between witnesses and unknown entities. God, she had rocked that crowd back on its collective heels! Scholars of the paranormal ranged from serious scientists to technogeeks to folklorists to gullible hobbyists to complete paranoid schizophrenics, and none of them were particularly glad to hear what she had to say. Especially since it was so persuasive.

Edgar had been mesmerized equally by her perspective and her person, this Cree Black whose name he'd encountered occasionally in the field but whom he'd never met. When he shut his eyes, he found he liked the music of her voice and the way her sober pronouncements could yield rapidly to a mischievous, ironic humor.

Yeah, yeah, like it was all totally rational, he chided himself. At one point, she had stepped to the side of the podium to demonstrate a witness's body language; when she'd finished, she'd paused for a moment with one fist to her waist, one hip a little out, and the sweetly curved silhouette had taken his breath away.

After her talk, he'd joined the small crowd that clustered around her at the edge of the stage. He'd waited his turn to greet her and then surprised himself by proposing professional collaboration: between his background in engineering and physics and hers in psychology, he said, they'd make a good team, come at the problem from both sides. She was in a great mood, riding the nervous high that most people felt after speaking in public, and her sparkling hazel eyes had seemed to dance with his. But up close he could see sadness in her face, too, and an existential hunger, and suddenly he felt that he *had* to know about that part of her.

She'd thanked him for his offer. Otherwise, she'd shown no more interest beyond accepting his business card.

But two months later, she'd called: Would he care to help her with a case in South Dakota? Since then, he'd witnessed her unique abilities too many times to doubt their reality or effectiveness, or the benefit to those needing her help. Still, in many ways he was no closer to putting them into any kind of rational perspective than he was that first day. Cree Black was an endlessly unfolding mystery, endlessly confounding. Always throwing some new challenge his way, demanding he expand his outlook. He loved that aspect of being around her. Even the problem of her lingering loyalty to Mike, though an obstacle to defining their relationship, intrigued and touched him. He knew enough about his own emotional constitution to know that, under similar circumstances, he'd have similar confusions.

Okay, so he'd be patient. She deserved that. But.

The ache came into his chest again, and he did his best to put the whole question out of his mind. There was work to be done. If only the sea didn't gaze into the windows with water the exact hue of Cree's eyes.

He finished mounting the last of the assemblies, then checked the portable power supply and turned on the system. He checked it by simply walking in a circle in the room. If everything was in order, the infrared would record the heat signature of his body, and the sensitive multiple EMF field meters would measure the minute electromagnetic activity of his nervous system. Sure enough, when he reviewed the readings, he saw that the gauges had responded in exact relation to his proximity to each array.

He checked his watch and realized it was time to head back to Gloucester to meet the Wainwrights for lunch. He knelt to open the last of his equipment cases and had just finished setting up the tripod when he heard a door open and footsteps in the entry hallway. Old Helen Wainwright, he knew, dreaming up another excuse to come out and see what he was doing. The uneven gait resulted from the lingering stiffness of her recent hip replacement.

"I'm in the music room, Helen," he called loudly. "I'm almost done, just have to get my video gear in place and we're all set for tonight. You're welcome to look, but please don't touch. It's all calibrated and a little delicate."

She didn't answer, but he heard her continue through the front hallway and into the echoing dining room. Edgar took out the visible-light video camera, slipped in a new data disk, then dug in the side compartment of the case for the right lens. Mrs. Wainwright stopped at the doorway.

Bent over the case with his back to her, he didn't turn. "It's a wide-angle lens, so it'll take in the whole room. Does make things look like a fishbowl, but it'll make darn sure we catch our ghost if it emanates visible light."

She didn't respond, so he turned to greet her. But she wasn't there. "Helen?"

No one answered.

"Mrs. Wainwright?" Edgar stood and went to the dining room door. The big room was empty, as was the long hall that led down the landward side of the house.

The skin up and down his spine prickled. He ran into the corridor, to the kitchen, then back to the front entry hall. Looking out, he saw only his rented minivan there, door-handle deep in the uncut winter-brown grasses of what had once been the driveway.

Edgar felt a little dizzy. It had happened! He'd experienced a ghost – heard one, anyway! He'd witnessed a paranormal phenomenon! It was eerie, and that sense of standing blind in a huge, mysterious place deepened. It was intimidating, awe-inspiring, chilling.

He recovered enough professionalism to note the exact time of the event, then went through the whole house just to make sure no one was there. For the first time the attic under the cobwebbed mansard roof struck him as creepy, and the basement was almost unbearable – that sense that anything, absolutely anything, could happen. Edgar Mayfield could fall through a hole in the fabric of space-time, a crack between dimensions, and vanish forever.

But nothing out of the ordinary happened. And there wasn't anyone there.

Calming a little, he returned to the music room, where he stood silently for a few minutes, listening. Beyond the erratic whistle and rattle of the wind, there were no more sounds. At last he decided he couldn't wait any longer, the Wainwrights would be wondering where he was.

Still, there was one more trick he liked to pull. Before he left the room, he opened the bag of baking flour he'd bought on his way over. He took a small handful and, working his way from the back toward the doorway, sprinkled flour until a uniform white film covered the floorboards from wall to wall. As an afterthought, he continued dusting through the dining room and down the hallway. It was a primitive but effective way to reveal whether a manifestation recorded by the equipment had a tangible, physical presence as well – whether it could disturb matter as it made disturbances in the electromagnetic spectrum. Also a way to snag would-be hoaxers: an entity that left, say, size-eleven Nike waffle-soled prints in the sifted flour would probably not be a compelling candidate for further study.

Getting into the van, he looked back at the house, stark and lonesome on its hill, and felt the shiver return. With it came a wild exhilaration. *Cree*, he thought, *I did it, it happened to me! I understand now! At least a little.*

"Yeah, but unfortunately, it isn't that simple," he told the Wainwrights.

Along with a mix of other local citizens and out-of-season tourists, they had taken a booth in the North Harbor Diner and were eating cube steak and haddock filets. Helen Wainwright was in her late sixties, a slim, tough old Gloucester native whose ancestors had been whalers and fisherfolk for many generations. Despite her hip replacement, she was fit and made a point of walking three miles every day, rain or shine. Her husband, James, was a little older and wasn't faring as well: emphysema. He had a habit of puffing out his cheeks, blowing his breath through pursed lips as they walked, and had taken to making every move, even lifting a water glass to his lips, slowly – a strategy to conserve oxygen. He'd been a fishing boat pilot for most of his life before buying in as part owner of a fish-processing plant in his later years, and he knew the waters of this coast as well as anyone alive. They were both practical people, sharp and alert. And very keen on the ghost they and their daughter had seen, very interested in the whole phenomenon of paranormal research. Not wanting to bias their stories, Edgar had decided not to tell them about his recent encounter. They'd been talking about what he hoped to record with his equipment, what he'd found in past cases.

"Well, why not? Why isn't it proof?" James huffed indignantly. "You say you've recorded physical evidence of ghosts. With all this high tech nowadays, what's the problem?"

Edgar had chosen the haddock, as he had every day since he'd arrived – it was the best fish he'd ever eaten, broiled with butter, salt, pepper, and nothing else, perfectly fresh and flaky white. He took a bite and chewed reflectively as he thought about how to answer.

"The advances in technology are a double-edged sword," he said finally. "It's true that they provide us with new ways to perceive and record anomalous or very subtle phenomena. But they've also raised the bar of proof."

"How so?" Helen asked.

"Well, think of technological changes in your own lifetimes. Once upon a time, a photograph was proof of something, right? Then, as our knowledge of the medium improved, we learned to fake photos so well you couldn't tell. Okay, then we went to film – surely, if you had a moving picture of something, it was *genuine*, right? And that was more or less true for some years. But you folks saw *Forrest Gump*, right? Tom Hanks talking to Richard Nixon and all that? To say nothing of, say, *Jurassic Park*. Nowadays the media of film, magnetic-tape video, and digital DVD are so easy to fudge that even a clean, focused recording of a ghost doesn't prove anything to anybody."

"But you've got your, your infrared things and all that business – "

"Oh, yes, I've got supersensitive equipment that'll record physical phenomena of all kinds – I don't have even a tenth of my stuff here now. But what can I *prove?* I can show a skeptical scientist the record of my near-field EMF readings, say, and a seismic record of vibrations in the floor, and I can claim they occurred at the same time as the video I've got of a spectral light moving in a room. But how can I prove they have any connection? And any one of them can be easily faked, especially in the digital era."

The Wainwrights toyed with their food, frowning.

"So, what's the point?" Helen asked. "If no one's going to believe anything you come up with, why bother?"

Edgar chuckled. "Sometimes I feel the same way! I get especially mad at these professional debunkers, those hypocritical pricks, lemme tell you –" Edgar caught himself getting wound up and had to make an effort to bring his righteous indignation back down to a dull roar. He gave them an apologetic look. "To answer your question, nothing'll ever be proved to die-hard skeptics until it can be shown to fit an encompassing physical theory, one that accommodates accepted scientific theories and applies also to other, accepted phenomena. So that's my long-term goal – to find the overarching patterns of paranormal events and test them against what we know from normal-world observation. My partner is a psychologist who studies the role of human emotion and neurology in paranormal phenomena. Between our two approaches, sooner or later, we'll put it together."

Mr. Wainwright looked at his wife. "Got his dander up about them debunkers, didn't he," he observed drily. "Can't say I blame the fella." He gave Edgar a wink of complicity with one rheumy eye. The Wainwrights had experienced skepticism from their community after they'd seen and heard the specter at the house.

Edgar felt a rush of affection for these two. He'd been here for less than a week, and already he felt as if he'd known them for years. Their daughter, the primary witness, was a different matter – she struck him as a chilly bitch with a big chip on her shoulder – but the elder Wainwrights felt like family.

"So what's on our agenda this afternoon?" Helen asked.

"Okay," Edgar said. "Sighting times. I need you folks, and your daughter and her husband, to tell me when you've experienced anything out of the ordinary at the house. I mean literally the day, the hour, the minute. Patterns – it's all about patterns."

Helen took her husband's wrinkled hand. "I think we can do that, can't we, dear?"

James nodded and squeezed his wife's hand. They'd been married, they told him, for forty-four years, and their closeness, that sense of being a team, moved Edgar. What would it be like to know someone that well?

And then he thought, *Damn it, Cree.* With the familiar ache came something of a determination. Maybe it was time to do something about this, be up front with Cree. Try to move past the status quo of their relationship, take it a step deeper. What would that mean – proffering a ring on bended knee? Maybe so. Maybe that's exactly what they both needed, maybe that would move their relationship forward.

Or maybe not. Maybe it would chase her away completely. And that was too dire a thing to contemplate. The indecision gripped him. What was needed, greater patience or more impulsiveness?

But Helen had opened her purse and taken out her calendar, and it was time to concentrate on the matter at hand.

16

AFTER LEAVING GUIDRY'S OFFICE, Cree tried to call Lila from the pay phone at the police complex. She got the machine again and hung up without leaving another message. Suddenly she knew where to find her.

Ten minutes later she arrived at Beauforte House, and, sure enough, parked at the curb was the beige Lexus SUV she'd seen in the garage at the Warrens'. The front door of the house was slightly ajar.

Two o'clock, and the Garden District hummed with its own low-key bustle: an occasional car driving slowly along the tree-shaded streets, a couple of tourists sauntering the root-buckled sidewalks. Grounds-keepers worked in flower beds or trimmed lawns, filling the air with the drone of mowers. Two houses down from Beauforte House, a team of repairmen were doing some work and the street rang intermittently with the whine and shriek of a circular saw.

Broad daylight, sunny and pleasant and ordinary, and all Cree could feel was seething fear. Whatever the source of Lila's problems, supernatural or medical, she wasn't safe here. Lila had no business coming here alone in her current condition.

She trotted up the stairs into the faint breath of cool, musty air that flowed out of the front door. She knocked loudly and pushed it open. The dim interior stretched away.

Her pulse jumped when she noticed a purse in the middle of the foyer floor, lipstick and keys spilling from it as if it had been thrown there.

"Lila? Are you here? It's Cree Black." The still house absorbed her words, and she called again, louder.

A scuttling sound upstairs.

She began walking up the long staircase, bringing each foot down hard to make sure her steps were audible. "Lila, it's me, it's Cree Black. You weren't at home, so I swung by here. Are you up there?"

A muffled shriek startled her before she realized it was the carpenters' saw down the street. And then the thought occurred to her that if Lila had screamed or called for help, no one would have heard it amid the chorus of noises outside.

She came to the top of the stairs and paused. There was more light up here, but she found the light switch and turned it on anyway. Overhead, the chandelier sprang to life, a galaxy of yellow sparkles. "Lila?"

The house looked fine and old and proper, yet its rooms seemed infused with that malevolence Cree had felt as she'd hung in the mirror tunnel. She hesitated at the top of the stairs, feeling almost incapable of going farther.

Quick footsteps thumped from the front of the house, and she turned in time to see a form cross the doorway of the middle front room and disappear. Lila!

Cree called to her again and started to cross the room, her eyes on the doorway. Halfway across, she stepped on something and felt a stab of pain as her ankle turned. She winced and looked down to find a woman's shoe, one of the slate-blue, square-toed pumps Lila had worn yesterday. She saw its mate flung into the far corner. Then she noticed that a lamp had been knocked off one of the side tables.

There'd been a fight here.

"Lila, it's Cree! Are you okay?"

Someone moved in the front room, and the window light shifted. Cree gimped toward it. Her sense of foreboding grew, that tornado weather again: She felt the sky's belly bulge and birth the dangling worm that would soon lengthen and swell. As she came into the doorway, she caught a momentary glimpse of Lila cringing behind an ornate desk to her left. And then Lila fled through the side door.

"Lila! It's just Cree! Don't be afraid! Please don't run away!"

Lila had looked like a madwoman. Her eyes were wide and mindless,

155

her face a checkerboard of red and white blotches, her hair ratted out on one side. Though Cree had barely glimpsed her, she saw that her skirt was ripped up one thigh, her blouse untucked and partially unbuttoned. Cree flung herself through the room and into the next, but Lila was already gone, into the central room. Cree heard her bare feet thumping across the big floor and then the different sound as she ran into the hallway.

She had to repress the urge to chase her. Lila was clearly lost in a nightmare in which she was being pursued, and Cree must not appear to be her pursuer. Instead, she limped slowly back through the big room toward the corridor. There were no more sounds from back there, so she didn't think Lila had gone down the rear stairs; she must have run into one of the rooms along the hall, maybe the master bedroom.

"It's just me," Cree called. "I'm just coming to visit you. Please don't be afraid." She continued taking measured steps, trying to ignore the ankle. Into the hall. Talking continuously, she found the light switch, flicked it on. "Lila, please don't run, it's just Cree! Please talk to me."

The only answer was the faint, grating screech of the circular saw outside.

The bathroom and the master bedroom were empty. Cree came to the doorway to Lila's old bedroom, the room she'd fled to to escape the boar-headed man. She felt the tension swell an instant before the attack came and had a flashing mental image of a pig's face, terrible small eyes and grinning snout, but it was too late. Lila lunged out of the doorway, screaming and clawing at her. Reflexively, Cree flinched away. Her injured ankle buckled, and she fell against the wall with Lila's hands at her face and chest, the compact body pummeling and pushing at her with astonishing strength. Lila's mottled face raged in animal desperation.

Cree managed to catch Lila's wrists as they went over, holding them hard despite the bruising fall. The breath went out of her, but she used her size and strength to hold on and roll Lila over. Lila tossed from side to side, kicking, her face terrified and terrifying. Cree held herself against the twisting and flailing, and managed to pin her arms against the floor. Raw panic leapt like an electrical arc between them.

And abruptly the plump heaving body went slack and the round eyes shut partially and slid to the side, defeated. Lila lay flat on her back, one pale thigh emerging from her ripped skirt, her blouse half open and showing the lace of her bra. The hands stopped clutching and relaxed, surrendered, against the floor. Somehow it was the hands that most wrenched at Cree's heart.

Cree lay half on top of her, trying to catch her breath, unwilling to let go of her wrists. The panicked rage faded from Lila's face, leaving only abject surrender, defeat, sorrow. Exhaustion, too. Her pumping chest slowed and then her breathing caught and went uneven, became sobs. Tears leaked out the corners of her half-closed eyes.

"Lila, it's Cree Black," Cree panted. Her voice came out a rough whisper. "It's Cree! I'm your friend! Don't be afraid. We're in this together, okay? I promise. You don't have anything to be afraid of."

Lila's head lolled to one side and she lay inert. Cree released one wrist and then the other, and still the hands lay limp and defeated against the carpet. Lila kept her face turned away, mouth open and eyes half shut.

It took Cree a moment to realize that she wasn't just dazedly staring but was focusing, looking down the hall toward the central room.

Cree followed her gaze. There was something strange just where the hall opened into the big room. Down on the floor, to the left: the tips of shoes. Someone was standing just around the corner. As she looked, the toes tucked themselves back, almost out of view.

Abruptly Cree felt him there, felt him wanting to be seen, wanting to be feared. That malevolent glee burgeoning with predatory lust and gnarled with unfathomable complexities. She caught the scent of his sweat again, an inky, testosterone musk.

She blinked rapidly, struggling to conquer her own fear and rage. The part of her that had become Lila wanted to explode at him, obliterate him. But that would do no good. It would only fuel his affect. You had to overcome it in yourself. You had to overcome it and find the link between what was good in yourself and the same in him.

"Who are you?" she asked. "What do you want? Do you know who you are?"

There was no change in his affect, no doubt or remorse. More than anything else she'd experienced near him, this terrified her. He had to be a memory spun away from a dying man, but Cree couldn't sense a perimortem dimension to him, none of the range of emotions she'd come to associate with the act of dying. Where was the link, the bridge?

Whatever he was, she was not ready to reach him. If he came at them now —

Lila stirred slightly, and Cree looked down at her. She had closed her eyes and now looked like she was asleep. When Cree looked up again, the shoes had retreated out of view. The sense of his presence dissipated.

Weak with relief, Cree leaned to stroke Lila's forehead. "You're all right now. Everything's going to be okay. You're not alone. You're not alone in this." It was all she could think of to say. It didn't sound convincing, didn't sound at all sufficient. Lila just seemed to drowse, a plump middle-aged housewife lying incongruously on the rich Oriental runner, ravaged and abandoned.

17

BY THE TIME CREE RETURNED to her hotel room, it was five-thirty. She dropped her purse, kicked off her shoes, and fell over onto the bed. Only after she'd lain there palming her eyes for a few minutes did she remember that she'd missed her four o'clock appointment with Dr. Fitzpatrick. The message light blinking on the phone was probably him, wondering where she was.

Too bad. Tomorrow maybe. She had a lot to discuss with him, but she was too drained to deal with it now.

She had sat with Lila in the hall for as long as she could bear to, fearing that the boar-headed ghost would return. Eventually Lila had stirred and opened her red eyes to look at Cree. The eyes were neither hopeful nor grateful nor even fearful. They were just desolately empty: *This is how it is. This is what I am.* It was a state of hopeless stasis Cree knew too well. She saw that same hollow resignation in the mirror, in her own eyes, after something had awakened her grief for Mike and the knowledge of how little she could do about his absence. How little the wound had healed despite the passage of years.

When Lila finally sat up, Cree retrieved her shoes, helped Lila get them on, and made her stand.

Downstairs, they picked up Lila's purse. Cree urged her out the door and down the gallery steps, and they went to sit in Cree's car, two utterly emptied women side by side in the heat. Cree's ankle throbbed, and she discovered that her elbows and thighs were bruised from the tussle in the hall. It was still bright daylight, the repair crew down the block was still at work. A few more tourists strolled the sidewalks, gazing around appreciatively and pausing to snap photos. Gradually, reality had re-assembled around these ordinary things, and Lila had begun to talk.

The hotel phone wheedled, and Cree's hand reflexively snatched the receiver.

"Cree? Paul Fitzpatrick. What's going on? I missed you at four, called your room, couldn't find you. Now I just got through to Jack Warren, who said – "

"She went over to the house. Alone. I came by while she was there. She was . . . it was bad."

"Oh, Christ! Why'd she go there?"

"To fight back. Confront it all. Show she was tough. Didn't quite work out that way."

"So she talked to you?"

"Yeah."

Fitzpatrick chewed on that for a moment. "Are you up for meeting with me tonight?"

"I don't think . . . I mean, we do need to talk, as soon as possible. But frankly, I'm . . . it was . . . grueling. I'm really tired."

"You sound like someone who could use a good dinner and a glass of wine. We could kind of combine our psychiatric conference with some R and R. I know the restaurants around here pretty well – I could introduce you to some regional cuisine."

Somehow, it didn't seem like a come-on. Fitzpatrick sounded straightforward, as always, concerned and reasonable. It had been an overwhelming day, and part of Cree felt that the last thing she needed was one more intense interaction. But it really was urgent that they compare notes on Lila. And Cree did need to eat something.

And, yes, Fitzpatrick was okay to be around.

"All right. As long as you know I'm more than a little out of it. I really am" – Cree groped for the right word – "kaput. Seriously."

"Kaput is just fine. Kaput is eminently doable. I'll pick you up in an hour."

The silver BMW swooped up to the hotel canopy only a moment after Cree made it downstairs. Paul Fitzpatrick waved, but to Cree's relief he didn't jump out and open the door for her or otherwise conduct any ceremonies that might make this seem more like a date. Determined to conceal her newly acquired hobble, she walked to the car, opened her own door, and slid into the leather interior.

Fitzpatrick gave her a small grin. "You look like hell," he said. "You look kaput."

Cree returned the smile. She had showered and changed, but she still felt like crap, and somehow it was just the right thing to say. "Thanks."

"Seafood okay?"

"Perfect."

"You want fancy, folksy, um — "

"Right now I want normal. I want simple."

He looked at her appraisingly for a moment, stroking his chin, then nodded and put the car into gear. "There are a lot of choices, but I think I know the right place for tonight."

Cree was grateful to have someone else decide things. She leaned back, accepting the easy pressure of the BMW's acceleration. Fitzpatrick swung the car north on Canal Street, away from the French Quarter. The sky was dark, leaving the boulevard lit only by street lamps, signs, windows, headlights. She laid her head against the headrest and looked out at the big, strange city she was just coming to know, and Fitzpatrick had the good sense not to say anything at all.

Deanie's Seafood turned out to be a casual place half a block from the lake, not too far from the park where she and Fitzpatrick had walked. Aside from the brightly lit fast-food place across the street, the neighborhood was composed of seafood distributors and light industrial buildings.

"Antoine's this is *not*," Fitzpatrick told her as they crossed the parking lot. "It's where you go when you're hungry and want very fresh fish and clams and crabs and lots of 'em. I like it because it doesn't go for the overdone Cajun or old-timey New Orleans themes you see too much of, and it's cheap. I thought you probably wouldn't be in the mood for anything too elaborate." He stopped, suddenly uncertain. "But if you are, we could — "

"This is just right."

The restaurant was an unpretentious place, just the kind of grounded, homey environment she needed: middle-class, mom and pop, guaranteed to keep existential anxiety at bay. The air outside was full of the smell of deep frying, reminding Cree how hollow her stomach felt. When they went inside and she saw people being served mountainous platters of golden-brown, battered sea things, her knees went weak.

They took a table at the far end of the back room, near the lobster tank. Cree dropped into her seat and watched the green-black creatures bumbling around the perimeter of their glass cage, claws held shut by rubber bands.

"I need you to tell me what you know about Lila," Cree said immediately.

"Don't you want to relax a bit? I thought you wanted to – "

"It's probably best just to get to it. I can't think about anything else right now. Dr. Fitzpatrick, if she were my patient, I'd be considering immediate intervention."

That brought his eyebrows up. "Not to digress, but could I ask you to call me something other than Dr. Fitzpatrick?"

"I'm not going to call anyone Fitz, I'll tell you that. How about Paul?"

"Paul will do." His weak smile faded quickly. "So Lila's really at risk."

"She spent the afternoon literally bouncing off the walls of Beauforte House, knocking over furniture." Cree glanced around to make sure no one was near enough to overhear, and then went on in a quieter voice: "She was in a state of absolute panic. Her clothes were torn and she had bruises and scratches all over. She was being chased by a pig- or boar-headed man who took sadistic pleasure in the pursuit, who drew it out, hiding, popping out at her, chasing her, and then hiding again."

Fitzpatrick looked aghast. After a moment, he spread his hands helplessly. "I have to admit, even from a psychiatric perspective, this is a little beyond my experience. More than a little. This is – "

He stopped when a waitress appeared, a harried-looking middle-aged woman who set down a bowl of boiled potatoes and then stood, one pencil behind her ear and another poised over her order pad. "Can I get you something to drink? Wine? Cocktail?" she asked.

"I'd like a whiskey," Cree said. "Bourbon, whatever's cheap. And a beer to knock it down with. Anything on tap, you choose for me."

Fitzpatrick ordered a glass of Chablis. When the waitress left, he looked at Cree with a mix of concern and amusement in his eyes.

"A family remedy," Cree explained. "My father wasn't a regular drinker, but he believed that extreme circumstances demanded extreme measures."

Fitzpatrick pursed his lips and nodded.

Cree leaned forward across the table. "It's beyond my experience, too, Paul. I can't explain the boar head, and I can't find any of the . . . 'handles' I usually look for. I can't find his dying experience in him, he's very one-dimensional. I've never even *read* of anything like it. Nothing legitimate, anyway. You'll think this sounds strange, coming from me, but this is almost like a – a fable, or a horror story. Something teenagers tell each other around a campfire. But it's very real to Lila."

"That's all it did? The . . . pig-headed ghost? It chased her?"

"It raped her, Paul. That's what it does when it finally catches her. That's what happened back in December. It scares her to death, and when she can't run any more, it rapes her. And it does it again and again." It was the first time Cree had said it out loud, and the enormity of it struck her. Cree believed Lila's account, but in one sense it made little difference whether this was a real manifestation or purely the savage hallucination of a tormented mind: Both were equally, deeply frightening.

Fitzpatrick was looking shaky, as if suddenly he'd lost confidence in his ability to cope with Lila's condition. He picked up his fork and played with it for several seconds, then dropped it with a clang as if he were disgusted with it.

"Hospitalization," he said. "I'll get her admitted tomorrow. Cranial diagnostics, sedation. A complete blood workup. I know a neurologist with an excellent reputation, we'll get him on it."

They both were quiet for another moment, and then the waitress came back with their drinks. "You ready to order, or do you need another few minutes?"

They hadn't even noticed their menus yet.

"Another few minutes, thanks," Fitzpatrick said.

Cree lifted her whiskey glass, sighted quickly through the amber fluid, and raised it toward Fitzpatrick. "*Skoal*," she said automatically. Before he could raise his glass, she tossed hers back. The unaccustomed burn brought tears to her eyes, but she swallowed it down and quickly followed with a draft of beer that replaced the fire with ice. Her eyes popped wide.

Fitzpatrick watched with interest. When she set down her half-empty stein, he tipped his stemmed glass and took a moderate sip. "You drink like a . . . Jeez, I don't know who drinks like that. My mother used to tell me, 'You burp like a stevedore.' Nowadays, people don't even know what a stevedore is, but – "

"I drink like a plumber. My father taught me."

"Does it help?"

Cree pondered the warmth growing in her midsection, the tentacles of anesthetic already reaching out to the nerves in her hands and feet. The ball of icy jitter in the center of her chest remained unthawed.

"No," she admitted.

"So what does a ghost buster with a Ph.D. in clinical psychology make of Lila's situation?"

"I saw the shoe tips. I didn't see the boar face. But I did see the shoes."

"Oh, man." Fitzpatrick moaned. He tasted his wine, made a face of disapproval, shook his head. "I don't know what to do with this. What the hell am I supposed to do with this?"

"Think back to your sessions with Lila. Before you knew what I've told you, what would you have said? Preliminary diagnosis?"

He gave it a moment's thought. "Well. So far, I've tagged chronic depressive tendencies, as indicated by low self-esteem, morbidity, indecisiveness, preoccupation with smaller problems. She told me she'd had a previous bout of depression around the time she went off to boarding school. My father was the one who treated her, actually – he was Richard's friend and physician back then."

"Did you know her when you were younger?"

164

Fitzpatrick shook his head. "Oh God, no. Lila's six years older than me. I was barely getting into baseball cards by the time she was getting into boys. We never played with the Beauforte kids. After my father died, about fifteen years ago, our contact with the family kind of fell off." His eyes narrowed and he looked at Cree with a touch of accusation. "If you're wondering if they came to me because of the old family connection, I like to think I have enough of a reputation in this town, on my own − that they came to me because I am *good*. Even if I didn't win the Christ-forsaken Haverford."

Cree grinned. "Never crossed my mind. I can tell you're good."

"In any case, I'm not surprised she got the blues back then − that's a tough time for any kid. But in Lila's case it was a particularly lousy period. Apparently her uncle had died in a fishing accident the year before, and just before she went off to school her father died of a heart attack." Fitzpatrick stared out into the bustling restaurant, drumming his fingers. "Beyond that, I'd have said I've got a patient in some kind of denial. A lot of repression, especially in her feelings toward her birth family, focused on ambivalences − pride and resentment, love and dislike. A yearning to live up to expectations and a desire to be free of them. Has a domineering mother who probably found her kids a bother and a disappointment and didn't mind letting them know it. Loved her father, his loss hurt her probably more than she admits, doesn't want to get too close to that. Poor self-esteem, probably based on a sense of failure. Guilt for those supposed failures." He thought about it some more. "But she's a patient who's hard to probe, reluctant to reveal too much. One minute she's defiant, her pride won't let her open up, the next her guilt and shame take over and she's too ashamed to talk about it. It's hard for her to let anyone near her."

Fitzpatrick glanced at Cree and then looked away. "I know it's not much. Could fit a lot of women her age. Doesn't explain what she claims to be seeing. I've really only had, what, four sessions with her," he finished apologetically.

Cree was thinking that the oscillation between poles of affect and response Fitzpatrick reported matched exactly Lila's behavior in the last two days. Going to the house alone was one such extreme act of defiance; the backside of it was hopeless collapse.

"Paul, what's your take on the repressed memory theory?"

He tossed an equivocal hand. "I've read both sides. I guess I'd say repression is possible, but the satanic ritual abuse business really discredited it. Recovered memories of buried trauma are too often programmed by the therapist. They say more about the therapist's unconscious fantasies and fears than they do about any experience of the patient's."

He stopped as the waitress appeared again. She regarded them with expectant disapproval.

"Sorry," Cree told her. "We'll need just another minute. We'll be good, I promise." She picked up her menu to prove it.

When she'd gone, Cree put the menu down. "I agree completely. But, Paul, *I* experienced something there. I know you can't readily accept my . . . approach . . . but I believe Lila is reacting to the presence of an entity at that house. It is interacting with her. I don't know who or what it is, but there's something there. I agree with you about conducting diagnostics, but don't be too surprised when they come back clean."

Fitzpatrick had turned sideways on his chair, staring with a frown at the lobster tank. One lobster was particularly active, climbing on the backs of its sluggish fellows, working its way clumsily up the glass and falling back.

"Can I ask you a question?" he said finally.

"Sure. I guess."

"Where'd you grow up?"

"Northeast and New England. Born in Philly, lived in eastern New York State and New Hampshire as a kid. Why?"

He tossed his head, puzzled. "Your accent. Listening to you tonight, if I didn't know better, I'd say you were a local. Lou'siana born and bred. I didn't notice it so much when we first met."

Cree felt a tingle of alarm. Part of her wanted to tell him the truth: that she'd been appropriating it from the environment, and most of all from Lila, as her borders seemed to dissolve. But by his standards that was beyond far-fetched. And even if he believed it possible, he wouldn't approve of it as a therapeutic process. She wouldn't blame him.

"I . . . I guess I just do that," she said lightly. "Pick up accents fast. I've been told that before. You know, we should probably look at these menus, or that waitress is going to throw us out of here." She tried to smile.

"You're duckin' me, Dr. Black." He turned toward her, looking straight into her eyes.

Cree returned the gaze, trying not to reflexively rebel against his probing. She liked his eyes: intelligent, honest, insightful. A sweet sensuality in their blue clarity and dark lashes.

"You *are* something of a medium, after all, aren't you?" he went on quietly. "You pick up on things. That's one of your skills, right? Your talents? You . . . resonate. You've got your . . . antennae . . . up there in Jung's transpersonal space, you probe the collective unconscious. Only you're not a medium just for ghosts. You do it for the living, too."

Cree took a breath, exhaled. "You're not too bad at it yourself."

"Not in your league. Not even close."

Their eyes remained locked. The hubbub of the restaurant seemed distant, and for a long moment they paused in a sudden intimacy. Cree felt a growing warmth inside her, a magnetism that was at once foreign and deeply familiar. It was alarming but exhilarating, and for once she didn't recoil from it.

And then the waitress reappeared. This time she didn't say anything, just stood flat-footed as if indicating she intended to stay there until they damned well ordered.

"I'll have the special," Cree blurted.

"Same for me," Paul said.

The waitress jotted something on her pad, snatched their menus, and spun away.

"Whatever the hell the special is," Paul whispered.

They attended to their drinks, as if the moment of intimacy, once shattered, had made them both shy. The warmth ebbed, leaving only the jitter ball in Cree's solar plexus.

"Why'd you ask about repressed memory?" Fitzpatrick asked. "Is that what you think this is about?"

Cree drained the last of her beer. "I believe Lila is the victim of some past trauma. If she was, the ghost could be someone who had a role in the original trauma. Or it could simply be that the ghost triggers her memory of it, and she conflates the two experiences. But there's some reason, psychological or situational, why Lila connects with it."

"Trauma like rape?"

"Rape, or the emotional equivalent of it, yeah. Some extreme violation of self, of boundaries, of self-determinacy."

Fitzpatrick nodded in agreement. "Her defiance-submission thing – a common affective polarity for rape victims. Especially incest victims."

They warmed to the topic, Cree speaking in her language, he in his, yet somehow able to ignore the divergences in their pursuit of a common goal. Fitzpatrick became more animated, and Cree knew it wasn't the wine. It was the joy of the hunt: Fitzpatrick was a fellow bloodhound.

The special turned out to be a mixed seafood plate, everything dunked in a slightly peppery batter and fried: soft-shell crabs, shrimp, oysters, and catfish, stacked carefully in a pyramid a foot high. Cree began eating tentatively, feeling simultaneously starved and a little sick, but the flavors soon got to her and she indulged her appetite. She'd never had soft-shell crabs before and couldn't get over their sweet, nutlike flavor. Fitzpatrick warmed to his plate, too, eyeing Cree with amusement between bites.

"I know," she said, "I eat like a stevedore."

"Or a plumber."

"Gotta eat." Cree held her fork in her fist and stuffed in an oversized mouthful.

The warmth burgeoned again as they laughed, and they set to in earnest, eating in preoccupied silence for a time. When they talked again, it was about other things; Paul told her some scandalous tales of New Orleans city politics.

As Cree's hunger waned, the exhaustion returned, ashes and shards. The active lobster continued to trundle around on the backs of its fellows and climb the glass, a tiny, muck green, coral-speckled dragon. Then a cook came from the back of the restaurant, hesitated briefly over the tank with a pair of tongs, and snatched up the most obvious and available choice. The lobster came up waving its legs and claws in slow-motion panic, a stranger to the air, and Cree looked away. Somehow it struck her as a dour omen.

Fitzpatrick seemed to sense her mood. He set down his fork, wiped his mouth, and tipped his head to look around the restaurant. "I gotta get you home. Where's our waitress? She was here every two seconds when she wanted our order, but when you want the check she's nowhere in sight. You know?"

They came out into a night chilled by a breeze that whispered in off the water. Over the top of the levee, a block away, the darkness of the lake's western horizon was stitched with a string of pinpoint lights that dwindled and disappeared into obscurity, the famous Ponchartrain causeway. Above, a few stars dotted the night sky.

Fitzpatrick frowned over at her. "Are you limping?"

Cree had forgotten it. "Had a bit of a tussle at Beauforte House. Sprained my ankle a little. It'll be fine."

"Jesus." He shook his head. "The rigors of parapsychological field-work. We got to get this woman to bed."

Cree didn't think he intended a double entendre. Paul unlocked his car and this time opened the door for her, solicitousness for an injured person.

They drove east along the lake, then dipped south through darkening neighborhoods, saying nothing. The silence was somehow pregnant but not disagreeable, and Cree relaxed and watched the city slide by. They had been driving for about five minutes when suddenly she sat bolt upright.

"What is *that?*" she asked pointing.

"Hm?" Paul was startled out of his own ruminations. "Oh − the cemetery. I think this one's Greenwood. Or Saint Patrick's, they all kind of run together here." He looked over at Cree, saw the intensity of her interest, and pulled over to the curb. "Another beloved peculiarity of

New Orleans. This isn't the best time of day to see 'em, though. Looks a little grisly now, but in daylight they're really very charming places."

Cree had never seen anything like it. Stretching off into the darkness was what seemed to be a miniature city. The streetlights cast an angular chiaroscuro of silver-blue and black shadow over a tightly packed, haphazard jumble of masonry walls, pitched roofs, gables, and columns. The crypts appeared to be built of white marble, their roofs just over head height – tiny temples, or giant doghouses, many topped with stubby crosses. Hundreds and hundreds were ranged along little streets that diminished in the distance and darkness. The architecture was Old World – probably, as Paul said, charming – but the streetlights on pollution grime gave them a stark, metallic look.

"It's a whole . . . city," Cree said.

"Yeah, that's what people call them – 'cities of the dead.' I should have realized they'd be of particular interest to a ghost hunter."

"No. That's folklore. Cemeteries are among the *least* haunted places – nobody's ever lived or died in them. I've just . . . never seen anything like this." Cree couldn't stop looking at the scene. The cemetery hung in the dark, its miniaturized perspectives confounding the eye like a theater set or museum diorama.

"You really didn't know about burial customs here?" Paul chuckled. "Well. It seems weird to an outsider, I suppose, but it all makes perfect sense. When the first Europeans came here, they tried to bury their dead underground, but New Orleans is too low and too wet. Whenever the river would rise, or after a good rain, the water table would come up and the coffins would float out of the soil. Pretty gruesome. So they had to start burying aboveground. You just build a little house, put your departed in there, brick up the door, fait accompli. Perfectly sensible."

He put the car into gear and drove on for half a block more, then turned onto another street to continue along the wall of the seemingly endless graveyard. "You see some of those bigger crypts?"

Cree could see a few larger structures, rearing square topped above the gabled roofs. Their flat facades held many panels, three or four rows tall and six or eight wide. Each panel was about the size of an oven door, just big enough to receive a coffin.

"They look like apartment buildings in a neighborhood of single residences."

"Yeah, exactly! Those're society crypts – kind of burial cooperatives. There are society crypts for fire departments, nurses' organizations, fraternal clubs, you name it. Say you were of Italian descent, you might have yourself buried in the Sons of Italy crypt along with a few dozen of your compatriots. Saves space and burial costs. And the wall here? Can't see it from this side, but it's crypt, too, with hundreds of vaults in it. That's kind of the low-rent district."

Paul turned again onto another, smaller street.

"Where are we going?" Cree asked.

"I'm hoping we'll get lucky," Paul said mysteriously. He was ob-viously enjoying playing the tour guide. He drove slowly, glancing often toward the cemetery wall. "This is Metairie Cemetery, now, biggest one in town."

Cree looked out the window, spellbound. "You said a few dozen could be buried in the society crypts. But that would have to be a pretty huge one. I don't see any with that many vaults."

"Aha! But the peculiarities of the tradition don't end with above-ground burial. See, space was at a premium in the old city – not much room in this swampy terrain for the living, let alone the dead. But they discovered that if you build an aboveground, closed masonry structure in this climate, it turns into an oven. In summer, lots of sun and hundred-degree heat every day, it gets *very* hot in those things. Reduction and decomposition are very fast, it's actually almost a form of cremation. So back when, they came up with the 'year-and-a-day' law, which is still in effect."

"What's that?"

Instead of answering, Paul yanked the wheel and pulled the car to the curb. They were at a break in the cemetery wall – a service entrance, Cree realized, judging from the functional shed and big Dumpsters ranged to the side of the iron gate. Sticking at odd angles out of the

Dumpsters were several rectangular shapes that looked familiar but were so incongruous it took Cree a moment to recognize them.

Coffins, she realized. Lidless coffins, plush interiors open to the city night. A couple more lay on the ground, lids stacked nearby.

Paul watched the involuntary start she gave at the realization. "Yeah – coffins. *Used* coffins. We practice multiple burial here. After a year and a day, you can bury someone else in the same crypt. You just pull out the old coffin, rake the remains into a plastic bag, shove the bag back in there, and you've got room for a new customer. Like I say, aboveground burial is more like cremation, all that's left is dust and chunks of bone. Doesn't look like there'd be room, but behind each of those doors are the remains of several people. All those individual crypts you saw? Whole families, many generations, are in some of them. Very cozy, very efficient. And since nobody's too keen on reusing a coffin, they go into the Dumpster."

Paul gazed with satisfaction at the scene: stained, shadowed coffin interiors emerging from the Dumpster in the streetlights, the eerie miniature city disappearing into gloom behind. Caught up in his narrative, he seemed oblivious to how nightmarish it might look – the Gothic, funereal elegance of coffins juxtaposed with the crude, industrial functionality of the garbage containers, all in the harsh mercury-vapor light.

"Do I detect a note of civic pride?" Cree asked.

Still smiling, he thought about that. "I guess so. We're fond of our own peculiarities hereabouts." He looked at her face for a moment and must have seen her fatigue there. "I'm sorry, Cree. I shouldn't have taken this detour. I guess I got carried away – I don't often get to initiate an out of towner to our quirkier traditions. Provoking that appalled and astonished look – it's kind of irresistible." He looked back to the coffin scene. "You're right, this probably isn't the best thing to show you right now. It's different in sunlight, really . . . I am sorry."

He resumed driving. The city flowed past and Cree was thinking and then she realized she must have dozed because suddenly the lights were bright and they were pulling up at the hotel. She stirred, momentarily disoriented.

Fitzpatrick turned to her. "I know you're kaput. But can I ask one more personal question?"

"I think so."

He hesitated, then reached out and with his thumb swept her hair up off her forehead, out of her eyes, and tucked it behind her ear. His touch was gentle, yet the contact startled her with what seemed an electrical charge. He looked at her, considered, then shook his head, smiling. "I changed my mind. No questions. Just, thanks for dinner, Dr. Black. This has been really fine. A real surprise. That's all."

Cree found her purse. She gave him a tired smile, opened the door, and got out without saying anything. She'd made it all the way through the glass doors and the BMW had pulled away before she realized she had leaned over and kissed him, quickly, good night.

18

MONDAY MORNING, CREE AWOKE disoriented, momentarily not sure where she was. When she looked over at the clock she saw it was nine-thirty; she'd been down so deep that even the jackhammers on Canal Street hadn't penetrated her sleep.

She'd been exhausted when she'd gotten back to the hotel, but she'd felt an irresistible desire to check in with home. She had called both Deirdre and Mom and had nice but somewhat stilted talks, as if they'd both been waiting for the other shoe to drop, for Cree to confess some catastrophe. Cree had compensated by forcing cheerfulness. It wasn't until she'd talked to Dee for a few minutes, unable to tell much about why she'd called, that she'd realized she wanted to talk about Paul. She wanted an excuse to say his name to someone close to her, not make a big thing of it, but just touch that connection ever so lightly. But she didn't. Too soon. Instead, she talked about the way the city looked, about the food. She told Dee New Orleans was great and so far not too scary. Dee told her the twins missed her and that she should take care.

Mom was different. Cree had been thinking about her anyway, and then meeting Charmian had begun a cascade of thoughts. What was it between Lila and Charmian – the love, the distance, the distrust?

Janet sounded tired when she answered, reminding Cree that even on the West Coast it was getting late. Cree told her she was dealing with a mother-and-daughter relationship. "I guess I want you to be my oracle after all."

"Great," Janet said unenthusiastically.

"About mothers," Cree clarified. "This woman, she seems so . . .

hard. About her kids. Mom, what do mothers really want for their kids? What's the most important thing?"

"I can't speak for anyone else, Cree. I want my kids to be happy and healthy and live good lives."

"Could a mother *not* love a daughter? Just want her to, I don't know . . . make her proud, or keep up the family image? Could it really be that simple?"

"Aren't you the one with the Ph.D. in psychology?" Janet blew out a breath. "My answer is, maybe that's possible, but I've lived sixty-four years and I've never yet met a mother whose first motivation wasn't to protect and nurture her kids. Every mother chooses different strategies, that's all. And each kid needs a different approach."

Cree thought about that. "Do all mothers keep secrets from their kids?"

"Of course!"

"*You?*" Teasing.

"I sure as heck hope so! If you don't have anything you want to keep private, you must not have lived much of a life."

Cree and Deirdre had often surmised, from a variety of small clues, that Pop had had an affair around the time Dee was born. They'd always wanted to know what went down, how their parents patched it together afterward, but had never figured a way to open the subject. Janet had certainly never given them the slightest chance to do so.

They talked about other things, Cree keeping it light, determined not to give her anything to worry about. She'd been about to say good night when Janet returned to the topic: "Of course everyone has secrets, Cree, and they're by God entitled to them. It's only when you keep them from yourself that you're in trouble."

Leave it to Mom to hit you with something profound on the backswing. Cree had chewed on that until she fell asleep.

A blast of multiple jackhammers reminded her again that there was a lot to do. She showered and dressed, made coffee with the hotel kit, and got to work.

First, a call to Delisha Brown, the *Times-Picayune* reporter who had written most of the articles on the Chase murder. She got Brown's voice mail and left a short message.

Next, the School of Architecture Library at Tulane University. The librarian told her she could look at the plans for Beauforte House, but it would take a day or two to process the request and retrieve them from the archives. Cree wouldn't be able to remove the drawings from the library, she said, but she could make duplicates on the library's big blueprint copier. Cree left her number and requested that she be called as soon as the drawings were available.

She set down the phone with the realization that she'd unconsciously started with the easy calls and was stalling on the harder ones. With some trepidation, she made herself dial the Warrens' number, half expecting to hear the answering machine pick up. But Lila answered with a bone-weary voice.

"How're you doing today?" Cree asked.

"As well as can be expected. Given that Paul Fitzpatrick is here, explaining that he'd basically like to have me *commit* myself."

"For observation, Lila!" Paul's voice said in the background. "For diagnostics."

"I think you should do as he suggests," Cree put in. "It's – "

"I'm sorry for yesterday," Lila went on. "And I wanted to thank you. Did I thank you? You probably saved my life. But I'm very, very sorry you had to get dragged into my – "

"Lila. There's nothing to be sorry for! Will you listen to me for a moment?"

"I'm listening to everybody." Lila's tone flattened. "I'm just listening away. I'm listening to my mother. I'm listening to my husband, and my brother, and – "

"We just want to eliminate medical possibilities."

"Oh." The single word conveyed Lila's feeling of betrayal.

Cree couldn't let it pass unchallenged. "You're taking it the wrong way! Lila, I saw his shoes. I felt him! I *smelled* him, damn it, I know what you're up against!" There was no way to tell her the full extent of her empathic connection.

176

"I'm sure." The flattened affect again.

"Please do as Paul suggests. I need to do some other research anyway. I'd feel better if I knew you were safe and were looking into the . . . the other possibilities."

"Oh, yes. The other possibilities." Lila's tone was a tired, diminished version of her mother's caustic irony. "Well. I will certainly consider what you say. Thank you for your concern."

The line went dead, and Cree hung up, feeling frustrated. While they'd huddled on the hall floor, gathering the will and energy to get up and out of Beauforte House, she'd stroked Lila's drowsing head and felt an almost overwhelming compassion for her, an inexplicably powerful sense of shared predicament. Hadn't Lila felt it, too? Cree almost hit the redial button, but then decided that with Paul and probably Jack there, the poor woman had enough advice, pressure, and persuasion going already. She'd check in with Paul later to see what clinic Lila had gone to, maybe stop in and see her.

She had two more calls to make, and she realized that these were harder still.

After the events of the last two days, her instincts were telling her to begin the full-scale investigation immediately. She'd seen the entity, she'd probed the outermost edge of its affective complex, and it was clear that this case had several important elements urgently worth pursuing. First was the degree of the ghost's interactivity: the hiding and chasing, his waiting, his purposefulness. This was no simple perseveration, but a much rarer phenomenon, an entity that had retained at least some level of awareness of its own existence, the environment, and living people – of Lila, anyway. Second, there were the many anomalies: besides the pig head, there were the wolf, the snake, the table, and the other change-lings. Some of that could be psychological, or even just medical, but Cree was beginning to think neither fully explained what Lila had experienced.

And finally, there was the boar-headed man's mysterious lack of a perimortem dimension. Even in extreme cases, where the dying person's primary manifestation was the reliving of intense memories, Cree could sense an "umbilicus" of connection to the death experience. But this one didn't seem to be reliving his dying, didn't seem to have a conscience. She hoped she would locate it as she got nearer to him, probably it was the vague affective locus she'd sensed in the library, that melancholy keening. But it was too soon to be sure.

Ultimately, it was Lila's state of mind that made it most urgent to commence a full investigation and remediation. After yesterday, Cree had no doubt that her life, let alone her sanity, was in danger. If Cree hadn't arrived when she did, Lila could easily have fled in panic through one of the second-floor windows. Or she could have been literally scared to death as the hormonal chemistry of mortal panic drove her heart rate to intolerable extremes. And there had to be a suicide risk.

It was good that Lila was going to spend some time under observation, but sooner or later she had to come out. If she were to be truly safe, somebody had to solve the mystery, provide her with some answers that made emotional sense, and eliminate the source of the haunting. And that meant calling Edgar and Joyce, getting them down here.

Ordinarily, calling them on a priority situation wouldn't be a big problem. In the case of Joyce, it still wasn't a problem.

The problem was Edgar.

Cree got up from the desk and paced a circle, limping only slightly now, approaching the thought warily.

Edgar. Good, wise, kind Edgar. Handsome in his stringy way, funny, smart, protective, supportive. Wouldn't think it to look at him, but he was a terrific dancer who when he took his shirt off revealed a tanned, hard abdomen cut with muscle that turned women's heads. She imagined that he was a fine lover, tender yet passionate. Certainly devoted to Cree.

It was stupid. One walk along the levee, pleasant conversation in the light of the setting sun. One night at a restaurant with that buzz of magnetism, partly fueled by exhaustion and booze. That brief, startling touch in the car, a quick kiss. She didn't know anything about Paul Fitzpatrick – for all she knew, he was married and had ten kids, and the feelings she'd experienced were not reciprocal at all.

178

Nah, an inner voice told her.

Okay, but this was a professional trip – business. Social involvements would only get in the way, destroy Cree's focus when someone else's life was at stake. She wasn't here to hunt for true love. She wasn't looking for romance. She didn't walk around with her heart on her sleeve, accessible to any single male who showed an interest. And she wasn't really available: She was a goddamned nun, married and still loyal to a man long dead.

Very much a widow, she thought again, hating Charmian.

And then the other blade cut at her again: *Mustn't waste the bloom.* Why *not* look for true love, singular love, lifetime love? Why shouldn't she actively seek something so beautiful and fine? Why should there be the slightest shame or reluctance? But if she admitted that's what she believed in and wanted, then she had to face that she'd already found that love, married that man – and lost him, nine years ago. So to believe in the one true love was to effectively deny it to herself for the rest of her life. Leaving the alternative: staying hard and skeptical, denying that such love could exist, killing daily her own romantic, lyrical yearnings.

Neither was a tolerable choice.

But Edgar. Whatever might or might not be possible with Paul, Edgar's presence would compound her already abundant confusions of loyalty. What *was* their relationship? How *did* she feel?

The phone rang and jolted her out of her uselessly spiraling thoughts.

"Hey, darlin', it's little ol' me." Male voice, an unfamiliar Southern accent. "And have Ah got some news fuh *ya'll!*"

"I'm sorry, who –?"

"Y'all don't rec'nize mah voice?"

Suddenly it clicked: "Edgar! Jesus. What a god-awful lousy accent! Nobody really talks that way here."

"Shoot. All that practice for nothing!" Edgar laughed. "How're you doing, Cree?"

"I was – I was just going to call you, actually." Cree felt some relief: Ed's calling had solved her dilemma for her. Fate intervening, saving her from making a fool of herself.

179

"That's nice. How come?" There was a suppressed smile in his voice, as if he had something important to say but was saving it: Edgar with a bouquet held behind his back.

"We need to get on this case. Full research and remediation. How soon can you get down here?"

"Uh, Cree, listen – the reason I called, I have just had the most amazing day and night of my *life!*" Once he let himself go, Edgar sounded almost breathless with excitement.

"Tell me."

"Guess what happened to me!" he practically sang.

"No shit, Ed! Really?"

"Yeah, *me!* Mr. Empiricism himself! I heard footsteps, Cree! I did! Clear footsteps coming through the whole house, somebody with a bit of a limp. Broad daylight, right, I turn around, expecting to see one of my witnesses, and – nobody! The hair rose on my arms, man, I got the chills."

Cree felt good for him. She could feel his pleasure in at last being able to share at least some small part of her experiences. "So what was it like? Did you experience a particular mood, a feeling – "

"Yeah, I felt I wanted to call you up and tell you! But Cree, that's not all! I'm onto something really *major* here. Listen, the cycles of manifestation, right? Why do people only see or hear this thing when they do? I come out here with my geomagnetic theory, which suggests sightings should occur at the same time of day or night, but the times of sightings just don't match the solar day. This one's been seen many times, by several people, so today I talk to all my witnesses and chart the times of the last dozen sightings, including my own? At first glance they look like they're scattered around the clock. But then I saw the pattern. *Tides,* Cree! Tides aren't on a twenty-four-hour cycle, it's about twelve and a half hours between high tides, which means they progress through the solar day! Tides mean a lot to the commercial fishermen here, so all the times are published in the papers? So I happened to spot the tidal tables and got thinking and then went and found almanacs for the last two years, and bingo, man – hundred percent correlation between tidal cycles and sighting times! I mean, this is seriously *large.*"

Ed used "man," "big," and "large" like that only when he was really, really into something, as if in his excitement he regressed to his teenage years in Santa Barbara.

"I guess I don't know much about tides," Cree admitted. "Would it . . . does it affect places inland, too?"

"Absolutely! Tides are a harmonic, a metavibration of the planet's matter, liquid and solid alike. The pull of lunar gravity meets the rotational dynamics of Earth, which has a fluid core, mostly nickel. The core bulges, so you get measurable fluctuations in gravity and geomagnetics." Edgar paused to take a breath and then went on intensely: "Cree, you get this, right? This could be the big one. This could verify the whole geomagnetic connection!"

It was impossible not to share his enthusiasm. His excitement came palpably through the phone, irradiating Cree, kicking her pulse up a notch. "Wow, Ed. This is fabulous!"

"Yeah. So I'm going over there again tonight, only now I know just when I should be there! I've got this guy Dickerson, from Harvard's geophysics department, coming tomorrow to take some readings. Give us five or six nights in a row, we should be able to verify the pattern." He paused and seemed to put on the brakes, as if just now remembering what she'd said earlier. "But you said you wanted me down there. What's going on? You didn't seem to be in such a hurry yesterday."

Cree gave him a summary of events. Ed grudgingly supposed he could call off Dickerson and drop the Massachusetts case for the time being. But she heard his reluctance: He had grabbed his own tiger by the tail and wanted very much to hang on for the ride.

"Can it wait until Saturday?" he asked finally. "Or maybe Sunday – I might be able to get there by Sunday night."

Cree hesitated. When he'd wanted to come, she'd stalled him; now that she had asked him to come, *he* was stalling.

At last she answered, "Sure, Ed. I'll see if Joyce can come down. But you stay there and keep after that. I'm good here." And for the second time in ten minutes, she thought, *Fate intervening*.

By the time Cree hung up, she was becoming very aware that it was nearly lunchtime and she hadn't eaten breakfast yet. Still, she dialed the PRA office in Seattle.

Joyce picked up on the first ring. "Psi Research Associates."

"Got time for a trip to the birthplace of jazz?"

"I am *out* of here," Joyce returned. "Bye–byeee!"

19

CREE STEPPED QUICKLY INTO the dim cool of Beauforte House, closed the door behind her, and shut down the security system. This time she went immediately into the front parlor and tugged apart the heavy drapes. Dust sifted down in the window light as she hooked the fabric back. She repeated the process at the four windows, and when she was done turned to look it over.

Oh my, she thought.

It was a lovely room. In natural light, the colors of the wallpapers and fabrics turned rich and vivid, the old woods took on a warm luster. The gloomy canopy of the ceiling became an airy height, the room's stately proportions were more evident, even the faces in the various Beauforte portraits seemed to take on more pleasant expressions. The window views of blossoming greenery and other houses nicely complemented the interior vistas.

So this is what Lila remembers, Cree thought. *What she wants.*

She went into the back parlor and did the same, opening the room to daylight that shifted and mottled as a breeze rocked the magnolias outside. From the back of the second parlor, she gazed through the length of the two rooms, a grand sixty feet or more, and had a second realization. She had wondered why Lila, or anyone, would want to live in a house that was virtually a museum. But though you might see this elegance in museums, separated from it by velvet ropes, it was another thing entirely to stand fully within it, have it all to yourself. Seen in old lithographs, stiff portraits, darkening landscapes, or fading grainy photos, the past seemed rigid and colorless. But that was due only to the failings of the media. The reality was rich, fully dimensional, and beautiful.

And very much alive.

She went through the rest of the downstairs and pulled aside every drape and curtain, then threw open every interior door so that light moved between the rooms and the house was full of long vistas. When she was done she dusted her hands together, savoring the look of the place.

Where to begin? It had to be just the right place.

Somewhere inside, a familiar shift had begun with the decision to bring Joyce and Edgar in. *You are something of a medium, after all,* Paul had observed, and it was true. Once Joyce got here, tomorrow, and Edgar presumably this weekend, Cree's best contribution to this case would be the internal process she undertook. All the other elements hinged upon that highly subjective, delicate progression toward the ghost and its mental world.

But the upstairs of the main house scared her. She couldn't banish the memory of yesterday's events: the sight of Lila careening madly away, the bruising impact of their fight in the hall, the sudden appearance of the malevolent ghost with his knotted, turbulent affect. Just thinking about it sent jolts of electricity down her nerves. Though she was tired from the events of the last few days, she felt hyperalert and ready to run. She had to massage away a tic that began hitching her shoulder up and down, and her hands kneaded her wrists like a pair of small, frightened animals trying to comfort each other.

No, she couldn't manage that hallway or the master bedroom. Not yet. It would have to be somewhere the boar-headed ghost was not likely to manifest. As she and Lila had regrouped in the car yesterday, Cree had painstakingly questioned Lila about every moment of her ordeal and had verified that she'd encountered him only on the second floor of the main block and east wing; he appeared to be spatially restricted. Some relief there.

Of course, with this ghost, you couldn't be sure of anything.

She went to the library, opened its curtains, and sat for a time, hoping she'd find a reprise of the keening feeling she'd felt before and hoping it would prove to be the strangely absent perimortem side of the upstairs ghost. But aside from the same mood, maybe the faint smell of almonds, she didn't come up with anything. The library wasn't the right place today.

What, then? There was still the lingering question of Lila's anomalous vital signs; she'd be wise to explore every point in the house where those had occurred.

She headed to the back of the house and went up the rear stairs, a shorter flight leading to the former slave quarters that occupied the north wing. After a moment of claustrophobia in the darkness of the narrow stairwell, she emerged onto a landing and then went out onto the long balcony that fronted the three second-floor rooms. In town, it had been a convention of the era to provide slaves with quarters on the second floor, each room accessed only by the narrow, outside gallery, like the balcony that served second floor motel rooms.

This was the only part of the house where the sun came directly into the windows, and though the rooms were far smaller here, Cree found them very pleasant. Richard Beauforte had done a good job of remodeling back in 1948. The rooms retained much of their rustic simplicity, with homey furnishings and details: rough, white plaster walls and dark, wide-board floors; an antique cast-iron woodstove for heat, a wooden chest of drawers, patchwork quilts on the beds. Hand-tinted lithographs of nineteenth-century plantation scenes and anonymous portraits decorated the walls, and each bureau held a bone-china washbasin and water pitcher. But Richard had wired the rooms for electricity and converted a storage room along the row to a bathroom, making the whole wing a functional, comfortable dormitory for servants or guests.

Cree sat on the bed in the first room, leaving the door wide to the sunshine. When they'd toured the house that first time, Lila had said only that this had been the bedroom of Josephine, the housemaid and nanny the Beaufortes had retained throughout her childhood. Why had her vital signs shown so much subconscious agitation here? She spoke of Josephine with great affection. And it was a wonderful room. Two squares of sunlight on the floor gave it a homey feel; through the open door, beyond the balcony rail, Cree could see the lawn and some bright flower beds, and then the hedge and the wall of the next house. To the left, the partially sunlit rear facade of Beauforte House seemed to glow.

In the pleasant room and buttery sunlight, Cree felt safely removed from the malevolent presence in the main house. She was increasingly sure he was spatially contained. Lulled by the serenity here, she found the fatigue of the past week stealing over her. She let it come.

Back here, surrounded by the yard and trees, there was no visible clue to what century this was. No phone lines, streetlights, or parked cars. She savored the feeling. It occurred to her that this feeling was more the norm of human experience: For most of human history, really, past and present hadn't been so different, the past was more evident. In the era before farms and neighborhoods were so quickly replaced with malls and highways, they often stayed more or less the same for centuries. People awoke in the rooms they'd been born in, walked past their ancestors' graves as they went to work, ate supper off the same plates their grandparents had eaten from. When things did change, they tended to do so gradually and incrementally, their essence enduring despite physical changes. Cree knew she'd absorbed some Eastern thinking in that regard, but it was by no means only an Asian philosophy. Even back in New Hampshire, she had found the same basic idea in a telling bit of Yankee folk humor: "Ayuh," the old timer says, "that there's a fine ax, had that same one all my life. Changed the handle four times, changed the head twicet, always been a good ax."

Funny, but so true: Things changed utterly yet continued perpetually.

Cree's thoughts spiraled and looped, and she let them lead where they might. The gentle whisper and buzz grew, not so much a sound or even a thought but a sensation around her heart and stomach. *Buzzle buzz zuzz.* The quiet, breathy, subliminal voices of times and people past, fascinating, lulling. No sign of the boar-headed man.

Nearly drowsing and a little sun dazzled, she stared out the open door into the yard. In a minute, she really should get up and go back to the library, get back to work. But this was so nice.

Really, she had always been fascinated with the Deep South, had intuitively felt it in some mysterious way all her life – had *known* it, known the rhythms of life and the cadence of Southern voices. The humid blossom scent, the heat of the days, fanning yourself as you sat in the shade of the gallery. The way an ankle-length skirt buoyed by layers of petticoats felt, broad and sweeping, the way you moved with it and tucked the folds when you sat.

During the Civil War period, when the house was young, there'd have been fewer neighbors – from here you'd have a longer view, across gardens and a small field that still remained from the original plantation. Immediately behind the kitchen, there'd be the vegetable gardens and cistern. The day the Union Army first occupied this house: the men gathered around the cistern, seeking the relief of a cool drink with jackets off, blue caps tipped back, shirtsleeves rolled and circles of sweat under their arms – not used to the heat here. Their manner was half the swagger of conquerors and half the uncertainty of strangers in a foreign clime, hostiles deep within the enemy's domain. And the Beauforte slaves, too, walked uncertainly, ambivalent: inspired by the prospect of the freedom the Yankees claimed to grant them but frightened at having nowhere to go, no confidence their liberty would endure. Not sure how to act around the family – to obey, still, or to disdain their former masters? Because everyone knew the war was far from decided, these soldiers could be gone in a day or a month, and what would become of the slaves then? Everything was coming apart and uncertain. No one really knew where to go, where they would end up – not the slaves, not the family, not the neighbors.

Beyond the cistern, on the far side of the kitchen garden, the officers' horses stirred in their makeshift paddock, and farther still, wavery in the rising heat, another unit of blue soldiers stood in loose formation at the side of the next house. Their rifles rested long on their shoulders as they watched the wife and the two children mount their carriage – evicted, their house seized, just like this one. It was too far to see their faces, but they would be crying or sad and defiant beyond crying. And soon it would be time for the Beaufortes to leave, too, and it might be the last time any of them would ever see the house again in this life, and it was too poignant and sad to bear.

Cree startled as she heard a door slam in the central block of the house. Reflexively, she leapt up and started to bolt for the door, then caught herself. Her legs were bare, no petticoats, and the skirt she wore rode above her knees, little more than a chemise – she couldn't go out of the room like this, virtually undressed! And then she was shocked to see that there was no cistern, no vegetable garden, no paddock or horses. The yard was thick with green, enclosed, with neighboring houses right on its borders.

The present broke suddenly over her with the colors and shapes of the early twenty-first century. Right, 2002. Cree Black, right.

She'd been daydreaming, indulging the kind of drowsing fantasy of the past she'd been having so often since arriving in New Orleans – so vivid, so real. She took a deep breath and shook her head to dispel it.

Faint sounds of movement came from the main house.

She walked stealthily along the gallery, opened the door, and paused to listen. Above the thud of her pulse, she heard voices – several people. A man. And a woman, maybe two women. In a moment, with a mix of relief and distaste, she recognized the male voice: Ronald Beauforte.

Cree went inside and made her way to the top of the stairs.

"Hello? Mr. Beauforte?"

Ronald Beauforte appeared at the bottom of the stairwell, looking up, startled. But he recovered quickly. "I'll be damned. I was wondering who opened up the drapes. Well, Ms. Black, I'm giving a little house tour. You're welcome to join us." His welcome sounded strained.

Cree went downstairs, where Ronald introduced her to three elderly ladies who he said were representatives of the New Orleans Historical Preservation Society. "And this is Lucretia Black, who's doin' us the honor of visiting from Seattle," he told them. He shot a dark glance at Cree. "Ms. Black's visit is an unexpected pleasure today."

The three women looked at her with poorly concealed expressions of distrust.

"I take it you are also interested in the house?" one of them asked.

"Very much so," Cree admitted.

The old women shared covert looks of dismay. For an instant Ron looked uncomfortable, but another expression quickly replaced the concern — an opportunistic glint followed by renewed confidence.

"Well. I was just talking about some of the portraits," Ron said, "but I know Mrs. Mitchell and Mrs. Crawford are particularly interested in the restorations my father did. Please follow me, ladies. Ms. Black, do join us, won't you?"

Cree did. Ron led them through the house, pausing to describe features of interest. He discussed several innovations the original architect had incorporated and then explained how careful his father had been to install central forced-air heating and air-conditioning so as to have minimal impact on the historical appearance of the house. When he unlocked the doors along the east wing hallway, Cree saw the interiors of the rooms for the first time. Ron explained that one had been the original kitchen and the other the larder; though now they were mostly empty, the Beaufortes had stored their most valuable antiques in them during the Chases' occupancy.

They finished with the former slave quarters. In the room where she'd drowsed, the sun squares were gone now, the three old women crowded the room and filled it with chatter. To Cree's dismay the sense of the past faded. She clung to the images and scents, missing it, longing for that shimmering summer air. But it sifted away and left her feeling oddly empty.

When they were done there, the three ladies conferred as Ronald took a moment to shut the doors along the balcony. Then, as he led the way to the narrow stairway, one of them turned back to Cree. It was Mrs. Crawford, a thin woman with a mesh of blue veins visible through the nearly transparent pale skin of her face, white hair spun fine as cotton candy, an expensive-looking, perfectly tailored suit. A woman of porcelain delicacy with a brittle, disapproving expression.

"I take it your interest is private, Ms. Black?" she asked. She looked Cree up and down and apparently found her unsatisfactory.

"Well, yes – "

"We are somewhat disappointed. We weren't aware Mr. Beauforte was entertaining other interest at this point. I do hope this doesn't mean we'll be competitors in a bidding war. That would be so unfortunate for both parties, don't you think?"

"Wait a minute – " Cree began, getting the drift now.

But before she could continue, Ronald Beauforte appeared again, looking up at them from the bend in the stairs. "Oh, there you are. We missed you. If you have any questions, I'm happy to try to be of assistance – ?" He smiled insincerely as he continued up, and Cree got the sense he was deliberately interrupting them.

Mrs. Crawford didn't take her eyes off Cree. "We were just discussing how important it is to keep houses of great historical significance accessible to the public. To preserve our cultural heritage for posterity."

"So very true," Ronald agreed. He took Mrs. Crawford's arm and steered her toward the stairs. "But I did so want to show you the carriage house – again my father was well ahead of his time and took pains with the restoration, bless his soul – " And he shepherded her into the stairwell before Cree could say anything.

"I supposed you're wondering what that was all about," Ronald said. He shut the front door and dusted his hands together. Outside, the three ladies of the Historical Preservation Society were making their way down the front walk.

"Yeah – I'm wondering why you're showing the house to prospective buyers even though your sister still hopes to live here."

Ronald crossed his arms and stood flat-footed, looking down at her and smiling. "What the hell were you doin' up there when we came in? Not to beat a cliché to death, but you looked like you'd seen a – "

"And why you intentionally let them think of me as another possible buyer. I assume having another buyer in the picture would help drive up the price?"

"Ms. Black, your presence was, to put it mildly, unexpected. What would you have me do, explain the whole sorry business to them?

'Ladies, this here is a ghost buster we've hired because my sister is going crazy and we're so afraid for her mental health we'll do *any* damned thing'? But no, I didn't mind them assuming that's what you're here for, and no, it probably won't hurt the price." He didn't seem at all disconcerted by Cree's scorn.

"What about Lila?"

"Oh, what *about* Lila?" Ronald's good mood vanished. He turned away, frustrated, striding into the front parlor and then wheeling back to face Cree. "First the woman takes it into her head that she's perishing to live in the old family home – last kid leaves the nest, and suddenly she comes up with the notion that there's going to be some great Southern dynasty reborn here? Hell, she'll be lucky if her kids'll even come visit after college. You see what she's doing? It's not just the empty nest thing, she's got some kind of a . . . a hole in her life, and decides living in this place is going to fill it. She's suddenly feeling her age, feeling alone, and so she's clinging to some kind of a dream or . . . fantasy that isn't real, never was. Just how seriously am I supposed to take it? And Jack! Well, we all know what Jack – "

"Doesn't she deserve a chance to see if that's what she really wants? Don't dreams deserve a chance to become real?"

Ronald stopped his tirade to drop his chin on his chest as if martyred by Cree's idealism. But when he raised his face, his huff had vanished and his expression was appreciative. "You sure get in deep, quick, don't you? We only been talking five minutes and look how *very* philosophical we're getting!" He clicked his tongue, looking at her admiringly, then sobered again. "No, Ms. Black, I am not immune to the idea that dreams deserve a chance. But let's look at what's really happened. Just as my dear sister is giving her dream that chance, all of a sudden she comes up with this big reason *not* to, doesn't she? See, what you don't know is, there's some history here. We've been having to deal with Lila's fits and starts, grand plans and self-sabotage – have I got the psychobabble right? – since she was fifteen! This time it's ghosts, terrors, I don't know what all, none of you'll tell me. And next time it'll be something else. Who knows where this thing'll end up? You see what shape Lila's in. Can you guarantee you're going to 'cure' her? That you're going to exorcize the . . . evil spirits she thinks this old place is stuffed with? That when the all dust settles, and you've come and gone, she's still going to want to move in here? You can guarantee that?"

"No."

"Fine. So what's the harm of having backup plans? You know, these old places cost money even when they're sitting empty. You got half a million dollars in antiques gathering dust and getting eaten by moths and mice. You got an acre of roof to keep from leaking. You're paying for security service, pest control, insurance, taxes, yard work, you name it, and all for what? To have something to worry about! Why not see it preserved for posterity, just like little ol' Miz Crawfish said?"

"How much does Lila know about your 'backup plans'?"

Ronald turned away to stride into the front parlor. "Are we done here? You want to help me pull these? Sunlight – they say it'll wreck up these rugs and whatnot." He unhooked the ties and tugged the front drapes together. The room dimmed, taking on one small shade of its former melancholy.

Ronald went to the next window but stopped before yanking the drapes there. Instead he turned back to Cree. "There's another thing. You're a psychologist – tell me how healthy it would be, living where you're afraid to sit down because you might wear out the genuine Louis Quinze upholstery? She going to keep the drapes drawn all the time? Put plastic runners over the rugs, or just never walk on 'em? You gonna tell me that's any way to live?"

"I hear you lost a bundle in the stock market last year. That liquid assets would be nice for you just now."

That stopped him cold, and for a moment anger flared in his eyes. But he got it under control quickly, shaking his head ruefully. "Momma. My dear, loving mother. Why's she telling you this stuff? What on God's green earth does it have to do with what we got you down here for? You want to see my stock portfolio, too? My tax forms?"

Cree shrugged, letting him hang for a moment.

Ron waited, too, and then made a dismissive gesture. He pulled the next drapes shut, bringing back yet another shade of gloom. He walked past Cree, then turned again with an expression she had never seen on his face: a discomfort, an urgency, as if something really did, after all, matter to him. His irritation was only the surface of a deeper disturbance, she sensed, a frustration and confusion. She felt a pang of sympathy for him.

"See, there're things here you don't understand. You've got me pegged now, the bad brother who wants to sell the house out from under his poor sister. Well, believe whatever you care to. But sometimes people don't know what they really want or what they really need. Lila'd be a lot better off leaving the past lie. Getting a new life, not trying to reclaim her old one."

"Why's that?"

"You are one irritating female, you know that? You won't let go of a goddamned thing! I can't even – "

Cree put a hand on his arm, wanting to defuse the antagonism between them. "Ron, you may well be right about what's good for Lila. But to really start a new life you have to make some kind of peace with the old, don't you? If there's anything in particular you think she should 'leave lie,' I'd like to know about it. So I can help her put it behind her."

Ronald brushed away her hand and strode past her to the entrance hall.

Cree followed. "You said Lila had a hole in her life. What's missing?"

"I'm not a headshrinker. You tell me." He opened the front door and fished in his pocket. He pulled out a key ring, pointed it at the Jaguar parked sloppily at the curb, and thumbed the door lock button. The car's lights flashed.

"You said she's been this way since she was fifteen – these fits and starts. Are you saying she was different before then? Did something happen to change her?"

Ron just headed out onto the front gallery without looking back.

Cree felt close to something, but she had no idea what it might be. Suddenly she was desperate to keep him there, to know what he might tell her. "You were very close to her once, weren't you? You loved your sister very much. What changed that?"

That hooked him. Halfway across the gallery, he turned. "'Course I did. And what makes you think anything changed? Where the hell do you get off even asking a question like that?"

"Then why do you hide your best feelings? Why don't you want people to know who you are?"

His eyes rolled in angry disdain, and he turned away again. "Why don't you go to hell, Ms. Black."

So many questions to ask. "Were you also close to Josephine Dupree? As close as Lila was?"

He wheeled on her one more time, his suspicion hardened into dislike now. "Now what the hell's *this* about? What've you got cooking *now?*"

His hostility hurt her, as did the vulnerability that hid just behind it. All she could think of was wanting to end the dissonance between them. "Ron, truly, I'm not trying to oppose you. I really have no wish to be your enemy, I'm just – "

He shook his head, done with her, and headed on down the steps. "I think it's a little late to worry about that," he tossed over his shoulder.

20

CREE DROVE TOWARD THE *Times-Picayune* offices, unsettled by the incidents at Beauforte House. A lot to think about but no time.

Ronald: so much hidden there, so much to understand. He was obviously motivated to sell the house and self-interested enough to do so in spite of his sister's desires. Could he be a hoaxer, faking a haunting to scare Lila away? The *Gaslight* scenario – where someone faked supernatural phenomena with the goal of upsetting someone else, making them appear "crazy" – was a possibility any serious paranormal researcher had to consider. But Cree had already encountered Lila's haunt herself, twice, and the damned thing was for certain no living human. No, Ronald was weak and narcissistic and many things she disliked, but he was not a hoaxer so much as an opportunist. And there was something touching about him, something wounded and compelling, perhaps even a grain of real nobility buried beneath the bullshit. The dynamic of hostility between them was so painful and so unnecessary.

It was her own fault. She hadn't dealt with him well. She'd been off balance, surprised and frightened at hearing someone in the house, and disoriented from pulling so suddenly out of that daydream. No doubt its detail and vividness were the result of doing historical reading in her hotel every night, of absorbing the history-drenched atmosphere of New Orleans.

But its poignancy, and her reluctance to let go of that time and those images – that was a potential problem. It was another indication of just how much the stresses of this case were adding up, how unstable and malleable she was right now.

But she was getting close to the *Times-Picayune* building. Time to put on the act of being sane and competent, to stuff her sense of urgency into a compartment of her thoughts and keep it there for now. She wound her way around and under a tangle of highway entrance ramps, parked in the visitors' lot, checked herself over in the visor mirror, and did her best to muster a pretense of professionalism.

Delisha Brown emerged from the depths of the building, crossed the modern, marbled lobby to where Cree waited at the reception desk. She was a woman of middle height, with skin a deep chocolate color and hair done in cornrows that ended in dozens of short braids lined with turquoise-blue beads and tipped with wads of tinfoil. Though she had a chunky, big-busted build, she was only in her late twenties and moved with an active woman's forceful stride that made the beads swing and rattle softly. She wore black slacks, a red blouse, striped jogging shoes, and a no-nonsense frown that she panned up and down Cree as they shook hands.

"I'm Brown," the reporter said, "and you're Black. Uh-huh. Right." A grin twitched the corners of Delisha's lips. She turned and beckoned for Cree to follow her. "Everybody calls me Deelie, you might as well, too."

"Thank you for returning my call. And thanks for finding time for me on such short notice."

Deelie's plump shoulders shrugged. She led Cree down a long corridor, through several sets of glass doors, and into the quiet bustle of the great paper's newsroom. It was a huge room containing dozens of cubicles and desks, about half of which were occupied by reporters or writers working in the state of sustained panic required to put out the paper every day. Computer monitors glowed from every littered desk. Along the far wall, a row of glassed-in offices faced the big room; inside, knots of harried-looking editorial staff bent their heads together over big tables. Cree had to jump out of the way of a cart pushed at a run by a young clerk who seemed oblivious to her existence.

Deelie's desk was messier than most, with a rusted automobile muffler encircled by an uneven wall of stacked papers and file folders. She gestured Cree to a plastic chair, took her own seat, and frowned at the muffler. "Temp Chase murder, huh. What's your interest?"

"I'm writing about the case – maybe an article, maybe a book. I saw your byline on most of the articles I read, and then Detective Guidry said you'd done a lot of research, so – "

"Bobby G. That little midget! He give you anything useful?"

"Mainly, your name."

"Flattering." Deelie's face split in a wide grin that took Cree by surprise with its warmth and energy. "Hey, come on, girl. Tell me the truth. You're no freelance writer – nobody writes on spec and doesn't know if it's a book or an article. Internet says you're a Ph.D. in psychology who does research on ghosts." When she said more than three words in a row, Delisha had a musical rhythm to her voice that charmed Cree.

Cree chuckled. "I guess I shouldn't be surprised an investigative reporter did some detective work before an interview."

"No, you should not. So, what, you trying to see if Temp turned into a ghost or something?"

"Maybe. It's a long story, and most of it's confidential."

"Ooooh, tempt me!" Deelie laughed, but the lines of her face quickly turned businesslike again. "Tell you what. We trade. I give you something, you give me something. I trade you Temp for some ghost-hunting material I can maybe put together for a feature later on. This town loves ghosts. And anything else good for tourism."

A young man came to the desk, slipped a file folder onto it with a meaningful raised eyebrow, and left without a word. "Shit," Deelie said.

"Doesn't look like you have time for such a trade," Cree said.

Deelie looked thoughtfully at Cree for a moment, then pondered her watch. "I got an hour for lunch – that'll give us a start, anyway. And for this, I think let's go out. I got about one good thing to tell you, and unless I'm mistaken it's right up your alley. But it got some context go with it, so we gonna serve the Seattle girl a slice o' life along with lunch. You drive, my car's waiting for an organ transplant to be flown in." She gestured at the muffler with disgust.

Deelie grabbed a small shoulder pack and the muffler as they left. Out in the parking lot, she paused to toss the muffler into the seat of a low-slung, beat-up maroon sports car, then gave the car a whopping kick that rattled its rusted quarter panels. "It's what I get, buying an Alfa Romeo. Vanity. Stupidity. Twelve-year-old import, can't find the parts. Where's your wheels?"

They got into Cree's rented Taurus and Deelie instructed Cree to head up Broad Avenue. As soon as they were rolling, the reporter worked the dashboard knobs and brought the air-conditioning up to maximum.

"Where are we going?" Cree asked.

"My home neighborhood. A fine culinary establishment called Chez Henri."

From Broad they turned left onto St. Bernard Boulevard, through the poor neighborhoods Cree had sought solace in the day before. Deelie explained the hubris and naïveté that had prompted her to take the Alfa Romeo junker as collateral on a loan to a now long-gone boyfriend, and the ongoing grief it gave her. Then, at Deelie's prodding, Cree talked about her profession, some of the hauntings she'd investigated. Cree could sense a sharp mind clicking away behind the laconic questions and disinterested expression, the reporter snapshotting, underlining, filing points for future reference.

After a few minutes more, Deelie told her to pull over. They had come to a block of tenements built of yellow-brown brick, two and three stories tall, each fronted by a green-painted stoop. The project stretched out of view to the north and east. Almost every window was covered from the inside with foil-faced insulation that reflected the merciless sun: With no air-conditioning and no shade, the foil was all that kept the apartments from turning into ovens. The atmosphere of decay and poverty was rich and deep here, as was the dense aura of human experience.

"This here's my home turf. Born and raised in St. Bernard Development. Figured that you looking into Temp Chase and the Beaufortes and their crowd, you're gonna get the uptown perspective. You're gonna need some thesis-antithesis here, a little dialectic – the African-American side of it. These people here? They've been in N'Orleans as long as any Beauforte, but their names ain't in no history books or social registers. Main exports from here're back labor, jazz, and boys to fill the prisons. Your tourists go to the Quarter and the Garden District, but they ain't coming here anytime soon, you can bet. Pull up there, le's park."

Cree took in the feel of the place. It seemed heat-beaten. The ground between buildings was flattened grass and bare earth, litter-strewn. People lounged on some of the stoops, avoiding the direct sun, or stood in pairs or trios looking bored and exhausted. Here and there, men squatted with their backs to the brick, hands loose on their knees, just smoking or doing nothing whatever. Mothers strolled lethargically on the sidewalks, kids toddling along behind or riding plastic trikes. Just down the block, a police cruiser had stopped and a pair of NOPD officers were talking with a group of teenagers. From behind the nearest foil-covered windows came the muffled pulse of warring beats, mostly rap music.

Deelie got out of the car, settled a strap of the backpack over her shoulder, and then stretched and breathed deeply as if luxuriating in the humid air and urban grit. She tipped her head to a couple of old men who sat in aluminum lawn chairs and they returned the greeting with gap-toothed grins. When Cree got out and joined her, heads turned to look her over: stranger, white woman off her turf.

Deelie led her down the street, her beads rustling as she walked. "Le's take a stroll. There's method to my madness, don't worry, this's all part of my half of our bargain. You know much about voodoo?"

"Voodoo? Not much. Sticking pins in dolls, that kind of thing."

Deelie looked at her incredulously. "No shit! You in the supernatural business an' all, I thought . . . Well, then, this's just right. See, people up north think voodoo's this fringe thing – weird cult, holdover from another century? Has to do with murdering people or, what, biting heads

199

off snakes or something, right? Fact is, it's a belief system that's concerned with reverence and doing good and protecting against bad, just like any religion. It's always been here, and it's growing. You just can't see it unless you know what to look for. But I'll show you. See there?"

This side of the street was lined with sagging wood-frame houses, fronts to the tenements of St. Bernard, backs to the roaring highway overpass a block away. Deelie had pointed to the left front window of a double shotgun, where a mournfully placid plastic figurine of Mary stood on the windowsill, bracketed by stubby candles in the shape of crosses.

"If you're thinking Catholic, you're half wrong. Voodoo, it's grabbed onto Jesus and Mary, and most believers mix and match 'em. It's all about *belief*, see, so voodoo appropriates what people are gonna believe in, that's where it gets its power. Look at the door. See that corner of dark cloth up in there? Means there's curtains just inside the door, got stuck in there when it was shut. The curtains keep bad spirits out. Whoever lives here's a believer or a practitioner."

They moved on. For Cree, what Deelie said explained one of the unfamiliar strains of the whispers here: the rich, dark, Caribbean-spiced undertone, the faintest echo of long-ago drums of Africa. Yet another thread of the ancient past weaving seamlessly into the present.

"And this has something to do with the Chase murder?"

"Yes, ma'am, it does." Deelie nodded, grinning broadly. "I'm about to tell you. But here we go, lunch at Chez Henri."

The gray-stained stucco two-story building housed several businesses that fronted the street with mesh-covered windows. They went through a doorway beneath a sun-bleached magnetic sign that advertised *EAT* in big letters, with *Henri's Po'boys* spelled out beneath.

"Yo! On-ree!" Deelie cried joyfully.

Behind the counter at the back, a man reading a newspaper lifted his head, then stood up. He smiled at Deelie without taking the cigarette from his mouth, the butt remaining magically suspended on his lower lip and bobbing as he answered, "Hey, Deelie."

"Henri, this here's my friend, brought her all the way from Seattle to sample your fine cuisine. She looks white, but she's black. Ironically speaking."

Henri shrugged. "Sho'," he said noncommittally.

"Henri's the master chef. I recommend the oyster, that's the best. Oyster po'boy for me, Henri."

Cree scanned the hand-lettered menu board above the counter. Po'boys were available with meatballs, sausage, ham, catfish, crab, squid, even beans and greens. "I guess I'll have the same," she said.

It was well after lunch hour, and they were the only customers. Henri's was a grimy place about sixteen feet square with a gray linoleum floor and five masonite-topped tables. A film of cooking grease made every surface sticky, so that Cree had to peel her feet up for each step, but the smell from the kitchen was delicious. She and Deelie sat at the table nearest the door, where through the service window to the kitchen they could see Henri working on their order.

"Okay, Chase murder, here's the connection," Deelie said. "Popular media personality murdered in historic house in Garden District. I'd won a couple journalism prizes the year before, so I got the story, you know? Great assignment, good for lots of follow-ups locally and likely to get syndicated all around, get my byline some national exposure. Lot of what I did was the background, the human interest angle. Oh, I followed out anything forensic Bobby G.'d give me, but I did a lot of other stuff besides – talked to their friends, family, associates. Sniffed around good."

Deelie glanced up as Henri lowered a basket into a deep fryer, making a tremendous sizzling. When she went on, she lowered her voice: "But everything I fished up didn't make it to the paper. That was the deal I cut with Bobby G. for him giving me a little inside track on his end – police had to have some say in what went in the paper? Standard procedure, they don't want the killer to know everything they're working on. One thing I found, I believe was a significant contribution to the case. Problem is, nobody can connect it back in yet."

"And it has to do with voodoo."

"You got it, girl." Deelie dug in her backpack and came up with a packet of photos. "I's walking around the house, trying to maybe take some shots I could use in my articles, you know? I'm out on the sidewalk, looking for an interesting angle of view, something atmospheric, so I push aside some leaves on one corner of the fence. And what do you think I see? There's a little hoodoo *hex* tied to the corner pillar!"

Cree took the photos out of their envelope and saw a number of views of Beauforte House. "There's really such a thing as hoodoo? I thought it was . . . I don't know, a vaudeville term. Like 'hocus-pocus.' "

Deelie reached across the table and fingered through the stack until she found the one she wanted. "Here – this one."

It was a close-up of a short stick lashed with strands of long grass or some other plant fiber to a bar of the fence at the corner pillar. Beyond, out of focus, Cree could see the green of foliage and a blur of yellow that was probably a wall of the house.

"Deelie, I don't know what this means. What's hoodoo?"

"Shame on you, girl! You come down here, don't do your home-work? Call yourself a researcher?"

"Order up," Henri called. He pushed a couple of paper plates onto the counter. "Som'in' drink wi' dat?"

They both asked for Cokes. Cree got the food and insisted on paying. A po'boy, she saw, was a big sandwich, like a sub, but in this case a crusty baguette stuffed with deep-fried, battered oysters, mayonnaise, and shredded lettuce. Back at the table, Deelie grabbed hers and took a huge, rapturous bite. So did Cree. It was delicious, the oysters crisp on the outside but hot and juicy inside.

"Didn't I tell you, best thing you ever ate?" Deelie leaned close and confided, "But you gotta come in early in the week, 'cause he change his fryin' grease on Mondays. By end of the week it get a little funky, you know what I'm saying?" She tipped her head toward Henri, who had settled back behind his paper, motionless but for the cigarette smoke curling up.

They ate in silence for a moment, and then Deelie was ready to go on. "Okay. Hoodoo's folk cures and conjuring. It's not a coherent form of religious observance, like voodoo, but it's connected. It's just the folklore of cures, hexes, charms, potions, herbs, curses, and shit that goes along for the ride with voodoo, about like Santa Claus and Easter Bunny go with Christianity. Roots go back to western African medicine and mysticism of the sixteenth century and probably much earlier. There's traditional general ways of doing things, but hoodoo doesn't have a fixed form, and every old root doctor or conjo woman got a slightly different set of remedies and charms."

"What does this one mean?"

"Hold on, I'm getting there!" Deelie held up a hand as she attacked her sandwich, chewed, swallowed. "Take a look at that close-up of the stick, you can see it's about as long as a stubby cigar, and it's got those two notches? I found one on three outside corners of the fence around the Beauforte lot. So I told Bobby G. about it, and, ooh you should have seen that white boy's face wrinkle up! He didn't want another problem to figure in. But he had his boys go retrieve the three outside, and then after I got some advice from this ol' conjo woman I knew about, they went through the house with an eye out for more signs of hoodoo. They found one more stick, up under the overhang of the mantel in the parlor. Just where the old woman said it'd likely be!"

They ate in silence for a moment as Cree pondered the hex. "So what's it supposed to do?" she asked at last.

"Oh, man, Bobby G., he wanted so bad for it to be a killing hex! Some person of the colored persuasion put a hex on Chase, then popped him when the hex didn't work? But the old conjo woman, she says it's a hex for 'confusion of mind,' like insanity or maybe forgetfulness. She said if someone got inside to put that fourth stick there, the police should look for other things, too – maybe something like burnt hair from Temp's head, maybe some graveyard dust or these commercial hoodoo oils and shit you can buy. But this was like a month after, they'd had so many people in and out, it was too late for Bobby's techs to go after that. The scene inside had been pretty well compromised."

"So, Deelie, let me get this straight – do you *believe* in hoodoo?"

Delisha hooted and turned toward the counter. "Yo, On-Ree! You believe in hoodoo?"

Henri's newspaper dropped and with his cigarette he pointed to the air-conditioner above the front door. A fist-sized cloth sack lay flopped there, dust frilled. "B'lieve in b'lievin'," Henri said mysteriously. The newspaper came up again.

"That his *gris-gris* bag," Deelie explained. "His protection charm. Got different herbs and powders and stuff in there. Wards off attack and theft. What he means is, he don't exactly believe, but he believes hoodoo got power over those who *do* believe, so he keeps his *gris-gris* there to protect him. You can see he keep a crucifix on the cash register, too. That's how most people do."

Henri's newspaper dropped. "Tha's how mos' people do," he confirmed. "And I ain't never been robbed by a b'liever yet!" Then he reached under the counter and with a wide grin pulled up a chunky, snub-nosed revolver. "For the rest, I got this here!"

Back on the baking sidewalk, stomachs happily full, they strolled toward Cree's car. There was a walk you did here if you didn't want to die of the heat, Cree realized, an energy-conserving, keeping-cool walk – slow, rolling, loose. It explained the seemingly lethargic gaits of the people on these sidewalks, so different from the comparatively tight, jerky strides of the sweating Northern tourists on Canal Street. An African walk, a Caribbean gait, sensible in this climate.

She had probed Deelie about the Beaufortes as they finished their sandwiches. Deelie said she'd never met Lila or Charmian, but she had interviewed Ronald to get a little color on owning a house where a prominent murder had occurred. She said she couldn't really imagine any connection between the Beauforte family and the murders or the hex. As for the organized crime connection, Deelie thought Chase definitely had a few shady friends, but she'd never turned up anything sufficient to provide a motive for murder.

Deelie was an amazing person, Cree decided, an amalgam of the innumerable cultural strains that came together here. Beyond the particular ancestry she brought to this city where French, Spanish, Afro-Caribbean, Acadian, English, and German history converged, she was a woman poised between two modern worlds as well: one predominantly white, relatively affluent, educated, the other black, poor, streetwise. Even her accent and vocabulary reflected the diverse social worlds she moved through, readily mixing academic terms and concepts with Southern black patois. It couldn't be an easy balance to maintain. Yet Deelie walked at her ease here, proud, her beads swinging and clattering softly.

"So, the hex. What do you think it says about the murder?" Cree asked.

"Bobby G., he'd say either there's a nigger in the woodpile somewhere, or there's somebody smart trying to make it look that way. Either way, it says this thing's more complex than anybody bargained for."

And none of it might bear on the haunting at all, Cree thought. So far, nothing she'd picked up seemed to have any connection to Temp Chase. But again, you never knew.

When they opened the doors to the Taurus, a belch of blast-furnace heat came out, and both women stood back to give it a moment before getting inside.

"We didn't get too far on your end of the deal," Deelie said. She slapped the sizzling metal of the car roof. "Means you owe me, right? In my line of work, this quid pro quo thing is serious."

"Girl, you just tell me when," Cree said.

Deelie grinned at her over the roof. "Not quite," she said. "But you gettin' there. Accent's still a little ironical, but you definitely gettin' there."

21

THERE WAS SO MUCH TO think about, so much to try to make sense of. And the house was calling her, compelling her to return: so many questions to ask it and its secret occupant, so much to learn. But after dropping Deelie back at the *Times-Picayune* office, Cree knew she had a couple of other priorities.

From a pay phone, she called Paul Fitzpatrick's office to learn the whereabouts of the clinic where Lila should be safely ensconced by now. His secretary patched her through, and the moment she heard his voice Cree realized she'd been hungry to hear it, curious to explore that warmth again.

But his voice was anything but warm. "She refused to be admitted, Cree. She's at home now. Or maybe she's back at Beauforte House, bouncing off the goddamned walls."

"What!"

"Look, this isn't easy for me to say. But maybe we were right the first time around – you can't present a patient with two conflicting modes of therapy. She said *you* believed her, *you* knew there were ghosts, you'd *seen* the damned ghost. She even pointed out that your fucking credentials are better than mine! That's pretty hard for me to overcome, Cree – someone validating, endorsing, a patient's delusions – "

"Paul, I told her she should do exactly as you said! I completely supported – "

"She didn't seem to hear that part, did she?"

"I'll go over there now. I'll tell her again!"

"Well, I'd appreciate that very much," he said acidly.

Cree stood on the sidewalk, looking at the phone, stunned. "I – I thought we would make an effective team, Paul. I thought we'd worked out ways our approaches could complement each other."

There were muffled voices on the other end of the line. "I've got a patient. I've got *other patients*, okay? I have to go now."

"Paul."

She wasn't sure whether he'd hung up, but after a pause he answered. "Yeah."

"Is this what you want?" She hoped it sounded ambiguous, but she meant, *with you and me.*

Another pause. "Not really."

"Me neither. I'm going over there now. I'll call you as soon as I can."

"Okay." Just one word. She wasn't sure if she'd heard a slight softening of his tone or not.

Cree's tension eased slightly when Lila opened the door at the Warrens' tidy neoplantation home. Her panicked flight through Beauforte House had left her battered, with bruises purpling on her face and several bandages on her arms.

"Are you going to yell at me, too?" she asked as she led Cree back into the house. "So many people to try to please."

"You don't have to please anybody. But you do have to take care of yourself. How are you feeling?"

"Sore. Aching. A hundred years old."

She looked it. She looked like a gray balloon someone had let most of the air out of.

Lila led Cree to the dining room, where she swept her hand toward a chaos of loose photos, albums, cards, yearbooks, and clippings spread out across the big dining table. "I was looking at some things. You'd said you'd want to see our photo albums and such, so I started getting them out. There's a lot. There're still a couple of file cabinets over at the house, but when Momma moved over to Lakeside, she gave most of it to me — damn sure wasn't going to give it to Ron, with his lifestyle. This is just the recent stuff. If you want the whole Beauforte history tour, I have a whole closetful."

"Do you enjoy it?" It sounded stupid the moment it came out of Cree's mouth.

Lila looked at her with a failed attempt at a smile. " 'Enjoy' isn't quite the word. Not at the moment."

"You want to show me some of it?"

They sat side by side at the table. The room was cool, half darkened, its windows dimmed by curtains. At one end, an antique-replica colonial hutch displayed decorative plates propped up in little brackets, and Audubon prints hung on three walls wallpapered in a muted fleur-de-lis pattern. Eight matching tall-backed dining chairs surrounded the table, which was lit by a small chandelier. Again, Cree was struck by the anonymity of the decor – with the exception of Lila's tiny watercolors, this could be a room in an upscale hotel suite. There were no mirrors, and the observation reminded Cree of the question she'd been meaning to ask.

"Lila, did you break the mirrors at the house?"

Lila's hands shuddered as she arranged loose photos and albums. "Yes." A tiny voice.

"Can you tell me why?"

"It was . . . mainly it was when I was . . . running. When I was fighting him."

Having seen Lila careening through the house in blind panic, Cree could easily understand how things would get broken. Still, she was sure there was more to understand here. "Did they . . . frighten you?"

"Yes."

"Was there something in them, or – "

"There was me, Cree! There was *me!*" She spat the syllable with disgust, looking at Cree with eyes beseeching understanding. She held both hands open, palms up in front of her chest, as if the explanation were self-evident: *Because I am this.*

Cree took the hands and brought them together in her own. Lila looked away, but Cree cradled them until, after a moment, the tension ebbed from them. When Lila's breathing had steadied, Cree gently freed the hands and began scanning photos.

"That's your mother," Cree said. She pulled over a black-and-white photo of Charmian, posed in a Jackie Kennedy–era dress and pillbox hat. Though she looked much younger, the imperious and slightly predatory look was the same. "She was pretty! She's still a beautiful woman."

"I've always thought so. Momma and I aren't what anyone would call close, we never have been, but I've always been very proud of her." Lila put the photo aside and pulled a scrapbook over. "She was very prominent in society, very active with all the civic organizations and clubs. She had the style for that. I know I sure never did – it was about all I could manage to be a housewife and a mom."

Lila flipped the plastic-sealed pages. There were a few photos of Charmian in domestic circumstances: in the kitchen at Beauforte House with baby Ron, in the garden with baby Lila. But most showed her at one social function or another – meetings, speeches, balls. One, clipped from a newspaper, showed her on a tennis court, dressed in whites, winging what looked like a savage backhand.

Cree drew over another photo. "And this one – your father?"

"Yes."

Richard Beauforte had a staid, boardroom look to him. In several photos, he stood at Charmian's side in a tuxedo, with a sober smile and dark eyes beneath heavy brows. One photo showed him in front of a small boat, dressed in a checked shirt, khakis, a billed cap. He was handing a couple of fishing rods to a slightly younger man who grinned rakishly at the camera. Behind him, a scrawny, towheaded, T-shirted Ron showed an eager gap-toothed smile.

"This is Ron, but who's this?" Cree asked. "He's handsome! He looks like Brad Pitt."

"It *is* Brad. My uncle Bradford, Momma's brother. He and Daddy were good buddies. We all loved him so. Uncle Brad. For Ron and me, he was more like, I don't know, our older brother or something."

"He's the one who – " Cree started to ask, then thought better of it.

"Yes. Who died in the fishing accident." Lila faded suddenly, then quickly flipped several pages. This was clearly not a good moment for recalling family tragedies. She turned a page, waited a few seconds without saying anything, then turned again and again. Snapshots of people and places past, little windows into bygone worlds. Richard and Brad in front of a new Thunderbird car. A black groundskeeper high in the branches of a fulsome magnolia, Ron and Lila grinning from the ladder beneath him. Various nameless faces whose resemblance revealed them to be Beauforte or Lambert uncles and aunts.

Another page showed a tall black woman bent over Lila and doing something to her hair while Lila grimaced. "Josephine," Lila explained. "I told you about her, didn't I? Our nanny."

The second photo on the spread showed Lila and Josephine standing together. Lila looked to be about twelve and was wearing a graduation gown and an excited, rather blitzed smile. Josephine was a slim, sinewy woman with a faint friz of gray in her hair, wearing a black dress with white polka dots and prim white collar. She looked at the young Lila with an expression of pride, possessiveness, and something else – concern, or maybe protectiveness.

Lila put her hand to Josephine's face. "Sometimes," she said quietly, "when this has been really bad? And all I want to do is go run to somebody, like I'm a baby again? It's her I want to run to." Lila's eyes went wide at the admission. "Don't ever tell Momma I said that! Please!"

Cree would have liked to ask about Josephine, but Lila had begun flipping pages again. Then Cree spotted a face she wanted more time with, and she put her hand on Lila's arm to stop her.

"That's you."

"Yes." Reluctantly, Lila let the page fall open. "I was somethin', back then, wasn't I? Uncle Brad always called me a real firecracker, and I guess I was."

One photo was a grade-school-era portrait of a clear-eyed, pretty girl looking straight at the camera with an expression of confident amusement. Another showed her on stage with a cello between her knees, sawing away intently.

"I had no idea you played the cello! Do you still?"

"Haven't touched it in . . . oh, so long I don't remember. I guess I gave it up when I went off to Excelsior – that's the boarding school they shipped me to over in Mobile. I did love it so, but I . . . didn't have the talent." Again Lila began turning pages as if fleeing the images, and then stopped abruptly. "Oh, I am so rude! I didn't offer you anything. Would you like something to drink? Coffee? Iced tea?"

"Actually, tea would be nice. I'm sure not used to the heat."

Lila stood up and went quickly to the doorway. But she paused there and looked back at Cree. "Everything hurts," she said, as if explaining her sudden retreat. "It's all *lost!* When life takes a turn like this, it's all . . . frightening. It's all pain. Every page, every face. I can't touch it. I can't go near it." And she turned away and fled into the hallway.

Cree sat alone in the air-conditioned cool, feeling overwhelmed by the sad feast of memories spread on the table. *I can't go near it:* Cree remembered too well the day she had boxed up the photos of Mike. Into the closet went any image that would remind her of their wedding, their vacations, the innumerable impromptu moments, the dogs, the parties, the new cars, the dinners with friends. The odd ones that really hurt: Mike lying on that awful plaid couch in their first apartment on some hot day, sleepy-eyed, naked beneath the newspaper he'd been reading. That Polaroid taken by a stranger they'd corralled for the job: Mike and Cree together on Cadillac Mountain with the misty depths of Mount Desert Island behind them – Mike's accidental look of tenderness.

She'd come to the point of locking things away only after, what, three years or so. But it never really worked. After that, she thought about that box all the time; she could feel it in the house, those years compressed inside it, as if it glowed with heat and pressure. Sometimes it seemed it was about to blow open again on its own like an undetonated bomb left over from some war, and then she'd flee whatever house or apartment she lived in to get away from it. Or she'd give up and spread it out like this and spend weeks of renewed grieving, trying to reassemble anything like a life. She couldn't blame Lila for her reluctance.

She had come here with the goal of convincing Lila to do as Paul said: to admit herself for a period of observation and treatment. But there didn't seem to be any way to ask that of her, even to open the subject.

Cree took a deep breath, reminding herself that in any case, she had to seize this opportunity to look through the Beauforte family archives. There were a thousand threads here; synesthesically, she could feel them almost as if they were tangible filaments beneath her fingers. Each led to some element of Lila's past, and she was sure one would lead her to the connection she sought: the link to the ghost, to Lila's vulnerability.

Randomly, she pulled over a school yearbook: Jean Cavelier Country Day school, 1969. Lila would have been in seventh grade. Opening to the index, she was astonished to find a long column of listings under Lila Beauforte's name: drama club, chamber orchestra, debate team, honor roll. She'd also been active in what sounded like school-sponsored community groups, Save Our Shores and Neighborhood Friends. Cree chose a page and opened it to see Lila with four other kids of mixed races, all holding the slender trunk of a sapling they'd apparently just planted. They looked proud and happy, Lila particularly – that wise, innocent spark of *joie*.

Cree heard the distant *chunk!* of the refrigerator door and the rattle of ice cubes, and suddenly she felt that there was something she had to do before Lila came back. She stood to rummage quickly through the materials on the table. She found several more yearbooks but not what she was looking for. Then she saw that there were still materials in one of the plastic file boxes under the table, and when she bent to open it saw that it contained what she'd hoped: yearbooks from the Excelsior Academy Girls' School. She opened the one from 1974, found Lila's name, and turned to the solitary listing. It was just a small portrait in a row of photos, a plumpish sort of girl staring out of the frame with a mix of uncertainty, hopelessness, and sorrow – an early version of the look Lila wore today.

Another reason for locking away the photos of Mike: having to face the difference between the Cree who appeared in them and the Cree she met in the mirror every day – the desolation there, the aching hollowness that refused to be filled.

Abruptly hopelessness descended on her like a heavy curtain falling.

Someone in her predicament had nothing whatever to offer Lila. She was showing too many signs of instability herself; she had too much emotional baggage of her own. Paul was right: All she was doing was compromising Lila's recovery process.

She heard footsteps in the hall and quickly dropped the book into the box. She was back in her chair by the time Lila came in with her little silver tray and two glasses of tea, a wedge of lemon clipped to each rim.

Lila handed her one and then held hers uncertainly, as if she wanted to apologize for the tea's inadequacy. Instead, she gestured toward the spill of photos. "I'm sorry," she said, "I know this is something you need to do . . . but I really don't know if I'm up for any more of it today."

"I was just thinking the same thing. Me neither."

"You? Why not?"

"Look, Lila, I – " Cree grappled with what to say. She swigged her tea but set it down quickly, frustrated at her inability to express what she felt. "You want to go for a walk or something? Just to get outside? I . . . I'm feeling a little cooped up, I think I have to get out of here."

"I don't know – "

"What do New Orleans women do when they have guests over? How about showing me your garden? I got just a glimpse from the levee the other day, it looks lovely."

Lila looked completely taken aback. "It . . . the groundskeeping service does it all. I used to love working in my garden, but I haven't even – I don't think I've even been back there since . . . you know."

Cree stood up awkwardly. "All the better. We can both explore. We can both pretend we're normal."

They went out through a rear door to a tall, narrow, columned gallery set with a white wrought-iron table and several chairs. Beyond, the grass stretched level for a hundred feet or so before the steep green slope of the levee began. A big live oak and a longleaf pine shifted in the lake breeze, and two palmettos rattled their spiky fronds. Islands of blossoming shrubs and flowers exulted in the dappled sun.

Without waiting for Lila's invitation, she stepped off the gallery and into the lawn. The mat of grass was deep and spongy, and she kicked off her shoes to feel it with her toes. Wishing the tea she carried were a beer, she headed back across the yard to the levee, found a spot of tree shade, and sat down with her back to the levee. It was better out here. She eased her back down against the grass and lay looking up at the heat-hazy sky. When she lifted her head she could see Lila, a little, forlorn figure still standing indecisively between the tall white pillars.

She laid her head back again. No question: Paul was right. She'd be better off quitting this case. She was showing serious indications of psychological instability. She was too tied up in her own knots, fighting with her own "ghosts," to do anything about the ghost at Beauforte House. She was just screwing things up. She'd do Lila a favor by leaving. Today. Now. Really, the only thing left was to tell her.

Lila's voice, nearby, surprised her. "I'm sorry, but the ground's probably moist. I'm worried you'll ruin you skirt." Cree looked up to see her standing anxiously a few feet away, holding her tea glass carefully. She was barefoot; her shoes were set neatly side by side on the steps of the gallery.

"Screw my skirt," Cree said despondently.

Lila looked slightly aghast.

"Don't you ever feel that way? You know? Screw it all, totally?"

Lila seemed to think about that. "Yes, I guess I do." She sounded surprised at herself.

"My father had an expression: 'Heck wit'.' He was a plumber, born in Brooklyn. It translates as 'the heck with it.' It meant, 'Sometimes you just have to let it go.' Or maybe it was 'You can't win 'em all.' Or, more like, 'It's not worth getting bent out of shape about.' It was actually a profound philosophical statement."

Lila nodded equivocally.

Cree dropped her head back and stared up at the sky, wondering why her father came back to her so strongly at moments like this. After another moment Lila sat primly down on the slope next to her, her glass in her lap. Behind and above them, a couple of women rode bikes along the top of the levee, chatting. Through her blouse, Cree felt insects move in the grass.

Cree was trying to think of how to say it: *I think Dr. Fitzpatrick is right.*
I'm lousing things up for your work with him. I've got too much shit of my own,
and some of the stuff I do, it's crazy. I have to quit. I'm sorry I can't help you,
but —

"Something happened to me." Lila said it quietly but with great
certainty.

Startled, Cree lifted her head again. Lila was sitting with her legs
straight out in front of her, flexing her feet. Her big toes angled hard over
toward the second toes, Cree saw: feet long imprisoned in a proper
woman's confining shoes.

Cree sat up to look at her.

"I don't mean the ghost," Lila said. "I mean a long time ago."

"What was it?"

"I don't know. But I know it changed me. Most of the time I run
away, or I shut it off in me. But sometimes I want to run right at it – chase
it away, or . . . or *know* it and take away its power. And you help me do
that. You're the only one who's ever helped."

Cree felt her face flush, trying to find the way to tell her, *I can't! I want*
to run, too!

"You act like . . . something happened to you, too," Lila went on.

"Yeah. But I know what it was."

"What?"

"Oh, I don't usually talk about it. Just something I have to get over."

Lila nodded at that. Sitting there side by side, gravity drew them
slightly down the slope, their skirts rising unavoidably higher on their
legs. Lila's plump, dimpled thighs looked unaccustomed to daylight, a
blue-white now marbled with awful purple bruises from yesterday's
violence. She stared perplexedly down at her legs, as if they were strange
to her.

"Cree, could a ghost be the, what did you call it – perseveration? – of
more than one emotion? More than one experience?"

"Yes. As a matter of fact, I count on that. It's always mixed. It's one of
the ways you release them – you find the part that's willing to let go.
Why?"

Lila tore up a tuft of grass and inspected it disinterestedly. "Because this one isn't all bad. It's hard to explain."

Cree thought about the affective locus in the library, which she hoped was a perseveration of the boar-headed man's dying moments. "Nobody's all bad or all good."

Lila nodded, accepting that. "Why can't you tell people what happened to you?"

"You know, Lila, I'm . . . I'm kind of unbalanced myself right now. I haven't been through what you have, but the last few days've been very draining for me, too, and – "

"I mean, maybe that's how you find the part that's willing to let go. In yourself. Does that make sense?"

They just looked at each other. For the first time, Lila held her gaze for a long moment, shy but not permitting of evasion, imploring yet somehow . . . what? Determined.

Cree felt a gust in her chest, a welling toward release. *Maybe*, she thought. She realized suddenly that on some level, Lila was bargaining. Seeking an equal exchange: *You try it, I'll try it. You dare, maybe I can dare.* But it was too big. The consequences of opening that repository of feeling could ruin Cree for this case. Right now, it felt as if it would rip her apart.

Again Lila startled her. "Do you know what Jackie did last night? He took away all the kitchen knives, right out of the house."

"What! Why?"

"And his shotgun, and most of the pills in the medicine cabinet. Even the single-edged razor blades in the hardware drawer." Lila paused to observe Cree's expression. "Because after I came home from the doctor, I had . . . thoughts. I told him I had thoughts."

That sent a chill through Cree. She had known all along that suicide was a real danger. A bad experience with a ghost could be like terminal disease, settling in along the nerves and synapses, gripping the psyche, killing the will to live. Cree could feel the impulse in Lila, brooding like a bruise-colored cloud at her center. Besides all the damage they wrought among the living, suicides made for the very worst kind of ghosts: an enduring echo of self- and life-hatred that poisoned the place where it happened, hard to banish.

"But I told him," Lila went on determinedly, "I told him I wouldn't. I told him there was a way through this. That the answer was, There's a ghost in that house, and we've got to understand why it's there and get rid of it. That you had seen it, too, it couldn't be just me going crazy. That you'd been through this before and you knew what to do about it. That no way was I going to give up before we'd given this all a try. So he shouldn't . . . worry."

Cree felt a sudden admiration for her – her concern for those around her despite her own predicament. And it dawned on her that, as if she'd intuited Cree's faltering resolve, Lila was consciously or unconsciously asking her to persevere, to see this process through. Again, she had challenged Cree and had proposed something like a pact: *You have to stick this out. If you don't, how can I?*

Cree was trying to frame an answer when the back door of the house opened, and there was Jack Warren, coming out onto the gallery, loosening his tie.

"Darlin'?" he called.

He looked toward them in bafflement, and for a moment Cree saw the scene through his eyes: two women sitting at the base of the levee with their legs awkwardly straight out in front, skirts bunched around bare thighs, looking at each other like frightened, battle-weary comrades-in-arms who had just forged a pact to charge out of the foxhole and face enemy fire together one more time.

22

I T WAS EVENING BY THE TIME Cree made it to the house. The air was cooling fast, and the darkening sky above the Garden District was lined with tendrils of high cloud that presaged a change in weather. She let herself in the front door, set her equipment case down to tap in the security code, and paused to allow her eyes to adjust. She faced the black hallway and the hush of the big house with a mix of reluctance and anticipation. She felt dangerously off balance and vulnerable, but the desperate thought occurred to her that maybe that was exactly the state this case required.

Yeah, she thought, *the way beating a steak with a tenderizing hammer prepares it for cooking.*

Whether or not Lila had intended to shore up Cree's resolve, she'd succeeded in doing so. It occurred to her that her sudden, intense desire to quit, her doubt of her own process, was just another way she'd taken on Lila's state of mind – another proof she'd taken her empathic process to an unusual extreme.

That was a cause for concern because in the rarified world of empathic parapsychology, the risks of extreme projective identification were well documented. Her process had always depended on balance. The way into the world of the ghost was through the mind of the witness, and to enter either one she had to surrender her own identity to a considerable degree. If taken too far, the process could lead to madness, but it worked for her and she'd proved she could survive it. The key was to retain a core sense of self during even the most poignant, consuming encounter. Only by keeping a sure through-line could she set either the haunt or the haunted free. On this case, that had evaded her from the start. Why? Her appropriation of Lila's ambivalences – that occilation between fear and retreat on one hand, and defiance and determination on the other – was only one explanation. The other was Paul Fitzpatrick: Their unexpected encounter had awakened a dormant part of her. And with that un-avoidably came Mike and all the emotional pain and rational confusion that had never been resolved.

After leaving Lila's house, she'd called Paul's office to report, but only the machine answered. Same at his house. The message she'd left at both places was curt and professional: "Lila agreed to go in for diagnostics tomorrow, on an outpatient basis. Best I could do. I hope it helps."

She hadn't asked for a follow-up meeting. It all left a sad ache of disappointment. But it was best to start getting over those yearnings, abort them early.

Cree sighed and picked up the equipment case again. If the vulner-ability was extreme, she told herself, it would have to be matched by an equally extreme degree of determination, some equally forceful way to anchor her identity, to find a foundation of stability. It would mean, she knew, facing into a lot of things she'd dodged for a long time. A daunting prospect.

She had decided earlier that the library would be her chief concern tonight, and anyway, as she'd feared, the upstairs was still too forbidding, the boar-headed man too near to nascence. Hoping again that he was indeed limited to the second floor, she passed the stairway and headed into the depths of the house. The curtains were still open in some rooms, letting in enough of the evening light to navigate by, and the kitchen was brighter still, especially the alcove where Temp Chase had died. For a moment she paused there, feeling a faint reprise of that cold breath of compressed whispers. It passed quickly.

The house was full of innumerable whispers and mutters, as any old house would be, the psychic "residuals" – just transient echoes, really – of all the experiences lived here over the years. But she instinctively felt that only the affective locus in the library had any prospect of turning out to be boar-head's perimortem component. If it was, it might well provide the handle she needed on his monstrous manifestation upstairs.

Through the kitchen, down the darker corridor to the east wing and the library. She passed the doorway to the storage room she'd glimpsed with Ron and the Historical Preservation ladies, came to the library door, then hesitated and turned back. It occurred to her the storage room was the only place in the whole house she had not yet spent any time. She tried several keys on the ring Lila had given her before she found the right one.

It was a fairly big room, perhaps twenty by thirty, mostly empty, with bare, wide-board floors. Its two windows were lined with security-system tape on the inside and barred on the outside; thick foliage pressed between the bars and against the glass, turning the dim light greenish. Only a couple of odd pieces of furniture were left: various mysterious humps under dust cloths, a little grove of ugly antique floor lamps, and a couple of oak file cabinets that hunkered against the far wall.

She pulled off one of the dust cloths to reveal what she'd expected, a hideous S-curved love seat. When she turned to sit in it, a flicker of movement across the room gave her a jolt, but she saw that it was just her own motion in a slender, full-length mirror that leaned against the wall. Looking back at her was her own face, dust muted and fractured by a single fissure. Another broken mirror.

The Cree in the glass looked alarmed and a little demented. And ghoulish, she realized. In the fading light, with the crack splitting her face into two mismatched planes, her brow naturally split with its crease of worry, and that . . . thing . . . forever in the eyes: yes, almost a mirror phantom, a ghost emerging from the mirror world's confusions and inversions.

Yes, Lila, she thought bitterly, *something happened to me. And I can't talk about it. And, yes, that's probably how you let it go — sooner or later you have to face it. If you don't, you become suspended between your yearning and your fear, and you're doomed to repeat the same sad acts without end, without completion or satisfaction.*

You become a ghost.

That thought struck her breathless. The face in the mirror could be nothing but a perseveration, lost and tangled, unable to fully live, afraid to fully die.

I'm becoming a ghost!

This had to end, she realized. She couldn't live locked into the constraints of emotion and memory she'd imposed on her world since Mike's death. She had to face herself. She didn't want to be a ghost, a fragment. She wanted to be alive, and whole.

She shut her eyes, took three deep breaths, then went to the mirror and turned it to the wall. It didn't help much.

She sat quietly, waiting for something to manifest, but after half an hour it became clear the only haunts here were her own. She stood, drew the dust cover over the love seat and left the room.

The library was very different. She knew it as soon as she turned into the big, dim room.

Moving in almost total darkness, she brought the equipment case to the far corner and repositioned a wingback chair so that from it she'd have a good view of the whole room and the black rectangle that was the door to the corridor. She opened the case and, working mostly by touch, set out the trifield meter, the remote temperature sensor, the ion counter, and the audio recorder.

She relaxed her hands into their *mudra* in her lap, listening to the almost inaudible hum of the recorder and breathing from her diaphragm. After a few moments she discovered a hard tension in her shoulders. By the time she was able to relinquish it, she'd found a deeper hitch or gathering in the center of her chest. That was emotional tension, the dam that held back the great reservoir of feelings that simply could not be allowed loose. But she did her best, relaxing around it and around it, softening its edges. So difficult. Its color was a deep rose saturated with bruise-blue diffusing to blackness. She kept her eyes open throughout, unconsciously watching the phosphene fizz in the dark, dots of pinpoint light so fine they looked like a mist. The gently glowing trifield meter read zero on all three gradients.

Time passed. The room turned black as the last light abandoned the sky outside.

Silence.

A long time later, she realized there were shapes in the mist of darkness. There was a person in the room. The person seemed made of phosphene mist and emotions. There was movement, a gesture, too: rising and falling. Rising and falling *hard*, cruelly hard: beating! A faint hump of light dust that had to be another person. Explosions of black crimson pain. Regret, anger. The terrible wrath was shot through with excruciating self-condemnation, and they fueled each other. The beating going on.

The hard part was not to pull away. Cree clung to her breathing, struggling to keep her eyes from trying to focus on the misty forms, to keep her heart from racing. One corner of her mind told her the trifield meter readouts were changing, but she dared not move her eyes to look.

The darkness convulsed in the beating movement, then abruptly passed into another mode, one of seeking. This part Cree had seen before on other cases: seeking, questing, asking something like forgiveness or understanding. Asking for refuge, wanting to explain. That was the opening, and Cree moved toward the desire, presenting her willingness to understand, intruding the tiniest degree on the ghost's reality. But then a sense of surprise supplanted the yearning, and another sensation, a physical pain in the middle and a sense of wrong, of desperation. A man shape fled toward the dark doorway but fell before reaching it, and the motion startled Cree so much she stood half out of the chair before she regained control of herself. The shape twisted on the floor: a man, a writhing puddle of dark and light, a man again, a cloud full of dark violet glints. In the corner of her eye she saw the flutter of the meter readout, changing rapidly as the scent of almonds – no, the sweeter, sharper odor of amaretto liqueur – became almost suffocating. At the center of the paroxysm was the seeking, the unresolved need, the need to explain or receive forgiveness or to say one more thing. And there was *love*, that was what needed explaining, and the love sought a little girl who went back and forth on a swing beneath sun-gilded green leaves. The love sprang from the dying man like an arrow released from a bow.

It seemed to bear directly upon Cree and everything she lacked and yearned for and regretted. She pulled away, denying it, hating it, and that strong good love spun away from the form on the floor and dissipated like gold dust in a whirlwind, unrequited. Her body convulsed with a sob of grief that caught jagged in her throat and made her cough. She sobbed and coughed wrenchingly for a full minute.

By the time she came out of it, tears were streaming from her eyes and the state of mind and the ghost were gone. The trifield meter was back at zero, the other sensors inert. In the aftermath of the piercing emotions, she felt only empty – hollow and disappointed with herself. She'd lost the ghost. She'd come so close, but she'd let her own fears intrude, she'd shied away at the crucial instant.

Swearing, she fumbled for the switches to the sensors and shut them down. When she pushed the glow button on her watch, she saw that it was almost eleven; she'd been in the chair for four hours.

She stood stiffly, stretched, and then blindly fumbled the equipment into its case. No point in trying further tonight. She'd gotten close, but she'd reacted too strongly and had put up resistance, had shut herself away from the ghost. If she'd sustained another few minutes, she might have been able to more fully enter its experience. But the sudden shift of mood and activity had caught her by surprise, and then that intolerable poignancy had struck her like an arrow aimed at her own heart and she'd reflexively protected herself.

She inventoried what new information she'd gained. There was some physical evidence, a digital record of increased electromagnetic activity from the trifield meter. But it wouldn't reveal anything about this ghost's identity or origins.

More important by far was the layered affect of the ghost. Later, this would be the crucial thing, but for now it didn't offer any clues to his identity, either. Any hopes she'd had that this presence would prove to be the perimortem dimension of the upstairs ghost were long gone. Because one thing was definitely *not* here: a boar-headed man and the affect of stealth, predation, sadistic glee, all the gnarled feelings scented with sweat and lust. The library manifestation carried none of those resonances. None.

He's not all bad, Lila had said.

It was true that nobody was all good or bad. But the reason the manifestations were so different was simply that there wasn't just one fully emergent, articulated revenant manifesting at Beauforte House. There were two of them.

She bumbled to the front of the house, let herself out, and locked the door behind her. When she turned around, she saw a dark figure move suddenly down in the shadows of the gallery. She dropped the equipment case with a clatter as the shape rose tall in front of her.

"Cree?" a voice said.

"Paul!"

"Didn't mean to startle you." The shadow backed toward the edge of the gallery, where in the better light it resolved into Paul Fitzpatrick. "I've been out here for hours. Couldn't reach you at the hotel, so I figured you'd be here. I came by and saw your car out front, but I knew you were probably into some . . . procedure . . . and didn't want to be disturbed, so I . . . I waited." He chuckled humorlessly. "I kind of fell asleep. You scared me as much as I must've scared you. Jesus! My pulse is racing!"

"What's going on? Is Lila all right?"

"I talked to her. She's fine. I assume. Nothing's going on. Nothing except I really wanted to see you. As I think must be evident. Man, I'd figured out something intelligent and hip to say, but I'll be goddamned if I can remember what it was!"

Relief flooded through Cree. She retrieved the equipment case and joined him at the edge of the gallery. Closer, she could see he was dressed in jeans and a gray sweatshirt. They stared at each other in the gray-blue streetlight glow. She was close enough to catch his scent, a clean sweaty smell only very slightly augmented with cologne, and she felt the magnetism stirring between them. He looked wide-eyed and unsettled, and Cree guessed she probably looked about the same. She'd had one of the longest, strangest, most difficult days she could remember, yet the prospect of being with Paul was attractive and energizing. The memory of her own cracked face in the mirror came back to her, and the determination to become something other than a ghost. The way he looked gave her a certain courage.

"One question," she said finally.

"Anything."

"Do you know anywhere to get something to eat this late? I'm absolutely starved."

He paused for just a heartbeat. Then he said, "I know just the place."

23

PAUL'S APARTMENT WAS ON THE third floor of a Creole-style town house on the far end of the French Quarter. Like the buildings adjoining it on either side, the tall, narrow building had a shabby-looking, flat facade that descended directly from roof to sidewalk, with wrought-iron balconies on the second and third floors. Paul opened a door on the right side and led Cree into a gangway that led straight back into the house. It ended at an interior courtyard, surrounded by high brick walls, open to the sky above and landscaped with flower beds and small trees. Exterior stairs led to galleries on the upper floors. A few scattered windows glowed and gently illuminated the greenery. It was lovely and strange, a tiny private oasis in the middle of the city.

"It's a condo," Paul told her. "Just bought the place about four months ago, and I'm doing some fixing up – you'll have to forgive the mess. But the kitchen is done, I can make you something good."

They went up the wooden staircase. From the third-floor gallery, Cree could look down into Paul's courtyard and the others on either side. This was the face of the French Quarter invisible from the streets, where the real lives of residents were conducted.

Leaning over the railing, Cree noticed a statue at the center of Paul's courtyard, only vaguely visible – a woman's pale form, smooth bare limbs and draped cloth.

"That's Psyche," Paul explained from behind her. "When the Realtor first brought me here and I saw her, I knew I had to buy this place. Given that I make my living studying her domain." She heard him unlock his apartment door.

Psyche, personification of the soul, Cree was thinking. *Also the lover of Eros, god of sexual love.*

The thought put her suddenly on edge as Paul switched on lights and stood aside to let her into the apartment.

"These old places were mostly left to rot for a long time," Paul explained, "and back in the fifties the city was going to tear down pretty much the entire district. But then a bunch of civic-minded people began a movement to restore and preserve them. And thank God. When you get them fixed up, they're like nothing else. Let's start in front."

He led her through the kitchen to the front by means of a hallway that ran down one side of the apartment. The living room was gorgeous. Ceiling fans spun lazily high above. The streetside wall was lined with floor-to-ceiling French doors that opened to the balcony. Paul's taste in furniture and art was mostly modern, with a few Asian curios here and there, but it went well with the high ceilings, faux-finished moldings, battered but nicely refinished wooden floors, crackled plaster walls. It all came together in a style like nothing Cree had ever seen: not quite a Parisian apartment, or a Greenwich Village loft, or an antebellum Deep South parlor, but rather a little of each.

When Cree stopped to tap a knuckle on a xylophonelike instrument, Paul explained that it was from Bali, where he'd visited some years ago; the tarnished gong and parchment shadow puppets above the bookcase were also Balinese. They moved on into the hallway, where he opened a door to reveal a room under construction: bare split-lath walls, piles of broken plaster, sawhorses, plastic sheets, scattered tools. "The once and future master bedroom," he told her. "And here's the bathroom. And this's my office – not where I meet patients, God forbid, I run my practice from a suite downtown, this is just where I do my homework. The couch is a convertible, that's where I've been sleeping while the bedroom's a mess. I know it's not Beauforte House, but my daddy was a humble physician and he had six kids to divide his inheritance. Let's head back to the kitchen so I can make you something to eat."

The kitchen had new appliances but cabinets and counters that were apparently original. The track lighting, fine cutlery, and built-in wine rack showed that he'd lavished some money on the remodeling here. A photo above the sink showed Paul in a some tropical-looking place, naked but for a knee-length sarong. Cree gazed at the articulation of his chest and stomach muscles before realizing what she was doing and snapped her eyes away.

"I take it you're an accomplished cook?" she asked.

"Huh!" he snorted. "No, it's something I keep thinking I'd *like* to do but never quite get around to. I'm afraid I don't have some great culinary genius to astound you with. Sorry. But I'm pretty sure I can whip up something reasonably palatable and nutritious. What're you in the mood for?"

"Whatever's easy."

"Wine?"

"Wine, definitely."

What was easy was an eclectic meal of a good baguette, pâté, mustard, some leftover jambalaya, Greek olives, several cheeses, a bunch of grapes, and a bottle of burgundy. Paul set it all out on a big tray, but instead of bringing it over to the dining area, he carried it to a door at the far corner of the kitchen. Balancing the tray on one knee, he opened it to reveal a steep staircase, almost a ladder, that led up into darkness. When Cree gave him a questioning look, he said, "The other reason I bought this place. You go first, hold the upper door for me. This is a little tricky with a tray."

She went up. At the top of the stairs she found herself in a slope-ceilinged attic, its dimensions invisible in the dark, still stuffy from the heat of the day. A faint square of light drew her, and approaching it she entered a narrow roof dormer with a small door at its end. When she opened it she found herself outside in the city night. The dormer gave to a wooden deck built over the roof, which Paul had set up with a makeshift trellis, several planters full of growing things, and a teak table and chairs covered by a Cinzano umbrella. There were no stars visible, but the city's glow lit the hazy sky in every direction, and rows of bright windows defined several of the tall buildings downtown. Though it was

Monday midnight, Cree could still hear the distant sound of a blues band from the direction of Bourbon Street. The varied peaks of nearby rooftops stretched away into darkness. The air had cooled considerably, but the roof still gave off some of the day's heat, making it perfectly comfortable.

Paul moved past her in the dim light to set the tray down. It clattered, the wine almost toppling, and as they both moved to catch it their bodies collided. Neither backed away from the contact. Without thinking about it Cree turned toward him, bringing her body against his, her arms going around him. One of his hands went to the bare skin at the back of her neck, the other slid into the incurve at her waist and found a fit there. Against her body she felt his breathing, a little quick from the climb up the stairs.

It happened so fast she was startled, but she just shut her eyes and felt the fascination of it. A man gave off heat, she realized, half surprised, as if she'd never known that fact. Her hands moved and found hard ridges of muscle where his back flared wide to the shoulders. The solidity of him seemed to give off gravity, too, and her body responded, falling toward him. They rocked side to side minutely as if they were dancing to each other's heartbeat. After a moment he turned his head slightly and put his lips to her ear. His warm breath tickled, and she thought he was going to whisper something, but instead he bit the rim of her ear – just with his lips, not a kiss at all but a way of tasting her or taking her a little into him.

In the dark, she felt vertigo. With the plummeting sensation came fear.

She pulled away, breathless. "Jeez. How much wine have I had?" she joked. "I'm dizzy already."

"None. But I know what you mean." He chuckled with her, but he'd heard her request for some time, a little distance. He let her go.

Cree took her arms back, though her hands were uncertain what to do.

They sat on either side of the table. Paul lit a couple of candle lanterns, poured the wine, and they clinked glasses. The wine was smooth and smoky. In the light, she could see the question in his eyes.

Why had she pulled away? A moment ago she was just free falling, and it was nice, it was . . . *fascinating*. This was what Joyce, Deirdre, anybody sane, would call a romantic situation. Soft rooftop air, the strange cityscape, good food, a handsome man, that undeniable charge of attraction and, yes, expectation. Two adults with that unspoken understanding that had been forged between them, by degrees, each time they met.

It should've been easy. It wasn't.

Cree found herself increasingly at war inside, wanting somehow to tell him, warn him, explain. Explain what? How unbalanced she was right now. How at odds this simple, sweet moment with nine years of habit. How long it had been.

"Weather's changing," Paul said, breaking what had turned into an awkward silence. "Supposed to get a couple of days of rain. This time of year, hard to believe, but it can be hot enough to boil crawfish one day, then turn truly nasty cold. I hope you brought sweaters and umbrellas with you."

"I'm from Seattle, remember?"

"Right. Of course. Where the biblical deluge never quite stopped." His smile flashed in the candlelight, and he tasted his wine. "You know, I've been thinking about what you do. On one level, I have this skepticism, I've told you that. But every time I think about what you've told me, I can see ways it makes sense."

"Such as?"

He sipped, looking over the rooftops. "In graduate school, I was fascinated with traditional healing disciplines, even wrote a paper on shamanism from a psychoanalytic perspective. I pointed out that all over the world, throughout history, healing traditions are remarkably consistent. I saw it firsthand in Bali, but you'll find the same basic ideas in Siberia or Central America or Congo. People with bad health or troubled circumstances go to the village shaman. To fix the problem, the shaman enters a special state of mind that allows him to make a journey to the underworld, where he intercedes on the patient's behalf with ghosts of the sufferer's ancestors or maybe spirits of nature. The affliction is always assumed to have a psychological as well as a physical element, and so does the cure. The shaman finds that some part of the afflicted person's soul is held hostage because he's offended some spirit by doing wrong in his life – there's some unfinished business. Say a son marries someone his mother disapproves of. Later, after the mother dies, he gets sick or his crops fail repeatedly. The shaman identifies his guilty feelings as the cause of his misfortunes, figures out an appropriate way for him to atone to her ghost. And it often works! Because the shaman allows the victim to have closure with the unfinished business. Same principle as psychoanalysis, just a different vocabulary!" He looked over the rim of his glass at Cree as if a little wary of her reaction. "But why am I telling *you* this? You're the modern-day shaman."

"I've observed the parallels. You're very insightful."

"So then I was thinking, how does your methodology compare with mine? And I realized yours has several advantages. Me, I see only the patient – I listen to his story, I probe, I ask questions. I accept the story, regardless of its literal truth, and help the patient formulate a constructive coping process. Conventional psychoanalysis is based on creating useful, therapeutic fictions, and I've never been comfortable with that . . . separation from objective reality. The issue of recovered memory you brought up is a perfect case in point. The patient may come to believe he was ritually abused by satanic parents, but if it's literally, objectively *not factual*, it creates a damaging schism between the patient and the rest of the world. But you, you do research on the whole picture, so you have much more information at your disposal. You not only talk to the patient, but you also talk to family and friends, you look at patients' home environment and family history, you observe how they live, you see their relationships firsthand. Which allows you to be more . . . objective. More reality based." He looked surprised at himself and then added with a grin, "I can't believe I said that! If one accepts that there are such things as ghosts to begin with, I mean."

"It's really a more intuitive process, Paul. I get pretty far out there, by your standards. I know ghosts to be a literal reality. And some of my processes – I doubt you'd appreciate them all in the same light."

"That sounds like something of a warning – 'Keep back! I'm weirder than you think.'"

"Paul, I am for sure weirder than you think." She said it flippantly, but it reminded her of just how much there was to warn Paul Fitzpatrick away from. It wasn't just issues of scientific credibility, things like empathic identification with clients and telepathic communion with ghosts. It was personal.

"But I didn't hear you say, 'Keep back,' right?" he asked.

Cree didn't answer. She was starving, and yet she was too tense to eat. A pressure grew in her, something that had begun when she first met Paul. How could she ask Lila to brave her own depths if she herself wouldn't? Wasn't this the first step to becoming a living person again? But it was so huge. It would have to begin with Mike and expand into metaphysics and psychology and life after death and professional commitments, and there seemed no end and no way out. Going into it now would twist her up inside and imperil her process.

"So you *did* sort of say it," he prompted, disappointed.

The wind was cooling rapidly now, bringing with it a coarse mist and the scent of the wet Delta lands to the south.

"I don't want to get into my own convolutions right now. I'd rather get a little drunk. Enjoy the view, unwind in good company. Cut loose a little."

"Fine by me." Paul poured her glass full and topped off his own. They both drank and looked out at the view.

That lasted about one minute.

"I mean, what?" he asked. "You're living with someone? You're HIV-positive? You're a lesbian? You belong to religious cult that forbids intimate relationships with psychiatrists?"

They were both able to laugh, that was nice, but Cree's trepidation grew. She put her hand over his, the best she could do for an answer.

Paul was looking increasingly unsettled. "Look, Cree, you want my marital résumé in twenty-five words or less? It's pretty humdrum – your typical postmodern tale of white-collar love. I'm thirty-nine. Lived with various girlfriends when I was younger. Finally got married about seven years ago, wanting to hang in for the long haul. Got divorced last year, some resentments and bruised hopes on both sides, but sort of semi-amicably. She relocated to Atlanta. It's one reason I moved to this place – get a fresh start, you know? I'm still a little rusty at living single. But I like to think I'm wiser now, I move more slowly into relationships now – " His eyebrows jumped as he looked down at their clasped hands on the table. "Present circumstances excepted, obviously."

It had all come out in a rush, and when he was done he paused to take a deep breath. "Sorry it's not more exotic or . . . *epic* or something." His face moved in wry self disapproval, but then he rallied and met Cree's eyes. "Your turn."

Cree thought about it. She was tired, and the familiar pit of despair opened and drew her toward it. It occurred to her that she faced a clear choice: She could give in to that dark attraction, stay confined within the limits she'd imposed on her life since Mike died, become ever more a ghost. Or she could yield to the sweet magnetism that filled the night air between her and Paul.

She sipped some wine. The blowing mist thickened and began to condense into drops that beaded on her face and rolled intermittently off the umbrella.

Paul gave her plenty of time but at last broke in on her confusion. "If it'll help at all, I can tell you that I haven't waited on a doorstep in the dark for anyone since I was . . . I don't know, maybe sixteen?"

"Mine is maybe a little *too* epic. You up for that?"

He tried to smile. "From you, I'd expect nothing less."

Maybe it was the need to honor that unspoken compact she'd forged with Lila. Maybe it was just the wine on an empty stomach, or the big, beguiling, rainbow ghost of New Orleans, the Big Easy. But she did, she began. It was the first time she'd ever tried to lay it all out in plain language. The words came haltingly at first but gradually began to pour until she couldn't have stopped it if she'd tried.

They'd met at U Penn, where she was getting a degree in psychology and he was studying art and film media. Mike was a dark-haired, blue-eyed Irish kid from Illinois whose goal was to get into animation production. They married while they were both still in school. He lingered around Philly for a year while she got her bachelor's degree, then they moved to New Hampshire so he could take a job with Imagitech, a Manchester firm that was producing a new generation of digital animation equipment and software. They lived in a ramshackle farmhouse outside of Concord, surrounded by abandoned hayfields that looked down on the back forty of a commercial apple orchard. They'd decided to have kids later, but they had two dogs and two cats and it was very much a family. They'd never had to think about their love, or getting married, they'd never analyzed it. It was just something that flowed, easy and uncomplicated; it always felt *inevitable*.

Mike adored his work. The technical side of it exercised his talents for math and engineering, while the cartoons and other visual fantasies he created expressed his whimsical, dreamy side and his absurd sense of humor. Cree admired the way the two sides balanced in him.

Cree worked for the county, helping counsel individuals and families in the social services system. She eventually wanted to go on for her master's degree in psych, get into research, but for now she felt her job did some good for people, and besides life was so nice. It all wove together. Deirdre and Mom were still in Philly then, and she visited them often. She and Mike had good friends in Manchester and Boston. For seven years, it seemed that this was how it worked, this was what life was about. Rather very much lovely.

Telling Paul about it now, she paused, unable to say some things. There was making love beneath the scraggly crabapple tree in the tall meadow grass they never mowed. Mike's broad, muscular body above hers, hard yet so gentle, the earth beneath her back and the grass parted around them clean and sweet, the timeless currents running through them both. Without thoughts, their desire and the ground's fertility and that inevitability all merged into one thing that was who they were and what life was —

"Can I ask something?" Paul said. "When you say you wanted to do research, you mean in parapsychology, or — "

234

"Oh, God, no! I never once thought about any of that stuff. If somebody had asked me about ghosts or ESP, I'd have said I was a skeptic. I was just fascinated with the human mind, and I was good at talking with people, empathizing with them . . ."

Paul nodded.

Suddenly Cree doubted she was up for this. "Look, Paul, that's the easy part. I've never . . . I don't know if I can – "

"Don't, then. Only if you want to."

Cree thought about that for only an instant.

So then Mike had to go out to Los Angeles. Big company meeting with some Hollywood heavies, Spielberg or Lucas or somebody. Everybody was excited, this was the big break not just for Imagitech but for the whole field of computer animation. Mike and the four other company principals flew out, intending to be gone for three days and to come back rich. Cree took the opportunity to go visit Mom and Deirdre in Philly. She had a great visit with Deirdre and the six month old twins, already demure and contentious, and talked to Mike at his hotel that night.

The next day she went clothes shopping downtown. Just after noon, she was making her way through the crowded sidewalks on Market Street when she saw Mike, of all people, standing forty feet away. After her initial feeling of sheer surprise, she felt delight – how nice he looked, how fun it would be to spend some time in Philadelphia with him. He was facing slightly away from her and seemed to be searching through the crowd, and before he saw her she took a moment just to admire him. He was wearing the suit that she had helped him pick out for his trip, a flattering cut, he was very definitely the most handsome man on the whole street. At last he turned her way and his face moved in recognition; she waved and smiled and began walking toward him. She thought of a salacious line to greet him with, as if he was a stranger and she was picking him up. He watched her intently, his eyes burning with feeling, lips moving as if he had something very important to say and was overcome with emotion. His intensity caused her to feel a rush of worry – for the first time, it occurred to her something must have gone wrong, maybe with the Industrial Light and Magic meeting, for him to have come back so early. But even as she thought that, she knew with certainty that together they could fix anything, whatever it was they'd ride it out, they'd be okay. She continued making her way toward him through the lunch-hour crush, and his intensity grew, and she felt a stab of fear, realizing something really bad must have happened. Maybe his mother had died, he'd flown back earlier and called Mom to find out where she was, came straight from the Philly airport on the off chance of finding her here. When she was only a dozen feet away, a vendor rolled a concession cart between them, and when he passed, Mike was gone. She turned around in a full circle, she ran after the cart, she scanned the street and the sidewalks and saw him nowhere. She called his name; no one answered. She *shouted* his name, getting frantic, and people around began to give her odd looks.

His sudden disappearance confused and scared her, especially when she thought of the intense, unspeakable feeling in his eyes. Suddenly she realized how wrong the whole thing was. She'd just talked to him on the phone last night, how could he have gotten here from L.A. so quickly? What were the odds he'd be able find her in central Philadelphia at lunch hour? From a pay phone, she called Mom's house. But she hadn't heard from him. She called their number in Concord and got their messages off the answering machine, but there was nothing from Mike. She called his mother, who said no, she hadn't heard from Mike since before he left on his trip, was everything all right?

Three hours later, she called Concord again and heard the message from the Los Angeles police. Mike had been riding in a rented car with three others from his company, the voice said, when they were hit broadside by a pickup truck that ran a red light. Two of the people in the car had been killed. One of them was Mike.

She knew it was a mistake, but it still scared her almost out of her mind. When she called LAPD and got the right person on the line, she heard the news again.

"No, there's been a mixup," she told the cop. "He's back here – I just saw him. It must be someone else."

But the policeman insisted he had personally recovered the identification from the corpse. The dead man's appearance, as he described it, was very similar to Mike's.

"Who were the other people in the car?" Cree asked, panicking now.

The names were Mike's colleagues at Imagitech. The other person killed was Terri McNamarra, Mike's fellow VP and good friend.

Cree said, "Maybe the wallets got mixed up during the accident – "

"I'm sorry, Mrs. Black. His boss – Mr. Lederman – was still conscious at the scene. He identified the body."

But but but. But she had *seen* him, here, alive! She had looked into his eyes!

For a full day, she refused to believe Mike had been in that car. She kept refusing, insisting there had to be a mistake – first because this *couldn't* happen to him, to her, to their marriage, and second because she had *seen him alive in Philadelphia*. She kept up the denial until she flew to L.A. to identify Mike's body herself. She later determined that he'd been pronounced dead at the scene only moments before she'd seen him there on the street in Philadelphia, three thousand miles away.

Cree stopped and found her way back to New Orleans, which seemed choked with fog, unreal. She'd hoped it would be easier, but it felt as though things were breaking loose inside her chest. The pain seemed impossible, open-heart surgery without an anesthetic.

She had never encountered him again. No physically manifesting phantom, not even a sense of his presence. For a long time, she wished she could. Just one more moment together. But it didn't happen. The only ghost that remained was the one that lived in her memory and that box of photos that had to be locked away.

Later, trying to make sense out of what had happened, she went over and over the scene, trying to glean every detail. The Mike she had seen that day had not been bloody and broken, but handsome, beautiful Mike wearing the new suit he'd bought for the trip and the tie she'd given him for Christmas, the breeze making his hair do that thing that irritated him but that she liked. Did he cast a shadow? Was the background faintly visible through him? Much later, having played the sight back so many times that the memory lost its integrity, she could see it any way she chose: Yes, he cast a sharp shadow on the sidewalk, no, he didn't; yes, he was solid as anyone else on the square, no, he had a slightly misty or translucent look.

One thing she knew for sure, though: It had been Mike, Mike and no one else, who had looked into her eyes that day with that inexpressible emotion. Somehow space and time and corporeality had permitted him to visit her in the minutes after his death. Mike had sought her and found her.

Much later, she'd learned that the occurrence was among the most common paranormal experiences: the spectral visitation by a geographically remote loved one at the moment of death. The survivor's conviction that the manifestation was physically real was also typical.

Of course, the statistics didn't explain how it happened. Nor help her come to grips with it.

In the end, all she hoped was that whatever he had experienced at that moment, he had seen the smile on her face, understood it for what it was: *Oh, my beautiful Mike is here, what a wonderful surprise! Hello, my sweet, how I love you.* Surely that was obvious, surely he couldn't mistake it for anything else. Whatever he took wherever he went afterward, she hoped he'd remember that.

It deflected her entire life, her whole being. Suddenly she was alone and heartbroken. Every simple assumption had been smashed. The days of anything clear and straightforward had died with Mike.

She also had a huge mystery right in her face, obstinate, undeniable. To cope with that, she started doing some reading. After a while she went back to school, studying psychology, philosophy, religion, anatomy and physiology, history – whatever seemed to promise hope of an explanation.

Or was it really explanation she wanted? Cree sometimes wondered. Maybe it was more a search for a way back to Mike. She spent her life looking through windows into other dimensions of the world, and into the past, observing and interacting with the ghosts that lived there. She claimed to be a scientist, but in the end maybe it all came down to the simple hope that one day, through one of those windows, she'd see Mike again. Just one more glimpse.

The night air had turned very cool, the breeze more insistent and now heavily laden with mist. The candles had burned themselves out, and Paul Fitzpatrick had become little more than a shadow in his chair. He didn't move or speak.

Against her will, Cree found herself laughing. Each laugh hurt, an explosion in her chest that burst up and seemed to come out her aching eyes.

"What?" Paul asked warily.

"Talk about a lead balloon! Talk about ways to put the chill on a date! Oh, man! Tell him you were married to the perfect guy whose shoes nobody could fill. Yeah, and better yet, tell him the perfect guy's not really, totally, quite dead, no, you're still pretty much married to him, so good luck, bud!" It really would be funny if it didn't hurt so much.

Paul didn't say anything.

Neither of them moved for a long time, and after another little while the coarse, blowing mist turned into raindrops that pattered on the umbrella and splashed on Cree's face. They were both well soaked by the time Paul leaned forward, put his hands on his knees, and stood. He came up stiffly, as if his joints pained him.

"Blowing up pretty wet," he said hoarsely. "We should probably go inside."

24

HEY. IT'S ME." A quarter to four in the morning. Poor Ed.
"Mmph. Hi. Yeah. I figured."

Cree had been lying for hours in the dark room, listening to waves of
rain wrap around the hotel and thrum at the windows. At intervals the
wind sighed vastly, a weather god from the gulf coming inland to die.
Mike's face came and went: Mike from days in Concord, nights in Philly,
road trips they'd taken, mundane moments, making love.

Between visits from Mike's memory, she replayed the scene with Paul.
They had fled the roof as the rain began to pelt down in earnest. Back in
his kitchen, there didn't seem to be anything more to say. Her hands
could still almost feel the topography of his back, the man shape of his
bones and muscles, and they wanted to go there again and explore
further. But that would be betrayal, and anyway the moment had gone.
Whatever Paul thought of their embrace or her narrative, he didn't voice
it. After a few strained moments, Cree had said tentatively, "Well, I
should probably be going." And Paul hadn't argued, only offered to walk
her to her car. She had declined. No point in both of them getting any
wetter.

"Sorry to call so late, Ed, you must be — "

"No, no. Actually, I w's gonna call you, but I . . . mm, got in pretty
late myself . . ." She heard the sandpapery sound of Ed massaging his
cheeks, trying to get his mouth working.

"I'm all fucked up, Ed."

Rearranging noises: Ed was sitting up in his bed in Massachusetts,
hunching over the phone. He'd scratch his head with his free hand and

leave his hair sticking out the way it did when he napped on his office couch.

"I disagree about that, but I'll gladly listen to why you think so."

Cree hadn't thought it through this far when she'd reached for the phone. She couldn't tell him about Paul, and that wasn't where it came from, anyway. "Oh, *Mike* stuff. You know."

"Yeah."

"I mean, I'm going around *talking* to him."

"Why's it happening now, Cree? What's bringing it on?"

She stumbled over the question. "I don't know. Nothing. I don't know." *Paul Fitzpatrick. Who reminds me that I want to live life and don't know how.*

They were quiet for a long moment. Ed probably heard her evasion. At the very least, he'd know Cree Black was never without complex explanations – if she wanted to reveal them.

"And my mind is doing some pretty strange things," she confessed. Partly a way to change the subject.

"Like?"

Where to even start? "Oh, I don't know. Like yesterday, middle of the day, I was over at the house. And I had this daydream. I had clear picture of what it was like during the Civil War."

"I do that sometimes. Everybody does, don't they?"

"No, this was . . . a particular day, a specific moment. I was looking out the window, across the lawns at the next house. The Union troops were taking the neighbors away, and . . ." Cree stopped. Telling Ed about it now, she suddenly remembered something she hadn't realized had been there when she'd been jolted out of the vision. Names: The neighbor woman was Mrs. Millard. The two girls were Lizzie and Jane and the little boy was William John. The Millards.

"Jesus," she said.

"What?"

"I remember their names now. And I wasn't me, I was a young woman, a teenager . . . and I was sitting in the slave quarters because they were making me wait there."

Ed didn't say anything for a moment. No doubt he was processing it the same way she was: Either Cree was getting very screwed up indeed, her mind running amok, or she had really visited the past through the mind of someone who had once lived at the house. And if that were true, poor Ed would have another huge theoretical problem to try to fit in with all the other crazy, freakish things Cree threw at him.

"Did the general have a teenage daughter then?" he asked.

"I don't know."

Ed was chuckling. "Oh, Cree," he said softly. "The marvelous Cree."

"What."

"The amazing and ever-astonishing Cree. Hey, I just remembered something I wanted to tell you last time we talked."

"What was that?"

"Sunday . . . it's a little different today, but Sunday? The ocean was *exactly* the color of your eyes. I'd glance out the window and it was like you were looking at me. Keeping me company."

His affection touched her and she had to flee from it. "Thank you, Edgar."

"Okay, so let's see if we can dig up the names of the neighbors. See if General Beauforte had a daughter. We can work on it when I get there. In the meantime, you gotta think of yourself differently. Not a problem, an opportunity, right? You gotta celebrate yourself, Cree. You're not screwed up, you're miraculous. However it works out, Millards or no Millards. Okay?"

She could hear the smile in his voice. His attitude helped. He was right, that was a good way to process it: *You have to welcome your own strangeness.* Good advice.

"I'll try," Cree said. Yes, talking to Ed always helped. The hard part was that you could love someone like this and still not feel the pull, the magnetism, that you knew had to be there. Which meant that as good as this friendship was, there were places it couldn't go, confidences it couldn't accommodate.

As if he'd heard her despondency, Ed didn't say anything for a long time. She began to feel very sleepy. The rain noise increased outside, bearing down hard now. Four A.M.

"You still there?" he asked at last. He sounded as if he had more to say.

"Barely," she mumbled. "I feel better. Thanks, Ed. You're miraculous, too. I should probably get some sleep now. Both of us."

"Yeah." He sounded disappointed. She was always letting him down.

They said good-bye. Cree lay in the dark and drifted away to the sound of the tropical rain from across a thousand miles of water, exploring and caressing the building in the dark like a blind lover.

25

Y ES, IT COULD RAIN IN New Orleans.

Cree clenched the steering wheel as the car hit standing water and sent an arc of spray slashing across Highway 10. She was running late, so blind from the whirling rain and the dirty mist tossed up by other vehicles that she was afraid she'd miss the airport signs. Blind also from the welter of facts and impressions and intuitions, the half-seen paranormal and normal-world insights that seemed to come at her just as hard.

She had awakened to find the hotel windows streaked and bleary. Below, Canal Street looked battered by the drenching gale. The awnings along the sidewalk fluttered and humped as if they'd rip off and fly away, and only a few pedestrians scuttled here and there. The road crew had apparently given up their mud pit for the duration.

The memory of last night made her wince.

Her visit with Lila this morning had been frustrating, distracted, pointless. The wild wind and rain seemed to pull everything apart. In the Warrens' neighborhood, so staid and placid on a calm day, the trees and garden plants tossed and gyrated in the stormy half-light like a frenzied disco crowd. Then she'd arrived to find a couple of tradesmen's vans parked in the driveway. Sweet, dear, Realtor Jackie's idea of a romantic surprise, Lila had explained resignedly: He'd scheduled the remodeling of one of their bathrooms to cheer her up. Which meant the house was full of the voices of men, the whine of drills, the thump of fixtures being moved around, and every few minutes a voice calling down the stairs, "Mrs. Warren, I don't mean to trouble you ma'am, but I got a question 'bout this heah shower stall . . ."

Understandably, Lila was also preoccupied with her forthcoming diagnostics; the desperate intimacy they'd established yesterday had faded. Still, she had dutifully pulled out more of the family archives, and they'd spent a difficult hour or so looking at photos. They had looked at faces of Beaufortes and Lamberts, of Charmian's brother Bradford, Richard's sister Antoinette and brothers Franklin and Alexander, of cousins, in-laws, family friends, servants who had come and gone.

Between interruptions, Lila had managed a few words about each one. All Lila's uncles and aunts were dead now. Bradford had been the only one to stay close to the family, and he'd died before having children. Richard's sister Antoinette had married and moved to Houston, where she'd had one son, killed in Vietnam, and a daughter who'd become a prominent oncologist before succumbing to her own specialty; Antoinette had died a few years later. Franklin had moved to Italy just after World War II and had stayed there, marrying into a large Tuscany clan. Alexander had died of a stroke; one of his sons had become a priest, the other had been killed driving home drunk from a keg party. His daughter, Lila's cousin Jennifer, was still alive; fifty-one now, she lived in Oakland, California, with her partner Ellen.

Lila told it all without excess emotion, in a tone that was almost formal, as if she were speaking for the benefit of the plumbers and carpenters who passed in the hallway.

With Brad's death in 1971, the future of both proud families had come to depend on only Charmian and Richard. And given Ron's distinctly undomestic habits, that had narrowed in the next generation to only one line: Lila and her three children. Lila admitted that the fact had contributed to her desire to reestablish the family roots at Beauforte House.

Many of the photos and clippings showed Charmian or Richard with influential people who Lila explained were good friends, neighbors, or fellow members of their country club or Mardi Gras krewe: a couple of mayors, a state supreme court judge, a governor, a police commissioner, the state coroner, various parish representatives, prominent restaurateurs,

other bankers, heads of charities to which the Beaufortes gave gener-
ously. Lila's memory of them all seemed quite good; if she were
repressing anything, Cree thought, it wasn't apparent from any systematic lack of recall.

Cree had her own distractions. The reassurance she'd felt after talking
to Edgar hadn't survived the conflicted feelings that accompanied it.
Uncomfortable memories returned: last night with Paul and almost
intolerable ones of much earlier. At moments, Mike's face materialized
in front of the Beauforte faces she studied.

And then after a while it was time for Lila to leave for Ochsner Clinic
and for Cree to head to the airport. Lila ended their session looking
battered, puffy around the eyes. Cree felt only frustration: The family
archives had shown her nothing, except to confirm that the Beaufortes
were indeed very well connected, well established. A distinguished
family without a blemish upon its name.

Cree gasped as a truck threw up a huge gout of muddy water that
completely obscured the view ahead. The car sped forward into absolute
murk, Cree bracing for a head-on collision but afraid to slam on the
breaks for fear she'd be hit by the equally blind car behind.

Her view cleared after only a second or two. But the sensation of
hurtling out of control, the sense of imminent danger from ahead and
behind, future and past, stayed with her.

Joyce came into the arrival gate wearing baggy beige pants, a tight white
tank top, open sandals that displayed her red toenails, and oversize pink
sunglasses pushed up into her ebony hair. With her gigantic handbag, she
looked every bit the Long Island tourist, and she barely made it to the
parking lot without buying cheesy New Orleans souvenirs from the
airport concessions.

"You look like something the cat dragged in," she said as Cree pulled
onto Route 10 and headed toward the occluded skyline of New Orleans.
"*You* are not living right."

"Hey, tell me about it."

Joyce peered out the car window. "This is not what I expected. I

didn't know it rained like this here. Not this time of year. My Gawd."
She had to raise her voice to be heard over the drumming of rain on the
car roof and the vehement *whack-whack* of the windshield wipers.

"I didn't either."

"Your sister says hi, by the way. And the twins. Such sweet kids!"

"You talked to them?"

Joyce bit her lips and looked a little caught out. "Well. She was a little
worried. Called me as I was going out the door this A.M. and asked me if I
knew how you were doing. Said you'd called her late last night, you had
the blues pretty bad."

"I'll get over it."

Joyce's eyes narrowed skeptically and her voice took on an excessively
neutral tone Cree knew well. "Of course."

Driving took all of Cree's attention.

"The borders thing?" Joyce asked.

"Oh yeah."

Joyce frowned. "This is me trying to check in emotionally, Cree. But
you're not helping much."

Cree freed a white-knuckled hand from the wheel, found Joyce's, and
gave it a quick squeeze. "I think I may have used up my allotted lifetime's
worth of emotions, got none left. I'm sorry."

"Well, you can tell me in excruciating detail when you buy me lunch.
And let me stress the lunch part. They served us these things on the flight
– I think they were supposed to be foodstuffs, but you could have fooled
me. Honestly."

"So what I don't get is why you're so sure you scared this guy off," Joyce
said decisively. "I mean, your story is overwhelming on so many levels.
Sounds to me like he did his best, you're the one who pulled the plug. If
he didn't argue with your decision to leave, that was out of respect for
your feelings – he didn't diminish them by trying to bring you out of it or
seduce you or something. What did you *want* him to do?"

Joyce was a tenacious researcher who was impossible to deflect if she
wanted information, and she'd skillfully coaxed and goaded the whole

247

story out of Cree. Joyce's idea of checking in emotionally had an inquisitional quality to it, Cree thought, but it sure got the job done. Now they were sitting in a Starbucks at the edge of the Garden District, rain blasting against the plate-glass windows in erratic gusts. The relentless sloshing and splashing made Cree think of the interior of a dishwasher on high cycle. Under the circumstances, she had given up on finding something regional to eat. Joyce had complained about having her first New Orleans food in a too-familiar, Seattle-based franchise, but access to a bathroom had become imperative, and it was only five blocks from Beauforte House; when they were done, it would be easy to swing by and give Joyce her first glimpse. They had ordered caramel mocha cake, apple crumb cake, and coffee. Between Joyce's familiar presence and the first food Cree'd had in twenty-four hours, she felt a little better.

"I mean," Joyce finished, "let's face it, for all your empathic talents, when things bear upon you personally you don't seem to understand the simplest things about human nature. Especially your own. The way I see it, not telling him was getting you nowhere fast, what was there to lose?"

Cree accepted the chastening. Joyce was enjoying the mother-henning, and Cree didn't want to spoil her pleasure by telling her that her relationship with Paul Fitzpatrick was almost something of a moot point. It was less his reaction than Cree's own that she feared. She'd made it through the night only by resolving to focus on the hauntings, on Lila, on her own internal equilibrium and process. That was the foundation on which she would have to rebuild, not on resurrecting some wan hopes about a possible relationship that had clearly gotten off on the wrong foot, probably irredeemably.

"Point taken," Cree said at last. "I'm screwed up, I'm working on it. This has all been particularly difficult for me. Now, will you assume I'm dodging the issue if I bring up the reason we're both here? Our commission from the Beaufortes?"

"Atta girl! Come right back at me, that's the way!"

They both laughed. Joyce was a pain.

Cree filled her in on developments: details of Lila's apparitions and state of mind, Beauforte family history, the Chase murders, the hoodoo hexes, Cree's experiences at the house. A legal pad materialized in front of Joyce and she started taking notes.

Cree outlined their research priorities. First, the architecture. Joyce would need to nag Tulane for the floor plans and go get them when they were available; as soon as possible, they'd need to go through the house, room by room, feature by feature, to look for divergences that would clue Cree to the ghosts' eras.

Next, history. The convulsive beating gesture she'd seen in the study could well be a link to the murder of Lionel, John Frederick Beauforte's supposedly troublesome servant, around 1880. Joyce should search newspapers of the period for references to the incident, seeking details of the murder and anything relating to Lionel's personal history. While she was at it, she might as well look for references to Richard Beauforte's death in 1972 — news reports, medical details, obituaries, eulogies, whatever.

Then, Josephine. Cree asked Joyce to try to trace Lila's long-gone nanny. If she were still alive, she might provide information Beauforte family members didn't know or were reluctant to share. If indeed she and Lila had been close, she might have an opinion on what had transformed the bright, confident girl in the early photos to the scared, reserved, repressed junior college student. At the very least, she might be able to explain why Lila's vital signs had shown such agitation when they'd toured the house and had come to Josephine's room.

Finally, Cree also asked her to keep her eyes open for any link between the Beaufortes and voodoo or hoodoo, anything that might make sense of the hexes Deelie Brown had found. She considered asking Joyce to research some of the details she'd recalled about the daydream in Josephine's room but decided she'd given her enough.

"Gawd, this is a regular smorgasbord! Missing persons, historical archives, voodoo, architecture – this is it, I've died and gone to heaven." Joyce turned an ecstatic face to the ceiling but quickly brought her eyes back to Cree and sobered. "I'll get on it right away. On one condition – You come with me to Bourbon Street one of these nights, eat some Cajun food, have a few drinks, and go dancing. And maybe, dare I say it, if you're giving up on Dr. Fitzpatrick, flirt a little? I'm serious, Cree, I'm gonna have to insist. You don't like this condition, fire me. You gotta live a little. This is not Muncie, Indiana, it's *New Orleans*, right? Seize the day."

Everyone close to Cree had some prescription; she usually acquiesced – for their sakes, not her own. Now she agreed with a pretense of enthusiasm she knew was unconvincing.

They dashed for the car and drove through the maelstrom to Beauforte House, where they pulled up in front and just sat in silence for a few minutes. The trees thrashed in the wind like creatures in pain; rain darkened the yellow siding in irregular patches and poured in wind-twisted runnels from every angle of the roof. The hollow upstairs windows gaped like the empty eyes of a cadaver. For Cree, the sight brought back the horror of the boar-headed man and that powerful sense of brooding secrets that surrounded both the house and Lila.

"This one is so hard for me," Cree found herself confessing quietly. "I . . . I don't know why. I can't remember being so . . . accessible, it's like everything *invades* me. I can't seem to get any control, it's gotten so I don't trust myself. The whole thing is . . . very disturbing."

Joyce didn't answer and didn't look at her, just stared at the house with eyes narrowed and mouth constricted to a tight line. After another moment she made a pistol out of her forefinger and fired it at the rain-smeared image. "We're going to get you," Joyce muttered quietly. "We're coming after your translucent white ass, and don't you forget it."

26

THE RAIN HAD SLACKENED by the time Cree made it to Charmian's house the next morning. Before going in, she sat for a moment in the car to gird herself for another encounter with the dowager. It wasn't easy. Inside, she felt like a port city in a hurricane, all the boats broken loose from their moorings and beating themselves against the shore. She was torn from her own identity, even from her anchor in the present. Adrift in too many ways, susceptible to every wind.

Yesterday afternoon, she had napped as Joyce had settled into her hotel room, three doors down from Cree's. Dreams of Mike troubled her. By the time she'd awakened, it was dark, and the rain still swirled madly outside. She checked her voice mail and found a message from Charmian Beauforte scheduling this meeting. She stifled a pang of disappointment that there wasn't one from Paul, and then the confusion of loyalties rose up to torment her.

Even Joyce admitted that it was not a good night for cruising the Quarter, so while she set up her computer and began doing some Web research, Cree drove over to Beauforte House.

The Garden District was battened down in the rain, its streets empty and few porch lights lit. The live oaks roared and groaned in the wind and cast thrashing patterns of shadow and streetlight against the walls of the big house. Inside, Cree took off her raincoat and left it in the front hall. *No high tech tonight*, she'd resolved earlier. Edgar would be furious if she had a good contact but missed an opportunity to record some empirical evidence of it. But the devices always demanded some share of her attention, and right now she didn't need any more distractions. She groped in near-total dark back to the study, feeling desperate for progress in this case. Identify the ghost or ghosts, release them before somebody got hurt. Go home, get a life.

Beyond the ubiquitous rush and hiss of rain, the house was full of little noises as the wind probed and bullied it: ticks and taps, groans and scraping noises. The windows of the kitchen were vague, mist-opaqued rectangles, the back hall doorway just a black rectangle. The library itself was a cave of darkness.

Cree knocked her thigh painfully against the arm of her chair before she knew it was there but otherwise managed to get seated without making a ruckus. She sat and tried to muster her professional discipline. Calm the breath, the mind will follow.

Much later, the darkness seemed to have a mist in it. It was turgid with feeling: rage and regret, a soul-wrenching confusion. A keening sense of betrayal and loss, replaced by outrage and wrath. The hazy phantom materialized again, stuff of mind and darkness, the outrage burst like a boil, the beating motion began. A paroxysm, a convulsion. There seemed to be a disturbance in the wind of darkness near the door: another figure?

Then she penetrated the beating, and she saw it was only the edge, the outer layer, of something more urgent. What was really happening was the sharp smell of almonds and that pain in the abdomen. This time Cree felt it, low in her gut, doubling her over, felt herself fall and become the writhing puddle on the floor. Then came the calling out, the seeking, as some part of the ghost's psyche homed toward what was most important to it. The arrow of yearning lofted toward the dying person's heart's desire: the girl on the swing, the house with patches of sunlight on its walls, the green canopy of leaves with blue sky behind, and a feeling of things being right and in their place.

Paradoxically, though she was better able to sustain the violence of the beating this time, she pulled away from that last part. It felt as if that arrow of poignancy could kill her.

Dismayed at her inability to overcome her own fears and self-protective reflexes, she pulled back from it, left the library, and returned to the front of the house. She considered trying to brave the upstairs, to challenge the boar-headed ghost in his domain. For a time she stood looking up the stairway into the patchwork light and dark, straining to hear through the white noise of the rain. All it took was a vague sense of his presence, a faint reprise of the dark lust and self-hatred, to make her realize she couldn't do it. She was still too afraid, exhausted and in turmoil and defenseless. She was being crazy and desperate and every-thing Edgar had warned her about.

She left the house hurriedly, returning to the hotel after two in the morning, feeling bruised and ragged.

And of course Charmian was sure to see her state and exploit it in some sadistic way.

"I've been thinking about you," Charmian said. She walked straight-backed ahead of Cree to the living room, mastering her limp almost completely. Today she wore a tailored beige pants suit, a yellow silk scarf knotted stylishly at her wizened throat, pearl earrings, a tasteful blush of makeup.

"I'm flattered. Why?"

"Paul Fitzpatrick tells me that you saved my daughter's life. I'm grateful."

"Really, I just happened to go to the house while she was there. I was lucky."

"And did you see the ghost?" Charmian sat herself in a wingback chair, poised and regal, crossing her good leg over the other at the knee. The tightening of her face gave way to a hard little smile that flickered at the corners of her lips, showing that she intended the question rhetori-cally, condescendingly.

"As a matter of fact, I did."

"Did it reveal its terrible secrets?"

Cree tossed her purse onto the couch and threw herself beside it. "You know what I think? I think *you're* the one with the secrets, Charmian. I can't make you tell me, but I'm not going to sit here and play straight man for your sarcastic wit. If you want entertainment, go watch another slide show with your geriatric buddies. I've got a job to do. Are you going to help me or not?"

"Why are you so out of sorts?" Charmian countered. "I hope this doesn't mean your budding romance with Dr. Fitzpatrick is going awry?"

Cree gaped.

"It doesn't take extrasensory perception to notice the way you two speak of each other. Your excessive 'professional' respect and consideration, the way your voices modulate when you pronounce each other's names. I'm pleased for you, really I am."

"Tell me what happened to Lila when she was fourteen. What changed her."

Charmian didn't gape; Cree thought she was probably incapable of it. But her lower eyelids ticced before her face stiffened into its inscrutable mask. "Her father died. They'd been very close. She went off to school. It was a very difficult time for – "

"Worse than that."

"She had something of a nervous breakdown during her first term. A battle with depression and anxiety. It was completely understandable. Two family deaths within one year, going away from home . . . I was a wreck and had nothing to offer her. Her world was coming apart."

"*Before* she went to school. Something that made her hate herself so much that now she breaks mirrors so she won't have to *look* at herself!"

Charmian held herself absolutely motionless. "I haven't any earthly idea. Why don't you ask your ghost?"

Cree returned the implacable stare. Then the telephone on the table next to Charmian rang, startling both women and breaking their locked gazes. Charmian answered it, spoke briefly, and hung up.

"I am going on an outing today," Charmian said drily, "a jaunt with some of my 'geriatric buddies' of the Garden Society. The van will be here in fifteen minutes."

"Why did you schedule – "

"I'm so sorry. We had planned a garden tour in Baton Rouge, but I'd assumed it would be canceled due to the weather. Now they say the rain is letting up and it's on again. I'm sorry for any inconvenience this may have caused you." Charmian stood, limped into the kitchen. Cree followed her. With her back to Cree, she began packing a large leather handbag: a pill bottle, a pack of facial tissues, an apple, a pair of fine calf-skin gloves.

Cree spoke to her back. "Do you have any idea where Josephine Dupree went after she left your employ?"

"None."

"Have you any idea who would put hoodoo hexes at Beauforte House? Or why?"

That seemed to bring a stiffening to the squared shoulders, but Charmian just said, "Of course not."

Charmian had clearly decided not to give anything, and Cree's frustration spiked. "There's something you should know, Charmian. Bad ghosts kill and maim people. Some do it directly, most do it by driving people to suicide. Or to incurable psychosis. Are you aware that this situation could kill your daughter? That information you give me could save her life? Do you even *care?*"

That brought Charmian around fast. "Don't you *ever* impugn my concern for my children! Don't you *dare* presume to educate me about my familial responsibilities! You know *nothing* about my feelings toward my children!"

The old woman was breathing hard now, and with the tendons on her corded neck standing forward, her brows arched and eyes blazing, she was physically intimidating despite her age and size. Cree felt the radiation of her emotion, a fierce, enormous, invisible energy like heat from a smelter.

"I think there are two ghosts," Cree persisted. "Do you know who they are?"

A flicker of the eyelids, something hitting the target, but no other response.

"A little girl in a swing," Cree blurted desperately. "A sunny day. One of the ghosts, that's his . . . his homing impulse, that's what he yearns for, that's the big unresolved thing for him."

Charmian's shoulders hunched suddenly as if Cree had punched her in the stomach, and she lurched forward a half step to keep her balance. It lasted only an instant; she drew herself back up with implacable will. Still she said nothing.

"Who are they, Charmian?" Cree asked, trying to tame her urgency. "Could the girl be Lila? Could the ghost be Richard?"

That didn't completely make sense, not with the beating motion, the other figure there, the affect of wrath and regret, but it was the only possibility Cree could think of. Two ghosts – one being Richard, dying of his heart attack and overcome with love for his daughter, and the other one the boar-headed man? But no, the figure dying on the floor was not having a heart attack: The pain had been too low, gut-deep.

Charmian's face changed. The angry blaze had given way to a look of shock and, for the first time in Cree's memory, uncertainty. But by degrees that faded, mastered with difficulty, to be replaced by the ancient, wise, hard look. She turned and limped away to the windows, where she stared sightlessly out at her garden. The rain had not fully stopped, but the overcast was broken now with brighter spots.

"Life is not a simple proposition, is it Ms. Black? It is mysterious, as you well know. It surprises us and confounds us continually. And all we can do is make the best judgments we can at the time and hope we've made the right choices and done the right things. But we are wrong at least half the time, aren't we? And then our mistakes compound our quandary tenfold. You of all people must know what it is to be something of a prisoner to one's own past. To one's own stubborn predilections." She gestured at the garden, where petals strewn by last night's winds spotted the glistening leaves.

"We're only prisoner to things we've left unresolved. Those haunt us until we deal with them." Cree wanted to press Charmian for specifics but stopped herself: better to see where the old woman took it.

"You're very talented," Charmian went on. "I can see now that I underestimated you."

She seemed about to say more, but the housemaid appeared in the doorway. "The van is here, ma'am. They waitin' out front."

Charmian flipped a hand and the maid vanished again. Still facing the garden, Charmian bit her lips and appeared deep in thought.

At last she turned, limped toward Cree, stopped in front of her, and gave her a penetratingly candid, curious look. "You're like a mirror, aren't you? You change around me — you become like me. I must admit it's quite remarkable, even if the reflection you offer is most unflattering!" The raying wrinkles revealed a flash of sardonic humor as she said that, but the expression passed and she became serious again. "And you do it for each person you meet, don't you? At moments I see Lila in you so strongly! Look at you now, the way you wring your wrists, that's one of her gestures! It's not really something you can control, is it?"

Cree took her hands away from each other but didn't say anything. The old woman seemed to be hesitating at the edge of some important decision.

The maid returned. "I'm sorry, ma'am, I tell him to wait, but he say they goin' be late they don't go soon — "

"Tell him I'll be right *there*, Tarika," Charmian ordered. When Tarika had gone again, she continued to look at Cree with that curious light. "I can imagine it would be difficult — that you could lose yourself in the process. And one has to wonder whether it is something you can do for yourself." The question didn't seem intended as just another of Charmian's provocations.

"I'm workin' on it, Charmian," Cree said gruffly.

Charmian limped past, looping the strap of her handbag over one shoulder as she headed for the door. She stopped at the hall doorway and turned again. " 'That which is unresolved lives on.' You're absolutely right — that's really what all this adds up to, isn't it? So true. In so many ways. If only we had all been wise enough to know that from the start."

She didn't wait for a reply but headed down the hall. Tarika stood at the open front door, waiting to help her to the van.

Cree caught up with Joyce at the Williams Research Center on Chartres Street, in the heart of the French Quarter. She had arranged to meet Lila at three-thirty, leaving just enough time for a few other errands, and then had called Joyce's cell phone number. Joyce told her she'd already had a productive day and that she'd be glad for a quick conference.

The Williams occupied a splendidly restored building that, according to an informational plaque, had once been a fire station. Cree rang the bell and was buzzed inside to a cool, spacious marble lobby, where a receptionist asked her to register and directed her to the main reading room on the second floor. This proved to be a two-story chamber with balconies on two sides, lit by huge hemispherical chandeliers and ceiling-height windows topped by gracious fanlights. Bookshelves lined both levels, and microfiche carrels lined a darkened alcove. Here and there, other researchers sat singly or conferred quietly together.

Cree recognized a familiar pair of big sunglasses on one of the bent heads and went over to the table where Joyce sat.

"Hey," Cree whispered.

"Aha." Joyce patted the chair next to her and slid a stack of photocopies toward Cree. "I'm about to hit the microfilm on Richard Beauforte. But I did get you some goods on that murdered servant. Take a look."

Cree sat and looked over the papers, which reproduced short articles from newspapers of August 1882. The first, from the *Times-Picayune*'s daily "Crimes and Casualties" feature, gave the basic information; a follow-up article filled in the details in the florid, opinionated journalistic style of the day. Lionel Daniels, a former slave who was now houseman for the Beaufortes, had responded violently when his employer – the papers still referred to John Frederick Beauforte as his "master" – accused him of stealing two silver candlesticks. In self-defense, John Frederick had "seized the fireplace poker that stood nearby and administered several blows to the negro's head and torso." Still, "a negro of in-temperate disposition and imposing physical stature," Lionel wouldn't desist, so John Frederick had beaten him further, inflicting a fatal wound. The Metropolitan Police found the downstairs library of Beauforte House "in a state of utter disarray that bespoke the vehemence of the servant's temper." "Court officers agreed that a clearer case of self-defense could hardly be imagined and expressed hope that the incident will provide a corrective example for others tempted by larcenous inclinations."

"There's your beating motion," Joyce whispered. "In the library, too."

Cree thought about that. It was possible, but the idea that the ghosts were John Frederick or Lionel created as many questions as it answered. For starters, she would expect to experience the scene from the perspective of Lionel, not that of John Frederick, who died during a business trip to Vicksburg many years afterward. And why would either ghost manifest now? And what explained Lila's suscept-ibility – what was the link to the Beaufortes of today? Not to mention the problems suggested by the boar-headed man, the wolf, the smoke snake.

She took out her own notebook and pen and was about to jot some notes when Joyce hissed, "*Put that away!* Jesus, Cree, no pens in here! Really, seriously, pencils only." Eyes wide with alarm, she tipped her chin toward the staff desk, where one of the archivists had stood up and was shaking her head at Cree. Joyce put her lips to Cree's ear: "She's very sweet and helpful, unless you use a pen. Then she turns into, I don't know, Helga the She-Wolf of the SS or something. They're fanatics about not getting ink on archival materials here."

Cree put her pen away and took the pencil Joyce offered.

"Obviously the articles reveal a certain . . . bias," Joyce went on. "So I went a little deeper. This place has a great collection of personal correspondence from members of prominent New Orleans families, nineteenth and early twentieth centuries. The Beaufortes are well represented. I was able to find one from John Frederick to a cousin of his, from the period right after the incident."

This was a photocopy of an elegantly handwritten letter that had faded with age, harder to read. John Frederick confided that he had grown impatient with Lionel for his "reluctance" to do some of his chores as instructed, and that he had resolved to "take a firm hand" with him. From the letter's tone, Cree inferred that while the beating was certainly intentional, Lionel's death was not. Still, John Frederick boasted that the episode had greatly improved discipline among the other servants.

Cree turned the pages facedown, feeling a little sick. "Joyce, I wanted to tell you – "

"*And*," Joyce whispered excitedly, "I got your architectural plans. Went to Tulane and nagged 'em." She handed Cree a key with a number tag attached. "They're in a big tube. Had to check it into a locker downstairs, but you can pick it up on your way out. We can do the spatiotemp tonight, if you like."

"Great. It'd be best to have one of the Beaufortes with us," Cree told her. "Probably Ron – if he'll stoop. Can you call and ask him to accompany us? I think he's a little angry with me right now – "

"The guy who came to our office? The handsome one? Great idea."

Cree sighed and put the key into her purse. "Joyce, I've got a favor to ask."

"Sure."

Still chipper, Joyce waited expectantly. But suddenly Cree couldn't name the favor. It had to do with what Cree was doing, the radical balance she had to find. But there was no way to describe that. And no way, really, to know what form it might take.

"I think I'll probably need to go a little crazy," Cree said at last. "To get to the bottom of this."

Joyce sobered. "I got news – you're already a little crazy."

"A lot crazy, then. And I need you to trust me when I do." Cree was shocked to hear an echo of Lila's voice in the plea: *Stay with me.*

"I'm not sure I – "

"Just that I've realized I have to take this case very personally if I'm going to make any progress. But I don't want you to worry too much. Don't . . . overreact or something."

"Don't worry? Don't *worry?* I'm worrying already! What does Ed think about all this?"

"I haven't talked to him. And if you do, tell him I'm fine, I'm doing great. No need to get him all – "

"I don't know what you're asking me to agree to, Cree. But I don't like the sound of it." Joyce's voice had risen, drawing the archivist's disapproving gaze.

Cree stood up and gathered up the papers and folded them into her purse. "Gotta go. This is great work. I'll see you tonight, okay? We'll look for some Cajun food. I promise."

The promise didn't seem to make Joyce any happier.

27

CHARMIAN COULD REMEMBER WHEN she'd actually enjoyed these outings. It had once given her pleasure to visit the marvelous formal gardens in and around New Orleans and Baton Rouge, to trade tips on planting and pruning, or where to buy the best bulbs or slips. It was an opportunity to get out of the house and see some countryside while you shared complaints about your servants and your grandchildren and your husband, if you still had one. Which most of the Garden Society did not, any longer: The van was full of puffs of blue-white hair.

My "geriatric buddies," Charmian thought sourly.

But over the last couple of years the outings had become nearly intolerable. She went along only out of a sense of obligation as their chairwoman. The rides were tedious, the van claustrophobic, the gossip savage and as small-minded as it was hugely irrelevant. The blue-haired blue-bloods looked refined, but Charmian knew *that* for what it was: a veneer of delicacy over a hard, ruthless core. They were vicious social carnivores only too eager to use their money and position against the less privileged or each other. After two decades of rising crime in New Orleans, most of them had even started carrying pistols in their purses – Charmian herself had succumbed to the fashion. The little ladies' guns were supposedly for self-defense against the criminal underclasses, but looking at the busy blue heads now she suspected it was only a matter of time before their disagreements about how to fertilize an oleander, or what dish to order at Antoine's, brought the guns out.

It was an uncharitable perspective, she knew, one sharpened by the knowledge that it applied to herself as much as the others. But now even the gardens had lost their appeal. Especially since the events of the last few months.

Still, this time she'd been actually relieved when the van had come, grateful that Tarika had interrupted her talk with Cree Black. An excuse to escape, to have time to think. She'd felt some of her resolve slipping, indecision stealing in as the woman probed her.

Inconceivable: Charmian Celeste Lambert Beauforte beating a retreat from someone of Cree Black's class and background!

Being undecided was an invitation to the world to wreak its worst upon you. Decisiveness was the foundation of strength. Even if you made the wrong decision, making any at all allowed you to act with authority, the certainty born of resolve. And that was always better than vacillating, hesitating, allowing the world to act upon you rather than you upon it. And you *never* retreated.

"You heard about Billie? Isn't it just too *terrible?*" Lydia Lanier whispered loudly.

Lydia was a plump, shapeless old thing with excruciatingly bad taste in expensive clothes, and her face showed that however terrible Billie's misfortune might be, Lydia was loving every minute of it. When Lydia had clumped aboard the van, Charmian had prayed that she wouldn't choose the empty seat next to her. There *were* other seats – only eleven members had opted for this tour. But she had, obviously because she was burning to tell Charmian this little tidbit. And she was a big woman, overflowing the seat next to Charmian, crowding her with upper arms the size of hams and thighs like sofa cushions.

"Terrible," Charmian agreed. Whatever it was. She turned her face to the window to signal her desire to be left alone with her thoughts. The van headed north through the city toward the Ponchartrain causeway.

The thing to do was to regain composure, take the initiative. Pull back to a different line of defense and consolidate it. Clearly, from what she'd seen and what Paul Fitzpatrick had told her, she'd underestimated Cree Black. The woman was not the persuasive charlatan she'd hoped would spread some palliative balm on Lila's problem, calm her down, help her past this crisis. She had some freakish talents of insight or perception, and she had a quality of . . . what? Not idealism, because she had clearly seen and experienced too much to be naively optimistic about the human condition. Charmian tried various words, and none of them quite fit Cree Black, that quality that made her so dangerous. Maybe *commitment* was the word: She had a deeply held philosophical belief that you had to get to the bottom of things, that doing so was always the best path, always the best foundation of healing.

So maybe she was naive after all.

"Not that we all couldn't see it coming," Lydia Lanier went on nastily.

Charmian turned to look at her, affronted at her intrusion, and gave her a gaze that would have withered a vase of zinnias. But Lydia was either too stupid to notice the look or too arrogant to acknowledge it. Charmian almost said something sharp, but there was no point: It'd only get passed around and cause a ruckus, get all the busy hens squawking.

"Tell me what you've heard," she whispered conspiratorially.

Lydia tipped her big head toward Charmian, lowered her voice, and told the tale. Charmian tried to look appropriately scandalized and tuned her out.

The van took them up the ramp onto Route 10, and the city dropped away beneath them. In few moments, the huge cemetery complex opened on both sides of the highway, the innumerable crypts mottled gray after the rain, squalid looking. The sight gave Charmian a charge of energy. A little memento mori.

Okay, so Cree Black was determined to get to the bottom of this. And with her abilities, there was some chance she just might. *What made Lila hate herself so much she breaks mirrors?* – that was too close for comfort. But she could be obstructed. Better, she could be channeled, directed down paths that led only to partial, manageable truths. Charmian would need to decide the most secure line of defense and stick to it. Paul could help there.

She had thought it through so long ago, had done her best to figure all the probabilities and angles, had made decisions, and it had more or less worked. True, Lila had become the weak little thing she was, and in carving away the rotten places in her memory she had left big holes in her

264

life; but she had managed to marry, to have kids, to have a halfway decent house. And Charmian had come to believe it was done, closed, that all the guilts and ghosts had been permanently sealed away.

Until Josephine had reappeared and changed everything! Who would have thought the woman would live that long? She was older than Charmian, eighty at least by the time she'd appeared at Charmian's door, two years ago: tall, broad-shouldered, her hair a cloud of frizzled gray, her long, sinewy arms as tight and creased as hard salamis, her dark face drawn long with that tiresome excess of piety, sobriety, contrition. Intellectually, Charmian had long since forgiven her, but still the unexpected sight of her awakened a surge of rage that she had barely repressed.

The recollection made the area around Charmian's breastbone tighten, and for a few seconds she had a hard time breathing. She deliberately mustered a full, slow breath, hoping that Lydia wouldn't notice.

After Josephine's sudden reappearance and that one afternoon of confession and accusation, she'd disappeared again without a trace. Once Charmian had sorted through the implications of her visit, she had even discreetly hired Crescent City Confidential Services, a highly recommended private detective firm, to locate her. But they'd come up dry. And then Temp Chase got himself murdered, and it had seemed best to just let Josephine fade away again.

Cree Black had zeroed in on everything, every question she'd asked had been relevant. And she'd been in New Orleans for only five days! She really was a sort of medium. She'd seen two ghosts; soon she would learn who they were. She'd pinned down the dates. She'd asked about Josephine.

Josephine! The tension gripped Charmian's chest hard. Surely Cree couldn't find Josephine, not if Crescent City Confidential couldn't!

Or could she?

How to stop or deflect her? According to Ron, Lila had now hired Cree herself, slapped down a check for her retainer; there was no way to fire her. Maybe they needed to consider more strenuous means to be rid of the woman — something to consider there. Ron might have some ideas on that score. He certainly knew enough lowlifes who might be willing to take on an odd job.

Charmian inventoried the ways Cree might penetrate to the truth. One was certainly the photos. They were not at the house; they had not been there when Charmian had looked for them after Lila had announced her desire to move back in. But Charmian knew who must have taken them, the only person who could have, and Cree Black would no doubt find her way there eventually. Had he destroyed them, as would have made sense, or preserved them for some devious future use? Hard to say.

"You are in dreamland this morning!" Lydia said. "I hope this doesn't mean you forgot to take your little smart pills this morning, darlin'? You haven't been listenin' to a word I've said!" The fat face loomed at Charmian, and suddenly she knew she couldn't do this, couldn't spend the day in Baton Rouge with the Garden Society and pretend that there was nothing the matter, and put up with Lydia and whoever else wanted to pour trivialities into her ear. She couldn't do it. Not when there was so much to be done. Not when the family was in danger.

That thought gave her resolve. But she'd have to act fast. The van had left the highway and turned north on Causeway Boulevard, and if she didn't get out now they'd get onto twenty-eight hellish miles of bridge and from the middle of the lake there'd be no turning back, she'd have to go to Baton Rouge and a day would be lost. And Cree Black would make more connections.

"I need to get out of this seat," she told Lydia. "Now. Stand up and let me out."

Lydia's eyes widened in surprise but quickly narrowed shrewdly as she sensed Charmian's urgency. The woman had a radar that picked up other people's distress, which she positively *fed* upon. "Why, Charmian Beauforte, whatever is the matter?" she drawled, speaking as slowly as she could. "You look like – "

"Get out of my way, you prize sow!" Charmian hissed. "This instant!"

Lydia gasped audibly, and conversation in the nearest seats stopped as the gray and blue heads turned. Charmian shoved at Lydia until the pig hoisted her bulk, moved out of her seat, and stumbled back a step, too shocked to speak.

Charmian gathered her bag and got up and limped quickly to the front of the van. She took hold of the driver's shoulder and shook it. "Stop," she told him. "Right here. I need to get out of this vehicle."

The driver, a big black man in gray chauffeur's livery, tried to mask his surprise. "Uh, yes, ma'am. Uh, is there something I can help you with, Miz Beauforte?"

"Stop. Open the door. Now. I'm fine. I just remembered another appointment. Go on to Baton Rouge."

"Yes, ma'am."

He braked hard and pulled the door lever, and when it hissed open Charmian climbed down into the street. The whole van of Garden Society ladies looked at her out their windows, shocked, curious, calculating. *Enjoy it, ladies. Something really juicy to talk about,* Charmian thought savagely. The driver looked down at her briefly, hesitating, but at Charmian's imperious gesture shut the door and drove on.

Charmian straightened her clothes. She spotted a street sign and got her bearings, then took out her cell phone to call a cab.

Ronald's apartment was in a newer office and residential tower on the downtown side of Canal Street. Charmian paid the driver, got out, and went inside. It was not even noon, Ronald would probably still be regrouping from whatever excesses he'd indulged in last night. If she understood his schedule correctly, he'd expect to do some on-line work after lunch and maybe swing by his office by one-thirty, flirt with his secretaries and schmooze with a couple of clients. Well, today would have to be different. She hadn't called because she wanted to catch him by surprise, off balance, bowl him over and roll him right along, make him obey her before he had a chance to think about it. She'd tell him she knew he'd removed the photos, and what that implied, and she'd tell him that Cree Black was finding out everything, and that he'd better start believing in ghosts fast because they were about to come back and make his life hell.

She took the elevator up to the twenty-first floor and walked down to his apartment. She rang the bell insistently and for good measure slammed her bag against the door a couple of times. After a minute she heard the muffled noise of someone coming. The peephole eclipsed, and she heard him swearing inside as the locks rattled and the door opened.

"Goddamn it, Momma, what're you doing here? You know, I would greatly prefer it if you showed me the courtesy of *calling* before – "

"Let me in. We have some things to discuss."

Ronald didn't move. He had his pants on, at least, that was good, but he stood holding the half-open door in one hand and didn't budge. "Tell you the truth, Momma, this isn't the best time, thank you. I have company at the moment."

She jabbed at his chest with her knuckles, backing him up, and pushed past him. "Get rid of her. Now. And then get dressed and get your wits about you."

She strode ahead of him into his living room, a huge expanse of floor furnished and decorated in what she thought of as playboy-modern. It was complete with the obligatory scattering of liquor bottles and glasses on every horizontal surface, and even a couple of little mirrors, lying flat and faintly dusted with powder, that revealed the more exotic tastes of Ro-Ro and his friends. One wall was all glass, filling the space with a big view of the nearer downtown buildings and then the darker, uneven rooftops of the French Quarter.

Ronald followed her, positioned himself in front of her with a defiant posture, and opened his mouth to argue. But the look she gave him shut him up fast. A door closed in the hallway to the bedroom, and after another glance at Charmian's face Ronald shrugged and headed down there. She heard their voices behind the closed door and the thump of things being moved around in anger.

Charmian waited for whoever it was to hustle past resentfully. She was thinking feverishly, the plan shaping up. She had always been afraid something like this could happen, but she'd supported Lila's moving back into the house because it meant there was at least the possibility that something like a family could be reestablished there. After Lila and Jack, one of Lila's kids, eventually grandkids. They wouldn't be Warrens, grandchildren of Jack's lineage of used-car dealers and barely two steps up from white trash. They'd be Beaufortes – the house would change them. But even that was the least of it, really. It was about Lila. Moving in would assert her victory over the past. It was worth the risk. Or so she'd thought, six months ago. Now she was no longer sure.

Rebuild, Lila, certainly, Charmian thought. *Restore. Re-create. Renew. Just don't remember.*

28

A MADWOMAN IN A CAR. *That's what people see,* Cree thought. *Screw 'em.*

She drove the Taurus toward Lila's house, having a one-sided conversation with Mike. "What's she doing, Mike? How would you call it?"

He'd always had a shrewd eye for people's motives. They used to talk about their family relationships or work contacts, trying to untie the knots that came with any human interaction. Playing detective with the human psyche.

The Mike in her imagination didn't answer. He wasn't there; he was a memory from a day in Concord, that first autumn at the farmhouse. They'd just discovered that grapes still grew along the stone walls at the edge of their property. In the dry fall air, that fine New England light, you could smell the winey sweetness of them as you came near the sun-warmed stones. Finding the vines among the scrub had excited him, and as he looked eagerly for bunches of frosted-purple spheres he looked much younger, like a kid. The wind tugged his cowlick over and down across his eyes like an errant windshield wiper and he pushed it away repeatedly, unconsciously, so intent on finding the fruit. The animation in his dark, alert eyes.

"It's like she's playing a game of chess with me," she told him. "She keeps me at a distance, she won't tell me what I need to know. But today I could swear she was close to telling me something. What? Why didn't she?"

Mike didn't answer.

"No, it's not like chess. This is a game where I don't know the rules. I don't know the objective!"

She had stopped at a light, and the driver in the next car over seemed to be looking at her strangely. Below the level of the window, she gave him the finger.

"Is she steering me toward something, or away from something? Or is she just really ambivalent, changing her mind? What?" Mike didn't answer. She looked quickly over at the empty passenger seat as if she might catch him there if she were fast enough. Of course, it was empty but for her purse. In the rearview mirror she caught a glimpse of her own desperate eyes: madwoman.

"Let's put 'em in a big vat and trample 'em with our bare feet," Mike said. "Stain our legs purple to the knees. A New England bacchanal." They had collected about two handfuls of grapes, and he held them up to the sun and gazed at them. "Naked among the mashed grapes. An ecstatic, drunken frenzy – "

"All that with a half pint of grapes?"

"Right. The hell with the grapes. Who needs grapes?" He gave her a lusty, wild-eyed look.

They had laughed and pitched grapes at each other. Laughed until his eyes changed, suddenly got very serious with a penetrating realization that she intuited instantly: *Jesus, I really love this woman. She really loves me.* It took her breath away.

Cree slammed on the brakes barely in time to avoid hitting the car in front of her. Mike's face vanished, leaving an aching void. This was dangerous, she decided. You couldn't get sidetracked like that.

Stick to the plan, she reminded herself. She stopped at a hardware store to pick up some gardening gloves. When she returned to the car, she turned on the radio, a country and western station, too loud, and got lucky: not a soupy ballad but a clever, upbeat ditty about lovin' your pickup truck.

After a big rain, New Orleans started up with a sputter and a catch before it regained its momentum. The winds had spread leaves and trash on the pavement, and boughs lay on the residential streets. Where storm drains had clogged, puddles made moats at the curbs. The weather reports announced that the front had swerved farther east then originally expected, and the sky was expected to continue clearing. Still, people paused often to gaze upward, as if skeptical that the weather had passed.

As she'd expected, the Warrens' yard looked battered, its shrubs stooped and blossoms blown. Leaves and twigs littered the front yard, and scatters of petals dotted the grass and stuck, rain plastered, to the pillars.

Again the house was full of the muted din of the remodelers. When Lila led her into the dining room, Cree showed her the gardening gloves she'd bought. "Let's skip the photos and stuff today – I don't think either of us is up for that. Your yard is a mess. We should go outside and try to spruce things up, don't you think?"

Lila was dressed in a pretty, prim housedress and pumps, and at first she looked dumbfounded by the suggestion. But after a moment she nodded.

"I have to change my clothes," she said.

Lila led Cree out to the garage, and they brought rakes, pruning shears, a little kneeling bench, and a two-wheeled garden cart out into the lawn. Though the sky was clearing rapidly, the grass was still wet and a pattering of drops fell from the leaves of the live oaks. Lila had put on jeans and canvas tennis shoes and gloves, but now she stood in her own backyard and looked around as if she were dazed.

"I feel like a stranger here," she said. "A stranger to my own life."

"I know the feeling." Cree took one of the wire rakes and began sweeping the grass.

"This is deliberate, isn't it? Getting me out here? You're thinking this might have some therapeutic value."

"Yeah. But not just for you, believe me. I am in serious need of some grounding myself."

Lila nodded. She picked up one of the pruning shears and studied it as she opened and closed it a few times. "You probably want to know what happened yesterday, at the hospital."

"Of course."

"They did all kinds of tests – I felt like a lab rat. They don't have all the results yet, but the brain scans were normal. There's still some blood work to come in, but they don't expect anything from it."

"Are you relieved or disappointed?"

"A little of both." A wry flicker of a smile moved at the corners of her mouth. "I think Dr. Fitzpatrick felt the same. He said you'd told him to expect it, though."

Cree resisted the urge to ask about Paul. Instead, she disengaged a fallen branch from one of the shrubs and put it into the cart, then began sweeping some more leaves together.

After a tentative start, Lila began to work more confidently. Her hands moved deftly among the bent leaves and ragged blossoms, testing, snipping. When given a task to do, Cree thought, they were competent hands whose skillful movements seemed at odds with Lila's habitual uncertainty.

"I had an interesting meeting with your mother this morning," Cree said after a while.

"Oh?"

"A remarkable woman. Also a hard nut to crack."

"Yes. She's always been a . . . forceful personality. But she got more that way after Daddy died. Harder, I mean. Distant. That's how she coped with it."

Cree nodded. "Sounds like they loved each other a lot."

"Oh, for sure. It was something of a famous courtship. Two old families, all that. Very romantic." Lila smiled at the memory, but then her hands hesitated among the leaves and the smile eroded.

"What was that thought?"

"Oh. Just that it's sad – the year before he died, they were having some problems. I remember her starting to sleep in the other bedroom, and wondering about it. Finally I realized it was because when Uncle Brad died, she was so close to him, she needed to be alone more to deal with her grief. But then when Daddy died, I knew she felt guilty about having been so distant. About letting something come between them during his last days and all."

"That's pretty perceptive for a girl of, what – fourteen?"

Lila's hands went back to work. "Once upon a time," she said, both bitter and wistful. "But I suppose everybody looks back at some golden era of their lives and wonders where it went."

Cree stopped raking, startled. "I used those same words just last night! Talking about my own 'golden era.'"

"To Paul?" Lila glanced sideways, caught Cree's expression, and again her smile flickered weakly. "Don't be surprised. You two — it makes sense you'd be attracted to each other. You . . . seem to have a lot in common. And he *is* easy to confide in." She worked for another moment with determination, then stopped and gave Cree a direct look. "Are you going to tell me your story?"

"If you'd like me to."

Lila thought about that briefly, and her confidence faded abruptly. "Does it have a happy ending?"

For a moment, Cree thought of contriving what Lila must have needed very badly, a compassionate lie: *Sure, I dealt with what happened to me and came through it just fine and so will you.* But it wasn't true. It wasn't that easy, couldn't be.

"I don't know what kind of ending it has," Cree admitted.

They kept working, removing damaged branches and exploded blossoms, raking leaves, picking up twigs. The sun came through more strongly now, drying the foliage and drawing forth the muggy humidity. An occasional jogger went by on the levee path. Cree told her about Mike's death and reappearance, and the way it had changed her. If she couldn't promise a happy ending, she thought, there might at least be some affirmation in hearing someone else's ghost story.

She had hoped it would be easier the second time, but it wasn't. Again she felt things breaking inside, jarring and grinding and rearranging.

They finished up the large, central flower bed and then went to the east side of the lawn to attend to the beds along the fence. Lila didn't say anything for several minutes after Cree finished telling her saga. She was working in a dense azalea, kneeling on her little padded bench with her head bent forward like a penitent.

"Thank you," Lila said quietly. "I know it can't be easy. To tell all that."

"It fucking kills me. Sorry for my language. But I keep thinking it's important. To talk about it. It was you who helped make that clear to me."

"If you're looking for me to reciprocate, I can't. I've already told you everything that happened."

"It doesn't have to be about the hauntings. Lila, today your mother told me you'd had a nervous breakdown when you went off to boarding school. An episode of depression. What was that about?"

"There's nothing to tell. I hated the school, my family was falling apart, my uncle had died not long before. And then my daddy died during my first year. I missed him horribly. My mother was broken up and drinking too much, and even Josephine had left, so I had no one to talk to. I got . . . unglued."

"That's a lot for anyone to deal with."

Lila nodded. "Ron, it wrecked him up, too, just in a different way. He's two years older than me, but he was still living at home – he went to the public high school here. You wouldn't think it now, but before all that he was a . . . a sweet person. He used to be my confidant, my protector. But it scarred him terribly. The lesson he learned was that loving your family too much can hurt you. If you take *anything* seriously, it'll hurt you. So he's never married, never settled down, never taken anything seriously. He's never let himself care about anyone but Ron Beauforte – that's how he protected himself. Now it's just . . . who he is."

Cree thought that was a fair appraisal. "So, you . . . did you get any kind of help back then?"

"Oh, I left school for a couple of weeks. I came home and Momma had me see Dr. Fitzpatrick – Paul's father, an old family friend. She wasn't going to let someone outside our immediate circle see a Lambert-Beauforte in the shape I was in, God, no! She told me to show some spine, and he did what doctors did back then: gave me all kinds of pills. Anxiety pills, depression pills, pills to help me sleep – it's a wonder I didn't become an addict. After a while they sent me back to school."

"When did it end? Your . . . breakdown?"

Lila tipped awkwardly back on her haunches, a plump woman unused to sitting on the ground. "End? It never ended. I put my problems and my feelings and my past into a . . . a Mason jar, sealed it up tight. And did my best to keep them there. I became *this*." She sat back into the wet grass, gesturing at her body, her house, and her yard, and her expression turned sad and hollow. "I didn't rock the boat or draw attention. That's what you were supposed to do."

Cree's breath went out of her as she was buffeted by an aching sympathy. She felt that self-containment in Lila, that holding back, that clinging to a safe, predictable life, that rigid rule of doing what was expected. It was Lila's way of protecting herself, not so different from Ron's – except that in her case it was reinforced by all the traditional, safe, domestic women's roles, and by Jack Warren's good-ol'-boy, chubby-hubby expectations, and Charmian's tyranny, and it all fit together. No one had protested when Lila had locked herself away and that bright, sparkling girl disappeared.

"Is that what you meant the other day? When you said something had happened to you?"

"Oh, hell, I don't know. I can't remember my past, Cree. What I remember, it's all from those clippings and photos. It's a movie of a life, not a life. Paul said you were thinking about repressed memory. Maybe that's what it is. But I don't know – it just feels like there was the life then, and there's the life now, and they don't have a hell of a lot to do with each other."

"Lila, there are two ghosts. I don't know what to make of the wolf or the snake or the table, but there are two more . . . human . . . ghosts. One is the boar-headed man who chases you and hurts you. The other manifests mainly in the library. He goes through some act of violent beating and then later dies and feels a sad, beautiful longing. They're not the same person. Do you know who they are?"

"No!" Lila's eyes had widened at the idea. "I thought there's only one! How can you be sure?"

276

"It's more than the difference in their moods or their affects. They spring from different impulses. They're completely different kinds of manifestation. Different . . . levels."

"I don't understand anything you're saying! I only know what happens to me!" Lila's hand were working busily among the leaves and stems, but she was clipping anything, hacking away at healthy branches and tops full of unopened buds. Cree put her hand on her arm and was alarmed at the tension she felt there.

"We don't have to go into that now. Lila, I . . . I've been taking on your susceptibility to these ghosts — you understand that, right? But if I'm going to survive, I've got to take on your strength, too. I've got to absorb your determination and your persistence and your stubbornness. I've got to know your desire to . . . fix what's wrong with your life. You've got to show me how you survive." Cree hoped any of that made sense to her.

Lila's arm seemed to shiver beneath Cree's fingers. "I know why you told me about you and your husband," she said in a darkly hollow voice. "And I'm grateful. But see, your story, it's . . . beautiful. Sad, but beautiful. Mine — it's *not*. And there's nothing either of us can do about that."

Cree didn't know what to say.

"And as for how I survive," Lila went on, looking more like her mother now, "I survive by doing the next thing that needs doing. And the thing after that. Which right now probably means working on the yard here. You're very right — it is a mess."

The plumbers had left by the time they went back inside, but the tilers were still at work and the house was filled with the sharp chemical smell of adhesive. As Lila conferred with the men upstairs, Cree spent a few more minutes leafing through the Beauforte photos. Nothing new caught her eye. When Lila came back down, they hugged good-bye wordlessly and Cree left.

She wondered whether she had accomplished anything at all. Her attempts to build upon their earlier spirit of companionship had failed.

Lila had closed down, especially when Cree had told her there were two ghosts. The idea had upset her greatly; the image of her hands rooting and clipping blindly, indiscriminately, seemed to bode ill.

The only ray of hope Cree could find was a subtle one. It had to do with why Lila had chosen to move back to Beauforte House in the first place. Yes, Lila was in a box, a jar, constructed equally by herself, her family, her society. But her original desire to move back to Beauforte House was a proactive effort to break out of her boxed-in life. She had sought to reclaim that depth, that richness of texture. To reclaim the past, too. Lila's determination to move back there had to have an unconscious element of wanting to come to grips with her sealed-away past. On some level she understood her fundamental predicament and was willing to face it. That motivation was the essential foundation of any therapeutic process.

Cree turned left at the street and walked along the front of the Warrens' yard. They hadn't gotten this far in their cleanup effort, and leaves and twigs still littered the shrubs and flower beds. She walked toward the Taurus, absentmindedly picking fallen twigs from the front plantings. At the corner of the Warrens' lot, where the growth met the side fence, a larger branch had fallen, crimping the shrubs beneath, and reflexively she stopped to disengage it. When she pulled aside the surrounding foliage to lift it free, she saw something that turned the world suddenly upside down.

Behind the leaves, lashed against the rail of the fence at the corner: a finger-sized stick. It was tied with long blades of grass, or maybe the thin fronds of a palmetto. It had one notch carved crudely into it.

A hoodoo hex, just like the ones Deelie Brown had found at Beauforte House.

29

JOYCE WAS IN A GOOD MOOD when Cree got back to the hotel. "Mr. Beauforte agreed to meet us at the house at seven. But he sounded prickly. What'd you do to get him so bent out of shape?"

"My job."

Joyce nodded without conviction. Then she looked Cree up and down, noticing the wet grass stains on the knees of her jeans, the many faint scratches on her forearms. "*What* happened to *you?*"

"Gardening. The storm kind of wrecked up Lila's yard, so – "

"I mean what's got you so upset?"

Cree debated telling her about the hex but thought she'd wait, try to fit it into the pattern that teased at the edge of her thoughts. "Listen, Joyce . . . I don't know if I'm up for going to the house tonight. I've got some thinking to do. You don't really need me for this, anyway, you're better at it than I am. You go without me."

Joyce nodded, suspicious but apparently not too dismayed at the prospect of spending an evening alone with a guy who looked like Clark Gable with some meat on him.

"And you're right that Ro-Ro has something of a grudge against me right now. I have a feeling he'll be . . . more responsive to you."

In fact, Joyce had put on a short, form-fitting cotton knit dress and shoes with heels higher than one would normally consider helpful for fieldwork. Her hair was loose, a smooth fall of burnished ebony around her shoulders and over one eye, and she looked stunning.

Yes, Ro-Ro was likely to be very helpful tonight. Cree almost commented further, then thought better of it.

" 'Ro-Ro'?"

"Nickname. Some fraternity or Mardi Gras thing, I don't know."

When they looked over the plans, Cree felt a moment's dismay. As far as she could tell, the original builder's drawings seemed to accord perfectly with the current floor plan. The absence of architectural discrepancies would make it much harder to narrow down a ghost's time frame, to name the individuals and identify their predicaments. But you couldn't always tell at first; it could come down to a matter of inches, and for Joyce's benefit she carefully diagrammed Lila's sightings and her own. Downstairs, the library would be their primary focus. Upstairs, Cree was particularly interested in the central room, the hallway down the left wing, and the doorways to the bedrooms along that hall – the boar-headed ghost's preferred hiding places and hunting grounds.

Joyce took notes and asked the right questions, all business despite her outfit. It wasn't until after she'd gone that Cree felt some misgivings about letting her go alone. The more she thought about it, the more she realized that the hex at the Warrens' house implied a solid connection between the Chase murder and the Beaufortes. Couldn't be a coincidence. But what was the connection? Did it mean that Lila and Jack had been targets of the killer, too? Were they still?

But in any case, that the murder was still unsolved, as Joyce had pointed out earlier, meant that there was a murderer on the loose. For all they knew, the killer would decide that Joyce and Cree needed some murdering, too, if they started turning up facts that implicated him or her.

For all they knew, it was Ronald himself.

The thought gave Cree a jolt. Joyce walking around in the big dark house, alone with Ro-Ro. Was he capable of murder? She thought not – he was at bottom too cowardly, too lazy. But again it was hard to say: The propensity seemed intrinsic to human nature, lurking inside everyone, waiting for the right trigger. When Mike died, Cree had discovered it in herself as she lay awake at night and imagined revenge on the drunken bastard who had killed him.

She showered long and hot, scrubbed her skin until it was red, as if scouring her outside could cleanse the inside. When she came out she spread a couple of towels on the floor and sat in lotus position. Back straight, hands in the *dhyana mudra*. Breathe. Clear the mind.

But it didn't help. Frantically her thoughts scurried in search of some place of comfort and gravitated toward Mike. She fought back by reminding herself sternly that she was alone in a hotel room in New Orleans, that Mike was just a tiny memory circuit in her brain, glimmering and now going dark again. And that was no help, either.

Enough of this, she told herself. She hadn't been this bad in years.

She dressed quickly and fled the room. Maybe there'd be surcease in the streets.

This time she let the flow of Canal Street carry her past the narrow streets of the French Quarter, toward the Mississippi. It was after sunset now, but the many bright windows, streetlights, and illuminated signs made a cheerful false daylight. Every view promised excitement and diversion. She was briefly tempted by the mindless glitter and bustle of Harrah's huge casino complex but got only as far as the door, where the cacophony of thousands of electronic slot machine chimes felt as if it would burst her eardrums. Instead, she went another block down and made her way through to the riverfront. The scent of muddy water and diesel exhaust surrounded her as she mounted the levee steps. Riverfront promenades stretched to both sides; on the right, the docked paddle wheelers were alight with life and music, but to the left she could see heavy freighters forging slowly along or berthed under lighted loading gantries. Tourists strolled Moon Walk, couples hand in hand. Beneath a street lamp, an elderly black man sat on a bench playing a tenor sax, sweet, melancholy slow blues that wove seamlessly into the river-scented breeze.

Better, Cree decided.

She walked the length of the lighted section of the walk, turned back, sat briefly, then decided to keep moving. Sitting still invited memories she didn't want; walking seemed to give her energy. She needed to stay in the present.

Two ghosts. A woman with a locked-up life and something buried in her memory. An overbearing, aristocratic mother with secrets. A playboy brother who wouldn't mind some liquid capital. The beating motion in the library, the man dying and yearning toward the girl on the swing. The Chase murder. Hexes at Beauforte House and at Lila Warren's. It was all a whirling constellation of unconnected dots, suggesting but never revealing a pattern. Dizzying.

And that was *without* trying to figure in the imponderable: the wolf, the snake, the living table claws! Most of all, the predatory upstairs ghost with his hateful affect and the double anomalies of his boar's head and his complete lack of a perimortem dimension.

After a while, the teeming streets of the Quarter seemed to call to her. She left the riverbank, crossed the streetcar tracks, and came to the terraced park just below Jackson Square. On the other side, she descended to the street through a crowd gathered around a trio playing something that sounded like bayou bluegrass.

Decatur Street, she discovered, was a more family-oriented version of Bourbon Street, a broader avenue that separated the narrow streets of the Quarter from the river. New high-rise apartment buildings and hotels dominated the south side, but on the north side it was lined with fine historic buildings that housed shops and restaurants, in better repair than elsewhere in the Quarter. Unlike Bourbon Street, there were no strip clubs or body-piercing parlors, and only a couple of the low-budget, black-painted voodoo shops. Most stores maintained cheerful windows and catered to the impulses of middle-class consumers, offering strings of beads, packages of Cajun and Creole spices, postcards, dried and varnished alligator heads and other bayou kitsch, bogus *gris-gris* bags, crawfish- and jazz-themed artwork, illustrated T-shirts and billed caps. The sidewalks were crowded, the restaurants and bars wide open to the evening, the cars bumper to bumper.

Better, Cree thought. Flux. All the appetites of the living. It did help.

Drifting, she window-shopped. She lingered for a few moments in front of a store that specialized in hot sauces. Its window featured hundreds of bottles with luridly illustrated labels and hyperbolic names:

Ass in Hell, Thermonuclear Holocaust, Liquid Lucifer, Mother-in-Law's Revenge, Pain & Suffering, Bayou Butt Burner.

She drifted to the next window and was admiring its contents when abruptly she felt as though she'd stepped through a hole and fallen and hit hard.

The store was crammed with Mardi Gras supplies: overflowing racks of beads of every description in sizzling colors, racks of gaudy gowns and capes and boas. Armies of manikins strutting in full-body costumes. Wigs and hats of every kind on Styrofoam heads.

And *masks*. Hundreds of them: faces grimacing, leering, snarling, laughing, conniving, drunken, murderous, seductive, imperious, pathetic, dead. Dainty eye masks, feathered face masks, and whole-head, pullover rubber masks of Nixons, werewolves, aliens, clowns, corpses, witches, Satans, queens and kings, kindly grannies, chubby babies, drag queens, vampires.

Bird heads, frog heads, dog heads, alligator heads.

No boar heads, true. And the idea didn't solve the mystery of the wolf, the snake, the table and other changelings. But here at last was a possible explanation for at least one of the anomalous aspects of Lila's experience. Of course that's how he would clothe himself in his thoughts. Of course that's how she would see him – half memory, half spectral being. She was appalled that the possibility hadn't occurred to her sooner, in this of all places. *City of masks*.

With the realization came another, meshing with the first like pieces of a puzzle fitting seamlessly. She'd spent hours pouring over the Beauforte family archives, and they had revealed almost nothing of value. But now she realized that what the material had to tell her lay not in what it contained but in what it omitted.

There were no photos or clippings relating to the family's Mardi Gras activities.

The Beaufortes had been involved in all kinds of civic activities, and from everything she'd read or heard from Paul, Mardi Gras was the ultimate civic function in New Orleans. It had been a family tradition for both Lamberts and Beaufortes: Lila had spoken of her father's involvement in one of the krewes, what was it? Epicurus. The Krewe of Epicurus. Uncle Brad had been a member. Ro-Ro was a member. Even Paul Fitzpatrick was a member, as his father had been. Yet Cree had looked at all the family records, and they showed no indication that the Beaufortes participated in Mardi Gras in any way.

No, she hadn't looked at all of them. She'd looked at the ones Lila had. But Lila had said her mother had kept some at the old house, that they'd stayed over there when Charmian had moved on to Lakeside Manor and they'd rented to the Chases. No doubt in the locked storage room she'd sat in briefly, pondering her own cracked image in the mirror: those two oak file cabinets against the far wall of the room.

She checked her watch as she hurried through the teeming crowds back toward the hotel to get the car. It had been more than three hours since Joyce had gone to the house to meet Ronald. She wondered if they were still there. She hoped not. Ro-Ro would not approve of what she was going to do. If Charmian heard about it, she'd have apoplexy.

She was relieved to find the house dark when she pulled up in front: Joyce and Ro-Ro must have finished the architectural comparison.

Inside, she locked the door behind her, reset the security system, and headed immediately through the black central hall to the back of the house. The hush wrapped around her, filling her ears with a ringing silence that seemed composed of a chorus of faint whispers and mutters.

Hoping the boar-headed man was indeed confined to the upstairs, she turned from the kitchen to the back hall, found the storage room door largely by feel, and used her penlight to sort among the keys on the ring Lila had given her. When she went inside, she flipped the light switch: This was a night for normal-world processes.

The central chandelier gave the room a depressing yellow cast but shed enough light to see the humped dust cloths, the mirror with its face to the wall, the big file cabinets against the far wall. The leaves reaching between the window bars seemed to press against the glass like desperate hands.

Cree crossed the room and yanked on one of the drawer pulls.

Locked, of course. She tried a drawer in the second cabinet with the same result. She fished in her jacket pocket and tried several keys from the key ring. None worked.

Who would have the keys? Definitely not Lila; that had been the whole point of separating these files and keeping them here. Ron, maybe; Charmian, definitely. But Cree couldn't ask her for them, couldn't reveal where her thoughts were leading her. Not until she knew more. Charmian would figure out some new level of obstruction, some new complication.

Her father's voice spoke to her from memory, another one of his humorous philosophical axioms: *Hey, it's nothin' that brute force and ignorance won't fix.* A comment on the human penchant for crude, stupid solutions, as well as an admission that you could outsubtle yourself and were sometimes better off keeping things straightforward.

Cree took a turn through the room, looking for a tool, something like a crowbar. The best she could do was the rack of fireplace tools beside the old coal grate. The poker was by far the strongest, but its head was too thick to insert between drawer and case, so she started with the ash shovel, wedging the blade into the gap and prying until it opened enough to receive the point of the poker. It was a murderous implement, with a thumb-thick steel shaft and heavy, elephant-goad head – for all she knew, the very weapon that had been used to beat Lionel to death. The long shaft gave her excellent leverage, and though her first two heaves just broke away the edge of the drawer, the third made something snap loudly inside the cabinet. All three drawers had been freed.

She slid open the first drawer, aware that she had truly started down a one-way street. The drawer she'd levered was gashed and broken, bristling with splinters of oak. Sooner or later, Ronald or Charmian would come in here and see that the cabinet had been broken into. There was no going back now, no way to hide the fact that she knew enough to go this far. She had better find what she needed here.

She used both hands to sort through the files crammed into the top drawer. The first few were not what she had expected: folder after folder about Charmian's tennis activities, photos and clippings from a fairly

285

successful amateur career. Bradford, too. One newspaper clipping featured photos of both of them in their whites, winning some minor event: "Teen Tennis Twins Terrorize Tournament Foes," the headline ran. There were more Lambert family materials toward the back of the drawer, featuring Charmian's mother and father and particularly her brother Bradford. Brad had indeed been a handsome devil, Cree admitted. He grinned from the backs of thoroughbred horses, frowned studiously as he worked on a tennis stroke. Here was Brad at some high school ball or prom, teeth as white as his starched collar, with some dark-haired teen lovely wearing the wretched Mamie Eisenhower hairstyle of the 1950s. Brad with fishing gear, sometimes with Richard, showing off the fish they'd caught. Brad with Lila and Ronald at some Christmas gone by.

She came to the end of the drawer without finding any Mardi Gras materials.

But the second drawer was different, and it drew a drumbeat from Cree's pulse. "Epicurus 1954," one file tab read. These were miscellaneous materials indeed: photos of parties, of floats being prepared, of parades. Notes of minutes of krewe meetings, financial statements. Invitation lists for Carnival balls. Glossy eight-by-tens and photos clipped from newspapers, showing costumed partyers, some with masks and some without. A newspaper photo of Brad atop a streetlight post in the Quarter, shirtless, strings of beads around his neck, arms raised exultantly to the sky. Another showed Charmian as Marie Antoinette raising a glass high to toast her masked Louis, presumably Richard.

Greek themes were prominent in Epicurus costuming, no doubt in observance of its namesake, the philosopher. Aside from the identification of his name with the pursuit of pleasure and the refinement of taste, Cree didn't know anything about Epicurus, and she suspected that most krewe members didn't either. But it gave license for lots of togas, beards, and dusty wigs. Here was a photo of Bradford wearing a toga and a crown of laurel, looking more Roman than Greek as he tipped his head to drink lustily from a flagon.

She moved on to the next file, "Epicurus 1955." This held more of the same and even included a small, sequined face mask pressed flat among the papers. Her fingers skipped through, piece by piece, impatient for the revelation that had to be here.

For the parades, all participants wore costumes appropriate to whatever theme had been chosen for the year, but for the private parties and balls leading up to Fat Tuesday, individuals wore widely diverse costumes. In the early sixties, the styles of Epicurus seemed to evolve: 1962 showed a preference for decadent movement figures like Oscar Wilde and Aubrey Beardsley. Later still, maybe as sixties trends caught up with the krewe, the costumes became more widely varied. There were a few hedonistic-looking psychedelic rock stars. Brad settled into a few years as a pirate, maybe Jean Laffite. Ron entered the scene as a ghastly child Nero, with toga and fiddle. Richard spent two years in the early sixties as some fat chef: a face mask with ballooning red cheeks, a towering mushroom hat, white clothes stuffed with pillows – presumably some icon of the pleasure principle.

From the materials here, she could see it was just as Paul had explained: A krewe was little more than a party club. You got together every year at Carnival to have parties and balls and parades, culminating in the extravagances of Fat Tuesday. Each year the krewe's activities were presided over by a king, chosen by the membership; from the records, Cree could see that Richard had been king of Epicurus several times. To be chosen krewe king was a mixed blessing, apparently, because along with the honor came the obligation to pay for everything: The files for years when Richard had been king included ledgers for the money he spent on lavish feasts, the best booze, exotic entertainments, and ostentatious decorations. One newspaper article suggested that though Rex and Comus were still the most prestigious krewes, Epicurus was the most expensive to belong to – due, apparently to the obligations of providing a truly epicurean standard of feasting and entertainment.

Cree came to the end of the second drawer and went on to the third. She leafed through 1967 and 1968, and then came up short. The back of the drawer was empty. The files from 1969 onward were missing.

Of course! she realized. Charmian would have taken them away before

Lila moved back into the house. Cree knuckled her head, furious at her own stupidity. This had all been a waste of time. Of course Charmian would have been several steps ahead.

On the off chance there was something more to discover here, she retrieved the fireplace tools and went to work on the second cabinet. The locking mechanism of this one was more stubborn, and eventually she just broke away half of the top drawer. She ripped away the oak slab and shined her flashlight inside. It was empty. Knowing it was pointless, she reached inside anyway and managed to release the lower drawers. They were empty, too.

That the crucial years were missing half proved her guess, but half wasn't good enough.

In frustration, she almost pitched the poker across the room. Clearly she wasn't going to find records for the year she was really interested in. It would have been 1971, maybe 1972, she figured, when Lila had been raped by someone wearing a boar-head mask.

30

IT WAS CLOSE TO MIDNIGHT by the time she turned off the lights and locked the storage room door. She headed down the hall, trying to loosen joints that had grown stiff with immobility and tension. The adrenaline high she'd maintained since her epiphany on Decatur Street had kept her tense enough to scream for more than three hours.

She'd made it all the way to the kitchen before she realized there was a sound in the house.

A voice, whimpering. Not weeping, but beyond weeping: the convulsive, involuntary utterances of an injured person. A woman's voice.

Lila! Cree ran down the dark central hall, following the sound, and stopped to listen again from the entry hall. It was clearer there, the sound of devastation. From upstairs.

Cree took the steps two at a time, turned at the landing, and came into the central room.

"Lila?" she called. She groped until she found the light switch and flipped it. The big room filled with the dull yellow of the chandelier, the doorways dark rectangles all around. "Lila, it's Cree. You shouldn't have come here. This isn't safe. We've got to get you out of here."

There was no answer, just the continuing squelched exclamations of misery. It was a wet sound of breathy exhalations and throaty vocalizations, ragged grunts and sobs, arrhythmic, constricted, forced. Hard to tell where it was coming from. Cree stopped to listen, and suddenly the awful quality of the whimpering suddenly made sense. Not an injured person. A person *being* injured, right now.

A woman being raped.

"Lila, where are you?" Cree shouted. She moved to the head of the hallway and thought the sound was louder here. Lila had to be in one of the rooms down the hall, the master bedroom or maybe the room she'd occupied as a child.

She ran down to the master bedroom, turned into it, slapped the light switch. No one. Now the whimpering seemed to come from behind: the other bedroom! She raced across the hall, flung open the door, and looked in. Nothing. No one.

The noise stopped.

Cree stood still again just outside the room, looking up and down the hall, confused. "Lila?"

The ceiling light in the central room went out, leaving it a cavern at the end of the hall.

"Lila?" she called toward the dark rectangle.

"Lila?" an echo came back.

The voice sickened her. It was a parody of her voice, a man's voice straining to reach a woman's range. It was mocking her fear and concern, ridiculing her, taunting her.

At the end of the hall, thirty feet away, just where the lighted corridor met the shadow of the big room, down on the floor: two brown shoe tips.

Suddenly Cree felt him, all around, the gnarled malevolent affect lit with manic glee and lust. His mental weather closed around her suddenly and completely, suffocatingly close. It was a trap, she knew instantly, a reprise of a long-ago game of predation and terror. Without knowing it, she'd fallen into Lila's role.

And the anguished, injured whimpering – that had been a ghastly parody, too, the monster mimicking and belittling the sounds of his victim's suffering.

"Lila?" the parody voice jeered again. *"Lila?"* Taunting her, savoring her terror.

Still frozen with horror, Cree could see now that there was something above the shoe tips: yes, the edge of coarse fabric, rising and falling with his breathing. And above that, at head height, something else. Glistening skin beneath coarse bristles. The side of his face.

The awful cheek moved. *"Lila?"* The voice had changed subtly, not so much a sadistic parody any more. *"Lila?"* Now he seemed to be just calling the name of his victim, twisting the nuance so the implicit threat was clear.

Cree heard the name as if it were her own, and maybe it was, maybe she had become Lila to a sufficient degree that she could draw him as Lila did.

The bristles moved as he turned his head. And there was the snout, just visible around the corner, and then the snout inched forward until the mouth and then the eyes came around. The mouth was wet and red, and the eyes were bright and small and gleeful as they fixed her. The nostrils hissed with his excited breathing.

Fear seared her. She broke and ran down the hallway toward the back stairs. Her body fled instinctively, by simple animal reflex, but her thoughts persisted, trying to find reasons, explanations, precedent, anything that would give her the slightest control. But she'd never experienced anything like this: the *intentionality*, the malevolent interactivity. His physical solidity. His one-dimensionality: no conscience, no dying man's regrets to appeal to. She heard heavy footsteps charging behind her as she plunged into the smaller back stairwell and flung herself down into the pitch dark. But before she reached the landing, he was there, in front of her, boiling up out of the stairwell. His shape congealed out of darkness: two legs, two arms, a man's torso with a boar's humped, muscular shoulders, an impossibly thick neck, bristled jowls, and pointed ears.

"Lila?" he sneered.

Cree stumbled and grabbed the bannister, almost pitching onto him as she stopped her downward tumble. He lunged at her, and she could smell the rank stink of him, male sweat and something chemical.

She hurtled up the stairs again, tripped, heard him right behind her, felt his hands flail at her heels as she got her footing and leapt upward. She broke out into the upstairs hall, dimly realized that the lights had gone out here, too, and began to run down the dark hallway, to the front stairs and down. But just ahead of her, at the doorway to the master bedroom, she saw his shoulder and snout emerge, his arms reach to grapple her. She twisted as she burst past him, felt his clawing fingers scrape her stomach and rip her jacket.

Into the central room. He was so close behind her she couldn't slow down to turn into the stairway. But through the doorways ahead, the windows of the front rooms were rectangles of streetlight glow and foliage shadow, and they struck her as beautiful, salvation, proof there was an outer world, a normal world, and she wanted to fling herself at them and through them, anything to get away from the tangled evil of the boar-headed man. But a shape broke from the shadows of the room on the left, the mirror-tunnel room, and darted at her, and without thinking she shied the other way, a reflexive action so strong it was as if some force field had repelled her. The thick-necked silhouette lunged and her legs kicked her backward. Her thigh hit the railing at the top of the stairs, and she pitched out into the open black chasm of the stairwell.

Something broke loudly, and her arms flailed in midair, hands grasping at nothing. In the instant of fear and vertigo she felt a tiny explosion of gladness, that she'd fall and die and not have to endure what the shadowed thing rushing to the railing intended for her.

31

JOYCE CALLED CREE'S ROOM again and got the voice mail for the third time. Where was she? Maybe she'd gotten her priorities straight for once and had gone to see the psychiatrist.

Joyce was feeling edgy after the day's events, almost enough to call the guy, Fitzpatrick, just to check up on Cree. But then she realized, no way, if that was where Cree had taken off to, no interruptions would be desirable. Ten o'clock was not late.

It would have been nice to go out for some drinks and some music, but no, here she was sitting on the hotel bed with the television exploding in bursts of canned laughter for jokes she was too distracted to appreciate. Surely Cree would return at any moment. She was eager to tell her the results of her architectural comparison, but she also couldn't wait to unburden herself about what had happened with Ronald Beauforte.

She had driven over to Beauforte House to find him pacing in the foyer, dressed in charcoal slacks and matching turtleneck. Definitely a good-looking guy, who definitely gave her a bit of the appreciative once-over and probably caught her doing the same.

She apologized for Cree's absence – unnecessarily, because he was obviously glad she wasn't there – and then told him, "We really appreciate your making time for this. Your knowledge about the history of the house will really help us out."

"How else was I gonna keep an eye on what you all're doing?" he grumped. "Let's just see the damn plans." She got the sense that his surliness was mostly an act, just doing what was expected of him.

He led her into a huge room to the right, the front parlor, where she got her first real sense of the house. The place was big as a barn, about half furnished, all of it old stuff that was no doubt valuable but struck her as a little ragtag, especially the carpets – apparently the ambience of faded splendor was the thing in New Orleans. And the closed-in, musty smell and the dim light from the chandelier didn't exactly help matters.

They made space on a table and unrolled the plans, holding the corners down with an antique inkpot and paperweights.

"There's nothing different. I didn't change a thing," Ron told her, tracing the kitchen floor plan with a well-manicured finger. "Had the walls painted and new tile put on the floor, but I wasn't gonna change the layout of the whole damn kitchen."

Joyce explained that they were not particularly interested in the kitchen, and that so far they had no reason to think Lila's ghosts had any connection to the Chase murder. She thought he looked surprised and maybe a little pleased at first, then a little disappointed. Cree would read his responses better, she knew, and wondered again what she was doing tonight.

They started with the library. Ronald switched on the light, and Joyce set up her tools and spread the plans on a table near the door. It was a big room furnished in antiques and lined with bookshelves, its dark woods and prehistoric carpets and book spines soaking up the insufficient light from the ceiling chandelier. Joyce tried to sense whatever it was that Cree felt here, and couldn't. It was just a mildew-scented, deluxe-type old-fashioned library room that looked like it could use a makeover.

Still, she felt obligated to flatter the place. "Such a nice room. Very . . . um, masculine decor." Somehow, being alone in the big house with a man she didn't know at all, that sounded more flirtatious than she'd intended, one of those door openers you had to be careful with. Especially since there did seem to be a little buzz going.

"Yeah. Mainly it was my daddy's room. Used the desk there as his home office. Also where he and his gentlemen friends would repair after dinner for brandy and cigars. To discuss politics, business, and women in the time-honored fashion." He looked around as if remembering, and then his face made that sourpuss grin again.

"Looks like you've got a few memories here," she prodded. "What was that one?" She had the sonic measure, but under the circumstances her instincts told her it would be good to keep Ron's hands occupied. So she gave him one end of the hundred-foot tape and with a gesture commanded him to take it to the far wall.

The long steel band sang as Ron started across the room with it. "Something I don't usually tell with ladies present."

"Relax. It'd be a bit of a stretch to consider me a lady," Joyce reassured him. And then realized how *that* sounded.

Ronald turned to face her appreciatively. "My daddy and Uncle Brad and me. They took me in here, shut the door, and told me about the birds and bees. Kind of tag-teamed me. Daddy soberly gave me the biological facts and lectured me about the sacred responsibilities of marriage while Uncle Brad enthusiastically filled in the more explicitly, shall I say, 'romantic' side of it. Needless to say, the latter was vastly more appealing. They also gave me my first drink of whiskey to acknowledge my initiation into the secret knowledge of manhood. I was eleven. They must have done a good job all the way around, because I've had an enduring appreciation for both subjects ever since."

He looked at Joyce to check her reaction and continued to the back corner with the tape. "How the heck is measuring this old place going to help you?" he called over his shoulder.

Joyce jotted down the length and then explained some of the nuances of spatiotemporal divergence as they lifted the tape and carried it to the opposite wall. "Has to do with figuring out which world the ghost thinks it's in. For example, a ghost seen emerging from a wall suggests the wall didn't exist when the ghost was alive. And the converse is true – if a ghost's movements reflect the current configuration of the site, and we discover that there have been alterations, we can reasonably conclude that the ghost lived since those alterations were made. And the more Cree knows about *when* the ghost was alive, the easier it is for her to determine *who* the ghost is. And once she knows who it is, she can better figure out why it's here. In this case, we're particularly wondering about any changes since 1882, when John Frederick Beauforte killed the servant in this room."

"You know about that? We're going that far back for this?" Returning with the end of the tape, Ronald looked around, eyebrows high and lower lip thrust out, as if seeing the room in a new light. Again, she got the sense he was pleased or relieved.

They measured the four walls of the room, then began taking distances between its significant features: the fireplace, the windows, the door. Ron *was* cute, Joyce decided as he crouched to hold the end against the edge of the fireplace coping. His slacks pulled taut against nice buns, and though he had a just bit of a gut it was more than compensated for by the good shoulders and hunky back.

"Ro-Ro," Joyce said. "How did you get afflicted with that one?"

He gave her that grin, just a little sharklike, sarcastic but cute. "My uncle Brad. Seems I had a bit of a stutter when I was two years old. 'What's your name?' he'd ask. 'Ro-Ro-Ronnie,' I'd answer. He started teasing me with it, and it stuck − Ro-Ro."

When they were done with the horizontals, Joyce took a moment to jot some notes. Ron came to the table where she stood and leaned across her to reach over and switch on the table lamp. It was only partly a courteous gesture, more of a flirtation, Joyce decided. The extra light was nice, but afterward he half sat against the table edge, too close, looking at her. She was acutely aware of how near he was, how big he was, how alone they were in the cavernous, dark house. And from this close, she didn't really like everything she saw in his eyes. Something calculating, and selfish, and indulgent. Something else, too . . . a little *afraid*, maybe, as if somewhere in him was a scared boy putting on an act. The combination frightened her, and she decided maybe it was time to cool the boy-girl games.

"So you really believe all this stuff?" he asked. "This psychotherapy for ghosts?" His expression made it clear it was intended as a good-natured, skeptical jibe.

"Of course."

He shook his head, amazed. "And your boss, she really *sees* ghosts?"

"She sees them and communicates with them, yes."

"Can I ask you something?" Ron leaned in confidingly. "What's her problem, anyway? She's got this . . . shall we say, *chilly* side to her. Has she got . . . relationship problems? A problem with men?"

Joyce took a small step sideways. "You know, Ron, I don't think –"

He held up his hands. "I know, I know. Sorry. I know she's your boss, you're loyal. No insult intended, honest to God – I think the world of that woman. I do. I was just going to point out that *you*, by contrast, most definitely do *not* seem to possess that, uh, particular problem." He paused to observe her response, grinning at whatever he thought he saw in her face. Before she could reply, he pushed himself away from the table and dusted his hands together. "Well. What's next, milady? I am at your service – what dimensions or proportions would you like to measure next?"

They took the vertical dimensions, plumbs, and levels. By the time they were finished, it was clear that the library had not changed in the one hundred and fifty years since it had been built. And given that the built-in shelves, the fireplace, and the windows and door largely determined the placement of furniture, the patterns of human activity would probably be unchanged as well.

Joyce felt a flash of disappointment: The physical room could tell them nothing about the ghost Cree had seen there.

They moved upstairs. Ronald switched on the lights in the central room and cleared a space on a table for the second-floor schematics. Joyce took a moment to study them and get her bearings, trying to ignore how close he stood as he looked over her shoulder. She didn't look at him, but she could feel his eyes on her body, as if his gaze traced an uncomfortable heat. She wondered what had possessed her to wear this dress tonight. From this close, his scent surrounded her, and she was dismayed at how attractive she found it.

She didn't tell him the details, but Cree was particularly interested in the juncture of hallway and central room, where Lila had first seen the shoe tips, and where Cree herself had seen them. The owner of the shoes had clearly been standing just around that corner, as if pressing himself against the wall.

It took only one measurement to find a deviation: The distance from the corner to the first doorway down the hall was eighteen inches longer than the plan's specifications. The central room proved to be the same amount shorter.

"Oh, hell, of course!" Ronald said. Frowning at himself, he walked along the wall, rapping it with his knuckles. The wall at the corner gave forth a hollower sound, and Ron nodded as if he'd found what he expected. "Heating and air-conditioning ducts. Daddy put in the furnace in the old larder, that's almost directly below us. This's where the main air duct comes up for the second floor, they'd've needed more room than the thickness of the old wall. So they'd've built out the whole wall another foot or so. See the vents there, and over there? Air-conditioning uses the same ducts." He gestured toward louvered grates on two of the walls. "Did a good job of matching the cornice and ceiling paneling, that's why it's not more obvious. Kept the historical appearance."

Joyce noted the measurements. When they moved on down the hall, they found another deviation immediately: The door to Lila's old bedroom had been moved about two feet to the right, apparently to allow space for ducts between the door and a load-bearing member in the wall. There was no question, from what Lila had described, that the boar-headed man used that corner and these doorways – in exactly their current location – to conceal himself.

The library ghost's period of origination might still be unclear, but this ghost had to be from after 1949. Or else it was a very, very unusual critter of some kind.

"Looks like this tells you something important," Ron prodded.

"Maybe."

"So, what – Lila saw something here? What the hell did she see, anyway? Or was it Miz Doctor Black who saw something?"

"Actually, I don't know," Joyce lied. "Cree keeps those details confidential. Sorry."

"You're really not gonna tell me *anything?* After the yeoman's service I've rendered tonight? Surely I get some little reward!"

Joyce just rolled her eyes and went about setting up the laser level for the second-floor work.

They spent another half hour at it, but she knew they'd gotten what they'd come here for. She was dying to get back to the hotel and tell Cree. Also, the ambivalence she felt about Ron's attention was growing, and it would be nice to get out of here before one of them did or said something awkward. She was glad when she was finally able to put the tools away and roll up the plans again.

Eleven o'clock and still no sign of Cree. Wouldn't she have called if she were going to spend the night at Paul Fitzpatrick's house? How much simpler this would be if Cree would just carry a cell phone. But no, she avoided using them because after listening to Ed yammer about electromagnetic frequencies she was afraid habitual use would affect her brain and impair her sensitivities. Natch. Of course. Leaving her friends and associates with dilemmas like the current one.

Joyce lay propped on the pillows of her bed, surfing through the TV channels. She skipped over innumerable true crime, unsolved mysteries, and autopsy shows and settled for an old Peter Sellers movie. She found an emery board in her purse and began doing her nails.

If only the evening had ended there! she thought. But then the thing on the stairs had to happen. *Gawd, of course, Murphy's Law.*

They had turned out the lights in the upper central room and Joyce was following Ron down the stairway. She had deliberately *not* let him carry the toolboxes or the rolled plans for her so as to not invite assumptions or patronizing displays. And as a result she was burdened and couldn't see the stairs as well as she might have. Ron had just reached the floor and she was about three steps above him. He half turned to say something, and at that instant she lost her footing and pitched forward and down. And big handsome Ronald adroitly caught her in his arms.

And as if that wasn't bad enough, she didn't pull away immediately! Ron held her firmly against his broad chest, arms around her, supporting almost her whole weight, and she was so shocked by her fall, by suddenly finding his face so close to hers, by how . . . interesting his arms and chest and thighs felt pressed against her, that she *hesitated*. For all of five wordless seconds, probably.

At last she regained her wits enough to pull away. Ron didn't resist, just sort of let his hands trail off her shoulders and hip to show he let go only reluctantly.

"My God, excuse me!" Joyce said. "God, what a klutz I am!" Completely flustered, like a teenager. She bent to recover the things she'd dropped and held them to her chest as if they'd shield her. "I'm so sorry!"

"My pleasure, I assure you," Ron had said. Then he went to the security panel, paused with his hand over the keypad, and said nonchalantly, "Remind me – what was it ol' Doc Freud said about accidents, again?"

"He also said sometimes a cigar is just a cigar," she'd rejoined. And then realized that for Ron, that would carry all kinds of suggestive overtones, too.

They'd gotten out the door without further mishaps. Out on the sidewalk, she'd declined his invitation to go out for drinks. "Some other time, then," he'd said as a farewell. "I'll most definitely look forward to it."

Joyce winced at the memory. She hoped that her own lapses of professionalism wouldn't impede this case in some unforseen way. Cree had described Ron as a womanizer – unnecessarily, because anyone could tell that within the first thirty seconds of meeting him. But he was handsome and rich and he smelled good and this was *New Orleans*. And though true love was a terrific idea, Joyce had been divorced long enough to know that a good roll in the hay with someone who knew how to roll could be awfully damned terrific, too – in many ways preferable to a "relationship" and the sticky complications that too often came with. Ron was no doubt a loser, but his confidence in dealing with women probably had *some* basis in experience. It could come across as smug, if you didn't have comparable confidence yourself. Which Joyce prided herself on having.

So why had she let the encounter fluster her? Maybe because there were other things besides weakness and lust in his eyes – something hidden, something dark and repellent. Dangerous? Maybe. More obviously, she decided, some kind of internal *desperation*. No, that wasn't quite right. Cree would be better at giving it a name –

Cree! Joyce glanced at the clock radio again and was shocked to find that it was eleven-thirty. She had to be definitive: Would Cree, or would she not, call to let her know where she was? Ordinarily, yes, she would: A, because she wouldn't want Joyce to worry, and B, because tonight in particular Cree would be very interested in the outcome of the architectural work.

Okay, so would Cree, or would she not, call to let her know she was at Paul Fitzpatrick's, either staying very late or spending the night?

This was tougher to answer. Being a considerate person, Cree would probably want to call, but in certain situations the opportunity to do so gracefully might not present itself. Joyce sincerely hoped exactly those situations had arisen tonight.

So the real question, Joyce decided, was: Would Joyce née Wu formerly Feingold, or would she not, solely on the basis of her current anxiety, call Cree's possible lover's house to make sure she was okay?

She gave it another ten minutes of rising concern and decided that damn straight she would. She dialed information and got the number for Dr. Paul Fitzpatrick, already rehearsing her apologies.

32

THE CLATTER AND BUMP of things falling, the jolt and jar of hitting and rolling, merged with another noise – a harsh banging and rattling that didn't stop when the other noises did. Cree's head lolled dizzily as the geometric pattern of dark and darker above her spun and stabilized and she realized that she was looking up at the open rectangle of the stairwell and the line of the balustrade. She was lying diagonally on the stairs just below the landing. Her breath left her chest as she felt the boar-headed man moving up there, but with the clacking and banging at the door he seemed to withdraw, like a toxic smoke sucked away, inhaled by the house again.

She moved one arm and slid bruisingly down another step, barely catching herself before she tipped and rolled the rest of the way down.

"Cree! Cree! Are you there? Open the door!" A muffled voice accompanied the clacking. That heavy brass door knocker, that's what it was. And Joyce.

"Cree" referred to her. She wasn't Lila. Some relief in that.

Carefully, Cree rotated her body until her feet were lower than her head, disturbing a couple of broken balustrade rails that slid noisily down. When she sat up, her arms and legs and spine felt as if their component bones didn't fit any more, as if she'd been wrenched apart and put together incorrectly. Her hips hurt and her head was bruised, but the worst pain came from her left index finger, which must have gotten bent wrong when she landed. It had taken only a split second: flipping over the balustrade, knees smashing the rails hard enough to break several loose. Flailing into space. Her hands and head had hit the wall an instant before the rest of her had landed half on the landing and half on the steps just below it. It was a drop of only about six feet. She'd been lucky she hadn't fallen farther toward the front of the stairwell, or impaled herself on one of the broken rails that fell with her.

Clack-clack-clack-clack-clack! Clack-clack-clack-clack-clack!

Not ready to stand, she moved her butt down one step and then another and then another. When her feet hit the floorboards, she lurched upright and staggered to the front door. It was hard to unlock in the dark with her uncooperative index finger, but after a moment of fumbling she got the door open and Joyce burst in with a shaft of blue light from the street.

"Cree! Are you all right?"

"There *is* a doorbell, Joyce. Jesus!" That didn't seem appropriate. Joyce had asked her something, and after a hesitation, Cree remembered what. "I'm shitty. But I'm okay," she muttered. Her jaw felt joined wrong, too. She turned to the security panel and reset it, feeling a little proud of herself for being so lucid. No point in bringing the *gendarmes* or whatever they'd be called here.

Joyce brushed past her, groping on the walls until she found the light switch. The chandelier came on and there was Joyce, face fierce, eyes wide, can of pepper spray at the ready. The stairway was littered with broken rails, and Cree saw one of her shoes there, too. She hadn't realized she'd lost it until that moment. She had only one shoe on, which helped account for some of the difficulty of standing. That was nice, she thought, because it meant you could put on your other shoe and then maybe your legs would work right.

"Sit down!" Joyce ordered. "Tell me exactly what happened. I need to check you out."

That's right, Cree thought appreciatively, Joyce had been an EMT in one of her previous careers. Amazing Joyce.

Loving her enormously, Cree said, "I'm so very glad to see you." It struck her as sounding formal and funny.

She told the story of being pursued by the boar-headed ghost as Joyce felt her limbs and tested her joints, inspected her abrasions, palpated her abdomen, found Cree's flashlight and checked the pupils of her eyes. At last Joyce made her get up, walk a bit, and balance on one foot.

"The finger's badly sprained, but otherwise I think you're all right," Joyce said incredulously. She looked up at the long flight of stairs, shaking her head. "You could have been killed! You're in shock, Cree. We've got to get you to a hospital."

"Nah. I'm great."

"Bullshit!" Joyce probably would have gone on more of a tirade, but another realization struck her: "Cree . . . you've never run away from a ghost before!" She sounded frightened.

"Not so good, huh? Not a good trend, no."

"Listen to yourself! Your being flippant just proves you're in shock."

Cree kept pacing, trying to flex out kinks, trying to get her thoughts together. At the rear of the entry hall, she caught sight of herself in the big, gilt-framed mirror there. Her hair was snarled, her jaw marred with a red swelling, her lips and teeth rimmed with blood. Both armpits of her jacket had sprung, and one pocket had become an upside-down flap of fabric. Her blouse was untucked and had lost buttons at top and bottom, and her knees had burst through the denim of her jeans. She'd been feeling almost giddy, opiated by shock and her unexpected rescue from the boar-headed man, but the image in the mirror threw cold water on that fast.

She looked like Lila.

Things were getting out of hand, she realized. There was work to be done, and there was a lot to tell Joyce. She whirled to face her just as a jarring buzz echoed from the dark hallway near the kitchen. Cree startled and retreated several steps before she realized it was the doorbell.

Joyce didn't seem as surprised. She opened the door to let Paul Fitzpatrick in.

The three of them sat on a bench in the emergency ward admitting room, waiting for someone to treat Cree's finger. In the nightly triage of New Orleans, Paul warned them, it might be a longish wait: the Big Easy had the highest violent crime rate in the country, and sprained fingers and contusions didn't rate against bullet and knife wounds. The finger throbbed and swelled to an obscene size despite the ice pack an orderly had given her.

Cree hated emergency wards. They were jagged, scary psychic spaces where a lot of pain and anxiety had been concentrated and where many deaths had taken place. The unending energy and determination of generations of medical staff were also here, a strong, bright river that cleansed and renewed, but nothing could wash away all the sorrows.

Cree concentrated on the welcome distraction of physical pain.

And on the growing excitement she felt. She knew it was partly the irrational euphoria of shock, but part of it was real, too: the thrill of the chase and the close encounter. Every new insight was costing her a lot, but she had grabbed a thread. It was more than the mask idea and the missing Mardi Gras files; she had learned something crucial from the ghost. This mystery was starting to unravel.

Back at the house, Cree's first thought upon seeing Paul was that she was not looking her best at the moment. But he came to her and warily held her shoulders, searching her face with concern. He looked good, Cree thought, in a frowsy, unshaven, hastily dressed sort of way.

But for all that, he struck her as diffident, too. Holding back. As they'd driven to the hospital in Paul's car, she'd told them the story of her realizations: the boar head as mask, the absence of Mardi Gras materials among Lila's family archives, the years missing from the Epicurus files at the house. Throughout, Paul had said next to nothing. When she'd asked him what he thought, he said only, "Right now, I'm just concerned about your health and your safety. We can worry about all that tomorrow." She got the sense he was stalling, giving himself time to appraise the situation from a psychiatrist's perspective.

Probably, she realized, he saw this as a psychological breakdown of grave consequence. Hysteria. Incipient schizophrenia.

That got her mad. Sitting here in the bright fluorescents of the waiting room, in that inimitable one A.M. emergency ward ambience, she knew she was emotionally labile from shock and exhaustion, and the best course would be to stay calm. But she couldn't let his skepticism be. Not after what she'd been through. The world owed her some credence.

"You're sitting there thinking I've flipped my friggin' gourd," she told him, "and that really pisses me off."

He shot a glance at Joyce, who just blinked expressionlessly. "I admit I'm trying to retain some objectivity here, Cree, but – "

" 'Objectivity'? How often has that been used as a euphemism for an unwillingness to face the obvious? How long did 'objectivity' keep multiple personality disorder, or Tourette's syndrome, from being properly diagnosed and adequately researched?"

"Only as long as it took for credible clinical evidence to accumulate," he said quietly.

His levelheadedness infuriated her further. "You want to see some friggin' 'credible evidence'? Lemme show you something!" And she lifted her shirt to show the four painful red stripes across her stomach, just above the waistband of her jeans. "That thing *grabbed* me, and I ripped myself out his grip, and he left some *evidence* right here!"

There were a dozen other people in the lounge, other triaged patients biding their time or tired family members waiting for news, and heads turned. Paul gently took her hands and made her lower her blouse. Cree felt suddenly ashamed of herself.

Joyce looked at the two of them, blinked again, then stood up and brushed her skirt smooth. "Well," she said briskly, "I think I'll go powder my nose." She gathered her purse and walked away.

Her absence changed everything as if someone had flipped a switch.

Cree got control of her breathing. "I'm sorry, Paul. I'm – I'm upset, I'm in shock. I'm all over the place."

"I've been wanting to call you."

The anger flared again, different this time: "Then why the hell didn't you?"

"I wasn't retreating. I wasn't hiding. I just had some things of my own to sort out, and I needed to think about what you told me. I thought you deserved that. I wasn't sure what I'd say when I saw you again."

"So did you figure it out?" Still angry.

"Some, anyway. But I don't want to talk now. Not here. I'd rather wait for . . . happier circumstances. One thing at a time."

Part of her wanted to rage at him again, part of her wanted to give up and cry and put her face against his chest and surrender everything and be comforted. But old reflexes kicked in, holding her back: Mike, and, yes, Edgar, who had sacrificed so many shirts to Cree's tears. Suddenly she missed Ed terribly. If he'd been here, Cree would have let it all go, it would be simple. He'd seen it all, she didn't need to impress him or pretend anything. It was too complex with Paul.

He was right, though: one thing at a time. She nodded, but still he was looking at her warily, as if *he* were the one needing some reassurance. He did look stubbly and funky.

After while she reached over and began unbuttoning his shirt. It was tricky with the sore finger. He didn't pull away or try to stop her, though he gave her a questioning eyebrow.

"You've got your shirt buttoned wrong," she explained.

He let her continue, and the moment felt very intimate.

By general consent a drink was called for, and of course Paul knew a bar for the occasion, even at two A.M. It was a battered-looking place in a charmingly decrepit district on Magazine Street. Even at this hour, there were at least a dozen other customers, making a soothing mutter of conversation. They took a table near the windows in front, and Cree and Paul ordered bottles of Jax beer; Joyce couldn't resist ordering a gaudy, oversized, New Orleans tourist drink. Cree's splinted finger stuck out awkwardly as she gripped her bottle.

The endorphins were wearing off, and the industrial-strength ibuprofen they'd given her hadn't kicked in yet, so every part of her body was starting to stiffen and complain. But that hot little flame still flared, blue-white, at her center – the hunger to understand and the sense that the mystery was at last becoming accessible.

The flame had an ugly green tinge, too: hatred of the boar-headed man.

"Paul, I need you to tell me some more about Mardi Gras. Particularly Epicurus. You're a member, right?"

"Yeah. I'm not the most fanatical participant by any means, though. Some of the society rites and traditions strike me as juvenile and they get old after a few decades. But it can be a lot of fun."

"So, what," Joyce asked, "a krewe is like a secret society? Like the KKK?"

Paul chuckled, shook his head. "Hardly! More of a civic group. Some of the more historic krewes cling to the trappings of mystery, the image of a secret brotherhood, but nowadays it's a halfhearted effort. Epicurus is like most krewes, pretty straightforward. Mainly, you just plan festivities at Carnival. Anybody can join Epicurus – if they can afford it. Meetings use Robert's Rules of Order, the secretary takes minutes, all very legit. Meetings are full of gossip and pranks, fraternal put-downs, and talk about money. You plan a few parties, build a float, do the Mardi Gras parade. That's it. Really, a krewe here is not so different from, oh, a softball team in other cities. In Seattle, you probably have gay teams and women's teams and office teams and all-lawyer teams, right? Basically the same thing."

"Give me a more psychological perspective. A more sociological one." Cree winced at the pain of talking and held the cold bottle against the bruises on her jaw.

Paul made a tired smile through a shadow of beard. "You know, I've never really thought about it – it's just what we *do* hereabouts? But let's see . . . The idea of a period of feasting before Lent is probably a Christian modification of older rites that go way back to pre-Christian times. Probably has roots in ancient fertility rites, that would account for the libidinous overtones here – the tradition of women baring their breasts and so on. Very sexualized. In New Orleans, it's an excuse to get together with people of your social sphere – in Epicurus's case, other rich people, or at least people from established families – and get plastered. You have masked parties at various members' houses. You indulge in extramarital flirtations, maybe even risk a quick fling. You make minor fools of yourselves, enough to show that though you're an aristocrat, your blood still runs hot, you know how to cut loose and have a good time. You provide yourselves with a year's worth of gossip that lubricates business and social transactions. There're status issues, too. You compete with other krewes for public profile and within your own membership for the role of king."

"The parties get pretty uninhibited?"

"In Epicurus? Not as extreme as some, not by a long shot. But, sure, that's the point. That's the psychology of the mask – you can act out in ways you wouldn't if people knew who you were. Of course, most people settle into the same costumes, the same roles, year after year, so everybody more or less knows who's who after a while. At this point, it's just part of the ritual of license or disinhibition."

Cree was trying to see how the boar-masked rapist theory fit with the social lives of the Beaufortes of 1971 or '72. Clearly, she didn't yet know enough. Charmian knew the answers, she was sure, but would never reveal them.

Joyce had been frowning at what Paul was saying or at her own thoughts. "I've got a question for you, Cree," she said at last. She sounded reluctant to bring it up. "We've talked about this over the years, but this boar-headed guy is going to stretch the principle. You always say experiences of the *living* can linger too, right?"

"If they're intense enough."

"Paul, you're probably skeptical, but just bear with me here, okay? Cree, this is a very *physical* ghost. He makes noise when he runs? You felt his hands on you?"

A shiver of revulsion shook Cree. "Yeah."

"And that's very rare," Joyce explained to Paul. "The most common manifestation of kinetic activity is poltergeists, which can move objects around, throw things, break things – "

"I see where you're going with this!" Cree felt a twinge of excitement. "Paul, poltergeist activity generally manifests around living adolescents, often girls in their early teens. They don't seem to consciously be doing it, but they are able to manifest psychokinetic activity. It's not a well-understood phenomenon. But Joyce's point is that poltergeists are an example of a living person manifesting a paranormal entity. Or paranormal activity, anyway. There's plenty of historical precedent for the idea – in the old days, it was considered one of the standard activities of witches. The so-called witches of Salem were supposedly able to manifest 'specters' that tormented the witnesses. There are a few contemporary examples in the literature, but I've always taken them with a grain of salt."

To his credit, Paul was willing to suspend disbelief and entertain the concept. "Meaning that maybe this ghost is not the . . . residuum of a dead person – he's an unconscious expression of some living person. Of someone's psychotic sexual sadism and anger." He tugged absently at his hair, pulling it into standing tufts, and Cree sensed he was frustrated at having his belief tested still further.

She felt the same way. True, the universe was a strange place, and human consciousness was the strangest thing in it. But this idea was getting very far out. It opened up too many possibilities. Yes, Cree felt the accumulated emotions and experiences of the living, but it had always been . . . impressionistic, a collage of synesthesic sensations, a "mood," an intuitive knowledge – not *seeing* and *feeling* a distinct entity! On the other hand, the specter idea would explain the most troubling aspect of the boar-headed ghost, the lack of a perimortem resonance. If Joyce was right, the answer would be that there was no echo of a dying experience because the creature's originator hadn't died.

Just thinking about it, she felt a reprise of that vertigo she'd felt in midair over the stairwell. Free fall.

But it was not without parallels or precedent. Even Paul seemed troubled by the idea, and they all seemed to need a moment to think about it. Then Cree wondered: the boar-headed ghost as an unconscious expression of some living person's psychosis – what had given Joyce the idea in the first place?

After another moment, she turned to Joyce. "I take it you had an . . . interesting evening with Ronald Beauforte?"

33

PAUL TOOK HIS TIME driving back from the Garden District, cruising the quiet three A.M. streets, thinking. The events of the day, especially the last few hours, had put him in a lousy mood. He felt compromised, tainted by ambivalences and conflicting loyalties.

He was very attracted to Cree, fascinated by her. Seeing her after her ordeal tonight had broken his heart — she was in such dismay, such a state of shock and disconnection. Yet he'd also found himself unbearably attracted to her — her wild hair, that look of wide-eyed alarm, and later, when they'd talked about Lila, her fierce concentration. Even when she'd blazed at him — the way her emotions were right there, her anger and need and hurt. He could still feel the sweetness of her light, fumbling touch as she rebuttoned his shirt.

But she was right about the other things. His feelings toward her *were* compromised.

The supernatural issue — the existence of ghosts, enduring noncorporeal impulses, whatever you called them — was a big part of it. Like a religious person, Cree was someone who had built her life on belief, who acted out of belief. You could argue that *all* belief was a kind of commitment to the invisible, the unprovable, and that Cree's was no different from faith in God, or luck, or democracy, or the stock market. But despite all the warmth and fascination he felt toward her, he couldn't get past his skepticism. The things she claimed she saw, heard, felt, did — they struck him as unscientific. Impossible by the laws of physics. The idea they'd batted around for a while, that maybe Ron Beauforte was manifesting a specter or poltergeist that raped his sister, showed just how far out this stuff could get.

The depth of her commitment, the passion there, was arguably delusive, obsessive, morbid. Many people believed in ghosts, in some vague way, but few made it central to their lives. That being the case, it radically affected the prospect of a relationship with her. This wasn't a little difference of taste or opinion, something you could chuckle over like whether one person liked Chinese food and the other Italian. It was central to her sense of herself and the world, and Cree demanded it be taken seriously.

And he did – as some form of psychological disturbance. For all of Cree's intelligence and persuasiveness, for all the insights her intuitions or supposed supernatural experiences had provided again and again, when push came to shove, he couldn't deal with it as anything else.

He wished he could suspend rational analysis and just go with his heart. What did his heart say? *One in a million*, it said. *Go to her.* It said, *Trust this.* How would Cree's synesthetic sensibilities describe the feeling he had when he saw her? Swallows swooping and weaving in the sunlit air.

No, it was bigger than that. Being around Cree made him feel as he had as a child, those three years when his father had taken a hospital administration job up north and they'd endured the dour winters of Michigan. He'd learned the way winter makes you appreciate the change of seasons. That first day in early April when earth and sky seem to celebrate, and your whole being opened to it. You became something of a blithe spirit in a new world. That's how being around Cree made him feel.

If he could forget the delusional pathology represented by her belief in ghosts.

He'd done his best to rationalize it. For all their unconventionality, her methodologies as a psychologist were slightly more defensible. Back when he was an undergraduate, he'd taken a cultural anthropology course that had briefly explored "etic" and "emic" approaches to understanding other cultures. Advocates for the "etic" approach insisted that you had to study cultures and belief systems from something of a distance, bringing an objective and comparative perspective to bear. The "emic" people argued that, no, you couldn't know how people thought, why they behaved the way they did, what traditions meant, unless you stepped inside. You had to experience what the subject tribe or group experienced, adopt their beliefs, see the world through their eyes. The best examples of the emic school were the anthropologists who studied the mysticism of Native American tribes by actually taking hallucinogens during traditional divinatory rites and vision quests.

Back then, he'd flattered himself by deciding that if he became an anthropologist, he'd combine the rigor and objectivity of the etics and the open-mindedness, the daring deep immersion, of the emics.

If you could apply the same concept to psychology, Cree was definitely the emic type. She empathically entered the world of her client, felt what the client felt. She learned the client's problems from the inside out, took them as her own. She *became* the client. She said she even became the supposed ghost, as much as she could stand to. Emic to the hilt.

Fine and dandy. Except that ghosts didn't exist. A woman who conversed with and communed telepathically with ghosts was not quite sane.

He crossed Canal Street and navigated through the streets of the Quarter. It almost always felt good to be enfolded again in those narrow ways, the balconies overhanging, the patchwork facades. It felt like home, especially at this time of night when even the die-hard tourists had petered out. Squint your eyes, and you could easily imagine you were here in 1840, or 1760. The old buildings and rough textures, the whole style of the place, created something of a refuge from the twenty-first century and its uncertainties.

But tonight it did little for him. He felt sour and depressed as he found a parking space and pulled the Beemer into it. He went upstairs, unlocked the door, kicked it open, and threw his keys on the counter.

The ghost thing was only one of the compromises, the conflicted loyalties.

He thought about what he had to do for a moment, then decided to fortify himself. He poured a couple of fingers of Jack Daniel's into a tall

313

glass, swirled it, sniffed it, and then tipped some back. It scalded away some of the sour taste in his mouth.

He picked up the phone, dialed, waited. It was after three in the morning, but she had insisted he call any time, day or night. Serve her right if it woke her out of a sound sleep. Or maybe she wouldn't answer. He hoped she wouldn't.

But the phone rang only once before Charmian picked up.

"She's very smart, Charmian. She zeroed in on the right years, she figured out the mask, she figured out the Mardi Gras connection. Then she deduced that there might be something in your files at the house, went over there, and broke into them."

At the other end of the line, Charmian spluttered in speechless outrage.

"Needless to say she didn't find anything," Paul went on. "But she will. She and her assistant are top-notch researchers. Even if they don't get at the Epicurus archives, there's bound to be something at the *Times-Picayune* records. And they're looking for Josephine."

Her voice, when she regained it, was acerbic: "And you are calling me at this hour because – ?"

"Because you told me to keep you informed of developments."

"And precisely what has developed at three-fourteen in the morning?"

"After she broke in the file cabinets, she says the boar-headed ghost chased her. She went off the stairwell, could have broken her neck. Her assistant called me, and we went over there. I just got back from the emergency ward."

"Was she badly hurt?"

"No, but – "

"How very unfortunate."

"I hope you've got a plan B. Because she'll be back at it tomorrow, Charmian. This isn't staying under the rug. Maybe it's time to tell her the truth."

Charmian thought about that a long time. Paul heard nothing but her breath, steady, controlled, for a full minute.

"You may be right," she said at last. "You are probably right."

"I think we've exhausted your attempts at deflection, Charmian. It's time to face the truth and start trying to figure out how to cope with the consequences."

Again, she needed to think about that. "Consequences," she said at last. "Paul, you're very drawn to her, aren't you? And she reciprocates, doesn't she?"

"That's irrelevant to – "

"No, it's not irrelevant at all. Because you two *would* be something very special together. And I think you really want that, and if you have half a brain, if you're even half a man, you'll go to her. But you've been something of a double agent in all this, haven't you? How do you think she'll react when she finds that out? If she has any trust issues at all, which we both know she does, you think that won't wreck any chances you might have with the oh-so-vulnerable Dr. Black?"

Now it was Paul's turn to be speechless with anger. It should never have gone this far. There seemed to be no limit to Charmian's willingness to intrigue, to control everyone around her, to bring anyone down if she didn't get what she wanted. At last he croaked, "You mean you'll tell her about our . . . arrangement . . . if I don't keep doing what you want."

At the other end of the line, Charmian made a pleased sound in her throat. "Exactly! And before you play indignant with me, Paul, let me remind you, you signed on from the start. You know what's at stake here. You're right, it's time for the truth. But even in your most self-righteous moments, you'll agree that it needs to be revealed . . . tactfully, right? So now I'm going to tell you exactly what we're going to do."

34

DON'T PRETEND TO BELIEVE ME, Paul. It's condescending. I don't need it right now."

She hadn't meant to say it like that, but the tension she felt was making her cross, impatient. She was leaning against the door of the BMW as Paul piloted it through the sunlit streets. Even with the sunglasses she'd put on, the light seemed too bright to Cree. She felt like road kill, but six hours of sleep, a scalding shower, and a half hour of cautious yoga stretching had taken away the worst of the pain and stiffness. Joyce was long gone to City Hall and the libraries, charged with locating Josephine Dupree. At Paul's suggestion, they were going to the office of Phil Galveston, the man who had been the Epicures organization's secretary for thirty years and who had charged himself with maintaining an archive of the krewe's activities.

If the Beaufortes hadn't kept records of the years after 1968, maybe Phil Galveston had. Maybe in his files they'd find photos of the man in the boar-head mask, and a name for him. If Cree's assumption was correct.

Paul shook his head. "I'm not pretending. I'm curious – I want to understand how the parts fit together. You seem to have an integrated methodology, you have your version of clinical observation and literature. So far, it looks pretty consistent and – "

"Yeah. The only hard part is the fundamental premise."

"That what we're talking about is the psychology of dead people? Yes. That's hard. Can you blame me? Put the shoe on the other foot, Cree. Suppose you'd been going merrily along with your private psychiatry practice, never had a paranormal experience in your life, and then you met *me*, and I told you the things you're telling me. How would you react? Would you revise your whole personal and professional belief system, overnight, on the basis of what I said?"

Cree shrugged and looked out the window, giving the point only grudgingly.

"So go on," he urged. "You were saying you learned something last night, something about the ghost's affective complex."

Cree sighed. "I have to give you some background first. I use the word 'complex' the same way Freud did, as in Oedipus complex, inferiority complex, and so on – a connected group of repressed ideas that compel habitual actions of thought, feeling, and action. My point was going to be that though every ghost relives the experience of the death to a large degree, the act of physically dying is not necessarily the foremost aspect of the dying person's experience. At the moment of death, people experience an enormous range of emotions. It's not just about pain or fear. They might remember or relive things that seem unconnected with the circumstances of death. They often yearn toward or call out to loved ones. They might feel lonely or ecstatic or serene. They might cling to, or retreat toward reassuring thoughts. Sometimes their concerns seem at first trivial or absurd."

"Okay. But you were saying something about 'distillation' – "

"A dying person's perimortem emotions and thoughts are not random. They derive from some central, overpowering concern or issue in his or her life. Death is a moment of absolute desperation and surrender, and a person's thoughts home in on a crucial, defining image, event, emotion, or concern life. If I can understand what that is, I can release the ghost."

"Example, please."

Cree took a moment to recall one that was appropriate. "A case in Arizona. The ghost – the man who had died – was a Hopi Indian, not particularly identified with Native American culture, who was making extra money stealing relics from historic Hopi sites. The physical circumstance of his death was that he'd gotten trapped in an underground kiva, badly injured after part of the rock ceiling fell in. So the immediate dying experience was one of physical pain, fear, and the frantic desire to try to survive, all very typical. The secondary experience was one of guilt at desecrating the holy place, and with the guilt came regret over having ignored his grandfather's lifelong pleas to understand and respect traditions – this accident and injury seemed like a punishment for that, for which he blamed and hated his grandfather. The ghost relived moments of conflict with his grandfather from twenty years earlier, an incident when he'd driven away from the grandfather's home after an argument, swearing at him and deliberately running over a couple of his chickens. That's the affect that witnesses felt when they saw his ghost, and that's what I first encountered, too – rage, impulsive violence, resentment, shame. Very scary. But deeper still was another layer, more affirmative – the knowledge that his grandfather loved him unconditionally and forgave him. That was associated with a look his grandfather had given him, literally a single momentary gaze, when they were out fishing when he was a kid. Sunset, just the two of them, a powerful glance of kinship and love. In its pain and remorse, the dying man's psyche yearned for, tried to flee to, that . . . sanctuary."

Remembering brought tears to her eyes, and she was very glad she had sunglasses on. She didn't look at Paul, didn't know how he was hearing it, but she decided, *Screw him, he can take it or leave it.*

"And that's what you used, right?" he said softly. "You helped him . . . find his way to that sanctuary? Helped him accept that the grandfather's love could overcome and transcend his transgressions?"

"Yes. I led him to his grandfather's eyes at the moment of that gaze."

Paul came up behind cars at a light and stopped. They sat there without talking, listening to muffled heavy metal music from the SUV in front of them.

"That's a beautiful story," Paul said, shaking his head. "Man! Every time I get around you, it's another . . . revelation. You . . . you kind of boot my brain into *orbit* every time we talk, so help me."

Cree didn't answer. She was glad he seemed to understand and appreciate. But it was becoming increasingly clear to her that their metaphysical differences were a real impediment to having a relationship. Last night, when they'd gone back to the Garden District to retrieve the other cars, Joyce had driven away immediately, leaving Paul and Cree standing together in the cool night, just down the block from Beauforte House. "Would you like to spend the night at my place?" Paul had asked simply. By then Cree had been on the edge of exhaustion. She'd put her arms around him and leaned her face against his. He'd held her softly, careful of her injuries, and for a full minute they'd just stood in the humid night air like that, and it felt very nice. He was warm, and she liked the rhythm of his bones, the way their bodies fit.

But other things didn't fit.

"Would you sleep with a woman you thought was presenting as schizophrenic?" she'd asked.

Against the side of her face, she'd felt his cheek move in a smile. "Not unless I was really head over heels. I'd have to be pretty far gone."

Yes, he'd framed it as sort of a joke, and it was a sweet way of affirming his attraction. But it had also been a deflection. Maybe she was still fleeing from her own ghosts, but Cree didn't think she could enter into any real intimacy unless it was truly reciprocal, equal, balanced. And as long as Paul believed she was at the very least misguided, and quite possibly in the grip of a delusive, clinically definable, aberrant mental condition, that equality wasn't possible.

She had pulled away, given his hand one last squeeze, and gone to her car.

"Here we are," Paul said, and Cree roused from her thoughts to notice her surroundings. Paul pulled over in front of a big brick building, three stories tall, with a Greek-revival-style entrance framed by four white columns. On the side of the building, a decorative sign in the style of the nineteenth century announced that it was Galveston & Sons Press.

"Phil's a fussy ol' fuddy-duddy," Paul told her as they went up the steps. "I don't know him well, but my father knew him, and of course I see him maybe twice a year at Epicurus functions. This is his family's business, since forever. It's a bindery, too."

A receptionist at the lobby desk told them how to find Phil's office; which adjoined the main press room. The noise of machines and the smells of ink and paper grew around them as they headed down the building's long central corridor. Cree's nervous anticipation grew with each step: This could be where they identified the boar-headed man. His identity, if her theory was correct, would make all the difference.

"For me," she finished, "that case was like watching three movies projected simultaneously onto the same screen – that raging moment of death, the fight with the grandfather, the long-ago evening of fishing. At any given moment, I had to figure out what image I was seeing, where I should start, which was most important. This case is the same way. When I experience the ghost, I sense many narratives at play at once – the affective complex of the ghost."

Paul nodded. They had come to a pair of wide glass doors that opened into a huge, high-ceilinged room lined with gigantic printing and binding machines. When Paul opened the door, the racket of the equipment enveloped them. Paul mouthed "Phil Galveston?" and a blue-uniformed technician gestured toward the back of the room, where a stairway led to a balcony lined with glass-enclosed offices. They walked along the rows of machines, skirting stacks of printed materials on pallets. Workers eyed them incuriously as they passed.

They climbed the metal stairs and entered a glass-walled lobby, where a secretary greeted them. She was a striking young black woman with the most elaborate hairdo Cree had ever seen, layers of oiled braids and curls woven and piled high on her head, and three-inch, curling fingernails. The sign on her desk said her name was Sharon Kincaid.

"Mr. Galveston is very sorry," she told them, "but he can't be here to help you. He got called to an emergency at our plant in Gretna." After all the rising expectation, the sudden letdown felt crushing to Cree. But Sharon smiled and went on. "So he told me to get you whatever you wanted from the Epicurus files. He got a whole room off his office just for those files. Sort of his hobby, you know? You all just have seat at the table there and tell me what you want, I'll go get it for you."

They told her they were looking for photos and clippings of Epicurus parties and balls and parades for 1969 through 1972. They didn't need dues ledgers, charitable donation receipts, float construction invoices, or the rest of it.

"I am sorry. Mr. Galveston is very particular, I'm supposed to bring out only one file at a time? It's a *lot* of stuff, the records have a way of getting mussed up. I'll be happy to bring you the other years when you're done with the first one."

They started with 1969. Sharon disappeared down a corridor between glassed offices, leaving them alone in the lobby.

Mr. Galveston was apparently an old-fashioned boss who liked the catbird seat. From this vantage they could see the entire printing room, the rows of web presses gobbling endless belts of white paper from gigantic rolls, the cutting and binding machines with their rhythmically rising and falling arms. Forklifts came and went with loads of bound books on pallets or giant spools of paper on spindles. The double glass wall kept most of the noise out, but the floor vibrated slightly.

"You look frightened, Cree," Paul said quietly.

In fact, she felt sick with anticipation. "I was going to tell you what I learned from getting so . . . close to the ghost last night. First, his pursuit and rape is not his dying experience. I can't get any sense of the act of dying. That's been bothering me from the start, enough that I'd almost consider Joyce's specter idea. But for now, I'm still going to operate on the theory that the boar-headed man is a memory – a crucial, pivotal memory that in some way defines his life. The memory perseverates because it was *so* intense an experience – a peak of sadistic indulgence. I have to assume he perseverates because the guilt and regret he feels are so extreme, even though I can't find them in him. He's reenacting his worst deed. His perseverating as this pursuit and rape is his *self-punishment*. In effect, he's condemned himself to reenact his most destructive, self-demeaning act."

Paul nodded thoughtfully, as if they were consulting about a living person. "That's how you'll reach him, right? That'll be your handle on him? Appeal to his contrition?"

"Maybe. It'd be nice if it was that easy." Cree slowed, feeling her nervousness spike, feeling suddenly not equal to the revelation that she was sure was imminent. "But there's one other thing I got last night, Paul. His arousal is predatory and sadistic as much as it is sexual. The pursuit and Lila's terror, the sense of power that gives him, are just as important to him as the rapes that culminate it. A big part of the thrill is the sense of *violation*. There's an element of that in all sexual encounters, even normal sexuality, the violation of social distance, right? But in his case, there's an acute sense of *violating taboos*. That really floats this bastard's boat."

"Well, sure, rape is pretty damned taboo – "

"I'm afraid it's more than that. I think it's the taboo against incest. He's related to his victim, Paul, he's aware of how taboo it is. That's part of the excitement for him."

Paul's shoulders slumped and his eyes fell to his empty hands on the tabletop. After a moment he stared out across the press room floor, a distant gaze oblivious to the activity below. Cree knew he was plugging the idea into his analysis of Lila; more, she could see genuine compassion in his face. He was as nervous as she was, drumming all ten fingers rapidly.

Below, at the far end of the press floor, a spindle lift driven by a young man approached a stack of paper rolls, each four feet in diameter. The shiny, six-foot steel phallus approached the holes in the massive paper spools, raised, lowered, found its way into the hole, backed halfway out to adjust its angle, went in again. *How many bad jokes that job must generate here*, Cree thought, feeling more than a little sick. It occurred to her that the incest probability didn't negate the specter theory. Ro-Ro's dark side?

And then Sharon was back, carrying a couple of fat, accordion-style folders. "Here we go," she said cheerfully. "Epicurus, 1969. Y'all take your time and enjoy." She gave them a stewardess smile and went back to her desk.

Paul seemed to share Cree's reluctance as they opened the first. It was a tidily organized file of photos of different sizes, some obviously done by a professional hired for the job, some three-by-fives apparently taken by

Mr. Galveston or other Epicurus members. There were also newspaper clippings, yellowing and turning a little crumbly in glassine envelopes.

They flipped photos for a few minutes. People in tuxes, people in costumes, people toasting, people dancing, people looking up from meals. Then a posed group photo, obviously done by a professional: around thirty costumed partyers standing shoulder to shoulder. Cree thought she recognized Bradford Lambert in the middle row, the swashbuckling pirate.

And then she saw the boar-headed man.

He stood at the left end of the back row, his bristled head turned to a three-quarter view. He wore a jacket of some coarse material, ragged and patched.

Cree felt the breath go out of her. Paul whipped the photo over. Penned in neat copperplate, row by row, were the names of the partyers.

Far left, back row, was Richard Beauforte.

35

CREE NEEDED SPACE. The interior of any building, even the city streets, seemed too congested, thick with sorrows. She told Paul to drive to the lake. The top of the levee, with its wide vistas of water and green, was the only place in New Orleans with any promise of respite. Human beings were insufferable. She didn't talk to him as they drove, but she did use his cell phone to call Joyce on hers.

"Where are you?" Cree asked.

"Right now I'm at the main library, looking through old city directories for Josephine Dupree. No luck so far. I've gone through the tax rolls, public housing authority, and social welfare records, and there's no reference to her. I even made calls to a bunch of Duprees in the current phone book, and nobody knows of any Josephine. I'd say she's probably dead, but I can't find a certificate of death in this parish, or any burial record in New Orleans. I might have to go to Baton Rouge for the statewide records."

Cree considered telling her to forget about Josephine, they'd solved the basic problem. But then it occurred to her that the old woman, if she were alive, might be useful in the next phase: helping Lila come to grips with what had happened to her. So instead, she added to Joyce's research agenda. "I need everything you can find on Richard Beauforte, Lila's father. I mean *everything*. Birth to death. Business deals, traffic citations, whatever."

"Uh-oh. Does this mean what I think it does?"

"We'll talk about it later," Cree said curtly. She folded the phone and handed it back to Paul.

He drove them to a lakeshore park not far from the Warrens' house. They left the car at the base of the levee, climbed the stairs set into the earthen mound, and stood for a moment, just taking in the views. It was just after one o'clock, the sun high; a wind sighed in off the water, drying some of the sweat on Cree's skin and rolling among the shore trees. The open lawns of the lakeshore park were all but deserted.

"How're you doing?" Paul asked. "You really up for walking?"

For a moment, Cree didn't know what he was talking about. She had completely forgotten the bruises and sprains that complained with every step. Something like fury drove her, anesthetized her. "I'm fine," she snapped. She turned west along the levee path, and yes, the breeze and the open sky and the relative absence of naked apes and their innumerable cruelties did help a little.

Paul followed behind for a time, then caught up. "So, Dr. Black, we have a problem."

"Yes."

"A fragile patient in denial over a severe childhood trauma. It's not just rape, and it's not just incest, it's worse than either. Beyond the violation of the rape, there's her betrayal by a loved and trusted family member. There's the frightening role reversal – a parent, a protector, turned into an attacker. All of it exacerbated by the mask, which made it more frightening and debasing – being raped by an animal who you knew was your father. It's all been repressed for thirty years, and the patient's ability to cope has been contingent on keeping it buried. Now the repression is breaking up. Why? And what's the correct therapeutic prognosis under the circumstances?"

They had found a number of other photos of Richard in the 1969 folder, wearing his boar's mask or holding it under his arm. Examining the boozy-looking gatherings, Cree had been struck by Lila, dressed as a twelve-year-old pixie or fairy of some kind: She was truly sparkling, a shining girl. *And why shouldn't she be?* Cree thought savagely. *After all, she wasn't due to be violently raped by her father for another couple of years.*

"The repression's breaking up because she moved back into Beauforte

House and encountered the ghost there. And you know, Paul, screw you if you don't believe in the ghost part."

"Can we get past what I believe or not? Lila's well-being is at issue here, not whether you or I agree on everything. You're a top-notch psychologist. Put your talents to use."

She rounded on him in rage, but she knew he was right. She closed her mouth before the anger could explode out of it and kept walking.

"Let's reconstruct the scenario," Paul told her. "What exactly happened? If we're going to identify all the dimensions of Lila's problem, we've got to know."

Cree walked fast, staying half a step ahead of him. They were speed-walking along the levee top, rage and frustration burning in Cree's limbs.

Suddenly she realized he wasn't there any more. She looked back to see him, standing in the middle of the path, twenty feet behind her.

"I am not Richard Beauforte," he called. "Nor am I some generic representative of 'all men' with their supposed rapine instincts. You're upset at what happened to that woman. But *I didn't do it.* I'm upset, too. I'm trying to help her. Accept that and I'll keep walking with you. Otherwise, I'm going home."

She couldn't answer. The best she could do was to turn aside and sit down on the slope facing the lake. It took another minute to call back to him, "I'm sorry." How many times had she said that today? She looked toward him and gestured to the grass at her side. "I am completely screwed up, Paul. I'm sorry."

He did come and sit, but not within arm's reach.

He was right, they had to determine just what happened. So she extemporized, stringing together what they knew with reasonable suppositions. Paul just listened, nodding now and then.

It was 1971; Lila would have been fourteen, and, according to the photos Cree had seen among the family albums, well developed for her age. The family went out for a typical Mardi Gras party at some other old family's house, wearing their costumes. Lila came home before the others; maybe she wasn't feeling well, or she was just sick of the party, or maybe being the youngest it was simply her bedtime. She was upstairs, maybe getting ready for bed, when she heard somebody come in. It'd been a busy, bustling day at Beauforte House, she didn't think twice about it. Or maybe she didn't hear anybody, she just came out of her bedroom or the bathroom and saw the shoe tips. They startled her, but it was a night of crazy behavior. Probably she thought it was Ron. But then she saw the boar head, peeking around the corner at the end of the hallway, trying to be scary. "Daddy, cut it out," she said. Maybe she laughed at him. She knew he was pretty drunk. But then he came all the way out, and the way he came toward her was creepy. It *was* piggy, he was being *too* real. Something startled her – his breathing, his eyes. Or maybe it started out as a game, some parody of a fatherly game of pursuit, the way they all used to love doing when she and Ron were younger. She skittered away, either playful or already scared. And he chased her. Maybe he caught her once and hurt her a little. And all of a sudden, however it had started out, it was no game: he had become a monstrous stranger, a real wereboar, no longer her father. After the first pursuit, he vanished into the house again, and she decided to try to go downstairs, get to a phone or go outside. But he cut her off before she could reach the stairs. He chased her through the rooms. She implored him to come to his senses. "What are you doing? Stop it!" He caught her and hurt her again, or touched her the wrong way.

He let her go because he had discovered how much he enjoyed the pursuit, even after she started crying and pleading. He called her name in scary ways, he mimicked her whimpers and cries, taunting her. Maybe he had started out just feeling a little devil-may-care, pushing the envelope with just a tinge of sadism, but anger or resentment burned in him from some business disappointment or loss of status, and here was catharsis. Probably he kept telling himself it was just paternal high jinks, but the wild dark hilarity, the temptation of the edge of the permissible, grew by degrees. He had never felt such power and freedom, such an absolute release of inhibition. He felt alive in ways he hadn't for years, he felt like a robust, rutting animal. His prey was lush and fresh and innocent. The feel of her blossoming body aroused him in ways he didn't anticipate. His control slipped another notch each time, and her fear gratified him.

Maybe he told himself that her terror was a pretense, part of the game. He chased her again, and vanished again, and chased her and wrestled with her, and finally his arousal was complete, he needed to cross the threshold, to break the ultimate taboo. And he did.

Cree had run out of air and felt dizzy. The details were all hypothetical, but somehow she knew the story was about right.

Paul was shaking his head, looking disgusted with himself. "It fits," he said. "It fits so well I should have seen it right away. She's classic. A textbook example of the psychology of incest and rape. All the behavioral patterns." For a moment he just sat, tearing up tufts of grass and tossing them into the breeze. Then he sighed and turned toward Cree. "And afterward?"

"I think she went to her mother and told her. Because Charmian damn well knows about this. She's withholding *something* from me, and this has to be it. And Lila told me that Charmian had stopped sleeping with her father right around then. Which I would bloody well hope she would."

"And Charmian's response was – ?"

"She told Lila to show some spine, reminded her that Beaufortes don't cry. Or she didn't believe her. So Lila tried to tough it out, and later she went off to boarding school. Couldn't process what had happened to her, had a breakdown, came home. They called in your father to treat her because they knew they could rely on his confidentiality. Your father drugged her up, did the best he could. Richard died of a heart attack in there somewhere. Once he was dead, and she was away from home again, it was easier to forget. Forgetting seemed like the only way out. Forgetting became the habit, the rule."

Paul sat with his elbows on his knees, squinting as he looked out over the water. "The love never dies, you know." He sounded very sad. "The abused child still loves the parent. She may hate and fear her abuser, too, but the love never goes away. Whenever her father has come up in our sessions, it's clear Lila admired him and felt very close to him. She has nothing but good things to say about him."

"All the more motivation to repress the rape. The ambivalence would be intolerable, the two emotions utterly irreconcilable. Burying the hate and sense of betrayal was the only way to preserve any of the love."

Paul was laboring over some thought. "Cree, let me ask you a very serious question. Please think about this, okay? Because it's stumping me at the moment. If we expose the memory, aren't we taking something away, too? Aren't we robbing the adult Lila of her father? Aren't we . . . killing the decent, loving man and replacing him with a monster?" He shook his head. "We can't guarantee a positive prognosis for Lila if we open up that wound. Jesus God, I never thought I'd hear myself saying this, but maybe in this case it *would* be better to . . . just let it lie."

They chewed on that for a while. Down in the park, an old man shuffled along the water's edge, head down, looking dejected. Far above, a jetliner caught the sun and blazed for a few seconds as it banked for its descent to New Orleans airport, bringing another load of happy tourists to the City That Care Forgot.

Cree was thinking that letting it lie was an option already lost to them. The spectral rape had started something irreversible in Lila. Somehow they had to do both: give Lila access to the anger and hurt so that she could start to rebuild, but somehow preserve the love she felt for her father, the love she still thought she felt *from* him. Possible? Remotely, maybe. It depended on the ghost. The outcome with the ghost would determine everything for Lila's future. Josephine might help, too, if she were alive, if they could find her. Lila had said repeatedly that in many ways she'd been closer to Josephine than to her own mother, that she had emotionally relied on the wise, patient nanny. And all the photos Cree had seen bore that out — their faces gave it away. A special connection.

But that brought up another thought. Lila had been so close to Josephine — wouldn't she have sought comfort in those strong, sinewy arms before she went to Charmian? Absolutely. Which meant the old woman would know the facts of that night. And Josephine would not have let the event pass without responding in some way. How? What had happened that night and in the following days? Josephine was crucial here.

Suddenly Cree knew she had to go help Joyce. They had to double up on the search for Josephine.

She stood up quickly, staggered as the forgotten pain exploded in her hips and thigh, and lost her balance on the levee slope. Immediately Paul stood, too, and she grabbed his outstretched hand. She let him help her back to the path, and when he didn't let go she didn't resist the continuing contact. He put his arm around her waist, and they started back toward his car that way, hip to hip. After a moment she put her arm half around him, too, hooking a finger into a belt loop.

She felt a little better. The open spaces had helped, and the thought that maybe in Josephine they had a resource to help heal Lila. Paul helped, too, she realized. The occasional soft bump and brush of their hips felt good, at once so casual and so intimate. Less scary and confusing than it would have been a week ago. For all her sense of urgency, she didn't mind allowing the moment to linger. They didn't race back. From a distance, Cree thought, they would look like lovers out for a stroll.

"So what do we do?" Paul asked quietly. "Do we approach Lila with this?"

Cree shook her head. "Not yet. I want to see if we can find Josephine. And I want to get to know Richard first. Maybe some therapeutic avenues will become clearer."

Paul nodded. After another minute he cleared his throat as if he had something he'd been wanting to say.

"Back at the hospital, I said I'd thought about . . . you know. What you told me the other night. About Mike. Is this something you're up for talking about now?"

"I think so." She tugged at his belt loop.

"I want to offer you a provocative suggestion, one you may not like. But I hope you'll think about it."

Cree chuckled humorlessly. "After the events of the last forty-eight hours, Paul, I think I can probably take just about anything."

He bobbed his head, uncertain. "Seeing Mike after his death was a huge thing. It changed your outlook, you had to radically adapt your worldview to cope with it. And it left you with . . . ambiguities about your marital status. If people don't exactly, totally die, is Cree Black still sort of married? Or is she single? Your situation was more extreme, perhaps, but it's not so different from the confusion that's typical of every person who loses a spouse. They grieve, and they often stay single and celibate out of respect for the dead loved one – the sense of connectedness and love, the desire for fidelity, doesn't go away. Staying loyal is a way to keep the lost one alive, just a little, and anyway, it just doesn't feel right to become close to someone else. And there's often the fear of intimacy, the fear that getting close to someone might just set you up for another such loss. Have I got all this about right?"

Cree nodded.

"So in searching for answers, you become, by degrees, a ghost hunter – a psychologist for the dead. Because you want to know how it works. You want to know what kind of beings we are! But you also wonder where Mike is. Some part of you has got to be hoping maybe you'll see him again? You'll find him again?"

Cree felt each word like a body blow. It was all too true, it was all too much to bear. "This isn't what I thought you were wanting to talk about," she said hoarsely. "I've just been through five kinds of hell. I don't –"

"Please, just let me finish. So you become a ghost hunter. Watching you dealing with Lila, I can tell your process just about kills you every time, yet you keep on doing it. Why? Just existential curiosity? I don't think so. I think the answer is right there, in what you really do with ghosts. Cree, no, don't turn away now! Listen to me! You get rid of them, you banish them! You 'free' them, you, what's your word, 'remediate' them! Don't hear this wrong, Cree, but maybe that's no accident? Maybe after nine years, part of you knows you need to 'remediate' *Mike?* Maybe that's the hidden truth of why you do this. You're unconsciously trying to free yourself from your *own* haunting. You're trying to – "

"You are *not* my psychiatrist!" All the anger had returned in a blinding blaze, and she shoved him from her so hard he staggered away. "How dare you!"

Paul stood just off the path, hands palm up, his face searching hers. "I'm just trying to — "

"You're trying to get me into the sack! You're being self-interested and opportunistic, and you're being intolerably condescending. You're thinking of me as some kind of psychological specimen under your microscope, Paul! You're violating a basic professional precept, which is that people *ask* you to analyze them, you don't presume to do so unless you are asked. And I most definitely do *not* want you to be my psychoanalyst!"

Furious, she strode away, leaving him standing there.

"What would you like me to be, Cree?" he called after her. "Maybe it's time to figure that out."

She stormed back to the car, tears burning on her cheeks. It wasn't until she saw the BMW below her that she realized that of course there were no clean exits here. She was dependent on Paul to drive her back downtown. A couple of other cars were in the lot now, trunk lids up as families unloaded picnic gear. She stumbled down the steps, ashamed of her red, tear-slicked face, of her predicament. She wanted to hide in the car, but of course the doors were locked and Paul had the keys.

So she leaned against the hood, her arms crossed hard, occasionally wiping her eyes with the back of her hands, doing her best to swallow the sobs before they could burst out. Everything hurt. The picnickers averted their eyes as they went past her to the stairs. Paul was a little figure at the top of the levee half a block away, walking along slowly, head down, hands in pockets, kicking at stones.

She hated him. She hated being wrenched open and exposed. She hated having to face that truth in her. She hated that Paul was right.

Oh, Mike! she cried inwardly. The rest was right there, the part she had never been able to say or even think: *Set me free! Please, my love.*

Paul came to the top of the stairs but stopped suddenly to dig his cell phone out of his pocket. He flipped it open, put it to his ear, and listened intently. His face changed.

Then he was trotting quickly down the stairs and jogging toward her. Whatever they might have said or not said was moot, because when he was fifteen feet away he called out, "That was Jack Warren. Lila has attempted suicide – he doesn't know, maybe she's succeeded. Cut her wrists. They've just taken her to the emergency ward."

36

THERE WASN'T MUCH TO BE done. By the time they got to the hospital, Lila had already undergone surgery to stop the bleeding and had been sedated. Now she slept in a private room with her wrists bandaged and strapped to the sides of the bed. Paul conferred with the surgeon and came back to report that she had lost a lot of blood, but that she'd received transfusions and was expected to be fine. Physically.

Of course, if she were really determined to do it, she'd try again.

Cree had no standing – she wasn't family, was not Lila's physician or psychiatrist, wasn't even licensed to practice in Louisiana. If Lila woke and asked for her, she might get in to talk with her, but otherwise not. And maybe not anyway: Jack made it clear that he blamed Cree for Lila's state of mind, and he claimed that given Lila's instability, he had some presumptive power of attorney that would allow him to prohibit future contact. The attending physician looked at her with suspicion and distaste.

Paul: She was pretty sure she'd blown it with him yet again, terminally. Or vice versa. *Whatever*, Cree thought viciously.

She slipped away while Jack and Paul talked. Downstairs, she found a pay phone, called Joyce, and went outside to catch a cab.

They met at the base of Canal Street, on the riverbank – Cree still wasn't feeling up for interiors. They found a bench in the narrow riverside park that adjoined the Aquarium of the Americas. The sun had become merciless, hard and heavy as hot bronze, so they chose a little enclosure shaded by oak trees and cooled by a weak breeze from the river. Today it carried a faint sulphur smell, pollution from some downriver chemical plant. Cree brought Joyce up to date on their discoveries in the Epicurus archives and described from a clinical perspective the many ways Richard's rape explained Lila's life choices and current mental state.

Listening, Joyce took on an old and world-weary look. But hearing about Lila's suicide attempt brought her eyes wide with urgency again.

"Cree, we're gonna have to step back a bit here. I mean, do you really need me to tell you how you look right now? It's not just last night, either – swear to Gawd, Cree, you've lost easily ten pounds since you got here, and you did *not* have it to spare. But last night, do I have to tell you how *bad* that was? How close you've been cutting it? When you tell me you've got to kind of go crazy, and when the person you're getting this super-empathic link with slits her wrists? What am I supposed to do? I keep telling you, this is a *job*, okay? It's not supposed to *kill* you."

"It'll only kill me if we lose it we fail to solve the problem. If I can save Lila, I can save myself."

"The problem is not just Lila! Look, Cree, I'm no psychologist, but it doesn't take Uncle Sigmund to tell that some of this is Cree and Mike and nine years of ambivalences. And you can't stake your survival on shedding all that in a matter of days!" Joyce shook her head, and her voice softened. "Cree. You know I'd do anything for you. I would. You're like . . . like a sister to me. More than a sister. We play this game, you and me, a lot of times I'm kind of the court jester with you, I'm trying to keep you happy and grounded?" Joyce's lips went into a trembling pout, and Cree realized how deep this went, how naked an admission this was. "But I can't find a way to do that here. Being the funny girl-buddy sidekick, you know, like in the TV sit-coms? It doesn't help, it's not enough. I'm scared. None of this is funny any more."

Moved, Cree reached out to touch Joyce's cheek. "You do keep me happy and grounded. Joyce, we're getting toward the end, I can feel it. We're beginning to get a handle on this."

"Yeah?" Joyce's anger rose again. "Well, I hope *you* are, because I've come up with just about squat that's gonna be useful. Richard Beauforte – there's a ton on the guy. He gave to charities. He was president of civic groups. He bought and sold properties. He entertained. He was buddies with mayors and other bigwigs. In the obits everybody called him practically a saint."

"He was capable of raping his own daughter in the most sadistic way imaginable. There has to be some indication of that elsewhere in his life. Somewhere we're going to find what we need to undo him."

Joyce opened her briefcase, took out a thick sheaf of photocopies, and shakily leafed through them, pulling one here and there to hand to Cree. "Well, you're gonna have to read a lot between the lines, Cree. Let's see – he got caught driving under the influence twice in his life. Got himself lawyered up, no convictions. Does that mean he had an uncontrollable alcohol problem and that he was out-of-control drunk when he raped Lila? Maybe, maybe not. Okay, here we got a sexual harassment suit by a female employee at his firm. He denied everything, fought it, settled it on some unspecified terms. A valid complaint, suggesting the guy had impulse control issues with the opposite sex? Or a frivolous thing by somebody who wanted a raise and didn't get one? Oh, and here he's doing some litigation himself, suing a former business partner, seeking damages and insisting the court revoke the guy's license to practice law. Was it appropriate, or does it show our man has a nasty, vengeful streak?" Joyce shrugged, flopped the sheaf against her leg. "If you want to know who this guy is from this material, you're gonna need more than empathic talents, Cree. You're gonna need to be *clairvoyant*. Because to me, this doesn't add up to a hill of beans."

Cree looked over the papers as Joyce tried to compose herself. She was right: For every little item that suggested a dark side, there were ten that showed Richard to be a pillar of the community, a good citizen, a dedicated family man.

At last she handed them back, beginning to feel defeated. "What about Josephine Dupree? Any luck at all?"

"Next to nothing. Her name *does* show up in the phone records for 1973 and 1974 – I have the service address here. Looks to me she moved there for a couple of years after she left the Beaufortes, but after that, nothing. The only other thing, I found in the *Times-Picayune* records –

exactly one, small hit for Josephine Dupree." Joyce rummaged in her briefcase again and extracted a single page.

It was a photocopy of an obituary-page article about the death of one Souline Dupree, who had died in 1975 at the age of eighty-two. "Queen Souline" had been a moderately well-known root doctor and conjure woman in New Orleans for forty years. The article described her as the last of her generation, having learned her hoodoo charms and remedies from practitioners who had once been slaves. As such, she was a repository of knowledge of Afro-Caribbean folkcures, quasi-mystical traditions, and oral histories; her loss meant the end of an era. She had once been a fixture in a tiny shop on the northern edge of the French Quarter, selling herbs and lore and advice. A lifelong smoker, she'd died of lung cancer, survived by only two of her seven children – daughters Jasmine Tricou, sixty, and Josephine Dupree, fifty-four.

The library photo showed an old woman with thinned gray hair and pouched eyes, wearing a small crucifix on a chain around her neck and holding a cigarette in a V of gnarled fingers. She bore an unmistakable resemblance to the photos Cree had seen of Josephine – that long face with its strong jaw, downturned lips, and resolute expression.

"So of course I looked for the sister, Jasmine Tricou, everywhere, too," Joyce said. "Nothing. Nada. I think they're both probably dead."

"No," Cree assured her. "Josephine is alive. And we have to find her."

The hexes, she was thinking. Here at last was a possible connection between the hexes and the Beaufortes. By all accounts, Josephine was a devout churchgoer, but as Deelie had pointed out, voodoo and hoodoo often coexisted with Christian beliefs. And Josephine must have learned something of the old arts, growing up with a mother who was a serious practitioner. Josephine had put the notched sticks at Beauforte House, Cree was sure, and had placed the one at the Warrens', with the goal of inducing "confusion of mind" in the residents there. If she knew about the rape, it made sense she'd want Lila to forget. But why the Chases? With everything she and Joyce learned, and with every new puzzle that presented itself, Josephine seemed to hold the keys.

"Okay. But, Cree – it hurts my professional pride to admit this, but

I'm kind of running out of magic here? I can't think of a lot more we can do to locate her. We could collect every phone book in Louisiana and call every Dupree to see if any of them know a Josephine. But for all we know, if she is alive, she moved to Chicago, or – "

"I know someone who might be able to help us," Cree said.

Deelie Brown said she had another appointment, but if they could get across town fast she'd be happy to hear them out. When they got to the *Times-Picayune* building, they found her waiting in the little park in front of the main entrance, sitting on a bench and pulling yards of magnetic tape from a cassette that was apparently stuck in a small recorder. Her face was folded in that glowering frown she'd first greeted Cree with, but when she saw them the smile came back, sun from behind the clouds. Cree felt a rush of affection for the solid, chunky woman, her mismatched clothes, the congruence between what she claimed to be and what Cree sensed she really was.

"Yo, my ghost hunter sister," she said. She tossed the mess aside and stood with a rattle of hair beads.

The highway ramps all around roared steadily as Cree kissed her cheek, introduced Joyce, and thanked her for making time to meet them.

Deelie's frown had returned. "You know, you don't look so good, Miz Black."

"I've been hearing that a lot lately, yeah." Cree tried to grin.

"Fight with your man? Or just 'fall down the stairs'?"

"Stairs."

"Oh, uh-huh, right." Deelie shared her skeptical look with Joyce. "So, what we got today? You need my help on a ghost hunt, you're talking my language, grist for the proverbial mill. What you need?"

Cree gave her an overview of why they wanted to locate Josephine, and she and Joyce told her the little they knew. The address Joyce had found from 1974, Deelie told them, was in Tremé, like St. Bernard Development a low-income housing project. "What you all out east call a black ghetto," Deelie said. At first, Deelie had looked a little disappointed to hear that she was needed to help find a living person, but when Cree explained Josephine's hoodoo connection, the possibility of a link to the Chase murder, she brightened.

"Money in the bank for me, it ties in with Temp." Deelie's eyes showed that her wheels were turning. "Yeah, see, now you're thinkin' straight. Out-of-town white girl and a Chinese not going to make a lot of headway doing a missing persons gig in black N'Orleans. You look like TV lady cops or welfare fraud investigators or something, people going to shut their faces they see you two coming. This Josephine got any connection at all to other voodoo and hoodoo people, I know where to look for her. If not, it'll be slower, but I got ways."

"There's one more problem, though," Cree said. "We . . . it's important that we find her as soon as possible. There's a certain amount of risk for several of the parties involved, and – "

"You mean like 'falling down the stairs.'" Deelie gave her a shrewd look and clearly saw the desperation in her face. "Don't want another 'accident' anytime soon? Yo, trust me, I'm on it already."

37

CREE SAT FOR AN HOUR in the relative calm of her hotel room. Joyce had ordered her to bed and then had gone off to her own room to call every Dupree and Tricou in the current phone book. For the first hour or two, she also called Cree every now and again, ostensibly to share some thought, but really, they both knew, to make sure she was staying put.

Paul's comments about remediating Mike gnawed at Cree's stomach. Now her memory conjured only their occasional fights, the miffs and tiffs and little hurts. Mike looked at her with reproach in his eyes. She knew it was true, and she couldn't live with her betrayal. *Damn Paul,* she thought. Another undoing.

She couldn't go on like this much longer. In her thoughts, she repeated a mantra she had cobbled together from bits of Zen and Taoist and yoga philosophy: *Out of weakness grows strength,* she chanted inwardly. *From confusion emerges resolve. In yielding is the root of resistance.*

These were the paradoxes, it increasingly seemed, by which she lived.

To be brave enough to face the boar-headed ghost and knowledgeable enough to understand its demented worldview, she had to become vulnerable enough to see it, to know it. To be strong enough to combat Lila's weakness, she had to know Lila's weakness in herself. To possess a strong enough sense of self to survive the encounters, she had to endure absolute uncertainty as to who she was. She had to find her husband so she could let him go forever.

And she had done these things, except the last. Surprisingly, out of all the confusion, all the wounds physical and emotional, she did feel a curious strength and resolve. It was as if the events of the last few days and nights had stripped away everything superfluous, leaving only this single, hard grain of defiance at her very center. It was tiny but durable – a starting place.

But there was a problem, an irritant to which her thoughts increasingly gravitated. It jangled in her mind like a discordant musical tone, a warning buzzer in the distance. The more she pondered, the more inconsistencies she found in her theory of events.

Richard Beauforte had raped Lila, that much was certain: the boar mask had borne it out, and it was perfectly consistent with Lila's psychological state and Charmian's attitude. But there was a clear divide between these normal-world facts and what Cree had experienced at Beauforte House. Something didn't fit. The simplest question was: If the boar-headed ghost was Richard, who was the ghost in the library? Who was the man who lay dying and sending his thoughts to that little girl on the swing? And what of the beating motion, the rage and accusation that went with it? There were a thousand shadings of feeling accompanying each manifestation, and they just didn't jibe.

And what of the other phenomena that Lila had described – the snake, that wolf? After finding that the boar-headed man was not an epiphenomenal manifestation brewed from Lila's subconscious, Cree had less confidence that the others could be so easily dismissed.

Obviously, the boar-headed man was not a perimortem experience, but rather a vivid, crucial memory replaying itself. But she'd never come near his dying experience. Could there be any truth to Joyce's suggestion, the idea that the ghost was a manifestation of Ron's subconscious? The idea didn't explain the boar mask, but at this point, disturbingly, she couldn't totally discard the theory. Anything seemed possible.

But Cree rebelled against the idea. Though she couldn't say why, she could swear the manifestation originated from a dying man. Maybe it was her sense of Ron, the lack of the psychic "buzz" she'd expect from a person with the capacity to project such a powerful psi phenomenon.

So maybe she should reconsider the ghost in the library. Could one dying man's mental processes manifest as two such clearly different entities – his death experience being played out only in the library, his paradoxical, self-punishing memories playing out only upstairs?

It was vaguely possible, but again her instincts rebelled. The two ghosts *felt* so different. The dying man in the library just didn't seem to be the sort of person who could do what the boar-headed man did. But more important was the dimensional difference between them, as clear as that between a video and a living person. The revenant replaying his death in the library was as emotionally rich and complex as he was physically insubstantial, and was rigidly locked into a very limited repertoire of acts, thoughts, and feelings. By contrast, the boar-headed man was narrow, one-dimensional, yet very solid and physical. He was also one of the most intentional, most adaptive ghosts Cree had ever encountered.

She puzzled over it for several hours, playing theories through to their ramifications. Only one stood up at all: that maybe there were indeed two ghosts but only one dying man. Maybe Richard Beauforte had been a Jekyll and Hyde personality, literally and clinically suffering from multiple personality disorder. One personality – internally consistent, probably not even aware of his alter ego – was the decent man, good citizen, loving father, who had died of a heart attack on the library floor. The other was the sadistic, lust-charged creature, in life always concealing itself from its benevolent twin and only occasionally set free to act on its own. And at Richard's death, that part of him had taken on an independent mental existence of a totally different order: physically substantial, kinetic, highly adaptive yet still locked into reliving the searingly intense act that had defined, distilled, its nature.

A multiple personality revenant: Cree suffered a sudden reprise of fear at the thought. How could you untangle such a sick and double being? At first glance, she thought that if you let the dying man in the library go free, let him finish dying, the ghost upstairs would vanish as well. But maybe not. Maybe it would continue on, so divorced from its origins as a living being and from its dying experience that it had no death left to accomplish.

The scenario also left the beating motion to figure in. Another dying memory? Or maybe the beating man was yet another entity, the much older ghost of John Frederick murdering Lionel.

Too many possibilities. None of them quite right, none quite wrong enough to dismiss. She stewed about it until she decided there was only one way to find out. Just the thought made her stomach clench.

But there didn't seem to be a choice. You had to fight back. Push the envelope. Couldn't run away with your tail between your legs.

She waited until almost midnight, when she was sure Joyce wouldn't try to call her. Then she dressed and quietly slipped out of the room and down the somnolent midnight corridors of the hotel. She felt scared to the edge of hysteria, but on another level she had never in her life felt more thoroughly ready.

She entered the now familiar hush of the house with an out-of-control pulse: The memories of the pursuit and the fall were too fresh to overcome. Leaving the lights off, she reset the security panel and headed back into the house, groping her way toward the library.

The silence screamed in her ears.

There was no guaranteeing her multiple personality theory was correct, but it was worth a try. If indeed both ghosts were manifested from a single man, the manifestation seen in its moment of death on the library floor would be the one most likely to reveal the key to the boar-headed entity. In any case, she knew she couldn't cope with the half man, half animal. Her panic was still right there, just beneath the surface. The fear reflexes were too strong. She'd only flee again, mindless, and be pursued and probably die, or worse, this time.

So she'd seek the dying man's experience. She'd have to pierce through those outer layers, find the core, the dying moment.

She found her way through the kitchen and down the hallway into the west wing, ears burning with the expectation of hearing that gut-wrenching, whimpering cry. But the house was silent, holding its musty breath.

The library was a cave of darkness. She walked slowly forward, found the piano, slid her fingers lightly along the smooth keys, veered a little left to find the back of one of the fireplace wingback chairs. From there, she went straight back until she bumped the claw-foot table. Moving to the right, she guided herself with her fingertips along the table's edge until her other hand found the chair she'd sat in the first two times. Deep in the corner, it would give the best vantage in the room.

Richard? she called. A thought like a secret.

She turned to sit in the chair and started to lower herself into it, then leapt up again with a shriek.

She had almost sat on somebody.

She was afraid to budge. Incapable of moving. She had seen two thighs, right beneath her, and they'd shifted as she'd glanced back.

She backed away two steps until she bumped into the bookshelves behind her. She'd have to run to her left, along the wall of the room. There was some furniture in the way, a table, a floor lamp, but she couldn't remember exactly where.

She could see him better now. In the chair. A man-shaped cloud, coalescing and taking on detail. A man in a dark gray suit. His head was turned, so she couldn't quite see his whole face from this angle, but clearly he wore no boar mask. On the claw-footed table at his side was a tray with decanters and bottles, and an ashtray from which he lifted a cigar. He put it to his lips, drew and exhaled a faint plume of smoke that Cree smelled. Then he took up a cut-crystal glass, and she tasted the liquor in it. Amaretto, fiery almond-sweet.

It gave the ghost no satisfaction. He was too unhappy, too preoccupied. He turned toward her, and Cree saw it was Richard Beauforte, who looked at his cigar with distaste and set it down. He sipped some more amaretto and put the glass down, too.

He stood up unsteadily and thought, *A little too much to drink.* He was unhappy. He was burdened. He was dealing with a problem that was vast and horrible, that made him too angry and sad to think about. Whenever his thoughts came too close, his mind sparked with rage and sorrow and regret. As Cree pushed herself back against the bookshelves, he walked slowly to the circle of chairs at the fireplace and stood for a moment just watching the gas fire that burned in the grate.

There has to be a way, he was thinking. *To piece a family together again. My fault, my responsibility to fix it. But how?*

Abruptly he wanted his cigar again, something to occupy his fingers. He returned from the fireplace toward Cree, and she could see his face clearly, a high forehead above the suffering eyes of a man who hadn't slept and who had terrible things on his mind. He lurched slightly as he walked, *A little drunk*, found the cigar, puffed it back to life. Saw the rest of the liquor in the glass and despondently thought, *What the hell*, and drained it. *Dull the pain.*

She will never understand. She'll never forgive, he was thinking as he walked away. *And she will never accept her share of the blame.* Cree saw the image of Charmian in his thoughts.

He detoured to the piano, where he stood and plinked a few plaintive notes. *How to piece together anything like a family again? How to recover the bond? Not to mention the Beauforte name, the pride, the posterity? I can't do it. Beyond me.* In desperation, his thoughts fanned out, seeking comfort, seeking an answer. Abruptly he thought of Bradford, the perpetually boyish, mischievous face, that offhand good humor, the needed leavening he had always brought to the household, the companionship for each member, and for an instant missed him terribly. *Irony of ironies, the one person who could help would be Brad. Brad who was dead dead dead, God damn him to hell anyway.*

Richard's emotions swirled red and black and sick green, anger and guilt and regret and loss, and he brought a fist down on the piano keys in a discordant explosion before he lurched away toward the fireplace again. There seemed nowhere for his thoughts to turn. He couldn't breathe right. When he got back to the circle of chairs there, he felt a twinge of pain in his gut, very strong this time, and thought, *Ulcer acting up. And no wonder.* Uneasy, he sat down on the edge of one of the chairs and checked his watch. The amaretto had left a displeasing, almost oily aftertaste. Or maybe it was the cigar.

Talk to Lila? Or do what Charm says and try to pretend it didn't happen? Maybe it will all heal over somehow. Only two hours until she goes back to school. Time to decide.

The thought of Lila hurt him terribly, an emotional pang that merged with the growing physical pain in his lungs and stomach and bowels, and suddenly he realized something was wrong. Cree could feel it, too: the paralyzed lungs, the burn in his stomach and the acid electric radiant pain shooting down into his lower belly and groin and legs. He stood up quickly, lost his balance, fell against the mantel to stabilize himself. *Not right,* he was thinking. *Not right, this isn't ulcer.*

He turned toward the door, realizing that his thoughts weren't right either, he was confused. *"Charmian?"* he called. He realized he didn't know if she was in the house, couldn't remember just when this was. The pain gored him again and he doubled over, went to his knees on the carpet. The cigar tumbled out of his fingers and he saw it there on the carpet and knew how angry Charmian would be if he put a spot in it. He ground out the ash with his fingers and only afterward realized it had burned him. Cree's fingers tingled.

"Charm, honey, can you . . ." and he didn't know what he wanted of her. *Where was she? ". . . help me?"* Or maybe she had gone out. Or was that yesterday? He lunged to his feet and took two quick strides toward the door but fell full out before he could reach it. *No air.* His legs refused to work, and the pain was everywhere now, he was a ball of pain. The amaretto taste was too strong and wouldn't fade and it surrounded him and it wasn't right, and abruptly he knew he'd been poisoned. Every labored breath was full of its suffocating stink. He flopped on the rug, trying to get to his hands and knees but the room tilted and he fell heavily on his side.

Josephine! his thoughts cried. Her face came clearly to mind. He was experiencing a telescoped, dreamlike memory, all of it rushing at him together, a flickering movie played many times too fast. Faces and names, Josephine and Charmian and Brad and Ron and Lila and further back, *Father!* and *Mama!,* and others Cree didn't know. And then the beating, beating, beating, the intolerable rage and the revulsion of it, the self-hatred and regret and compassion and fear of what the future held and the beating going on anyway, completely out of control. The horror of feeling such abandon, letting go into something so animal, knowing it had always been there and was impermissible but unstoppable, too.

And abruptly he knew for certain he was dying.

Cree had felt that recognition before, at once deeply familiar and impossibly strange. With the knowledge came the sense of everything being interrupted at just the wrong time: all the gestures of life, so desperately needing closure, so unresolved and incomplete. So wrong.

"Charmian!" he shouted. He doubled again on the floor like a grub brought out of the soil and contorting in the sunlight. *"Charmian!"* And there was no answer. No, she was gone today. *"Josephine?"* Another call for help. *"Josephine!"* This time more of an accusation – he felt betrayed by her. But she was gone, too. Or was she, yet? He didn't know when he was, time was folding upon itself in liquid, doubling loops. *"Josephine! Charm, don't let her go! She – "* And he didn't know what he was going to say. It was urgent, but it had vanished from his mind.

Again Cree saw a glimpse of the nanny's mahogany-dark face, her resolute mouth, her steady, relentless eyes. And there was no refuge in her, or in Charmian. His thoughts fled to Ron with concern: poor innocent Ro-Ro. Ro-Ro would never understand – this would destroy him just as it destroyed Lila. He'd failed his son, too.

And then he was just dying and all the thoughts fused into one thing, his life distilled down into what really mattered, and it was Lila, and Lila was a little girl, that day when the air was so nice and they'd found themselves in the backyard and for once there wasn't something else pressing that had to be done, and they'd both just been there together, father and daughter.

Overcome, Cree took a step toward the convulsing figure. "Daddy?" she blurted. "Daddy!" He couldn't die, not now.

Now the ghost existed only as a memory of that moment. He'd pushed her on the swing, so high, up into the branches, and they'd both laughed and it had been so complete, just doing that. So simple. There was no need to say anything and she was so happy and he was so complete. A moment of simple harmony that wrote its shape on his soul.

Richard arched in a last wave of pain, clinging to the memory, the one refuge for his tortured heart: the image of her way up and giddy on the swing, hair and skirts trailing behind, skinny legs stuck out straight and mouth wide with laughter. He sent his love toward her on her upward free arc, hoping she'd know it and carry it with her always, praying that in some way *this* was what she'd carry with her. This and not the other.

And then the form on the rug stopped convulsing and the girl on the swing broke into a million crazy fragments, shards of a broken mirror. After a moment the solid-looking man became a haze again, his body-ghost dissipating. The room seen through his eyes faded and it was dark and Cree was alone again, weeping. She sobbed so hard it felt as though she'd turn inside out. She fell to her hands and knees and cried until it was as if she'd vomited and she was weak and empty but it was done with for now.

She used her flashlight only once, to search the floor where she'd seen him fall. And she found the little burn mark in the splendid, faded carpet. She put her finger on it and almost felt the searing ash again. Then she put away the light and groped her way out of the room, blind from darkness and tears.

38

"THE RAPE WAS A BOMB THAT exploded that family," Cree told Joyce. "All the relationships blew apart, people scattering like shrapnel. Charmian learned of it and couldn't be with her husband any more but couldn't decide how to preserve anything like a family if she accused him publicly. So she started sleeping apart from him but otherwise made a pretense of normal life. Lila couldn't cope with what happened or with her feelings toward her father. She suffered from posttraumatic stress and became acutely depressed. Went off to school, broke down, came back, got medicated up, went away for good. Ron, I'm not sure how much he knew, but everything was going crazy, everything was wrong. He 'went away' by abdicating his role as scion of the illustrious family he now knew to be a complete hypocrisy. He retreated into self-absorption and self-indulgence. And Josephine left, too, fled the collapse of the Beaufortes – and probably the wrath of Charmian."

Joyce nodded thoughtfully. "So you're thinking it was Josephine, not Charmian? Who poisoned Richard?"

Of course Joyce would put it together fast, Cree thought. "Yes. Oh, Charmian would've wanted to, and she would've been capable of it. But her pride wouldn't have let her risk a public scandal. Above all else, she'd protect the family name."

Joyce didn't seem so sure. She sorted among her carefully ordered files and pulled out a page. "Richard's obituary says he died on January 7, 1972. Lila could have been still at home for Christmas break, or maybe she'd gone back already. How can we verify when Josephine left?"

Cree took the sheet from her and read it closely for the first time. "I don't know that it matters. Either she was still working for them, or she came back just to put something in Richard's drink. She might still have had a key."

"You think cyanide? Isn't that the one that smells like almonds? All I know is the old mystery movies."

Cree shrugged. It didn't matter.

They were sitting in Cree's room, drinking the hotel kit's anemic coffee with chalk dust in it. The curtains were wide to the morning light and the throb of activity on Canal Street below. When Cree had told Joyce she'd gone to the house again, Joyce had been furious at first, then merely negative and resigned. Only after a lot of reassuring had Cree been able to rekindle the spark of curiosity in her, her bloodhound's instincts.

Joyce tapped a pencil against her lips, thinking. "One question, though. Coroner said it was heart failure. How'd that get by?"

Cree had already found the answer. She showed Joyce a line from the obituary. "Dr. Andre Fitzpatrick – Paul Fitzpatrick's father – was the New Orleans parish coroner at the time, and he's who certified cause of death. He was Richard's physician and a good friend of the Beaufortes – I've seen his name on the back of probably a dozen photos in Lila's albums. He was also the doctor Charmian called in to treat Lila when she fell apart. My guess is Charmian prevailed upon him to cover it up to protect the Beauforte name. She probably told him *why* Josephine killed Richard, and he agreed that it was justified, that punishing her would serve no interest. And that charging her would only make the scandal public."

Joyce poured herself the last of the coffee from the little pot, swigged it, made a face. "So you're thinking Richard really was, clinically, a multiple personality? That he's both ghosts?"

"It's the only way all the parts fit together. It fits with what I've learned from the ghosts and what we've learned from conventional research. It fits Lila's psychological state and Charmian's secretiveness. I know it's a pretty radical idea, but I'm going to assume it's the correct theory."

"So what's next?"

"Well, we hope Deelie turns up Josephine. Part of me wants to go confront Charmian, tell her what I know, plead with her to cooperate. But first I think I need to talk to Dr. Fitzpatrick again. We need to figure out a prognosis for Lila based on what we now know."

"So it's *Doctor* Fitzpatrick again? Here I thought maybe you guys – "

"Joyce. This isn't the time for – "

"For what? Life? Or just love?"

Cree bristled and stamped her foot in anger and frustration. "Damn it, Joyce, you are simply going to have get off this thing of – "

"Oh, no! Uh-uh, Cree – don't you even *dream* of getting angry at me!" Joyce shot out of her chair and stood defiantly, startling Cree with her intensity. She turned three-quarters toward Cree, legs apart in almost a martial arts stance, her narrowed eyes shooting black sparks. "Yeah, Cree, I remind you that we are *alive*, okay, and that life goes *on*, and you should *never* let all this stuff interfere. Well, excuse me! My attitude is you need a dose of life once in a while. No, actually, let's cut to the chase here – my attitude is that getting *laid* would do you a world of good. There, I've said it. You don't like that, I quit. Seriously, Cree, I walk out of this room right now, and you go ahead and turn into some kind of walking dead, zombie bitch. The metaphysics here are a complete no-brainer, and I'm sick of going over it and over it!"

Cree had never seen her like this. She stood open-mouthed, unable to respond.

Joyce was shoveling her files into her briefcase in a blind fury, blinking back tears. "Plus you owe me two weeks' back pay and severance."

Cree's heart felt wrenched in her chest. "Joyce, it's not that simple with Paul – "

"It never *is* 'simple,' Cree, not even for people with discernable body heat and a few remaining mammalian instincts, okay? But you've forgotten all that, I guess." Joyce snapped up the briefcase but then looked at it in surprise. "What am I doing? I don't need this stuff. Here, you take it." She flung it at Cree's feet. Then she grabbed her purse, slung the strap over her shoulder, and strode to the door. "All yours. And good luck."

"Joyce. Please."

Joyce stopped with her hand on the knob, her heaving back to Cree. "What," she said after a moment.

"Listen, you're probably right. But it's very hard for me to be with a guy who . . . thinks I'm nuts. It means we're not . . . not equals. How can I be with someone who sees me that way? Half the time he acts as if I'm a . . . a patient, a *case* . . . not a woman."

Joyce spun back to her. The anger was still bright, but it was conflicted and starting to come apart. "Well, I can think of some real easy ways to shift his perspective. It doesn't take a genius. A short skirt, a snug tank top, and the *right attitude*, Cree, does wonders for a guy's outlook! Suspends all that rational judgment damned fast. Every time."

Cree shook her head. "Paul doesn't believe in what I do. He doesn't believe in what I see, what I am. His worldview won't allow him to see it any other way."

Joyce took a step back from the door, biting her lips as her fury broke apart. She was still breathing hard as they looked at each other for a moment. Then her face puckered. She put out her shaking hand to Cree's cheek, a cool, tentative touch.

"Then you're just gonna have to change his worldview, aren't you?" she said softly.

It took an awkward half hour, but they patched things up. They were both shell-shocked, but Joyce had called it right, it was the kind of battle and reconciliation sisters had: Afterward, the combatants mustered on and somehow the relationship endured. They talked about the case for a time, then Joyce went off to do homework – mainly, to chase down a few leads Deelie had suggested for finding Josephine.

Finally, Cree also requested that Joyce call Edgar and ask him if he could come sooner than planned. She didn't specify why, but Joyce clearly got the message: If Ed wanted a shot at this ghost, he'd better come soon. Cree would need to move straight into remediation; they couldn't delay for a period of technological verification and physical analysis. This ghost had to be dealt with fast, before Cree fell apart or Lila succeeded in killing herself. Or both.

After Joyce left, Cree put in a call to Charmian. She spoke to Tarika, who said that she was out; Cree left a message requesting a call back. She called the hospital and asked to speak to Lila but was told she was asleep. She was recovering well, the floor nurse said, but she was on a sedative drip that kept her groggy. Medically, physically, she could be released at any time, but her psychological health was another matter; Jack and Lila's physician were arranging longer-term treatment at a psychiatric facility. She called Jack to arrange a meeting with him, to persuade him to allow her access to Lila, but he hung up on her. She called Deelie to check in about progress on Josephine, got her voice mail, left a message.

That left her just about out of initiatives. True, there was much to be done at the house – too much, in fact, a daunting task. Joyce was right, she needed some recuperative time. The mere thought of the boar-headed man sent her thoughts scuttling like panicked mice; her hands shook. She was afraid to go back to the place alone.

Of course, there was still Paul Fitzpatrick to deal with. For an instant, Cree remembered the reassuring yet erotic contact of his hip as they'd walked on the levee, his arm firm around her waist. The sensation had touched a deep ache of longing. Should she sleep with him? No, the fundamental barriers were still there. Anyway, it was probably too late: They'd fought too hard, too many times. And Edgar would be here soon, and there was no way in hell Cree would subject him to witnessing her having an intimate relationship with someone else.

But Joyce was right that she had to change Paul's worldview. Cree couldn't stay in New Orleans forever to be available to Lila in the long term; Cree might be able to banish the ghost, but she couldn't banish what had happened when Richard was alive. And neither Paul nor any other therapist could effectively treat Lila unless he or she accepted the literal reality of the ghost – if for no other reason than that Lila did not need one more person urging her to deny, diminish, "selectively reinterpret," or forget another crucial and traumatic experience.

No. With bone-deep certainty, Cree knew the opposite was true: To survive, Lila had to face the ghost herself, to achieve her own victory over or reconciliation with her tormentor. Exposing her to the ghost again would put her in mortal danger, but so would pretending that the original or the spectral rapes hadn't happened.

Which meant she had to go back to the house. And there would be no way to get Lila back there, over the objections of Jack and no doubt Charmian, without Paul's help.

Cree stared at the phone for a moment, feeling the pulse accelerate in her throat, and finally dialed his home number. Machine. Then she called his office and was told by his secretary that he was not in today. She had just set down the receiver when it rang, making her jump. She snatched it up again.

"Paul?"

"I sound like a Paul to you?"

"Deelie!"

"No, it's the ghost of Jean Laffite!" Deelie's voice sounded a little hoarse, but there was definitely warmth and a smile in it. "Hey, Miz Black, I been up half the night. Legwork, my specialty? Mainly talkin' to a *lot* of old, old ladies. And, girl, you do now owe me major big. I believe I've found your Josephine!"

39

HIGHWAY 23 RAN STRAIGHT southeast from New Orleans, following the Mississippi almost to the point where it divided into multiple channels and petered out in the Gulf of Mexico. It was a flat, wet country. The shapes of land and water on Cree's road map told the story: Depositing its silt over millions of years, the patient river had extended the coastline by two hundred miles, leaving a lacework of low lying Delta soil, brackish bayous, and meandering channels.

Just south of New Orleans, the road ran through a seemingly endless series of commercial strips separated by areas dominated by heavy industry and shipping. From the relative height of highway overpasses, Cree could see horizons defined only by rearing loading gantries, the superstructures of gigantic freighters, and tall chimneys spilling smoke.

Farther south, the countryside became less cluttered. On the right, the land was empty, scrubby fields; on the left, when the levee didn't block the view, Cree could see a dense, snarled low-growth forest. Chemical plants rose out of the landscape every few miles, industrial necropolises of towers, pipelines, vents, rail tank cars, and razor-wire-topped fences. For two miles on either side of the Oronite plant, the air stank so badly of chemicals that she had to breathe through her handkerchief, yet just beyond it she passed orange groves and strawberry plantations, complete with cheery roadside stands. Road-kill armadillos broiled on hot highway asphalt.

From the map, Cree figured that Port Sulphur was about fifty miles southeast of New Orleans. One long, long hour from Canal Street.

Deelie had done what only a black woman, smart and personable and persistent and skilled at interviewing, could do: She'd gone back to Tremé, Josephine's last known address, and, starting with friends and relatives and acquaintances, had identified the oldest residents of the project. From there, it was a matter of going door to door, talking to old people who might have been around in the 1970s. At last she found a grandmother who remembered Josephine, describing her as a tall, serious woman who had a worked for some rich white family for many years. She vaguely recalled that Josephine had lived next door only a few years, until her own mother died; then she'd moved back down to where she'd been born, some no-count town 'way deep Delta.

It took a few hours more to find another old woman who had attended Josephine's church back then. She even remembered the minister's name. Josephine had been a true believer, a good Christian woman, and this Reverend Washington had won her lasting loyalty with his fiery piety and commitment. Deelie then called the church offices until she found someone who could tell her where Reverend Washington was; the answer was that he was dead. But looking through their records, the church secretary found Josephine: She'd moved down to Port Sulphur, where she attended an affiliated splinter church, Mount of Olives Sunrise Congregation. Deelie called and spoke to the minister, Rev. Bernard Huggins, who told her that, yes, Josephine Dupree was still a devout member of the congregation, a mainstay of the church community.

No, Josephine didn't have a phone. But she did have an address.

"Piece of proverbial cake," Deelie crowed. Then her voice darkened. "Gotta warn you about one thing, though. Couple people said there'd been some white guys asking about this same Josephine, like two years back? They went around saying she'd inherited some money, could anybody help them find her so they could give it to her? I don't have to tell you how well that flew in Tremé. You black in New Orleans, you know when to open your mouth and when to keep it shut. Rule one is you keep it shut when a white guy in a suit comes asking."

"So who were these guys?"

"Nobody knew. Not cops exactly, maybe like private dicks. Whatever, it suggests that this Josephine's messed up in something, and you're not the only one trying to find her. I don't know what this is all about, but, you — watch yourself. You know?"

Deelie had let Cree off the line only after she'd sworn a blood oath to give her first access to the story. If indeed there was any story.

Cree's curiosity grew as she drove, and she had to make a conscious effort to keep her foot light on the accelerator. Josephine was deeply connected to this; she was the key that could unlock the whole case. But would she tell Cree anything? Cree had debated asking Deelie to come with her, but the reporter had other obligations, and besides, this had to be a very, very confidential meeting.

Beyond the basic distrust between black and white Deelie had pointed out, Josephine would certainly not want to talk about her murder of Richard Beauforte. And then there was the apparent tie-in, whatever it was, to the Chase murder and the fact that others were looking for her. Josephine would probably feel too at risk to say anything at all to anyone — black, white, or green.

Here and there along the road, Cree saw the remains of old plantations: sagging, magnificent pillared houses deep at the end of tunnels of massive live oaks. In their weary-looking, moss-stained roofs and hollow windows, their overgrown grounds, Cree could still feel the history that saturated this place. There was the public history of Southern chivalry, decorous soirees, and great events, and there was the hidden, very different tale of intimate lives lived in the long days and steamy Delta nights.

In both cases, time had moved on, and the old mansions were few and far between. Now most of the houses were small and poor, desperately ramshackle, sharing their lots with buckling sheds, dusty truck gardens, and abandoned vehicles. Every fifteen miles or so she encountered new enclaves of gigantically ostentatious, upscale new mansions in pseudo-Tudor or Creole-modern style, safely isolated by perimeter walls and guardhouses.

And always, just over the levee, the marine terminals: gantries, mountains of coal, huge conveyors, fuel tanks. And a chemical stink the car's air-conditioner couldn't hide. Cree mistook the first cemetery she saw for a self-storage place: neat rows of little white buildings with gabled roofs.

When she'd told Cree how to get to Port Sulphur, Deelie had called this "Religion Alley," and faith did run strong here, Cree saw. For miles, every telephone pole wore a blue-and-white plastic sign that said simply *JESUS*. The same sign appeared on lawns, in storefronts and living room windows, something like an election sign. The declarations of faith brought up another question: If Josephine believed in that return from the dead, would she accept that other ways were possible, too? What if Josephine refused to talk to her on the basis of her beliefs?

It struck Cree that there were a lot of reasons for Josephine to say nothing, and only one reason for her to talk.

Port Sulphur wasn't much: the Tennessee Gas pipeline, a dead opossum in the road, Fremin's Foodliner and a few other stores, lower-middle-class and poorer houses. Residential streets branched to the left and right of the highway, lined with trailers, aluminum-sided ranch houses, or ragtag shacks. The streets all ended at the levee, a sloped wall of green at the end of each tree-shaded corridor. It took only a minute to find the Mount of Olives Sunrise church, a one-story wooden building with scaling white clapboard siding and a squat, humble steeple no bigger than a camping tent. From there, she followed Reverend Huggins's instructions to Josephine's house on the last cross street, out at the edge of town. Beyond it, the tangled forest and scrub fields began again.

There were no numbers on the houses, but Reverend Huggins had been clear that Josephine's was the last one on the right, an old place up against the levee. Cree cruised slowly past dilapidated one-story houses, drawing the attention of residents who paused at their tasks or came to screen doors to give her suspicious stares.

Josephine's house was an old wooden building in an overgrown lot, windows dark behind shrubs and vines, porch roof sagging under the weight of leaf detritus, screens patched or rusted through. Cree pulled into the driveway behind an old Ford and got out into heat that hit like a body blow. The smell of the bayou just over the levee was humid, rich with the smell of rot and carrying just a hint of some exotic spice, and it brought to her forcefully just how far from home she was.

Josephine had not visibly aged much from the photos Cree had seen: tall, straight-backed, her corded neck emerging from a floral-patterned dress, flat chest and sinewy arms, long dark face with a sober expression carved into its lines and folds. Coming close to the screen, she regarded Cree in silence for a moment. Her eyes were steady, deep brown irises in rheumy yellow sclera. Cree could feel her presence, a deep gravitas, somber, dark.

Josephine pushed the screen door out and half turned to make way for Cree. "You can come in. I been waitin'." Her voice was deep, almost a man's voice.

"You know who I am?"

"No, don't know who you are. Just know what you after. Been expectin'."

Cree followed her into the dark interior. The floorboards were uneven but were mostly covered with fine rag rugs Josephine had no doubt made herself. Josephine led Cree through a dark living room of sagging furniture covered in patch quilts and handmade white lace. It was clearly the room of a person who made the best of very little income, clean and well ordered. A television took up most of one small table, but it didn't have the altarlike status of most living rooms. No – in one corner stood a real altar, dominated by a large Bible surrounded by candles and a collection of crosses of different sizes; above hung a portrait of a chestnut-haired, Anglo-Saxon Jesus framed in a wreath of thorns. Near the door to the back hallway stood a small bookshelf, topped with half a dozen photos propped in plastic frames.

One white face stood out from the dark faces, and when Cree recognized it her breath caught in her throat: Lila Beauforte, aged twelve or thirteen. When she still gave forth that glow.

The old woman led Cree through a hallway and past a couple of dark bedrooms to a kitchen that was a little brighter. The tired yellow linoleum had worn through in paths of brown. A vinyl-topped tube table and four chairs stood in the center, and clean-scrubbed wooden counters lined two walls, along with a deep zinc-plated sink, an electric stove, and a round-topped refrigerator from the 1940s. Another portrait of Jesus hung above the sink. Above the counter, open shelves held a few dishes, some canned goods, and jars of preserved vegetables and plants. Dried herbs and roots hung in bunches tacked along the shelves. Cree spotted a little *gris-gris* bag nailed above the back door.

Josephine gestured to the window, where through the screen of the back porch Cree saw a powerful, shirtless man working a garden bed with a mattock.

"My grandnephew helpin' me with the garden today," Josephine explained. She went to the stove to poke a spoon into a jar of steaming dark fluid. "Just makin' tea when you knock," she said. "Offer you some, but it a remedy for my joints, taste like the devil." She stirred it, sniffed the steam, and turned back to Cree. "How'd ol' Miz Beauforte find me? Huh! Real question is, What she gone do now she find me?"

"You mean Charmian? She doesn't know I'm here. Nobody knows I'm here."

That surprised Josephine, and she looked at Cree with heightened interest. "Then who are you? What you want here?"

"I need your help. I have to learn more about what happened at Beauforte House in 1971 and '72."

Josephine considered that, eyes dubious. "What make you think I know anything at all about anything? Can't remember anyhow."

"You do know. You do remember. You came back two years ago and put those hexes at the house. You – "

"I don't gotta tell you nothin'. I don't *know* nothin'. You wastin' your time here." She turned back to the counter, brought down a smaller jar, and began pouring the tea into it through a patch of cheesecloth. Her movements were clumsy: The gnarled hands were stiff, Cree saw, with tension or arthritis.

"I don't believe you. You would never forget. I think you're just afraid of me."

"Oh, and why I be 'fraid of you?"

"Because you killed a man. And you're afraid you'll get in trouble for it."

The board-straight back didn't flinch. "Don't know what you talkin' 'bout. You sounding like a crazy. I'se eighty-one years old. Can't kill nobody!"

It was going as Cree feared. Josephine wasn't going to tell her anything.

There was only one solution, only one way to break through her resistance. Cree walked back into the living room, found the little oval photo of Lila, and returned with it to the kitchen. Josephine had turned and watched her, distrusting and disapproving.

"I'm sorry," Cree told her. "Let me start over. Josephine, I'm trying to help Lila, and I can't do it without you. I know how much you cared for her, and I think you still do. I don't care that you killed him. I just need you to help me find a way to let Lila go free of what happened."

Cree held the photo in front of her like a talisman, and Josephine stared at it for a moment before returning her eyes to Cree's face. "You some kind of doctor? Some kind of psychology doctor? Lila got so sick now she need a psychology doctor?" Then the yellow eyes narrowed as she seemed to see something in Cree's face. "No. No, you different. You a . . . healin' woman. You a seein' woman."

"Are you a seeing woman, Josephine? Is that how you know what I am?"

"Don't got no sight. Don't *want* no sight – all it ever bring is grief, I know that much. I know 'cause my mama was a healin' woman, you got some her look 'bout you."

The relentless gaze probed deep, and Cree felt a growing discomfort. "I'm a parapsychologist. A ghost hunter." Josephine's eyes widened slightly, and Cree felt she had to hurry on or she would lose the old woman again. "Lila tried to move back into Beauforte House. She was . . . troubled . . . by a ghost there. It attacked her. Lila asked me to investigate. I've seen the ghost, I know who it is. But Lila has been badly shaken up. She tried to kill herself yesterday, Josephine! If I can't figure out exactly what happened back then, if I can't help her be rid of the ghost, she'll just try again and again until she succeeds. Charmian won't tell me anything. You're the only one who can tell me. Please, Josephine!"

Josephine's rigid stance didn't change as she considered that, but the news of Lila's suicide attempt clearly hurt her, and suddenly she looked very old and brittle. " 'The truth shall set ye free'?" she rasped.

"Yes. Exactly." Cree allowed herself a tiny welling of relief: Josephine had not resisted the idea of ghosts or hauntings in the slightest.

"And you gone help Lila 'cause you know the *truth*. You help her see the truth what happened, she gone get all better."

Cree nodded, feeling the relief spread. Josephine understood and would cooperate. "I hope so."

Josephine took the photo from Cree's hand, stared at it with that ancient look for a moment. Then the creased lips turned down, the wooden face moved on its bones, pain and sorrow and love all worked together. Leaving the tea on the counter, she turned and walked stiffly to the door to the screened back porch. Cree felt the disturbance in her: The old woman was burning up inside.

The man hacking at the soil paused to look over at them, his sweat-sheened forehead creasing when he saw Cree. "You okay, Auntie?" he called across the yard.

"You just go on workin', Hiram. I'se talkin' to this lady."

Hiram hesitated, doubtful, then dutifully went back to his mattock work, his powerful back and shoulder muscles banding with each stroke.

"You can sit, you want to," Josephine told Cree. Three wired-together wooden chairs stood on the canted deck, facing the backyard. Cree sat, but the old woman stood looking out at the expanse of weedy grass, the garden plots where Hiram worked, and trees that stretched away into the scrubby forest beyond. One of her stiff hands knotted and kinked in jerky, painful motions.

" 'The truth shall set ye free,' " Josephine intoned again, shaking her grizzled head slowly. "You just a baby, ghost lady. You like me, way I was. Got the same idea. But what if you wrong? What's left o' your faith, you wrong? What you do with your faith? How you live, after that?"

"I'm not sure what — "

"You want to know why I killed that man."

"I know why. I need to know the details of what he did to Lila and what Charmian did when she found out about it. I need to know more about him, what kind of person he really was, so I can figure out how to set his ghost free." *And why you left the hexes. And how it connects with the murder of Temp Chase. And . . .* But that would come later, if the old woman seemed willing to go that far.

Josephine digested that for a moment, her eyes losing their immediate focus as some internal view took precedence. When she spoke again, it was with a quiet, impassioned urgency: "You gotta understand how I loved that girl. She was a . . . like a *star*, so bright, even when she a baby." Josephine put a hand to her hard, hollow stomach. "I had a sickness when I was a chil', couldn't have no chil'ren my own. Maybe she was that for me, closest I could have to my own daughter. But that not all of it. She every shinin', pretty thing you could ever think of. Strong, determined, she take on the whole worl', she got to! Biggest heart there could be. I love that girl, do anything for her. Oh, Charmian, she love her chil'ren, too, don't ever doubt that! But a different way, more like a lady lion love her cubs, teach 'em be strong hunters, be kings an' queens. She never see inside Lila like me. Lila, she knew that. We close."

"Lila has told me that many times. How important you were to her."

"An' what happen to her was so bad. What he do to her."

"It was the worst thing that could happen. That's why Lila has hidden it from herself. But it isn't staying down, it isn't staying forgotten. His ghost chases her and rapes her again. It's all coming back, and it's killing her now."

Josephine looked at Cree with an unfathomable grief in her eyes, and something else — a look directed at Cree herself, something like pity. "That the worst, huh? That what you think? That the worst?"

It was clearly a rhetorical question, and the way Josephine asked it gave Cree a chill. What could possibly be worse?

But Josephine had opened the screen door and was beckoning Cree to follow her. Hiram paused again, shaded his eyes to look Cree over, then wiped his brow and went back to work. By the side of the steps, the old woman found a gnarled stick that she used to help her hobble over the uneven ground.

"Hiram, this here lady's a healin' woman. You don't mind if I's soundin' upset, you just keep workin'. We got stuff to talk about, you hear?"

"Yes'm," Hiram said.

Closer, Cree could see that he was a huge man and was older than he looked from a distance, in his forties. The look he gave Cree contained a clear warning: *You on notice – you don't do nothin' to hurt my old aunt.*

"This my family house," Josephine said as they walked on. "I's born here in 1920. When Mama moved to N'Orleans, I went with her, but one my brothers stay on here – he Hiram's gran'daddy, Hiram get the place when I's gone. When I lef' the Beaufortes, an' then Mama died, I moved back. She a root doctor, Mama. People call her a conjo woman. Had a little shop on St. Philip Street, made her livin' at it. Knew all the ol' medicines, cures, charms. Learned from her momma and aunts. Some these plots here, still the same one she made when I's a girl."

"I read about her in a newspaper. You must have learned a lot from her."

Josephine tipped her head ambiguously as she walked on to the end of the grassy area, where several dirt paths led into the scrub. The view to the left was closed by the wall of the levee, overgrown with bushes and vines; above, the tree canopy cast a mottled shade. The smell of the bayou was stronger here and mixed with a sharp smell like insecticide – the ubiquitous stink of chemical factories.

Josephine started down one of the paths, stiff and slow. "You know how he wore that pig mask? How he chase her an' let her go and chase her again? How he torture her?"

"Yes."

"I's out that night. Should have been home, never would have happened. Some the other colored servants in the distric', they go their own party, I go along." Josephine's voice was bone weary with self-condemnation, sepulchral. "Lila come home, she feelin' a little sick and besides she never like seein' her folks so drunk."

"Did she tell you? Is that how you found out?"

Josephine stopped beneath one of the windy, scaly-barked trees. Her eyes were beyond sad and beyond angry now, more like the eyes of a dead person. "No. Not the first way I know. Come home, there's things knocked over. I figure it's party night, maybe some Beauforte friend extra drunk and cuttin' loose, I straighten things up before Charmian gets in. But when I see Lila in the mornin', she's *walkin'* wrong an' her *eyes* are wrong! Her *fire*, see, her fire was different! Mos'ly it was out, but then it burn *too* hot. Then it out again. An' she *scared* – scared to talk to me, even look at me! An' later I'm doin' my job, I'm changin' her sheets an' I see the blood. After that I ask her an' she tell me."

Josephine was vibrating slightly, a shiver that shook every inch of her gaunt frame. The habitual control had vanished as the ancient pain and rage took over again, and now her voice was just a rasp, coming out under great pressure: "I's a Christian woman. I knowed to kill's a sin. But I knowed he had to be punished. Couldn't do anything right away, seemed to take forever, havin' to wait. Even then, didn't mean to kill him. Didn't go into the lib'ary thinkin' to kill him. But when the time come, Lord Jesus, I did it, I took that iron an' I hit him. He layin' there, movin' around like a snake with its back broke, an' that exactly what he was, a snake, an' Lord forgive, I took that poker an' hit him in his head. Hard as I could. Did it again! Didn't hardly know I's doin' it. An' after that, that snake didn't move no more. No he didn't. No he didn't. God Jesus, help me an' forgive me!"

Josephine had gotten breathless and unsteady, and now she sort of swooned as her eyes rolled up and the tall straight body toppled into the bushes. Cree rushed to her and held her, lifted her out of the tangle. They limped together to a fallen log and Cree helped her sit, folding her body in long rigid sections like a hinged thing.

A terrible sense of alarm shrilled in Cree's nerves, the awareness that something was very wrong.

"Josephine, I don't understand. Richard Beauforte died of *poison*. You poisoned his drink. Something in his amaretto."

Josephine looked up at her with those frighteningly dead eyes, eyes

365

that had looked for answers and had found none. "Not Richard. Talkin' 'bout *Bradford*. Bradford the one chased Lila, raped her. Bradford the one I killed. Richard, he help me. Richard beat him till he down, mos'ly dead. I just finish it."

Cree felt suddenly dizzy herself, and she caught at a nearby branch to stabilize herself as she sat down on the ground. "No, Josephine, I saw the photos! *Richard* wore the boar mask! Brad, he was a pirate, he – "

A pair of military jets roared by overhead, deafening, making the foliage shiver and startling a flock of blackbirds from the bushes thirty feet away. The birds scattered like buckshot but then swarmed together again as the thunder diminished.

And Josephine explained: Yes, Richard had worn the boar head and the tattered swamp rat clothes for three or four years, and Bradford had worn the pirate getup, the patched and bearded face mask, the wig and low-slung three-cornered hat. But of course everybody knew who everybody was, so that year the two of them had worked out a prank to play on the other Epicurus partyers, even on Charmian and Ron and Lila. They switched costumes. Only Josephine, who had helped Richard get done up, knew about the joke. For the whole evening, they played not only their masked parts, but they played each other, a disguise within the disguise. They avoided talking, but when they did their voices were muffled by the masks and camouflaged by the outlandish accents they each put on. It was a big success, and later in the evening it took everybody by surprise when they unmasked. But Lila had gone home before then. And it had been Bradford, wearing the boar mask, who had slipped away after her, so drunk, so abandoned, so angry inside, that night.

There was no question that Josephine told the truth: She was implacable, beyond doubting. More, it made sense at last of the differences between the two ghosts, two ghosts after all, and the beating motion in the library.

It was a horrifying story, but as Cree thought it through, she began to realize it was in many ways the best possible discovery. This alone made coming down here worthwhile. The fact that she could now identify both ghosts and their issues was the least of it. Knowing the truth brought a huge gust of relief and hope: It wasn't Lila's beloved father who had raped her! Richard was, after all, the good man he seemed. Lila could recover memory of the night and cope with it, and, crucially, live on with a sure knowledge of her father's love. She could love him in return without the nagging ambivalence, subconsciously blaming him for the long-forgotten violation. She would learn that far from being her attacker himself, Richard in outrage had helped kill her real violator, her real betrayer. And if Cree could bring her to share his dying moment, to receive into her heart the arrow of love Richard lofted her way, she would be strengthened enormously.

Cree played through therapeutic scenarios, feeling hugely relieved, grateful for the truth.

But then a lingering problem occurred to her. Josephine had fallen silent as she let Cree sort through the ramifications, just watching her, clearly anticipating where it would take her.

"But . . . but Richard *was* poisoned!" Cree cried. "If you didn't kill him, who did? Charmian?"

Josephine looked at her with that implacable sympathy. "You poor baby. You poor girl. Now you got to grow into a ol' lady. Now you gon' know what's worse'n Lila got raped by her daddy."

"Nothing's worse!"

"Worse is, *Lila* killed her daddy! Lila burnt hot, she thought it was him had raped her, she stood up for herself, she put that poison in his drink. And she'd be right to! 'Cept Richard di'n't do it. He love her like I did! He the one beat Bradford near to death for it! But Lila didn't know. She killed her own daddy for somethin' he di'n't do. An' now you know why she got to forget."

40

THE HEAT WAS STILL INTENSIFYING as they hobbled along the paths in the dappled tree shade. Cree found herself limping, too, all the injuries of the past weeks coming back to pain her. She felt almost too weak to carry her own weight, as old as Josephine, as stiff. Behind them they heard the rhythmic *whunk!* of Hiram's mattock, and to the west the faint rush of cars on the highway. Here and there in the little ragtag wilderness were partially cultivated areas, Josephine's extended garden of wild herbs.

Broken mirrors, Cree was thinking. Murdering your own father, even if you believed him guilty of the ultimate betrayal – yes, that would freight you with enough subconscious guilt and self-hatred for a lifetime.

For the life of her, she could not imagine a way to free Lila. In this case, the truth set no one free. She walked numb and stiff and speechless as Josephine filled in the story.

Bradford had always been wild and reckless. The kids loved him because he was charming and funny and let them do things their parents didn't and because Charmian and Richard both adored him. Brad was smart, affectionate, and engaging – he quickly understood people and their feelings and motivations. Richard and he were very close. Josephine thought it was because each provided the other with a counterbalance for the excesses of his nature. Where Richard was responsible, overcommitted, staid, dutiful, Brad was freewheeling, pleasure seeking, risk taking, free of constraints and obligations. Around Brad, Richard could have fun, let his guard down, feel young and free and easy; around Richard, Brad could feel more important, useful, legitimate, connected.

They could talk about Charmian, they could talk about women in general, they could talk about Ron's development. Their fishing trips together were a chance for both to leave behind their habitual roles and connect in some primal male way, as equals. Richard sometimes helped Brad out in business matters. Brad occasionally helped smooth over arguments between Richard and Charmian, or served as mediator between Richard and his sometimes rebellious son, his spirited daughter. Over the years, they had forged a deep bond, more like brothers than brothers-in-law.

But Brad had grown up with too much money and privilege and good looks. For all the shallow social successes his charm bought him, he harbored the nagging sense that he was worthless, that he lived off the Lambert family's accomplishments and not his own, that he used his sister's family to anchor him because he lacked what it took to create one of his own. As he got older, he noticed changes in his relationship with other scions of the aristocracy: He became less of a peer than an icon of perpetual immaturity, the one who never quite grew up. People liked him, but they didn't respect him, didn't trust him in business dealings; as a result, his entrepreneurial efforts never panned out. The same was true in his intimate life. Women of his class learned he was fun for a fling but not any kind of candidate for marriage. Aside from his connection with his sister's household, he found himself increasingly outside the main channel of New Orleans social and business life.

Except for Carnival – that was an arena in which he could earn respect. Carnival had different standards. Status then was measured by the very things that jeopardized it in daily life: hard drinking, pranks, flirtations and risqué talk, sexual escapades and braggadocio, wild dancing, lavish spending, showing off, pushing every boundary of acceptable behavior. Fat Tuesday was almost a competition to see who could cut most loose, especially among the younger men. And here Bradford excelled.

Josephine's implacable rasp painted a clear portrait: For Bradford, the Mardi Gras of 1971 folded together the toxic psychological elements required for the sadistic rape of his niece. The lust-charged exuberance and abandon combined with the frustration and rage at his growing sense of irrelevance, his impotence in other spheres of life, an unending string of failed romances.

And Lila had turned into a beauty. At fourteen, she had already grown into a woman's shape, with fuller breasts and broader hips than her friends, and that *confidence*, that assertiveness, that spunk. Brad had long since begun injecting playful sexual innuendo into their conversations, flattering and teasing her, and Lila had thrown it right back, vamping and scorning him. The family laughed at the whole thing.

The morning after, when Josephine had seen the blood on Lila's sheets and had put it together with the change in Lila's affect and the mess in the house, she had gone straight to Lila. Lila had at first denied that anything was wrong. But after only a few moments of Josephine's probing she broke, crawled crying like a toddler into her nanny's lap, and told the story.

She was afraid to tell Momma, she said. She hurt inside. He had said things that suggested it was her fault, her own secret wish. It was 1971, the miniskirt had finally hit New Orleans, she had taken to wearing one over Daddy's objections, and she and all her friends were dancing to that kind of music he disapproved of. Maybe he was right, she deserved it, she had sort of asked for it? When he'd made those animal noises, pig noises, the whole time, it was like he'd wanted her to feel like an animal. And she did, she felt filthy and disgusting. She hated herself.

In that moment, Josephine learned that she herself was capable of the worst sin, that she could kill a man.

Lila couldn't face Charmian, so Josephine went to her. She was sitting in the study next to her bedroom, hungover, nursing her coffee and going through some Polaroids from the night before. Charmian confirmed that Richard – dressed as a pirate, dressed as Brad – had never left the Hardings' last night, and that he and Brad had revealed the costume switch near the end of the evening, as planned. And the proof was right there: the partyers grinning at the camera, Richard smiling ear-to-ear after lifting off his pirate face mask and wig. And Bradford, the boar mask under his arm, hair wet with sweat, mouth smiling but eyes to one side as if the enormity of what he'd done was catching up to him.

Charmian's rage had been terrifying to behold, and Josephine recognized the blood look in her eyes because she'd felt it in her own only moments before: Charmian, too, could kill. And yet Josephine knew she was also wounded, in agony over her daughter's distress and staggered by the fact that her younger brother was capable of this.

Telling it, Josephine had to sit down again. There was a stump among the maze of paths, and Cree helped her fold her length onto it.

"Before I lef' that room, she tol' me one thing. She say, 'You don't tell anyone.' I knowed that woman, know she hurtin' for Lila, see, but she thinkin' of Ron, too, she thinkin' of the Lambert name an' the Beauforte name. Me, I can't get past thinkin' 'bout that sweet baby girl and 'bout somebody could do that to her. But Charmian, she thinkin' ahead. She playin' it out in her mind. I says, 'No, ma'am,' but she know I don't mean it and she stop me at the door. She tell me to look at her. And what I see, I never forget. Never forget that woman's eye. She say again, 'You don't tell *anyone*. You don't talk to Lila. You don't talk to Richard. This is *my* family, and this is *my* respons'bility.' She say, 'Don't underestimate me, Jos'phine. What I will do to keep this from doin' more damage than it already done.' And I know she mean she kill me or anybody, not just the man raped her daughter. I b'lieve it down to my shoes."

Cree could easily imagine Charmian saying it, the cold steel in her eyes, the saber of her voice.

Later, passing by the door to Lila's bedroom, she several times overheard Charmian talking to her daughter in hushed, urgent, hard tones. But Josephine couldn't be quiet about it. The anger and concern were too great. She tried to talk to Lila, but Lila wouldn't open up again, and Josephine thought maybe that was a good thing, she was hardening herself as she had to. It took another week or more to find a time to tell Richard. She was shocked to learn that Charmian hadn't told him. But he admitted he had seen the difference in his beloved daughter, and now he was outraged to learn its reason. He stormed off to talk to Charmian.

Another two weeks went by and the household started to fragment into secrets, quiet hatreds, hushed conversations, and tense silences. Poor

Ron, knowing nothing, was especially confused. Lila grew increasingly distant, her light dimming, the lid coming over her.

Bradford had not returned to the house, but Richard and Brad's regular three-day fishing expedition was coming up. The night before the trip, Richard came to Josephine, told her to help ready his gear for their early morning departure. The way it always worked was Bradford got up early, came to the house at three-thirty or four A.M., they'd drive down to the private dock where Richard kept his boat, then continue by water the last ten miles or so. The place was an old trapper's cabin Brad had won in a card game years before, deep in the brackish swamps of Terrebonne Parish, back where water and land merged in a labyrinthine lacework.

Three in the morning, and Richard woke Josephine up. The rest of the household was fast asleep as she joined him in the library. When Brad came in, Richard locked the library door and confronted him. Brad looked sick with nervousness, but at first he pretended he thought Richard was joking. Richard threatened him and then had Josephine confront him as well. Brad shifted strategies, claimed it hadn't really been rape, it didn't get that far, it was just horsing around. When that didn't stick, he shifted again, saying it was Lila's fault. She was a ripe one, a hot one, a little slut who knew perfectly well what she was doing; he wasn't the first, she was lying if she said he was.

At that, Richard's rage built in him until he became a human bomb. At first he just demanded that Brad admit what he did, apologize on his hands and knees to Lila, and then leave New Orleans forever. But Brad resisted and anyway it wasn't enough. Richard bulled him, pushed him, took up the poker and threatened him with it. And Brad, afraid now, admitted, wept, swore he was sorry. But it was too late. The admission only inflamed Richard, the bomb had been triggered. Richard's face was a knot of red bulging veins, the enormity of it was catching up with him; he hit Brad, he kept beating Brad, he couldn't stop himself. At first Josephine was shocked, but when Richard finally came to his senses and looked at the poker, appalled, she took it from his hands. Bradford was lying on the floor, maybe already critically injured. And Josephine struck him, too – once, and then again, with all the strength her capable arms could muster. And then he stopped moving. Josephine's heart rose up, joyous in vengeance.

There was almost no blood, and what there was they worked quickly to clean up. Then they had another task.

Josephine had never been clear if Richard had envisioned everything from the start – the murder and then the concealment of the murder – or whether he had just been overtaken by his own rage and had improvised a solution afterward.

Whichever, in New Orleans, as nowhere else, there was a convenient way to dispose of dead bodies.

They packed Brad out through the former carriage house and into Richard's car. They drove to Lafayette Cemetery, only five blocks away, and carried the corpse quickly inside. Josephine moved the car away from the gate as Richard carried the body to the Lambert family tomb, deep in the center of the mazelike necropolis. When she rejoined him, they unbolted the crypt's marble front cover and used a small sledgehammer to batter away the bricks behind it. When they'd opened a hole big enough to squeeze the body through, they stuffed Brad onto the top of his mother's coffin, then bolted the cover back on.

So within half an hour of Brad's death, he had disappeared for good. Josephine and Richard knew no one would ever open the Lambert crypt to find the gap in the bricks or the remains atop the coffin. Because there would never be cause to open the grave: Brad was the last of the Lambert name. When her time came, Charmian would be buried in the Beauforte tomb. Anyway, in only a year and a day Bradford would be baked to dust and flakes of bone.

It wasn't yet sunrise when Richard dropped Josephine off at the house and went on down to the shack just as he and Brad had done so many times over the years. He came back two days later with a terrible story. The lie he'd told the police was that they'd separated in the cypress labyrinth, Brad taking a little pirogue he favored and Richard using the larger boat as they fished for black bass and flatheads. Later, when Richard arrived at their planned rendezvous, he'd been shocked to find the pirogue floating untethered and untended. Some accident must have happened. Police rescue teams combed the area, but no one could say for certain how far the pirogue might have drifted before Richard found it, and in the endless maze of cypress lanes, the tangle of roots groping down into coffee-dark water, it was no wonder they couldn't find his body. With all the alligators around, there probably wasn't much to find.

It made the newspapers as a tragedy for one of New Orleans's oldest and most respected families. At the church ceremony they eventually held, Brad's survivors – Charmian, Ron, Lila, Richard – appeared much distraught.

A family grieved.

41

THE MAN WHO PICKED UP Charmian wasn't from Crescent City Confidential Services. His two gold teeth, the checked shirt, those too-small oval sunglasses, and the posture of deliberate negligence showed him for what he was. As variously described by Ronald and the people he'd referred her to find him, he was a "fixer," a "hitter," a "handyman" – someone willing to do dirty work for pay. Just how dirty, Charmian wasn't sure, but the way he looked, slouched behind the wheel of his beat-up Cadillac, driving with one wrist, she wouldn't put much past him. He was a scrawny, chain-smoking, hatchet-faced Cajun swamp rat who leered when he told her his name was Pierre Lapin – Peter Rabbit. When he'd first taken the driver's seat and tugged his jeans up, Charmian saw the end of a switchblade over the top of his pointy, ankle-high, bayou lounge-lizard boots.

She wasn't sure how you went about asking his type if murder was part of his résumé. She wasn't sure she could bring it to that in any case. Three people had died already, her *daughter* had almost died yesterday – the swath of pain cut by that long-ago act was more than broad enough. But it was an outcome she was willing to accept if it proved necessary, and they'd have to discuss it before they got to Port Sulphur.

The Crescent City Confidential man she'd hired to watch Cree, after Charmian's last conversation with Paul Fitzpatrick, had phoned from Port Sulphur to say that Miss Black had located Josephine. As Paul had predicted. It infuriated her that in ten days this out of towner, a woman, a parapsychologist, a Yankee, could find a person the region's supposed top detective firm hadn't been able to. She let him hear her fury for a moment before telling him to wait there, that she would be there in just over one hour, that he was to follow Cree if she left Josephine's house and report in on the cell phone if she did.

Cree's finding Josephine meant that she would know the truth – most of it, anyway. There was only one fallback position now. If Cree didn't go for it, if she didn't agree on the solution, Pierre would be given an opportunity to become one very rich swamp rat.

It was bad enough that she had to spend over an hour with Pierre Lapin in his cigarette-reeking Cadillac. But the real problem was that there was nothing to say to such a lowlife, even if she did have need of his services, and the silence left time for her thoughts to whirl. The image of Lila, pathetically asleep in the hospital bed, her arms at her sides and bound to the bed, interposed itself between images of the past.

That night, and the following days, chiseled into her memory, replayed itself as it had so often in the past few months. It was becoming an obsession: searching every detail, every word said and every assumption made, in a hopeless quest to find ways she might have done it differently, done it better. With the wisdom of hindsight, she found many. But no amount of second-guessing or soul-searching could change what had happened.

It had been a particularly good party at the Hardings' that year, and the revelation of the ruse pulled by Richard and Brad had topped it off perfectly. Charmian had danced several times with her own brother, not knowing who it was, thinking only that Richard was affecting a different style of movement. She had watched the ostensible "Brad" stealing caresses from women old and young – only to shock them later by revealing himself as the ordinarily staid Richard! The only flaw in the otherwise perfect evening had been the way Brad looked, after they had taken off their masks: so sweaty and uneasy, his skin pasty. At the time, thinking she knew the reason for his poorly concealed misery, she'd felt a pang of sympathy for him. Susan Lattimore, Brad's most recent flame, had been noticeably absent from the party. Earlier, he'd confessed to Charmian that he was considering proposing to Susan, getting serious at last. Her absence, and Brad's appearance when he unmasked, suggested what her response had been.

And of course he'd been drinking heavily all night, lifting his boar's-head mask just enough to tuck tumblers of whiskey to his lips. They'd all had too much to drink. Excess was de rigueur at the Hardings'.

And then the nightmare of that morning: Josephine, storming into her bedroom study with a basket of laundry, her grave countenance afire with righteous anger. She was panting, so worked up that her voice came out more a scraping sound than a whisper: "Bradford come home crazy, he rape Lila when you's all still at Hardings'. He hurt that girl worse than anythin'."

"What are you talking about?" Charmian's headache pounded, and all she felt was irritation at the nanny's irrational outburst.

"He rape her! He chase her and rape her and scare her half to death and now you got to do somethin'!" Josephine threw the laundry at her feet, and Charmian saw the sheets, the blood on them. "You look here and see what he done!" There too were Lila's pajamas and underpants, ripped, spotted with blood.

Charmian's world rocked in something like an earthquake; the room seemed literally to tilt and shake as shock after shock hit her. First and foremost, concern for Lila – an agony of sympathy and fear for her future. But immediately after came fear and pity for Bradford, her beloved, charming, ne'er-do-well baby brother who had now truly become a lost soul. And then a thousand other shocks: a shrieking sense of failure, for having failed to protect her daughter. For having failed to help Brad become something better. For not having seen how far Brad had fallen. For having failed to protect her family, now gouged with a deep wound that could never knit. And then the shame of it! And the shame of knowing this servant knew of it. And fear of Richard, what he'd do when he found out, and –

And in that moment she knew that she had to take control. It was up to her to repair this, to manage it. Josephine was never again going to act as Lila's mother, that had gone on long enough. She, Charmian, and she alone, was going to do that now. And she'd never fail again.

Charmian groaned out loud, causing Pierre Lapin to turn his buglike sunglassed gaze to her. Charmian inched away from him, up against the door, turning her head to look out at the disgusting commercial strip that had sprung up along Highway 23 in the last twenty years.

Another wave of pain came, but this time she weathered it silently: yes, she'd vowed never to fail Lila again. But only five minutes later, she had done so, maybe the worst way.

She found Lila in her room, sitting on the floor, cocooned in private misery, her body rocking slightly. One look told Charmian that, yes, her light had changed; that was the most awful thing, worse by far than the bruises on her face. She didn't return Charmian's hugs and caresses, but sat with arms at her sides, closing herself in hard. Charmian saw herself in the reaction: the strength of it, the determination. The anger and shame that fired her resolve to yield nothing to no one, to trust no one. And clearly, Lila blamed her mother for some share of her pain. She was right to. Charmian damned herself to the lowest level of hell.

Charmian knelt two paces away, as close as Lila would allow her. "Lila, tell me what happened."

Delayed response, an accusatory look: "You already know. Josephine told you."

"I want to hear it from you."

Delayed answer, eyes not looking at Charmian, or anything. "He chased me. I wasn't sure at first."

Charmian waited. "Sure of − ?"

"Sure what he wanted! I thought he was playing! The way we used to. But then he really hurt me and wouldn't stop when I told him to." Lila's lower lip was trembling so that it shook her whole, soft, child-round face. Her rocking intensified, growing desperate as determination warred with defeat in her features. When Charmian came to her again, Lila pushed her away. It was a short, hard push, the small hand flat on Charmian's chest. It left a brand she felt there for months.

Lila began to sob and moan but would not let Charmian touch her. So Charmian decided the only course was to provide an example of mastering bad things. She had to tell her daughter, *show* her that her pride could endure, her sense of self could endure. That if she sought it and asserted it hard enough, she'd still have some control.

"Lila, listen to me. There are times when you have to be strong. At some point, every woman has to deal with something that hurts her, very badly, very deeply. Every woman! Sometimes the only way through is to act like nothing happened! If you act it hard enough, it will become true, because you'll show yourself it can be done."

Crying, crying, crying, and still not letting Charmian near her. Crying, crying, crying, as her mother spouted more useless homilies on strength and self-control and stiff upper lip and time healing all wounds, crying and crying until Charmian grew too frustrated, too frustrated with herself for having let her relationship with her daughter turn into this, where in the poor girl's moment of greatest need she couldn't turn to her own mother. Frustrated with Lila for keeping her away. Crying, crying, until Charmian hissed at her, "Lila! Stop crying. Right this minute! You have to stop crying. If you can do it now, you'll prove to yourself you can do it anytime you choose to. Show yourself that. This is *not* the end of the world! Show some spine! You are a Beauforte! You *can* be strong. No one can take away the strength inside you unless *you let them!*"

She must have groaned again, because Pierre Lapin turned to her once more, throwing his left wrist over the wheel as he used his right hand to take off his sunglasses. He peered at her with small, bloodshot eyes. "You sick or somet'ing? Don't go t'rowing up in my car, just had the interior done."

"I'll bear that in mind, thank you," Charmian told him witheringly. "Frankly, it would help if you didn't smoke so much."

He put the glasses back on and kept driving. After a moment, he used his free hand to tap another cigarette out of its pack, then flicked it expertly so that it spun up and into his lips. He made sure she'd caught the move before he lit it with the dashboard lighter. Charmian bristled at his impudence but admired his reflexes. Small, but wiry and quick, that was good.

They were past the strips now and into the open country, the downriver land of po' white trash and po' black trash and nouveau riche trash in their taseteless, ostentatious houses. The flat, scrubby fields drifted endlessly past, dusted with pollution from chemical plant chimneys. This area had always been Charmian's idea of hell.

"Can't you drive any faster?" Charmian complained. "At this rate, it'll take us two hours."

The sunglasses only half turned. "Tell you what. I don't tell you how to be a rich bitch, you don't tell me how to do my job."

And she realized he was right. You drive the speed limit or under so that you never, ever, elicit the notice of the police. It was another slight demonstration of professionalism that reassured her. But, still, it wouldn't pay to let the help get uppity. It was time to take control of Mr. Lapin.

She didn't raise her voice, but she put an edge into her tone that would etch glass. "Don't you ever talk to me that way again." He swiveled his head to look at her and would have come up with some other insolent wisecrack, but she cut him off: "You don't know who you're dealing with," she hissed. "You see an old lady with a limp. But this old lady has more money than you could imagine. This old lady has more resources, more friends in high places, more clout than trash like you ever *dreamed* about. And Pierre Lapin is cute, but I really much prefer Loup Garou, your nickname at the Bayou Cane bars you frequent. I know which trailer you live in. You think I'd get in a car with garbage like you if I didn't know I could bag you up and discard you anytime I choose?" That begat some resistance, so she opened her purse to show him the glint of stainless steel there. She put her hand on it and through her teeth continued, "I am also an old lady with a Smith & Wesson CS9 automatic in my purse and I will kill you with it. Act right, and you end your day with more money than you usually make in a year. Talk to me like that again, or do *anything* other than exactly as I tell you, you are dead. Your place in the scheme of things is four classes lower than my yard boy. Know your place, Loup."

He had sobered up when she mentioned his local nickname, Werewolf, and the other information she'd paid her Crescent City Confidential man to obtain. Now he didn't answer, just turned his attention back to the highway. It took a while for his grin to sneak back. It looked a little forced, she thought, but not entirely: There was some grudging admiration there.

"Okay, Gran'mère, you the boss for sure," he said at last. "Make my own gran'mère look sweet, you."

She smiled, glad he had taken it in stride, thinking that maybe he was indeed worth his pay.

Putting him in his place gave her a moment's satisfaction, but actually, she *did* feel sick. And it wasn't caused by his cigarettes or even the chemical air down here. It was what she'd said. How it must have sounded to Lila.

Charmian had been on the verge of crying herself, that choking ache that grew and you tried to swallow and it wouldn't go down. But she had to set the example. Lila looked as if she'd go truly to pieces, turn into a puddle of tears and quaking flesh. Charmian had to prove you could stave off triumph in collapse if you just kept your back straight. So she did. She did not let herself appear overly emotional. Not ever during that whole awful time.

She didn't become aware of Lila's misperception until another week had gone by. Richard had been out of town on business for several days. Charmian had tried many times to reach Brad, had driven over to his apartment, but he never answered his phone or the doorbell. She hung in an agonizing indecisiveness. No, paralysis. Bradford had to be punished, that was clear. But Charmian couldn't decide what to do, how to begin. Call a doctor to look at Lila's injuries? Old Andre Fitzpatrick was loyal, they could count on him to be discreet. Call a psychiatrist to deal with the emotional aftermath? Call the police? She could probably prevail upon Commissioner Deelay to keep it out of the press.

But every choice had ramifications, and all the ramifications were bad. A family's reputation *was* a valuable thing, and not just from the standpoint of appearances. Recovering from this would require recovering some small share of family identity and coherence and pride. True, for something this unsavory to get out would hurt Richard's business relationships, and it would sully the Lambert name forever. But what mattered was that if there was any hope Lila could get past it, she couldn't have everyone she met knowing all about it, she couldn't see the knowledge in the eyes of her friends, her teachers at school, all their family friends. And Lila *had* to get past it.

She and Lila were having another talk. Lila had alternated between a slumping, spiritless despondency and a bristling rage that let no one near. Charmian was trying again, trying to reach out to her, trying to help her find a way of coping.

Lila had started out hard but had caved in again, crying, crying, crying. "Why did he do that to me? How could Daddy do that to me? How could you *forgive* him!"

Charmian was confused. "Do what? What did Daddy do?"

Lila's eyes were outraged when they turned to her. "What he did! What he *did!* When he hurt me!"

"No, baby, Daddy didn't hurt you – "

"He *did!* He chased me all over, he threw me down! He *ripped* my – "

"No, Lila, wait – " The revelation shook Charmian to her marrow. The enormity of the oversight. The enormity of how poorly they'd communicated. The enormity of the pain and sense of betrayal Lila's misperception must have caused her.

"He didn't even take off the mask! He kept making the pig noise! It was like he wanted me to feel like – "

"Lila!" Charmian shouted. "Stop! Stop saying that!"

"And you act like you *forgive* him! You act like it doesn't *matter!*"

"Your father would never hurt you! You were so upset, you were so scared, it makes sense that you'd see things the wrong way, or think that – "

"So I *imagined* everything?"

"Your father *never raped* you!"

Lila was backing away, her mouth agape, seeing only utter betrayal in Charmian.

And the moment came, the moment to set it straight, to make it perfectly clear. And Charmian failed it. She couldn't say the words. She couldn't say Bradford's name. She couldn't make her mouth say, *It wasn't your father, it was your uncle Brad. My baby brother.*

As she hesitated, choking on it, Lila grabbed a book from her desk and pitched it at her. It hit Charmian on the cheek and shocked her, and she shouted, "You get a grip on yourself, young lady!"

Lila fled past her and out of the room.

It wasn't until the next day that Charmian cornered her again and told it straight out: "It was Bradford, not Daddy." She explained the mask switch. But by then Lila was a sort of demented creature, hollow eyed, sleeping on the floor because she couldn't bear to touch the bed where the first of the rapes had happened. She had become torpid and depressed, unresponsive, with only flashes of rage. A veil had come over her eyes, hard to see through. She nodded her head, but skepticism and accusation were the only emotions Charmian could read in her face. There were many questions Lila could have asked, such as, *Then why don't you tell someone about Brad? How can you protect* him? But she didn't. And Charmian was grateful, because she had not yet figured out the answers.

"You understand now, right?" Charmian persisted.

"Yes, Momma, I understand," Lila had said in a monotone. She was telling the truth. What she understood was betrayal.

Then Richard returned from his business trip, and they discussed it and agreed that before they went to the police or anything else that would come to public attention, he'd confront Bradford. After a time, he managed to make contact with Brad, and they supposedly went on their regular fishing trip, and Bradford didn't come back. And later, when Richard told her what he'd done, that he'd killed Bradford in the library and lied to the police about his drowning, Charmian understood why he'd done it. Of course she did. She even knew how it hurt him to have done it.

But she hated him for it, too. She couldn't bring herself to sleep with the man who had beaten her brother to death, couldn't bear to be touched by the hands that had swung that poker.

And so yet another crack formed in the family, another piece of it broke away. Another kind of distance intruded.

Charmian couldn't do anything about that, either. What — go to the police and tell them her husband had murdered her brother? They'd ask why, they'd find out why.

And the converse was also true: Now they really would have to keep the rape secret. There was no longer any choice about that. The police would put the rape and Brad's disappearance together, and Richard would go to jail for murder. The family would be destroyed. Ironically, Brad's death was what really sealed the secret of the rape — it cemented the family's complicity in the lie that it never happened.

So she hammered the lesson into Lila: Sometimes a woman just has to be strong. To move on. To act like everything is all right until the act is so habitual that it's just like real. To try to forget the bad things that happened. To remember that the family is more important than any one member's pain.

And she took her own advice. Drinking helped the forgetting.

In there somewhere, poor Ronald had come to her in his own misery. Not yet sixteen years old, very much an innocent boy, troubled by seeing so many inexplicable, bad things happening in the family. He missed Uncle Brad terribly. But he'd felt the changes even before the "drowning," he'd heard the hushed conversations and hard voices, felt the dissonances and distances. And yesterday Lila had said something that scared him. She'd said that sometimes she thought about killing herself. She even told him how she'd do it: She'd use one of the poisons Josephine had told them about, long ago when she used to tell them stories about her mother's voodoo magic. There was a recipe you made with the seeds and flowers from the wild black cherry tree, it tasted like almonds — like amaretto, Daddy's favorite drink. Why would you do that? Ro-Ro asked. His sister had been frightening him for weeks now, with her hollow eyes, her numb lassitude alternating with that disjointed, crazy, sudden heat. Because of what he did, she told him. Who did? he asked. You mean Dad? What did he do? Nothing, Lila said. He did nothing. Ask Momma, he did nothing.

So he'd asked Josephine, and Josephine had told him to pray to our Lord Jesus Christ and to strive to emulate His life through acts of compassion and charity.

Hearing this, Charmian concealed her bitterness that not just Lila but also Ro-Ro would go to Josephine before he came to his own mother. She did her best to calm and reassure Ronald. She fired Josephine, telling her if she valued her life she'd never come back or attempt to contact any of them again. She made arrangements for Lila to go off to boarding school. She talked to Lila again and again, and made her promise she'd never do anything like suicide.

And she drank like a fish, trying to drown her sorrows, Charmian thought feverishly. *She pretended to have self-control while inside she wallowed in confusion and self-pity. She missed all the crucial signs and signals.*

For a time she thought her efforts were succeeding. With Josephine gone, with time passing, Lila began walling up her knowledge in a secret vault in her memory. She stopped speaking of the event. Then she went to school, fell apart, and came back home toward the end of the first semester. Charmian brought in old Dr. Fitzpatrick to treat her, and she did seem to improve through semester break. The holidays were dismal, but Charmian felt a glimmer of hope that they were beginning to recover, that you could survive even something this extreme. Brad had paid in full. Lila could recover.

And the very day Lila was supposed to return to school, she poisoned her father for an atrocity he would never have been capable of.

Charmian had been upstairs, trying to get everything ready for Lila's departure. She went downstairs and into the library, and there he was, dead on the rug, curled like a baby, a thin foam of vomit trailing from his mouth. The room reeked of almonds. And though she'd so recently been through two heartbreaks that she had thought to be unsurpassable, this was far worse. This broke her. She found herself on the floor. She moved up behind Richard's body and pressed herself against his curled back, tucked her knees in behind his, and lay with him the way they slept together, one arm around his chest, her face against the back of his neck.

That's how Lila found them when she came looking.

"Hey, Gran'mère, wake up," Loup Garou said. "Wake up now."

"I am awake, trust me," Charmian told him drily. "I'm just thinking."

"Yeh? I'm stoppin' for gas. You need to pee or somet'ing, this is it. Port Sulphur's ten minutes down." He swung the car over into a gas station, stopped at the self-service pumps. He reached down to pull the lever that opened the gas-fill cover, then stayed hunched as he dug under his seat. Charmian looked down to see two license plates slide out, facedown, and then a big black automatic pistol that Loup held between his knees and did something to before he slipped it back out of view.

He caught her look and returned it with a little grin. "Listen, this's your trip, gotta pay travel. Need some cash for the gas."

Charmian acted as if she did this every day. She opened her purse again and handed him a twenty, chiding herself for her reaction. Of course he'd have stolen somebody's license plates and replaced his own with them before starting this trip. Of course he wouldn't rely only on the switchblade in his boot. Good.

The Werewolf went to the back of the car to lean jauntily against the fender as he filled the tank. Then they were on their way again.

Ten more minutes, Charmian thought.

Richard was dead. In the worst possible way. And again, there was nothing Charmian could say or do except to manage it, minimize the damage. When she'd recovered to the point where she could physically let go of Richard's body, she had called Dr. Fitzpatrick, New Orleans coroner and trusted friend, and, swearing him to secrecy, told him the many reasons why he must misrepresent the cause of death. Old Fitz had come through and had presumably taken the secrets with him to his own grave.

One image burned in Charmian's memory from that day on: the sight of Lila's face as she saw them on the floor, the mix of feelings there. It would be at the center of everything she did for years to come. It would wake her from the deepest sleep. It would startle her when she was working in the garden, come between her and any rose. It would motivate her to anything at all. She knew she owed a lifetime of atonement for having allowed her daughter ever to wear that expression, feel those feelings.

And then they went their own ways. Ronald was suspicious of the death of his father, and she'd had to tell him, only him, the whole story. He understood completely why he must never, *ever* speak to his sister of her rape and the death of their father. If she ever found out she'd wrongly blamed him, wrongly avenged the rape, it would destroy her. It would be a cruelty heaped upon a cruelty. Another irony: The concealment was the only way through, but it also served as something of a collective, tacit admission that Richard *was* the guilty one. That the family, what remained of it, agreed he'd deserved it.

Ronald did his best. He remained devoted to his sister even as he deformed inside and became what he now was. Lila went off to school, having killed her father, half strengthened by this victory over her presumed attacker and half dying with guilt and grief. Between the drugs Andre had prescribed, and the distance, and the inconceivable enormity of it, she stayed numb. Something like a scar thickened over that part of her mind, that part of her past. The first few times she came home from school, Charmian thought she was faking forgetfulness, putting on the act as her mother had instructed and punishing her with how dutifully she did so. But after a time, as she became by degrees softer, weaker, sadder, Charmian began to believe the forgetting was real. Some of her sweetness returned, and she talked with sincere fondness about her childhood – about Daddy, about Uncle Brad. She became a good, dutiful, emotionally distant adult daughter. She managed to concoct a semblance of a normal life. Jack Warren was no great catch, but they did seem to care for each other, and Charmian deemed it best not to try to derail the relationship. Lila got pregnant, had kids. The past faded. Sometimes at night, Charmian lay and mourned them, all three: her beloved insouciant brother, her dear, good husband, and the splendid, brilliant daughter who was also gone for good. But Lila had survived, more or less. All three of them had, more or less. No one had ever found out. With the passage of years, Charmian let herself think it was done with.

And then, twenty-seven years after she'd disappeared from their lives, *Josephine* returned to ruin everything. The messy Temp Chase business happened. And then Lila's ghosts entered the picture, and that horrible

387

Cree Black with her relentless prying, that frightening supernatural instinct that allowed her to discover exactly that which must be kept hidden.

Rage gripped Charmian. Josephine, again, still, forever! Always trying to take her children away from her, win away their affections! And then coming back after all those years wrapped in her smug virtue to confess everything to Temp Chase and open up the whole thing again. It was her fault this had all happened. When would she *ever* be free of that disapproving, accusing, pious face? And Cree Black! At the thought of the ghost hunter, Charmian's hands curled into scratching claws, and it seemed a red filter came across her vision, rage and contempt and fear. She mastered it with difficulty, willing her fingers to unclench.

Pierre's voice startled her: "Time we talk about how this goes down." He jutted his chin toward the sign that said they were entering Port Sulphur.

42

H IRAM'S MATTOCK HAD FALLEN silent, and neither Cree nor Josephine said anything as they hobbled back toward the house. Now that the wind had died, the afternoon heat hung under the trees in suffocating layers. The silence felt strange, charged by the buzz and fizz of flies and the distant rush of cars on the highway.

It had cost Josephine a lot to tell the story. Cree realized that the old woman, for all her determination, was not well; she seemed fragile, hollow, like something made out of straw or reed.

"I got to tell you about Temp Chase," Josephine said. " 'Fore we get where Hiram gone hear us."

"We don't have to do it now. You're tired. I'm tired, too, maybe we should wait – "

"No." Josephine shook her grizzled head decisively. "No time to wait."

"Then let's at least go inside, get out of the sun, get something to drink. You didn't drink your tea."

So they went on. Hiram had quit the sun, too, and now sat in one of the chairs on the back porch, drinking water out of an Army canteen. Nobody said anything as Cree helped Josephine up the steps, but as Josephine passed through into the kitchen she said, "You do good work, Hiram. Yo' great-auntie's thankful."

The big man nodded dourly, eyes on Cree.

Josephine got her tea and ran a glass of water from the tap for Cree and they went into the living room. It was hot here, too, the air unmoving, but the relative darkness was a relief. Josephine lowered herself into a chair and shut her eyes, recharging. Cree sat nearby, tasting her water, waiting, feeling little rivulets of sweat move under her clothes. The blind eye of the television screen reflected back the motionless room in miniature.

"Reverend Huggins," Josephine rasped after a time. "He always been sayin' how we got to come clean before Jesus. Tells us the only way you gone do that is confess yo' sins to all you's injured, try to atone. Says you got to take the consequences here on Earth, or you gone take them on Judgment Day – and you know which gone go easier for you! And I b'lieve he right. He right about that, no question."

Cree nodded. The terminology was not what she'd use, but the basic philosophy mirrored her own.

"So right 'bout then, this's two years ago, I get a scare. Doctor says I got breas' cancer, it gone kill me. And my sins come back to me, knowing I's goin' to die. The cancer, later I got a operation and chemo, thanks to Reverend Huggins doin' a collection for me. But the sins, they stay with me."

"Sins like helping kill Bradford."

"Killin' Bradford, oh yes." Josephine leaned forward, eyes hardening. "But worse is, knowin' it was a sin and *knowin' I'd do it again today!* Knowin' I got that in my heart. Rememberin' how *good* I feel when he go still – that just sit there in my heart like a devil. I got that in my heart." She leaned back, appalled at herself. "An' I di'n't want to come before Jesus with that contamination."

She knew that Richard had died not long after she'd left the Beaufortes' – a heart attack, the newspaper said. She was fairly certain that Richard had never told Charmian her role in Brad's death, because Charmian had never taken it up with her, and that woman surely would have. But now, thinking she was dying, Josephine knew she had to tell her. She welcomed the idea of receiving Charmian's rage, taking whatever punishment might be her due, if that's what Charmian wanted. She knew she owed. She had failed to protect Lila. She had killed Brad. She had exulted in killing him.

And, something she'd never admitted to herself before, she had savored her primacy in the children's lives, having their affection and denying it to Charmian. She had a rotten place in her soul, and it must be cut away; she would take what Charmian gave her. Only remotely did she hope she might receive her understanding and forgiveness.

She was still driving then – the old Ford in the driveway that Hiram used now. So she drove up to New Orleans for the first time in many years. She went to Beauforte House, knocked on the big old door, and waited in an agony of expectation. She was brimming with the need to confess and atone, overflowing with it.

But it wasn't Charmian or even one of the Beauforte kids who answered. It was a man, and she recognized him: Temp Chase, the TV newsman. She'd watched his show several nights a week for fifteen years, even back when he was just the weatherman. When she told him who she was, he welcomed her and explained that the Beaufortes still owned the house but that Charmian had had a stroke and now lived over in Lakeside Manor. Lila was married to a man named Jack Warren and lived out by the lake; Ron lived downtown, still single.

Temp's wife was out, but he would be happy to make her some iced tea if she'd like to come inside for a spell. Josephine was tired from the drive and the anticipation she'd been living with, and flattered to be talking to this celebrity. She accepted his invitation.

They sat in the front parlor she remembered so well. Though the furniture was different, there was an air in that old house, unchanged from all the years she'd spent there. The memories rushed back upon her, made her want to weep. It was as clear and painful as if it had all happened yesterday.

Temp was very respectful and kind. They made pleasantries for a time, and then Temp put down his tea and asked, "So what prompted your visit today? After all this time?"

"Just been a long time," Josephine told him warily. "Just wantin' to know how . . . things ever turned out."

Temp was very understanding. He smiled at her and said he was a very close friend of the Beaufortes. When Josephine raised her glass to her lips, her hands shook so badly that the ice cubes rattled, and Temp cocked his head slightly. "You have something on your chest, don't you?" he asked. "Something you'd like to talk about."

"Talk 'bout with Miz Charmian," she specified.

"I think I know what troubles you," he said, looking concerned for her. "But you're welcome to talk about it with me, if it will make you feel better. If there's any way I can be of help. I have a deep personal loyalty to the Beauforte family, as you can imagine." He gestured at the familiar room, then knit his hands in a patient gesture. "I know Charmian wouldn't mind your telling me. She has told me the whole story herself, and I assure you, she feels much as you do. I suspect you two are on the same page here."

Josephine felt a little relief to hear that and was flattered by his solicitousness, but she shook her head. "Miz Charmian don't know all of it. She don't know I's the one really killed Bradford. Mister Richard never tol' her."

If Temp Chase's interest quickened, he hid it well. He didn't prod or pressure her. He just nodded gravely, the picture of journalistic integrity and compassion, and waited.

Maybe she trusted him because she'd watched him so many times, presenting the news or interviewing important people, so sober, wise, dignified. Maybe it was that he treated her as an equal in this house where she'd always been a servant, and that he was part black, what her mother used to call octaroon, and could sympathize. Whichever, Josephine found herself confessing her crime to him. It overflowed out of her, she did so want to purge that devil from her heart, the words she'd held in for so many years just came pouring out. Of course, she admitted, Richard had his share of responsibility, too. But it wouldn't be right to condemn him, any father would do the same after what Bradford had done to Lila. Couldn't blame him.

"And no one could blame you, either," Temp reassured her. He took her hand in his two big hands and held it firmly, reassuringly. "Josephine, you mustn't blame yourself any more. You loved her like she was your own child."

Yes, yes I did, Josephine wept, grateful to him.

By the time Josephine left Beauforte House, she felt better. Temp Chase's understanding and sympathy helped. Releasing the secret from the place where she'd hidden it for so long was like a purification. Reverend Huggins had been right.

But of course her task wasn't complete until she'd talked to Charmian. So she went to the address Temp had given her, that retirement place for rich people.

Charmian was shocked to see her. In the instant she opened the door, Josephine saw it all on her face: She still had not forgiven Josephine for being so close to her children. Nor for knowing the dark secret about the Beaufortes.

She told Charmian that she'd been to the old house and had gotten her address from Temp Chase. She told Charmian she was here to tell her something about what had happened back then, to ask for her understanding.

Charmian brought her into her living room but didn't invite her to sit. She walked with a limp now, but Josephine could see that the years had done nothing to abate her scorn for her social inferiors.

"What are you here for, Josephine? Money?"

Josephine was deeply insulted. "No, Miz Charmian. Just the doctor says I's prob'ly dyin'. I got to come clean for my redemption."

"Come clean about *what*, precisely?"

When Josephine told her about her role in Brad's death, Charmian was enraged; clearly, Richard had never revealed that Josephine had a hand in it. And when Josephine said she wanted to go talk to Ron and Lila, too, Charmian took her arms so hard her nails made bloody crescents in her skin.

"You old *fool!* You shut your black face about this. You want to confess your sins? You don't even know what your sins are! You don't know half the damage you've done! You killed my husband, too! Telling my children stories of your darkie potions and superstitions — "

"What you mean?" Josephine gasped.

Charmian worked her nails in deeper. "I've done my best to accept that Bradford deserved to die," she hissed. "And I've told myself that you couldn't have known Lila would someday use your stories to kill her father. I think I have forborne admirably, Josephine, all these years. But I *won't* forgive your coming here and stirring this up. Lila has truly forgotten, and Ronald and I have done our best to. If you ever try to contact Lila, and she learns the truth, I *will not* forgive you. Do you understand?"

The truth about Richard's death shocked Josephine. She tore her arms from Charmian's taloned grip and fled in fear for her life.

Now her conscience was doubly, triply burdened. Charmian was right: If Lila found out she'd killed her father wrongly, that'd be the worst thing. After all she'd been through. That baby girl didn't deserve that. No one could live with that.

Josephine hated herself. In her selfish quest to seek forgiveness for her sins, she'd sinned again, worse than ever. Like some dumb country nigger, she'd spilled her story to Temp Chase. He'd lied when he said he was a friend of the Beaufortes, that he knew the story already; he'd used his wiles to get her to talk and she'd fallen for it. Now the truth was no longer completely buried. If Temp ever spoke of it, reported on it, Lila might remember and have to face the terrible mistake she'd made. What Charmian would do if she found that Josephine had told Temp was the least of her worries. In her vanity and weakness, her selfish concern for her own salvation, she had done the last thing she would ever want — she'd put Lila in danger.

Now Lila needed to be protected.

So before she left New Orleans for good, she performed some hoodoo craft her mother had taught her long ago: She cut little sticks of hackberry tree and notched them twice, one notch for Temp and the second for his wife in case he'd told her, and left them at Beauforte House. Some practitioners used the technique to induce craziness in an enemy, but Mama had always prescribed it for making people forget, like if a woman knew someone had seen her with her lover and wanted them to forget so they couldn't tell her husband. She put one hex at each corner of the grounds, then waited until no one was home and used her old key to get inside and put one under the mantelpiece. She looked up Lila's address and left hexes at the Warrens', too.

She thought it was probably just superstition, an old woman's fool-ishness, but her mother had always sworn it would work.

And anyway, there didn't seem to be anything Jesus could do about this.

As for herself, she no longer sought forgiveness. She didn't feel she deserved it. Oh, she did pray to God for Temp to forget, for Lila to keep forgetting. She went on her knees every day and pleaded for that. But when she heard on the TV news that Temp had been murdered, not two weeks after her visit, she knew that neither God nor Jesus nor hoodoo nor anything else on Earth or in heaven was going to stop Charmian Beauforte from remembering and from protecting her family however she felt she had to.

43

JOSEPHINE'S RASPING VOICE CEASED suddenly, and Cree felt the light in the room change. She turned her head to see a dark silhouette at the screen door, eclipsing the light from outside.

In another instant, Charmian Beauforte had opened the screen door and stepped onto the porch, and then she was coming through the open inner door. She was dressed impeccably in a beige suit over a white silk blouse, holding her ostrich-skin purse close to her side. She didn't have her cane, but she mastered her limp almost completely as she came into the dim room, stood regally, and fixed them with her raptor's gaze.

"Can't just come in my house like this!" Josephine gasped.

Charmian ignored her. "You know why I'm here," she said to Cree. "We need to end your investigation. One way or another. Today."

"My investigation *is* over."

"Yes, it certainly is. Now, you two are going to do exactly as I say. We're going to make a deal, right now, the three of us. Your lives depend on making this deal and sticking with it."

Josephine stood up from her chair, mustering a formidable power of her own. "Miz Charmian. This my home. This my family home. You don't come here an' tell me what I do or don't do."

Charmian didn't back down as the taller figure approached her. "Josephine, look out the window. See the man leaning against the big car? His name is Loup Garou." For Cree's benefit, she translated, "That means 'Werewolf,' and they call him that for a very good reason. There's another man, just down the street. So get it through your head, right now – I *do* tell you what to do. Here or anywhere else."

Cree turned in her chair to look out the window, and it was as Charmian had said. An older Cadillac had pulled up, right at the end of the front walk. The man leaning against it wore an oversize checked shirt, parted enough to reveal a mat of dark chest hair above a sleeveless T-shirt. A big automatic pistol was stuck in his belt. Though he wore sunglasses, it was clear he watched the door of the house with interest.

"How did you know where I was?" Cree asked.

"Paul Fitzpatrick has been most helpful to me throughout this escapade. He told me you'd locate Josephine. I just had you followed." Charmian must have seen the astonishment come into Cree's face, because her mouth hardened, the tiniest smile of gratification at revealing this betrayal.

Josephine had studied the man at the car, and now she looked back at Charmian. They locked eyes. Cree could see the arc that leapt there, the ancient antagonism between these two old women, the bitter contest over which would possess Lila's heart, the unforgiven failings they accused each other of. After a moment, Josephine took two steps to the kitchen hallway and called down it. "Hiram! Go get yo' uncle's shotgun from out my closet. Then you come on out the front room."

But Hiram must have heard some disturbance earlier, because immediately Cree heard the sound of a shell being jacked into the chamber, and then Hiram was coming out of the hallway with the big gun leveled. He was still shirtless, his dark skin still glistening with sweat, and he towered over Charmian with a baleful look.

Charmian looked him up and down with contempt.

"Hiram," Josephine instructed, "you go sit on the porch, an' you watch that man at the car. He start to come up here, you shoot him dead. I call you, you turn around shoot this ol' lady dead. She like a witch, you don't trust her neither, you understand?"

Hiram moved silently past Charmian, out onto the porch, where he took a chair facing the street, the shotgun held low but aimed at the man outside. When the Werewolf saw him come out, he straightened out of his slouch and one hand strayed to his pistol.

The guns scared Cree. The powers of the two women held each other in a tense stasis. The motionless air was charged with latent action, and the guns made any shift of balance potentially lethal.

"You don't tell me what I do," Josephine said quietly. "No more. You not my judge, and you not my maker. You not even my boss. And this is *my* home. This be a good time you learn humility, Miz Charmian."

Charmian eyes blazed at that, and she seemed to inhale, swell with rage. If she upped the ante another notch it would all blow apart.

"Charmian," Cree broke in. "What deal? What do you mean?"

"I will protect my daughter," she said through her teeth. "That's the deal. The only deal." The compressed fury in her had only grown in the face of Josephine's resistance and Hiram's dark presence twelve feet away. Against her will, Cree had to admire the strength of her.

"We *all* want that! But how, Charmian? You told her to forget. She did her best. But the ghosts won't let her."

"Ghosts!" Charmian snorted contemptuously and looked to Josephine. "What do you think? Does Ms. Black have powers, the gift of sight? What would your mother say?"

"She know what you done. She know why you done it. She seen Richard's ghost and Bradford's, too. She a healin' woman, can fix Lila if you let her."

"And what about you, Josephine?" Charmian's face moved in scorn. "What about your forgiveness you need so badly? Can she give you that?"

Josephine turned her face away. "Me, I'm not too worried about no forgiveness no mo'." Her voice was a dull, hopeless echo in her hollow chest. "How 'bout yo' own? You know how you done, how you lost yo' daughter."

Charmian pretended to ignore the question, but her eyelid ticced, and she went on hurriedly. "The deal is, I confess to killing Richard. I say I poisoned him with a preparation of black cherry seeds. I can prove it – they can open the crypt and find traces of it in his remains. I confess and you don't tell anyone anything different."

"Detective Guidry will ask why you killed him."

Charmian improvised: "Because he . . . he let my baby brother die in that swamp, let him go off on his own, drunk, and I lost my head and took revenge! Or he had an affair, or – "

"No." For a moment Cree had thought maybe Charmian was right, maybe this one lie was the route through, but she quickly came up against another wall. "Charmian, if you want Lila to survive, she has to face the ghosts – both her father's ghost and Bradford's. She might be able to buy in to your killing Richard, and that's what's most important. But when she faces Bradford, she'll know how he died, she'll know he died at the house and not in some bayou. She'll know he's the one who raped her. She'll know you lied. It'll all fall apart."

Charmian snorted. "You're assuming I believe in ghosts."

"Lila has to face them whether you believe or not."

Charmian's desperation grew. "You don't understand! If I tell about Bradford, it will be the end of the Beauforte name, the Lambert name! It'll reach every scandal-mongering journalist in the country! We'll – "

"Decide, Charmian. Decide whether it's your daughter you want to protect or just your family name and your control. It's something you should have decided long ago."

The dragon eyes looked baleful and wounded, but still Charmian held firm, said nothing.

"And then there's Temp Chase," Cree said.

For the first time, Charmian looked frightened. She mastered the expression quickly, but a shiver shook her, and Cree realized she'd reached the limit of her self-control. Just beyond was collapse or violence. "What about Temp Chase? He has nothing to do with this!"

"Temp came to you after Josephine's visit. He wanted to blackmail you. His career was falling apart, he'd had financial setbacks, he was desperate. Josephine had told him almost everything. He came to you and said he could feature it in an exposé, or you could pay him a lot of money not to."

Josephine's face folded in pain. "I am sorry, Miz Charmian. Didn't know 'bout Lila killin' her daddy, I wouldn't have said *nothin'* to him. But he say he already know about it! He say he your friend! I take it on my shoulders. This all on my shoulders."

"I didn't kill Temp Chase, that's absurd!" Charmian was truly terrified now, breathless and trembling from head to foot.

Cree let her hang for a moment. The heat was stifling, and the smell of so many fears in the small room was choking her. Charmian's reaction now would determine the outcome of the whole case, for Lila, for all of them. "No. I know you didn't."

Hearing that, Charmian's body shook. The straight back seemed to falter, and she groped toward a chair, grasping its back to stabilize herself.

Out at the curb, the swamp rat had heard Charmian's raised voice and had stepped away from the car. His narrow face lifted toward the house as if he were straining to see into the shadowed interior, and both hands now rested on his gun. "Hey, Gran'mère!" he called, just loud enough to be heard. "Is it time? Nigger on the porch don't scare me, you jus' tell me when."

Loup Garou took another easy step forward. On the porch, the shadow that was Hiram didn't seem to move, but the glisten along the barrel quicksilvered as the shotgun tracked Loup.

"Save me something," Charmian whispered. "Don't do this. Don't bring my son into this. Don't make this part of the deal. Don't make me protect one child only to lose another."

Loup Garou took another step toward the house, calling Hiram's bluff by degrees.

"Call off the Werewolf. Tell him to go back to the car."

Wide-eyed, Charmian shook her head, *no.*

God damn *the woman for her stubbornness!* Cree thought. "Temp is *dead.* His killer has to pay!" She said urgently. "Call him off!"

"Temp Chase stays out of it. *Ron* stays out of it! If it ever comes up, I'll confess to that, too. You know I will. Their investigation has gone nowhere in over two years! They already looked at Ronald! I can prove I had reason to kill him! You can tell Guidry anything you want, nobody can prove it, nobody'll bother. Not with me confessing!"

Hiram stood up as Loup Garou came another step closer. The barrel of the shotgun shook with his tension. Cree gave the shotgun the edge, but Hiram was no gunfighter. One hesitation and Loup Garou would have the advantage. Either way, the house would have bad ghosts forever and another generation of pain would be born. And nothing anyone could do would help Lila.

"You tell Guidry you killed Richard because he killed Bradford! And you tell him why Richard did it!" Cree insisted. "You have to tell him about the rape! That much has to come out or it won't hold. And you tell Paul Fitzpatrick to cooperate with me on treating Lila whether he believes in ghosts or whatever the hell. And I don't bring Ron into it. Okay? Now *call him off!*"

Charmian hesitated for three more heartbeats, calculating, not breathing. Then she called, "Loup! Go back to the car!"

He paused, only a few steps from the door.

"Now!" she shouted. "Go back to the car! Get inside and wait." She held herself there until he began backing away. Then she quickly took a seat and let her back fold.

Only when the Werewolf had gotten inside the big car did Josephine move again. Straight streaks of tears lined her face beneath both eyes. "You doin' good, Hiram," she called softly. "Yo' great-auntie thank you. Better put it down now."

44

"YOU HAVE TO REALLY FIND IT IN YOU," Cree repeated softly. She'd already said it five times in five different ways. "You can't fake it or force yourself to feel it. You've got to offer him a real window of escape. Encountering you has got to provide resolution for him, and that'll happen only when you provide yourself some resolution – when you really accept what happened and let go of it. The promise of that closure must be so real and attractive that it draws him toward you, and then your reality will war with his obsession. It'll show him his world is unreal. Does that make sense?"

Lila nodded minutely.

The three of them stood beneath a streetlight on Washington Avenue, looking across at the walls of Lafayette Cemetery. Behind them, the lush streets of the Garden District settled into the relative tranquillity of a Tuesday evening. Though the cemetery was closed now, Paul and Lila had prevailed upon its staff to open the gate for one after-hours visit to a family tomb; the Beauforte name still carried enough weight for such favors. Now the dark figure of a cemetery attendant waited behind the main gate. Beyond, the innumerable low roofs and gables of the crypts were tinted with sad twilight blue.

Lila looked pale in this light, her skin almost transparent, as if the blood she'd lost had not been restored to her. Her physical health was not bad, but the revelations of the past forty-eight hours had wrenched her open, exposing her past and her hidden self. Charmian had gone to the police, had confessed to killing Richard, and had told them why: because he'd killed her brother. And she'd explained that, too: the rape. Not trusting

Cree to keep the deal, she'd also confessed to murdering Temp Chase when he attempted to blackmail her; she was right, it was an effective way to keep Guidry from any suspicion of Ron. The story would cause a fabulous scandal when Deelie's scoop hit the newsstands, the kind that cropped up in New Orleans only once every few years and helped preserve its exotic reputation: great names fallen low, the sordid underbelly of the aristocracy exposed, ancient secrets come to life.

Still, Lila looked determined. Knowing what had happened back then, who the boar-headed man was, had strengthened her. She admitted she was terrified by what they were about to do, yet she took Cree's word that within the cemetery gates lay the promise of closure and the beginning of healing.

If everything went as Cree hoped, anyway.

Paul appeared to waver between confusion about Cree, and, she hoped, shame for being a lying, deceiving son of a bitch. Also worry for his patient and distrust of tonight's enterprise – he had come along only because Lila had insisted.

And Cree – how did Cree feel? she wondered. For starters, she wished Edgar had made it here, as much for moral support as for gathering physical evidence on the boar-headed man. But when Joyce had spoken to him on Saturday, he'd told her he just couldn't make it, after all. Things were really heating up with the Gloucester ghost, he needed to extend his stay a few days. Ordinarily, Cree would have waited on the final phase until Ed had a shot at these ghosts, but remediation couldn't wait.

But more than anything else, she was scared for Lila. Hopeful for her, too. A little sick with apprehension at the prospect of what they were about to do.

For Cree, the most difficult decision of the last two days was whether Lila should begin with Bradford's ghost or Richard's. On one hand, she felt that if Lila came to Richard's ghost first, she'd emerge strengthened, cleansed of subconscious guilt – just maybe strong enough to face down her uncle's monstrous revenant. But she worried that bringing Lila back to the house when the creature still roamed there would undo her before she got anywhere near the library. Anyway, before she went to the library, Lila needed to *know*, absolutely and at the deepest level, the truth of who her rapist had been. She had to purge any lingering subconscious accusation of her father if she were to meet him and accept the love he offered.

So maybe she should face Bradford first, conquer him, release him, to prove to herself that her father was not the guilty one. But Cree had no confidence she was strong enough to face the dark halls of Beauforte House, the spectral wereboar that hunted her there.

For most of the night, she had gone back and forth, agonizing. It had to unfold just right. If anything went wrong, Lila could emerge from the encounters crazy, permanently unbalanced, lost.

The biggest problem was that Cree really had no idea how to alleviate the boar-headed phantom. How could they reach him? He was too intentional, physical, awful. And he was too *simple* – a powerful revenant existing in a very narrow band, with an almost one-dimensional affective complex. For the thousandth time, she puzzled over the absence of the perimortem experience in his manifestation. She knew his predations were a memory recalled intensely at the moment of death, but she'd never sensed the "umbilicus": He was almost completely devoid of any connection to the man's actual experience of dying. And it was under the duress of dying that each individual most fervently sought to settle his accounts, sought emotional refuge – and therefore was most vulnerable. That's when he was most likely to allow a living being to intrude upon his perseverating universe. But Cree had never sensed the library beating in the boar-headed man. And if he felt any remorse, it was only a tiny, dark thing, a grain of ash.

But late last night, thinking through every step of the scenario yet again, an epiphany had come to her. A curtain had fallen away, her vision clearing so abruptly that at two A.M. she'd leapt out of the hotel bed. She had dressed and slipped away from the hotel and come here to Lafayette Cemetery. She'd slid between the iron rails of the gate and gone deep into the center of the city of the dead. It had taken a long time to find the right crypt, but her guess had proved correct.

Paul looked at Cree, a question and an accusation. She had not told him the specifics of what was to happen, only that this visit was necessary and that he damned well owed her this much faith after all she'd accomplished so far. Not to mention the little matter of his secret collusion with Charmian. She had refused to listen to his excuses, and she'd made no effort to hide her contempt: He was as deceitful as anyone else in this city of masks.

"What do you think, Lila?" Paul asked. "Are you really up for this?"

"I think so," Lila said. "I can try."

"You'll do fine," Cree assured her. She took her arm and went with her across the street, Paul following reluctantly.

The attendant swung the gate open to let them in, then closed it after them. " 'Bout how long?" he asked. "I got to stay on to close up after."

"It might be two or three hours," Cree told him. "I'm sorry to keep you late. We're very grateful."

He cheered up when Paul tipped him with a twenty. He nodded, checked his watch in a shaft of streetlight, and went to sit on a block of masonry to one side of the gate. Cree looked back to see him light up a cigarette, its tiny orange pulse the last beacon of the ordinary world beyond the cemetery walls.

Near the gate, the cemetery was arranged in major lanes lined with the little temples. Farther in, the lanes branched and wandered, narrowing, and the crypts stood closer together. In the dim light, the faux-marble surfaces took on a misty quality, rectangles and triangles pale against the night. Here and there, statues stood guard at crypt doors, patient and sorrowful.

There were a thousand faint ghosts of grieving here, the lingering feelings of the living who had come here to bid farewell to loved ones. But otherwise, it was a tranquil place, Cree felt. The densely clustered crypts blocked the noise of the city, broke its sounds on a million facets of masonry so that the wandering avenues were bathed in a soft white whisper. It smelled of old brick, old cement, and the faint, musty breath of vault interiors. The air was cool now, but when she passed close to crypts Cree could feel the glow of the heat they'd stored during the day.

They walked slowly on. Lila was gripping her arm hard. Paul still followed behind, saying nothing. Cree had instructed him to be quiet, not to voice his skepticism, to bring a flashlight but not to use it unless she told him to. It was crucial that they let Lila find her own way through this.

Near the center, they hesitated at an intersection of narrow paths. At first Cree wasn't sure she remembered the way, but finally she decided they needed to go left, and only a few steps farther brought them to the crypt. As befitted an old and prestigious family, it was larger than most, a Greek temple about the size of a prefab backyard storage shed. In front, two fluted pillars held up the roof of a shallow vestibule that cast the vault's cover into shadow. The back was wedged only a hand's width from neighboring crypts, the gaps between completely lightless.

"What do we do?" Lila whispered so quietly Cree could hear the pulse in her throat.

"We wait. Might as well sit." Cree gestured toward a squat urn to the left of the door. "You'll find him."

Lila sat, just a shadow within the shadow of the overhang. Barely more visible, Paul hung several paces back, shifting uneasily. When Cree had proposed this visit, he had warned her that New Orleans cemeteries were dangerous places at night, and not for supernatural reasons. The enclosed, labyrinthine little cities made good temporary lodging for homeless people and had become favored places for crack deals to be made, for junkies to cook heroin over candle flames and shoot up. Night in the cemeteries was too often a time of predation.

"If you're too scared," she had told him acidly, "then don't come." The look on his face had given her a pang, but he damned well deserved it.

The air turned gradually cooler. Cree stood until her legs tired and then sat cross-legged on the floor of the vestibule. Paul's shadow shifted uneasily from foot to foot. Lila was a mound of darkness that rocked ever so slightly from side to side.

Sometime later, Cree felt it coming: the impulse growing toward its eerie nascence. It began with a faint sense of movement and feeling that coalesced only inches away, on the other side of the vault cover.

Paul sensed it, too. His shadow froze, as if he were listening.

"I'm scared, Cree," Lila whispered.

Something moved audibly inside the crypt. It started as a faint scraping noise, like a rat gnawing, but it soon changed. Something larger shifted, making a rustle of cloth and then a faint, dull thump. Even knowing it was coming, Cree felt a feather drift up her spine.

"There's someone coming," Paul whispered urgently.

"Shhh."

"No, there's someone . . . this is no joke, Cree, these crack heads – "

"Paul, *shut up!*"

The shadow of Paul looked down one side of the crypt, saw nothing, then stepped to the other side. Then he mounted the apron and put one hand against the marble crypt cover. He snatched it away as if it had burned him. No doubt he felt the faint vibration in the marble. Afterward he stood motionless again, indecisive. Cree couldn't see his face, but she could hear his breath, a short, sharp panting.

Lila hadn't moved. Cree let herself fall into sync with the burgeoning manifestation in the crypt and felt Lila coming with her.

And they found him there.

He had just awakened in utter darkness, confused. At first it seemed that he couldn't open his eyes, but then he realized they *were* open, he had either gone blind or there was simply no light for them to register. A waterfall of pain originated in his head and poured down his neck and back. Something was wrong with him, he realized. He'd been hurt. It took a while to make sense of things, but he became aware he was lying on his back on a hard, smooth, slightly rounded surface. With an effort, he lifted one hand only to discover a coarse masonry ceiling just inches above him. The discovery shocked him and his whole body jerked reflexively. The movement caused him to slide to the right, down the slight incline of the curved surface. Abruptly he felt a gap beneath him, and he rolled partly into it.

He was wedged there in the dark, his forehead against rough stone, the back of his head against the thing he'd been lying on. One arm hung beneath him, his fingers trailing in some kind of rubble – dust and crumbly chunks and sharp pieces. An incomprehensible place.

The movement had caused savage arcs of pain to streak through his whole body, and with it the memory came suddenly to him: Richard had been beating him! He had fled the purpling face of his brother-in-law, cringing from and yet welcoming every explosion of pain as the poker struck. Now was some time after that, and he was somewhere dark and small and musty smelling.

The arm beneath his body could hardly move, but the other was free, and with his fingers he traced the surface behind him. Beneath a film of grit it felt smooth and metallic. Something was digging painfully into his back, and when his fingers found it he discovered it was carved in low-relief designs. A flange or fixture like a decorative fist gripping a pole or rail that felt like, it *was*, a handle!

It was the carrying rail on a coffin.

At the realization, Bradford's ghost ignited in sheer terror. The hand wedged beneath him scrabbled in the remains of his Lambert ancestors. His free hand clawed the wall and bloodied itself. He got it above him, past the end of the coffin, and found only more of the same: bricks with bulges of mortar between them.

Bradford screamed. He was in a crypt. Richard must have done this. Richard and that black witch Josephine had buried him alive.

A groan squeezed out of Lila, and Cree knew she was experiencing the ghost's terror. The silhouette of Paul had put its hands over its ears.

Bradford tried to pound on the wall. Somebody would hear the thumping. They'd let him out. But he found he was too weak to pound long. Two useless blows and his arm fell back against his side, muscles exhausted. The darkness swam in whorls of sick yellow light. He tried to inch himself forward or backward beneath the low ceiling but found he couldn't. He was wedged in the narrow gap between the coffin and the rough wall and he had no strength and he was damaged, badly damaged.

"Help me!" he mouthed. He intended the words but had not enough breath to make them sound. "Help me!"

He pounded the wall for another few seconds and nearly blacked out from the exertion. Confusion took him, and he lost track of where he was or why. It had to do with Lila, he thought. *Lila* was an idea that was all pain. He had to do something for Lila, she was hurt. Somebody bad had hurt her. He had to get free to do something for Lila. Why? Then he remembered chasing her, and the giddy craziness of it, the way his anger and envy had risen and converged with his lust and that strange sadistic abandon, and how he'd let them go, let it go on. Breaking the boundaries was a thrill that fueled itself. In the boar mask he was a rutting animal, powerful and brutal and free, given power in all the ways his daily life deprived him of power. How good her fear of him felt, how supple her flesh when he forced himself on her, how exciting her struggles beneath him. Even in his pain and remorse, the memory was sharp and clear and spun out of him like a creature with its own separate life, savage and exultant.

Then it got distant and he forgot it again. A sharp tooth of mortar seemed to screw itself into the flesh of his forehead, and he couldn't pull away even a fraction of an inch.

"Charm? Charm!" he called, and this time his heard his voice work. Charm would always help, she had always helped. For a moment the thought of her gave him reassurance, but then he lost his place in time again. He kicked with his free leg and hit something hard. The crypt door. He kicked again, and that was all the strength he had.

The sound of Bradford's spectral shoe against the inch-thick marble door was clearly audible outside the crypt. Paul retreated several steps from the crypt, stumbling as he came off the apron, hands still over his ears, and despite her anger Cree felt a pang for him: His world, too, would come undone tonight.

Bradford's ghost scratched at the bricks with his free hand until he felt his nails come away and he became too weak to move any more. He lay there in the dark, mostly unconscious for a while.

When he awoke again, it was with a start. Something had changed.

The bricks he was wedged against had gotten warmer. The air he struggled to breathe was getting warm, too.

Cree fought to keep calm, knowing the agonies that would follow.

The sun must have risen at that point, beginning its daily slow incineration of the occupants of the aboveground crypts of New Orleans. Inside, Bradford's ghost would relive the dying man's panic. His body would arch minutely as he began to be cooked alive. It would go on for some hours yet. It had been happening for almost thirty years.

Even in his wrath, Cree didn't think Richard would have intentionally condemned Bradford to this – surely he hadn't known Brad was still alive when he'd stuffed him in here.

She hoped Lila would intervene soon.

Cree could help, but Lila would need to find strength enough to offer him the window of escape. She had to enter his world dream and offer some promise of release.

Now the dying man was distilling down to his rudiments. There was regret – somewhere far away was a movie of memory that wouldn't stop, a wereboar taking its angry pleasure upon a girl. And Bradford hated the wereboar impulse. It lived in him like a huge tapeworm, fastened into his mind and feeding on him. It punished him. He wanted to be free of it.

You're dead, Bradford, he heard. The voice intruded on his solitary nightmare and startled him: Lila's voice! *Go away now*, it said. *Just go away.*

Cree looked at the dark shape of Lila. She was holding herself very still, but around her a dirty purple aura jittered.

Lila? the ghost thought. Its world became confused, and the presence of his victim, the source of his guilt, terrified him. The world of the crypt began to break up, unsustainable.

Cree held her breath, hoping Lila would find in herself what was needed.

"Go away, Bradford! Let yourself go away now!" Lila was saying it out loud. There was no forgiveness in her thought or her voice, but there was pity and there was acceptance. "You're dead. You're a long time ago. You're over with. The whole thing is over now."

The best thing she could manage to give him was to get over him. And it was just right, Cree realized.

It was all the window the tortured ghost needed. He fled from his nightmare in the crypt toward her hard pity and resignation. In the mind of the ghost, past and present clashed, irreconcilable. Lost, the ghost spun away. The boar-headed memory broke apart and became an echo of a memory of a dream and then just dust in a whorl of darkness, and even the walls of the crypt, oven hot now, weren't real. Nothing was.

45

B Y THE TIME PAUL SWUNG wide the iron gate at Beauforte
House, Lila felt as if she were floating. The night air of the Garden
District seemed to buoy her just above the ground – not a light, good
feeling, but detached, emptied. The familiar streets struck her as alien.
Meeting Bradford's ghost, sharing his dying moments, trying to find her
own reconciliation with what had happened, she felt as if she'd been
scraped raw inside, hollowed out.

Poor Paul had vomited wrenchingly after the encounter. Of the three
of them, only Cree had been able talk during the short drive from
Lafayette Cemetery. Cree had said that the coming encounter was the
crucial one. Meeting her father would be the way she'd become free and
strong.

Thank you, Cree, Lila thought, *I knew that.* They were all being so
kind.

"One other thing," Cree whispered. She put her hand on Lila's arm
and the three of them stopped, halfway up the walk. "I can't be
absolutely sure the boar-headed ghost is gone. Bradford's perimortem
ghost is gone from the crypt, but his perseveration of the rape was highly
independent. If we sense anything at all of him, we have to leave the
house immediately. If you don't feel you can take the risk, we shouldn't
go in at all."

Lila thought about that for a moment, weighing what was to be gained
and what could be lost. "I want to go in," she said finally. "Come with
me into the hall. But I want to go into the library by myself."

Even in the half-light, Lila could see the doubt in Paul's face. Cree looked wary but pleased. Of course Cree would know it was the only thing to be done.

They opened the door. Cree had insisted they leave the lights off, and for a moment the yawning darkness of the rooms frightened Lila. Maybe she couldn't do this. But though they waited at the bottom of the stairs, neither she nor Cree could feel the boar-headed specter, no echo or whisper. In fact, his absence was palpable. The house *felt* different: That coiled-spring feeling, that about-to-snap feeling, was gone. The boar-headed ghost was dead.

She drew one breath and realized it was the first clear, unconstricted inhalation she'd taken in many, many years.

Paul waited near the open front door as Cree walked her back through the dark hallway and through the kitchen. They turned into the long south wing hallway. Cree squeezed her hands at the library door and left without a word.

Lila went in. She could see almost nothing, but her body remembered the room's contours so well it almost didn't matter. She took small steps, feeling as she had when she'd performed on the cello as a little girl, going out onto the stage in front of a vast auditorium to perform some intimidating work she knew she hadn't mastered.

"Daddy?" she whispered.

The library smell reminded her of him, but she saw and heard nothing. Of course, Cree had said it might take a long time.

Her thigh found the piano bench and she sat backward on it, facing the room.

There were many varieties of fear, Lila decided. She was scared shaky now, but it was not the same as the fear she'd felt upstairs and in all her solitary moments in the last four months. That had been torn out her like a tumor at the Lambert crypt. No, this was more like the fear you feel from some mountaintop you've climbed, where the fear of height chills you even as the long views make you joyful. There was a state where fear and hope met, she realized, where they were indistinguishable. The impulses sprang from the same well inside in you.

It helped that everyone was so kind. Cree was so good-hearted. Paul had been dubious about this, but clearly he cared, he really wanted her to recover, as a human being as well as a psychiatrist. She hadn't seen Ron since all the revelations, but she knew he had done so much to protect her from what had happened. Even Momma, in her inimitable way – confessing to killing Daddy and Temp Chase, taking all the blame. She'd played the tyrannical dowager to the hilt, even refusing to see Lila when she'd tried to visit her at the jail earlier. She'd done it so that Lila couldn't sympathize too strongly. So that Lila could stay angry at her.

And so that she wouldn't see the lie for what it was.

It was so touching. They'd been protecting her for so long, she couldn't bear to let them down.

Cree and Paul had explained what had happened to her: the boar mask, Brad and Daddy switching costumes that night, the rape. Daddy beating Brad and, thinking he was dead, hiding his unconscious body in the Lambert crypt, where he died of his wounds the next day. Charmian's rage at Daddy for killing Brad, last scion of the illustrious Lamberts, and her vengeance by poison.

She could almost believe it. Certainly she would put nothing past Momma, and a tiny, awful part of her gloated at Charmian's having to pay the piper at last, for these and other sins. But as she'd thought about it afterward, it didn't quite make sense, and during that last long night awake in the hospital room, her memory had unsealed itself. It was like discovering a hidden door in the house, one that opened into a long, dark hallway. That secret corridor of memory had always been there, she'd always sensed it, running parallel to the traveled ways of her life, her daily acts and thoughts. She had knocked on the walls and heard the hollow echoes, but she had never been able to find the way inside.

But as she thought about what Cree and Paul told her, she suddenly found the door, swinging open unexpectedly. It made sense out of Ron's inexplicable comments in the kitchen that afternoon. *If you knew there was something I did – something that put me in danger. Something I could barely live with . . . something I could never even do again. Wouldn't you try to protect me?*

He hadn't been talking about himself. He was talking about her.

She began to remember: believing Daddy had done it to her. Secretly making the poison from the wild cherry seeds and blossoms as Josephine had told them years ago, and putting it in his amaretto. Coming down later to find Momma with him on the floor, and all the feelings she'd felt. Though she'd been kind of crazy since that night with the boar-headed man, it was that moment in the library that she'd gone truly insane. That searing instant had cauterized her mind, closing the wound and sealing off her memory.

Knowing what she'd done, she wanted again to kill herself. After Cree and Paul had left the hospital room, she'd raged at herself, and at them for trying to deceive her yet again.

But the girl who had done it was so long gone; Lila could not fully blame her. The emotion was weary, it had worn itself out. And all around her now was the kindness of those who sought to protect her. Didn't she owe them the consummation of their kindness? That was what won out, what gave her strength. That much kindness was something of a redemption, wasn't it? People were at least sometimes capable of fine deeds and noble hopes, weren't they?

She made up her mind to pretend she didn't know. Cree had helped her at every step of the way, but this step she decided she'd take on her own. She'd see if she could find Daddy tonight. She'd ask for his forgiveness. She'd try to let him free. Then she'd keep the secret for the rest of her life.

Time passed. She wondered now how long she'd been in here; it seemed like hours, but in the dark it was hard to tell. Cree had said it might take a while, and that Daddy's ghost was a subtler sort of manifestation; she might not experience him as strongly as Brad's ghost, at least not visually. It might be only her heart that perceived him, so she'd have to observe her feelings closely. *Be gentle with yourself*, Cree had said. *Be patient with yourself.*

She did her best. She tried to relax, and she stared open-eyed around her in the dark. The room wasn't totally black – a little light crept around the edges of the curtains. She could see the vaguest of forms: the dark flat of bookshelves, the lighter walls on either side of the fireplace, the looming lumps of darkness that would be the wingback chairs. Invisible at the far end of the room was the table that had scared her so badly and that throughout the many ordeals with the boar-headed man had lingered in her thoughts and figured in her nightmares. She'd worried that it would persist as the boar-headed man did, it would arise to torment her in some unforseen way. That other things in the house would start changing, too.

But Cree had explained that, too, along with the snake and the wolf. When Cree had asked Josephine about it, down in Port Sulphur, Josephine had shown her a book she'd kept since back then. Again, Lila remembered it the moment Cree told her about it. She and Ro-Ro would go to Josephine's room and huddle up in their pajamas on the quilted bed cover as Josephine read to them. Sometimes it was Bible stories, sometimes fairy tales, but their favorite was an old volume of supernatural stories, illustrated with lurid full-color plates, called *Terrors of Devil's Bayou*. Daddy called that kind of thing "pulp." The book had heavy, flaking cardboard covers, and just the smell of it when they opened its crumbly pages gave them a delicious thrill of terror. Josephine said it was from back in the 1920s. They'd make her read it, and though she'd always resist she always gave in. It would scare them terribly and they'd come trembling back into the main house to lie wide eyed and quaking in bed, imagining all its lovely horrors.

There was the gigantic water moccasin that dwelt deep in the cypress swamps. It came at night to the scattered houses of Cajun trappers to eat their children, right in their beds. Nothing could stop it: It was able to seep like smoke through cracks in walls, down chimneys, around doors. The old people knew that the black mist that sometimes gathered and glided along the bayous at sundown was the snake, beginning to take form, and that its appearance meant someone would die that night.

The wolf was a *loup-garou* that terrorized the swamps. He could lope through the night over land or water or swamp and turn into a man or a wolf at will. The scariest picture was when he was halfway between. When he came to the house of his victim, he became as stealthy as a shadow and took great pleasure in stalking his unknowing victim. Before he struck, he'd whisper the name of his intended prey at his door cracks and keyholes.

The living table was pictured in the book, Cree said, claw feet and all. Lila remembered the story: An evil rich man in some small town oppressed the men who worked in his sawmill and was cruel to their wives and children. He lived alone in a huge house, and while his neighbors suffered in poverty he indulged himself by buying jewels and baubles, importing fine furniture from France, drinking only the most expensive wines. Eventually the townspeople asked a local witch to put a curse on him. The house and the rich things in it came alive, attacking him, driving him mad, and devouring his soul.

These things happened when you were really haunted, Cree had said. She had a term for it: "epiphenomenal manifestations." Your mind was triggered and generated other scary things, cobbled together from memories and imaginings. The proximity of the unknown could awaken a lifetime's worth of fears.

Lila shivered, remembering the nightmare of the snake's visit, the wolf, the table. But as Cree had predicted, once they'd taken a place in the architecture of her waking, normal world, their power had begun to ebb. She had some control of them.

Cree was very smart, Lila thought again.

But still there was no sign of Daddy's ghost. Cree had told her nothing about what the ghost did, what it felt or needed, only to say that Lila would emerge from the encounter strengthened and freed.

Lila's back ached from sitting on the hard rosewood bench, and a tension pain sank talons into her shoulders. She got up, stretched, took a few steps in the dark, turned to survey the room. The darkness was ordinary darkness, as far as she could tell. It wasn't about to explode at her, or strike at her like some snake. It was just a quiet room where her father had spent many hours of his life. Until that awful table had come alive, she'd always felt a nice feeling in here, safe and calm, and she felt a bit of it now. Did that feeling count as a ghost? She wasn't sure. Daddy used to read in here, smoking his cigar, and he often did his business at the big desk. Sometimes she'd come in here to be with him. Sometimes he'd let her pester him, sometimes he'd shoo her away so he could attend to his affairs.

She repressed the urge to look at her watch. Instead, she recited Cree's parting advice like a chant, a prayer: *Don't worry about mechanical time. Take all the time you need. Just let your mind roam. Remember things, if they come to you. Feel what you feel, cherish each feeling, and then let it pass if it will. Keep your eyes moving in the dark, scanning, but remember it could start with a mood, an emotion, or even a smell.*

You might get afraid, but just remember this was someone who loved you. His ghost still does, very much. You'll see.

But he wasn't coming. It made her very sad.

"I'm sorry," she said out loud. "We all went kind of crazy. No one knew what to do, did they?" The room just absorbed her words. "I'm sorry I poisoned you. I wasn't really sure it would even work. I didn't know about Brad. I didn't mean to betray you. I love you so much."

There didn't seem to be anyone listening.

She went back to the piano bench and settled herself on it. Her hands started kneading each other, kneading the opposite wrists, but she made them stop.

Right now Cree would be sitting in the dark entry hall with Paul. They wouldn't be saying much; they'd both be listening hard for sounds of trouble from back in the house. Cree would have her weird, empathic radar going. Those two were so drawn to each other, you could feel it in the air between them. But Cree was angry with him for some reason, probably because for all her insights and courage, she was afraid of the things he showed her about herself. Everyone had things inside they couldn't easily face. Paul, too. Right now, he was reeling inwardly, feeling sick and uncertain about everything after what he'd experienced at the Lambert crypt. Lila knew just how it felt.

What would happen to the two of them? Cree would go back to Seattle tomorrow or the next day. Paul – who knew? She hoped they wouldn't give up, wouldn't waste the good thing between them. It was too rare in life to waste.

More time passed.

She worried about Jack. He'd be sitting at home, still awake and sick with anxiety, or fallen asleep on the couch. He hadn't wanted to let her go without him tonight, but she had insisted. She was determined to be a new person, to break out of her old roles, but she wasn't sure what that really meant. It was all so new, and she needed time to decide just what she'd do differently. Jackie had never met this new person – would he love her? She kind of hoped he would; for all that he was not high class or exceptionally intelligent, he was a sweet man, earnest, funny. He had sure stuck through some tough spots.

Again, she recalled Cree's advice: *Don't worry about Jack. Just trust that where you lead, he'll follow.*

She felt her back grow tired of sitting. The fear abated, replaced by exhaustion. She struggled not to drowse. Her mood drifted toward a sweet sort of nostalgic melancholy. The past looked and felt different now. Cree said everyone did this – that important events, even just of the normal world, changed your view of yourself and your history and your family. You were always revising them.

Lila found herself returning to a memory she'd long ignored or forgotten, an afternoon from when she must have been six or seven. It wasn't anything particularly special, just her and Daddy wandering in the yard. He was always so sweet but so seldom had the time. He'd gone out to look at the eaves or something, and she'd hijacked him. She had led him around by the hand, Daddy in his suit pants and business shoes and shirt with suspenders and tie, Lila wearing her favorite dress, a frilly sort of thing that made her feel pretty. She showed off by naming every flower and then swore him to secrecy and brought him to the elf house she'd made under the bushy, arching branches of one of the hydrangeas. It was really little more than a collection of sticks, but Daddy seemed very impressed. After a while they went to the swing he'd hung from one of the big live oaks, and when Lila sat in it he began to push her. It felt so nice. She couldn't stop laughing, not because anything was funny, just because she was happy. She felt like she could go up into the green, right through the leaves and on into the sky. At the same time, it was nice knowing Daddy was there to catch her if she needed him to. The sun came through the branches and made everything so green and intricate and mysterious. You could easily believe in fairies. Daddy seemed very happy, too. She remembered feeling good that he was having as much fun as she was.

She savored the recollection for a little while. When she came away from it, she could swear there was more light coming in around the curtains. It startled her, and she wondered at the source of the glow. She got up, went to one of the windows, cracked the curtain, and was astonished to see that it was the sky, paling toward dawn.

She had been in here all night.

Immediately, she felt sorry for Cree and Paul, who must have gotten very uncomfortable, waiting for her in the hallway for, what, seven hours! She had asked enough of everybody. It was time to go. She had failed to make contact with her father's ghost. If she wanted that strength and freedom Cree had promised, she'd have to find it without him.

She stood up, every muscle and joint stiff. At the doorway she turned and faced the empty room once more. The memory of that time on the swing, the green aerial mansions above and having Daddy all to herself, was ebbing; she was sad to see it fade.

"Daddy, if you're there and I just can't see you? I just want you to know I turned out all right. So you don't have to worry." She listened and got no answer, and then corrected herself: "There was a bad time," she said quietly, "but now I'm all right."

Then she turned back to the door and went out to make it true.

46

DEIRDRE'S HOUSE WAS CHAOS. The girls had hatched a scheme and had answered a flyer they'd spotted on a neighborhood telephone pole. The dog they'd come home with was a small, scruffy, miniature terrier mix, no puppy but a middle-aged dog they were calling Arthur for the time being. Now he skittered and biffed around the living room, kicking up throw rugs and terrorizing the cats, who watched him with loathing from the top of the piano.

"Tell me the other half of the plan," Cree insisted. Deirdre rolled her eyes.

Zoe took the lead: "It's the only way, Aunt Cree. If you don't want to do it, leave it to Hy and me. Who'd suspect two innocent kids of a scam like this? We go to where that old woman lives, right? And we give her Arthur somehow."

"Somehow like how?"

"That's kind of the hard part," Hyacinth told her. "Maybe we wait until she goes shopping and then we casually come up and ask her if she'd mind holding his leash for a minute while we go into a store or something. And then we never come back."

"Or maybe we just tie him to the fence in front of her house, and she sees him there and after a while figures he's been abandoned. And she'll take him in."

"Or we go up to her and say, like, 'Excuse me, ma'am, our dog is just *drawn* to you, like he knows you or something. Gee, it's almost supernatural, the way he keeps pulling us back over here. It's like he belongs with you – maybe you better take him.' Something like that."

Cree nodded doubtfully, trying to picture Mrs. Wilson's reaction.

"Well," Deirdre told them, "we're going to have to do *something* with him. He's a charming little guy, but he's awfully macho, and he's not meshing with the cats. He's also very set in his ways – he's a fussy eater, and he insists on sleeping only on the couch or on our bed. Don and I shoo him off, but – "

The dog yapped piercingly at the cats, who didn't move except to tick their ears back a notch. To distract him, Zoe began teasing him with a chewed-up leather belt, making him run in circles.

Deirdre gave Cree an accusing glare: *You got me into this, you get me out.*

"It's a terrific plan. We'll figure out something," Cree said. Actually, she thought, depending on the details, it might just work. And the habits that made Arthur less than appealing for Deirdre would probably be the very ones that melted Mrs. Wilson's heart.

" 'Innocent' kids?" Cree asked.

"Well, *Hy* is," Zoe clarified. "And I'm innocent *looking*."

Deirdre clapped her hands to get things moving toward the door; they were running late. Cree had just stopped to pick them up and had already distributed the beads, voodoo dolls, alligator teeth, and hot sauces she'd brought from New Orleans. The plan was to meet Mom at the gym, take her out to dinner. It was something of a ritual: Whenever she came back from a ghost-hunting trip, she needed to reconnect, nestle up against the family, touch every base, reaffirm every contact. She was trying to remember where she was in life, *who* she was. This time it was particularly hard. She had to reclaim herself.

Not everything, though, Cree reminded herself. Some things were best left behind.

There was no league play tonight, which meant that Janet could leave her assistant to oversee the casual hoop shooters or pickup game. While she did a few last-minute errands in the building, Zoe and Hyacinth shed their street shoes and skated out into the yellow floor. They found a ball and began tossing it around. Cree and Deirdre watched them from the sidelines. Zoe had more zip on the boards, but Hyacinth had a better eye for shooting.

"This was a tough one, huh?" Deirdre asked quietly.

"It shows?"

"Let's see. You called me three times, usually at around midnight. You're ten pounds skinnier. Finger's in a splint." Deirdre eyes narrowed as she appraised Cree's face. "Bruises and scratches. Eyes are different."

"I'm good, Dee. I learned a lot." She returned Deirdre's close scrutiny, afraid for just an instant. You had to check each connection when you came back, see if it was the same, or if maybe the way you'd been changed had put your loved ones out of reach. But no, she saw with relief, not with Dee. Not this time. "It put me through some changes," she admitted, "but a lot of them are really good. Things I've needed to look at for a long time."

Deirdre nodded skeptically. "Well, you'd better have some believable and reassuring explanation for Mom. She'll worry. And she's got enough to worry about right now."

It was eight days until her procedure, and Deirdre was getting nervous.

Zoe got a basket and aped the prancing, self-congratulatory dance the professionals did, hand over head, limp wrist, chest convulsing. "Sha-quille O-Neeeal!" she cheered.

Janet appeared at the back of the gym, pulling a windbreaker over her uniform shirt. She caught a pass from Hy, dribbled, and flipped it to Zoe. They came across the floor like that, triangulating.

"Okay. I'm a free woman," Janet told them. She bowled the ball back into the gym. "Lordy, it's so nice to see all my girls! How are you, Creester?" Her voice was cheerful, but her eyes looked old and concerned. Behind her, Dee gave Cree a glare.

"I'm great. I'm better than I've been in a long time." Cree hoped she heard the truth in that. "New Orleans was terrific. I ate a lot of great food, and I got drunk on Bourbon Street, Mom. I didn't whore my way down the other side, though." She grinned.

"What's *that* about?" Deirdre asked.

"Later," Janet commanded. Zoe and Hyacinth walked ahead of them and gave no indication they'd heard. "And, what, you got into a catfight with some drag queen? Good God, Cree!" She meant the splinted finger and fading bruises.

They came through the double front doors. The girls skipped down the steps ahead of them. Deirdre and Janet kept an expectant silence.

"I met a guy," Cree blurted, surprising herself. It was the only easy explanation or excuse she could come up with. Inwardly, she corrected herself: *Met him and unmet him. And he turned out to be a bastard.* But it was a truthful explanation for many of the changes, and truly they were not all injurious. Too bad it ended with Paul's deception. Just one of many in the city of masks.

The twins stopped dead, their pretense of obliviousness dropped.

Janet just snorted. "What, and that's supposed to make us feel better? Who is this bruiser?" She kept the facade of disapproval, but Cree knew she was just playing the role. Her curiosity had been aroused.

"Actually, he's a psychiatrist."

"Worse and worse," Janet growled.

Deirdre tugged their mother's arm. "C'mon, Mom. This isn't the McCarthy hearings, it's 'welcome home, Cree.' Cree will tell us about it if she wants to. We'll never get a table if we don't get going."

Cree tried to make Friday a regular day. She went to the office early, typed up some notes from the Beauforte investigation. Personal stuff aside, this had been an enormously instructive case, and she wanted to record her observations and impressions while they were still fresh. Also, Ed would be coming in later, and she wanted to be able to put it in some kind of order for the mutual debriefing they always conducted after doing solo work.

The thought of seeing Ed made her nervous.

At ten, Joyce came into Cree's office and they sat in the easy chairs facing the windows as they went through two weeks' worth of mail together.

One manila envelope bore a New Orleans postmark, and Cree opened it hurriedly to find that, as she'd hoped, it was from Deelie. The reporter's affectionate note was accompanied by several clippings of front-page articles she'd written about Charmian's arrest and confessions. Apparently, scooping the story hadn't been too bad for Deelie's career: Her byline now included her photo and carried the tag, "award-winning investigative journalist." Just the sight of that good face brought a smile to Cree.

One letter informed Cree that a monograph she'd written had been accepted by a prestigious scholarly journal, and another turned out to be an invitation to speak at the University of New Mexico's "Horizons in Psychology" conference. Very gratifying, a nice welcome home.

Several promising inquiries had come in, too. In Wyoming, a group of ranchers had asked PRA to look into persistent hauntings in a ghost town. In Nauvoo, Illinois, a Methodist minister solicited their perspective on what he believed might be ghosts of Mormons killed there during the persecutions in 1845; all over town, children were having dreams of hangings and burning men. In New York City, a police investigator wanted help with an unexplained seepage in the apartment of an unnamed celebrity; the fluid tested as human blood, but when they'd taken down the stained ceiling they'd found no source for it, and as soon as they'd rebuilt the ceiling, the seep returned.

In other words, the world went on as it always had, its seen and unseen dimensions maintaining their uneasy coexistence.

Sunlight came and went as an endless flotilla of little clouds moved across the sky: The Sound and the Olympics were dappled with cloud shadows that slid down the near slopes and skated across the blue-green water. *The Emerald City*, Cree reflected. It was good to be back.

They'd been going over the finances for half an hour before Cree really noticed Joyce's excess of professionalism. She was dressed in a snappy pants suit and was being businesslike to the point of brusqueness, and though Joyce could be very efficient this wasn't like her.

Cree put down her pencil. "Joyce. What?"

Joyce looked caught out. "Nothing. What do you mean?"

"What'd I do *now?*"

Joyce let her shoulders slump. She stared longingly out the windows as if wishing she could escape to the open spaces. "You *asked* me. So don't blame me when I tell you, okay? The same thing I've been saying, Cree."

"We've been over this!" Cree moaned. Joyce had been in Cree's room when Paul had called the hotel, the day before they left. When Cree had refused to speak to him.

"Yeah. Let's see . . . first you couldn't be with him because of the Mike thing. Then you told him about Mike, and he understood, and it was good for you to get it off your chest. Okay, so then you couldn't be with him because he didn't believe in ghosts and thought you were nuts because you did. But then he had a doozie of a convincing experience at the crypt, and he's a believer now. So what's the latest excuse?"

"He was a . . . double agent, Joyce! A hypocrite, a . . . a liar! The whole time, he was *spying* on my investigation and talking to Charmian! He nearly got Josephine and me killed! Jesus, he – "

"Stop. Cree, you wouldn't *listen* to him when he tried to explain! You told him to shut up. But after you hung up on him, he called me in my room and explained everything. Look at it from his perspective. He's recruited by old friends of his family to help Lila. He's a highly regarded psychiatrist in New Orleans, he stands by old family loyalties, so he says, 'Sure.' "

"He knew everything right from the start! He could have – "

"He didn't know anything except he's got a patient who thinks she's seen a ghost! He starts therapy, but before he gets very far, this ghost buster comes to town and starts shaking things up." Cree started to speak, but Joyce raised a hand to cut her off, eyes savage. "Before long, you find Lila bashing around the house, and he's very concerned – she's at risk, he may need to have the family's cooperation to get her into appropriate treatment. Naturally, he talks to Charmian – "

"He had no business talking to Charmian, to *anyone* outside the confidential relationship with his patient!"

"His patient was in crisis! He thought there was a good chance he'd need the family's help! Anyway, Cree, hey, talk about the pot calling the kettle black? *You* do it all the time! You're Cree Black, the mystic maverick shrink who has some special dispensation to take every kind of license with the therapeutic process, remember?" Joyce waited until Cree gave one small nod of contrition. "Charmian's realizing she underestimated you, you're onto something. She tells Paul his father once helped the family in a time of crisis and asks if he'd do the same. 'Of course,' he says. 'What sort of crisis?' 'Nothing that bears upon Lila's situation,' she assures him, 'but something that if it turns up in Cree Black's prying, it'll damage the family name. And that wouldn't be good for Lila, would it? Given how shaky she is?' 'No,' he agrees. All she asks is that he keep her generally informed of where your investigation is heading. He thinks that's not unreasonable."

"Bastard."

"He believed Charmian to be an upstanding community member, as her husband had been. Anyway, however screwed up her efforts may have been, she was trying to protect her daughter."

"He deliberately steered me toward Richard. He brought me over, had me look just at the Epicurus photos from 1969!"

"He thought that was the truth, Cree. Charmian had told him what you'd find if you looked in the 1969 files. He thought he was showing you the real story at last. Charmian set him up! Paul didn't know it, but it was her last line of defense – you were finding out everything. Suppose the ghosts revealed to Lila or you that Lila killed Richard? The only way to mitigate her guilt was if he *had* raped her, if he *did* deserve it. But Paul didn't know about Brad, or Richard's murder. He brought you to the archives because he really wanted your help to deal with what he believed was Lila's rape by her beloved father."

Joyce went on, methodically, logically, remorselessly. Cree was feeling her carefully nurtured, righteous anger unraveling, and it scared her. It had been sustaining her for a week.

"Joyce. The fact remains, he *cut a deal* with Charmian. They concocted these half-truths, they deceived Lila!"

Joyce gave her the dead eye. "Unlike you, of course. Who didn't cut a deal with Charmian. Who didn't agree to any half-truths to protect Lila."

Cree's resistance suddenly ran out of gas. She turned her own eyes to

427

the window. Somehow she hadn't seen it quite that way. It really was simple, wasn't it? Joyce was right. Joyce was always right.

The problem with accepting any of it was that it left her with only one grievance with Paul: his terrifying, penetrating insight. The hard truths he'd told her about Mike. And she couldn't think of a good excuse to flee that.

Joyce knew she'd scored a direct hit and was smart enough to know when to leave it. She gathered her papers and went to the door.

"So what do you recommend I do about it?" Cree called softly. "Given that it's a little too late."

"No way, Cree. No more advice to the lovelorn, it's not in my job description. You're the one with ESP or whatever it is, you figure it out."

Ed got into the office around noon. Cree heard him bumping through the outer office door with his equipment cases, heard him greet Joyce, heard the big kiss he gave her even through the partially closed door. Cree decided she needed one of those, too.

They hugged in the outer office, a solid, thorough hug, as Joyce busied herself with paperwork. The familiar length of his body felt good against her, but the kiss felt rather *measured*, deliberately administered. She realized she had been worried about him. They made small talk as she helped carry some of the cases back into his office, then helped him put things back on the shelves.

Ed had thrown himself slouching into his desk chair. He was looking around his big room, looking vaguely dissatisfied and drumming his fingers on the desk. "You want to take a walk? I haven't eaten lunch. We could take a stroll and then find a bite."

"You don't want to debrief?"

He hesitated. "Sure. Yeah. But let's do it as we walk."

They turned south on First Avenue, ambling toward Pioneer Square. The weather was cool and changeable, and at cross streets where the long views broke through, they could see the clouds rolling in from the west, sending shadows down the piebald slopes of the mountains. After a few blocks they turned downhill toward Alaskan Way, with the assumption they'd talk for a while and then grab lunch at Pike Place Market. They hadn't even discussed it, but of course Ed would know Cree needed the ambience of flux: The energy and flow made a safe haven for an empath. Both were new enough to Seattle to enjoy the bustle and color of the market's stalls, the endless variety of fresh fish and fruit and vegetables and breads, displayed so beautifully and temptingly.

Cree told him about her last days in New Orleans. They agreed that Richard's ghost had had a very typical double aspect – his memory of the beating, and of Lila in the swing, had been clearly linked with his experience of the moments of dying. But Bradford's doubleness was a different matter. The boar-headed phantom had been a remote generation. Its lack of an apparent link to its origin as a memory of a dying man, coupled with its high degree of independence, troubled them both.

Cree talked about the red herrings she'd considered: the idea of Richard as a multiple personality, and Joyce's all-too-plausible idea of a specter generated by a living person. Though those hadn't proved true, the boar-headed man still gave them a whole new category of manifestation to fit into their respective schemes of things.

Of course, the remote generation idea was only one of many troubling aspects of Bradford's second ghost. His solidity was one of them: Cree lifted her shirt to show Ed the faintly lingering scratches his hand had made on her stomach. In some ways more disturbing was his adaptability: He could perceive and interact with living beings in the current time.

Both features were as frightening for the fieldworking ghost hunter as they were challenging for the paranormal theorist. Together, these two aspects of the boar-headed man affirmed what many witnesses and parapsychologists had long claimed: that ghosts *were* capable of inflicting more than psychological injury upon a living person, and that ghosts *could* pursue something like an intentional, interactive agenda with the living, adapting to circumstances. It gave strength to the premise of folk legends all over the world, that ghosts sometimes pursued vendettas on those who had wronged them.

As they continued along Alaskan Way, Ed began to look increasingly troubled. Part of his dismay, Cree knew, was his concern for her, knowing that ghosts could hurt or kill a ghost hunter. The other part was theoretical. His lovingly constructed geomagnetic theory, now buttressed by the tidal-cycle evidence he'd brought back from Gloucester, might explain very limited perseverations, but it would never explain the phenomenon of the boar-headed man.

Nor, she knew, of Mike, that day in Philly.

"So," Ed asked, "how did she come out of it? Lila."

"She wouldn't tell me much about how it went with her father's ghost. She was exhausted. But she definitely emerged much stronger. She'd always had a core of strength, really, it was just a matter of putting her parts together, you know? She's a very different woman now. There's a *calm* in her now. A resolve. Hard to describe."

"Weren't you worried she'd learn the truth when she met him – that she'd killed him?"

"A little. But Richard was mainly an . . . emotional ghost. He was as affectively powerful as he was physically insubstantial. Remember, he didn't know who had poisoned him. And he never really thought about it as he was dying, he just wanted his kids to be all right. I was less worried that he'd reveal something than that her memories would spontaneously awaken from being around him. But it didn't happen. No, if Ron or Charmian don't tell her, I'm pretty sure she'll never know. And her psychiatrist is in on the deception, so I doubt he'll dig it up if she keeps working with him."

Ed's brow remained wrinkled.

"What else?" she prodded.

He shook his head, looking depressed and worn. "We go out on these expeditions wanting to figure out how the world works. We're trying to map this hidden terrain. We make terrific progress every time. And yet every time we come back, we have more questions than we have answers. We have new phenomena we can't integrate. Logic fails us. Our categories and taxonomies and theories all fall apart. When are going to *know* something, Cree?"

"Dunno," she admitted. She squeezed his hand.

"Speaking of which, what ever happened with that 'episode' of yours? The Civil War daydream?"

"Joyce and I checked it out. The house I saw across the gardens was definitely there, as I saw it, in 1862 — it's on all the plot maps of the period, and we even found a portrait of it the owners'd had painted. The original house burned down in 1954, but the family rebuilt and still lives there. Another old New Orleans family, the Millards. I even found their family crypt, not far from the Lamberts'. The names of the kids of that generation are all on it. Elizabeth — I thought of her as Lizzie — and Jane. The youngest was a boy named William John, who would have been six in 1862. Just as I saw him."

"Oh, man," Ed groaned.

"We checked the old Beauforte House site plans, too. They show the old cistern, right behind the kitchen garden. Just where I saw the soldiers drinking."

Ed was making such hyperbolic expressions of overwhelmedness that she had to laugh: His knees went wobbly and he staggered all over the sidewalk, clutching his chest as if having a heart attack.

"I think we even figured out whose mind I was seeing it through, Ed! General Beauforte had one daughter still living at home in May of 1862. Her name was Claudette, and she was fifteen when the Union Army took over the house. I was seeing it through her eyes as she waited in the slave quarters for them to take her and her mother away. It would have been a powerful moment. The experience lived on and I . . . I found it. I relived it."

Ed was looking around with theatrical paranoia. "Don't tell anyone!" he whispered. "We'll lose all our credibility. Or the CIA or somebody will kidnap you and make you do remote past viewing or something. Goddamn you, Cree! So help me, I'm going to catch up to you. I'm going to give *you* something that throws your theories into a tailspin. So help me."

She came to his side, put her arm around his waist; he did the same, and they walked on with matched strides, hip to hip. "You know, it's not too early to get a Bloody Mary with lunch," she told him. "Take the edge off these outrageous slings and arrows. Celebrate us both getting home. God, it's nice to see you!"

"Cree." His tone killed the exuberance dead.

"Yeah?"

"Tell me about the psychiatrist. How he fits in."

Cree saw it all in his eyes. "Joyce," she managed, feeling betrayed. "Joyce told you. That's why you didn't come to New Orleans."

Ed just blinked once.

She was at a loss. "He was . . . he and I worked on Lila together. Compared notes. He doesn't 'fit in.' He and I, we – "

"What's this? What're we doing?" He gestured at the two of them, the street, the sky. He meant the good feeling that came so easily with them. "This is nice, isn't it?"

"Of course! It's lovely! It's – " But Ed was walking on, and she had to jog to keep up with his long strides. She took his arm to slow him down, but he didn't look at her.

"So what's *wrong* with this?" he insisted. This time he sort of meant *me*.

Nothing! she almost said. *This is as good as it gets!* But her heart seemed to cleave inside her as she knew it wasn't quite so. "I don't know, Ed," she said.

They walked on for another minute, silent, not looking at each other, side by side but utterly distant.

"You should probably try to figure it out, Cree," he said at last. "Do what you have to. You know? We all gotta do what we gotta do. Let me know how it comes out."

He was offering some sort of permission, and she loved him fiercely for it. But when she tried to figure out what it was she had to do, no answer came. She clung to his arm, almost panicking, afraid he'd get away. "Okay," she told him. "I'll try. Thanks."

They kept walking. They reached Waterfront Park, looked out at the water for a time. The Highway 99 overpass roared behind them as the Bainbridge Island ferry came in from the Sound, its hull banded in white froth. Excursion boats took off from the piers immediately to the south, and beyond them a couple of freighters hove slowly to the forest of

432

gantries of the lower port. After a time they climbed the steps to Pike Place Market, got sandwiches, sat in one of the public seating stalls. They talked about other things. No Bloody Marys; the giddy sense of celebration was gone. Their conversation felt stiff, obstructed, but they forged along with determination. Ed said he'd heard about several other interesting cases in the Gloucester area: Various friends of the Wainwrights had heard about his prelim in their house and cautiously approached him with accounts of their own hauntings. It seemed everybody had some brush with the mysterious.

He said it reminded him again that, for all its weirdness, the world beyond vision was awfully close and immediate. Life – you really never knew what to expect, he said. What would come at you next.

Cree's heart felt as if it would break. Life was indeed strange, she agreed. She shook her head, feeling it: an ache.

Ed bit his lips and nodded his agreement.

47

B OURBON STREET HADN'T CHANGED.

It was still a circus, a perpetual mini–Mardi Gras packed with tourists seeking abandon from purveyors offering a thousand varieties of it. Lights bounced in the bars, shadows of dancers played on the windows, blaring rhythms battled as Cree walked past doorways. She'd had the airport shuttle drop her on Canal Street right at the end of Bourbon. Her flight hadn't gotten in until five o'clock, and now it was well past dinnertime. She was hungry and thirsty and still a little stiff from sitting in jets and shuttle buses so long.

Tuesday. She'd been away only twelve days, but New Orleans seemed to welcome her back like a long-lost friend, the kind you've formed a deep attachment to not because you've known each other for a long time but because the times you shared were so hard and so revealing. You know each other well. You greet each other with a certain gritty, guilty, wry intimacy. Cree liked the feeling.

She went into a cheap restaurant and ordered a sausage po'boy, which she washed down with a beer from a plastic cup.

Better, she decided.

Back on the sidewalk, her hunger stilled, she let the flow of the street pull her. She window-shopped, stopped to listen to street musicians, tossed quarters into the cardboard box set out by two little boys tap dancing. For a couple of blocks, curious about where such a person would be going, she followed a towering, muscular black man, glorious in tight pink skirt, feathered boa, and sequined platform shoes. He disappeared into an anonymous doorway between strip clubs, leaving her wondering at the mystery of his life.

Continuing up the street, taking her time, she bought a Jell-O shot, just to see what they were like: They were said to be lethal, but though it didn't taste too bad in a cloyingly sweet sort of way, it didn't affect her as much as she'd been led to expect. She bought a dozen strings of beads and a mask made of sequins and brilliant scarlet feathers that covered just her eyes and forehead. She stuffed the mask into the outer pocket of her shoulder bag, but she put the beads around her neck immediately. They sparkled and spangled with every step she took and made her feel good; men gave her appreciative once-overs and even a couple of double-takes. She stopped at a sidewalk concession and bought one of the infamous Hurricanes in a to-go cup. It was about a quart of icy liquid and it froze her palate; she made it only halfway through before she got too full and too chilled and had to drop the remainder in a trash basket. She was feeling a little looped anyway, as much from the whirl of the street as from the booze.

From windows and doors, attics and courtyards, she could hear the whispers of the ghosts of the living and the dead, forever and ever. In the night air, she could smell the big, slow Mississippi, just to the south, hugging the city in its big bend, and below it the miles of flat, wet land stretching away to the Gulf.

New Orleans.

Halfway down Bourbon Street she chose a club at random and went into the dancing throng. The band was playing Zydeco, raucous accordions and bass and piano and a pair of washboards whose rhythms put an itch into Cree's bones and made them move. She danced by herself for a time, then floated through the crowd, taking an occasional partner for a number or two. She wondered if she were stalling or just having a good time, but the music was so loud she couldn't really think about it.

Not thinking wasn't too bad. She resolved to try it more often.

After a while she'd had enough noise and body odor and cigarette smoke. She left the place and cut south two blocks to Charters Street, which was tranquil by comparison to Bourbon. A few more blocks east and she could feel the glowering, festering aura of LaLaurie House, one

435

block north on Royal, but she stifled the tremor it gave her. She passed into the quieter parts of the French Quarter.

Better. But her anxiety mounted as she drew closer.

She had deliberately not thought about this. She'd just made the decision. But when she got to Paul's place, she realized didn't know what she'd intended. The windows of the first two floors were dark, but Paul's lights were on. He was probably at home. But there was no way to get to the courtyard and his stairs without ringing the bell. He'd answer through the intercom and she'd have to say something, and she didn't know what. She'd have preferred just to appear at his door.

She pressed the button and waited. Nothing. She tried again, longer, and waited again as a falling sensation swooned in her chest. If he didn't answer now, she wasn't sure she'd have the brass to do this again. But after another long moment the buzzer went and she opened the door and walked through the pitch-black *porte-cochiere* to the courtyard. Suddenly afraid, she took out the feathered mask and put it on as she climbed the stairs. The statue of Psyche seemed to watch her from the dark garden.

When she saw him at the kitchen door, Cree recoiled slightly. He was shirtless, and his face and shoulders and chest and arms were uniformly filmed with white dust, cut through with runnels of sweat. The white emphasized the shadows made by the cut of his pectorals and his corrugated stomach muscles, and he looked like some pagan tribesman, interrupted at some wild ritual. His forehead and hair were white, too, but the skin around his mouth and nose was clear, vividly flesh-colored, as if he'd painted himself with skin tones there. When he opened the door and saw her, his frosted brows rose, but with his odd whiteface it was hard to tell what his expression was. He stood back and let her come inside.

"You," he managed.

"Probably," she said. She'd meant to say, *Of course.*

They stared at each other for another heartbeat or two. Cree knew that the eyes Paul saw in her mask's eyeholes were wide and disturbed. She couldn't resist another glance at his torso.

Paul glanced down at his own chest, put his hands to his powdered cheeks. "Oh. You're wondering why I look like this. I was just doing some renovation work – knocking down plaster in the bedroom. Hot and dusty in there. My downstairs neighbors are gone this week, so I can bang away at night if I need to. I seem to need to. It's . . . cathartic. Sorry if – "

"No, you look good," she said. And he did. God, yes. Another man dusted with white might look ghostly, but Paul looked like Nijinsky in *L'après-midi d'un faune*: wild, intense, and very physical. She could picture him, raging at the walls with his sledgehammer, angry at the new disarray of his once orderly world, chunks of plaster falling in clouds of dust.

He dipped his head, acknowledging the compliment. He stepped to the kitchen table, cleared away a dirty plate and a paper dust mask, gestured to a chair. At the counter, he grabbed a bottle of wine and a glass and turned back.

She stayed standing.

"No apologies, though, either way. Right?" he asked.

"Right." However they'd upset each other's worlds, whatever they owed each other, it evened out. He was pretty perceptive.

"How're you doing?" he asked.

"Mixed, I think. You?"

"You know. Why mixed?"

"You know why."

That caught him, pleased him. He put bottle and glass aside without looking at them and came straight to her. When he put his hands on her hipbones, the touch took her breath away.

"I made a bet with myself," he told her. "That you'd come back."

"Oh? How'd you know?" *Given what a shit I was.*

"I figured that if you were at all the person I thought you were, you'd come back." He hesitated, cleared his throat. "Well. Actually, that wasn't the whole bet."

"What was the rest?"

He smiled. "That either you'd come back here and find me, or I'd go to Seattle and find you. I couldn't lose." He watched her eyes, and the smile became a frown. "Why're you wearing a mask?"

437

"Just trying to fit in on Bourbon Street," she lied.

He kept looking at her.

"Hiding," she admitted, scared again.

"Take it off, Cree."

She mustered some false bravado: "I will if you go take a shower."

He nodded. When he let her go, she could still feel where his hands had pressed. His white back disappeared down the hall. Cree waited in the kitchen, listening to the water running and feeling her pulse thud in her throat. She debated tossing back a slug of wine to steady her shaking hands and then decided not to. After a few moments, she went out to the rear gallery and leaned against the railing. *Better*, she thought; it was cooler out here. The mask was hot and it pressed too hard against the bridge of her nose, but she left it on as she looked over the dark courtyard and the surrounding roofs and walls and hidden gardens of the French Quarter.

When Paul came back, he was wearing only a Balinese sarong, a bolt of batik wrapped snugly around his waist and falling like a skirt almost to his knees. Above it, his skin was clean now, tan and warm looking, shower scented. As she'd imagined, his legs were carved with the corded sinews of a runner.

They stood side by side at the railing, looking out at the night. They had both come a long way to get here. Paul looked at her expectantly, and then Cree remembered her part of the bargain. She slipped the elastic band over her head, took off the mask. After a hesitation, she flipped it over the railing, and it fluttered down into the darkness like some night bird.

Much better, she decided.

ACKNOWLEDGMENTS

First and foremost, sincere thanks to the good people of New Orleans, for making me feel so welcome in their wonderful city.

Special thanks go to my friends Margaret and Eric Rothchild for being such superb companions, hosts, co-conspirators, and tour guides to Seattle.

I owe thanks also to my readers and advisors in matters great and small, Amie Hecht, Willow Hecht, Stella Hovis, and Verbena Pastor; and to my "experimental subjects" at the Seattle Women's University Club, particularly Marjorie Reynolds, Joan Shirley, Isabel Falck, Cherry Jarvis, Deborah Lewis, and Margaret Rothchild, whose suggestions greatly improved this book.

Sincere thanks are due to Dr. Lucinda Mitchell, for helping me untangle matters of psychology with such insight and broad-mindedness.

A number of New Orleans institutions deserve particular recognition. Chief among them are the Williams Research Center for providing such an excellent historical resource; Deanie's Seafood for providing sumptuous feasts to hungry writers; and the New Orleans Police Department for open-minded help and advice. Any errors or omissions in this book are the fault of my own license or ignorance, not the fault of the many fine people who did their best to set me straight.

Thank you Karen Rinaldi, Lara Carrigan, Greg Villepique, and everyone at Bloomsbury; and thanks and xoxx to Nicole Aragi.

A NOTE ON THE AUTHOR

Daniel Hecht was a professional guitarist for twenty years. In 1989, he retired from musical performance to take up writing, and he received his M.F.A. from the Iowa Writers' Workshop in 1992. He is the author of two previous novels, *Skull Session*, a *USA Today* bestseller, and *The Babel Effect*,

A NOTE ON THE TYPE

The text of this book is set in Bembo. This type was first used in 1495 by the Venetian printer Aldus Manutius for Cardinal Bembo's *De Aetna*, and was cut for Manutius by Francesco Griffo. It was one of the types used by Claude Garamond (1480–1561) as a model for his Romain de L'Université, and so it was the forerunner of what became standard European type for the following two centuries. Its modern form follows the original types and was designed for Monotype in 1929.